THE RIBBON WEAVER

by

Rosie Goodwin

Magna Large Print Books
Long Preston, North Yorkshire,
BD23 4ND, England.

British Library Cataloguing in Publication Data.

Goodwin, Rosie
    The ribbon weaver.

    A catalogue record of this book is
    available from the British Library

    ISBN   978-0-7505-3553-3

First published in Great Britain in 2010 by
Headline Publishing Group

Published in Large Print 2012 by arrangement with
Headline Publishing Group Ltd.

Magna Large Print is an imprint of Library Magna Books Ltd.

Printed and bound in Great Britain by
T.J. (International) Ltd., Cornwall, PL28 8RW

THE RIBBON WEAVER

This book is for Jack Aaron Yates, a beautiful, much wanted and long awaited baby brother for Charlotte. Welcome to the family, little man. You are a gift after a time of great sadness, especially as you were born on Mum's birthday!

Also for my Nikki, 18!!!!!!!! A proper little lady now, and for Dan, who looked so very handsome and grown up on the night of his prom.

I'm so proud of you all and I love you millions xxxxxxx

Prologue

Nuneaton 1830

'Come on, Molly gel, let's be havin' yer. It is Christmas Eve, yer know, an' some of us have homes to go to.'

Molly grinned as Amos Bennett's good-natured face poked through the opening into the great attic where she was working.

'I'm just finishin' now, pet, I'll be down in two shakes of a lamb's tail,' she promised, barely taking her eyes from the intricate length of fine gauze ribbon she was weaving. Nodding, Amos disappeared back the way he had come.

Slowly, Molly stopped treadling and after placing down the shuttle she skilfully steadied the weight that hung beneath the loom. As the machine came to a creaking halt, she stretched stiffly and glanced up at the skylights that ran the length of the attic. The snow that had been threatening to fall all day was now coming down with a vengeance, and all she could see was a thick white coating of it that covered the glass and cast an eerie glow into the room. She shivered. Apart from herself the huge attic was deserted, the looms silent. The women who worked them had long since scurried away to begin their Christmas preparations with their families. However, it suited Molly to work late. Since losing her husband Wilf almost three years before, she had no one to rush

11

home to, and for her, apart from the loneliness, Christmas Day was much like any other.

She was never short of invitations admittedly, but Molly Ernshaw was known for keeping herself to herself, just as she had when her Wilf was alive. Back then, she had considered she needed no one else but him and now, at the age of forty-five, she felt it was a bit late in the day to teach an old dog new tricks.

Standing, she slowly straightened her back; it was aching from the long hours bent across the loom.

Gazing around the silent ribbon factory, she shuddered. Now that she had stopped working, Molly was suddenly cold and tired. If she had allowed herself, she would also have admitted to being more than a little sad at the prospect of the lonely Christmas before her.

Still, she consoled herself, there were a lot of folks much worse off than she was, and on that thought she pulled her thick woollen shawl more closely about her. Taking up an old tweed coat that was draped across the back of her chair, she pulled that on too. Then, after lifting her bag, she made her way painfully down the crude wooden staircase to the floor below. Amos was hurrying about, turning off the gas lamps and making sure that all the doors were securely bolted.

It was almost like descending into a rainbow. Everywhere she looked stood boxes and spools of ribbons of every shade and hue, all ready to be transported to the hat factories in Coventry, where the majority of them would be used to adorn headgear for the ladies of fashion. There were silk

12

ribbons, satin ribbons, pearl-edged ribbons, finely worked gauze ribbons, and tartan ribbons, all of various widths and colours, and Molly never tired of seeing them. She herself was one of the best silk weavers in the whole factory and proud of it. Her Wilf had taught her all she knew. His old loom now stood silent in the attic of her little cottage, and she could quite easily have worked from there as many of the local people did, but she preferred to work here in the factory for company.

As she picked her way amongst the boxes, Amos hastened across to open the door for her.

'A Merry Christmas to yer then, Molly.' He beamed, and she wearily smiled back.

'And the very same to you and yours,' she returned, then stepped past him into the almost deserted street. The bitter cold took her breath away. 'By God above, it's enough to freeze the hairs on a brass monkey out here,' she muttered to herself as she pulled her old coat more tightly about her. Head bent, she then began to pick her way across the slippery cobblestones.

The snow was falling in great white flakes, and the few people that dotted the streets passed her as if she was invisible as they scurried along with their heads bent, keen to get back to their firesides and out of the biting cold.

By the time Molly had turned out of Abbey Street and towards the empty stalls of the cattle-market, she was breathless and cursing. 'Bloody weather,' she said irritably, intent on trying not to slip on the treacherous cobbles. 'Why couldn't the snow have waited till I was safely home?'

All she could think of was her cosy fireside and

13

a good strong brew of tea, and the thought made her press on. The snow seemed to be falling faster and thicker by the minute, and by the time she had left the town centre behind her, it was falling so densely that she could barely see a hand in front of her. She was lost in a silent white world, the only sound being the putt, putt, putt of the gas lamps as she hurried past them. The snow had now risen above her old leather boots, and her feet and the hem of her coarse calico skirt were sodden. Street lamps cast an eerie glow on the thick white carpet, making it sparkle as if it had been sprinkled with diamonds, but tonight, Molly could find no pleasure in the sight. All she wanted was the comfort of her little cottage and her feet immersed in a tin bowl full of nice hot water.

As she approached the Parish Church she decided to cut through the churchyard. There were those that feared the graveyard at night, but the dead held no fear for Molly. It was the living she worried about! There were some that would cut your throat for sixpence in these hard times, as she well knew. Besides, this short-cut could save at least five minutes from her journey and she regularly took it.

The gravestones leaned drunkenly towards her as she hurried as best she could along the pathway, and soon the gas lamps and the little light they cast faded away as the great yew trees that bordered the church surrounded her. It was hard to keep to the path here, and occasionally Molly stumbled on a rock buried beneath the snow, but she ploughed on.

When she finally reached the dark doorway to

the church, she paused to catch her breath, leaning against the cold stone wall inside. The wind had picked up now and the yew trees swayed beneath their heavy weight of snow. Here and there, the scarlet berries on the holly bushes shone through, and it was as Molly stood watching them that a noise from the deeply recessed doorway came to her. It sounded almost like a moan, and suddenly nervous, she held her breath for what seemed like an eternity in case the sound should come again. After some time, Molly dared to breathe, chiding herself, 'You're goin' soft in the head, gel, hearin' noises as ain't there. Why, you'll be scared o' yer own shadow next if you ain't careful.'

Still unsettled despite her brave talk, she pushed herself from the wall and was just about to set off again when the noise came once more. Molly knew now that she hadn't imagined it, and her heart began to thump painfully against her ribs. Her eyes sought about for someone to help her, but there was no one – nothing but the snow and the swaying yew trees that stood as silent witnesses to her distress. Even as she stood there, uncertain what to do, she heard the noise again, louder this time ... much louder. Someone was in the doorway with her and, if Molly judged rightly, that someone was in great pain.

Chewing nervously on her lip, she stepped cautiously into the deeper darkness. 'Is anyone there?' Even to her own ears her voice sounded frightened. Her heart was thumping so loudly that she feared it would leap from her chest, but nevertheless she forced herself to stand there

15

listening intently.

'*Help me ... please.*' The voice that finally answered her was so weak that Molly had to strain her ears to hear it.

It was a woman's voice and so, calling on every ounce of courage she had, Molly edged a few more timid steps towards it.

After the glare of the blinding snow it took her eyes some seconds to adjust to the blackness, but gradually as she peered into the shadows she saw a shape, right at the back of the porch. It appeared to be lying against the huge, heavy wooden doors of the church.

Cautiously she advanced, and as her eyes gradually became accustomed to the inky blackness, her fear was instantly replaced with compassion.

A young woman raised her hand imploringly towards her and without a moment's hesitation Molly now dropped to her weary knees beside her. Realising at once that the woman was in a bad way, Molly took her outstretched hand and gripped it comfortingly. She was distressed to note that despite the bitter cold the girl's hand was feverishly hot and she was shivering uncontrollably. Molly's kind heart went out to her, and her eyes filled with tears at the poor soul's plight.

'Hold on, me love, I'll go an' get help,' she promised as she tried to rise, but the girl shook her head and gripped Molly's hand all the tighter.

'No, *please.*' Her every word was an effort. 'It's ... too late to help me now.'

Molly's heart was aching as, fumbling deep in her coat pocket, she pulled out a white linen handkerchief. She could sense that the poor girl

16

was almost at her end and a wave of helplessness washed over her. Leaning, she began to dab at the beads of sweat that glistened in the darkness on the girl's forehead, searching her mind for words of comfort, but finding none.

The young woman was gasping for breath now and struggling to tell Molly something. Molly leaned closer to try and hear what the girl was attempting to say. She suddenly turned imploring eyes to Molly, and the older woman's heart skipped a beat as she stared back at her. The girl was breathtakingly beautiful, with tangled auburn hair, a perfect heart-shaped face and huge dark eyes fringed with long dark lashes. Even in her pain, she was easily the prettiest girl that Molly had ever seen.

'Please ... take my baby.' The girl's voice was genteel, and Molly's eyes almost started from her head with shock at her words.

'What did yer say, love? What baby?' Molly cast her eyes about the freezing recess, sure that she must have misunderstood what the poor lass had said. The only thing her eyes could pick out in the darkness was a large tapestry bag tucked close to the girl's side, but there was no sign at all of a baby and Molly guessed that she was delirious.

'There ain't no baby here, love,' she told her gently, but even as she uttered the words the girl was becoming more and more agitated and, with what appeared to be the last of her strength, was trying to push the bag at Molly.

'*Please,*' she begged again as the tears coursed down her ashen cheeks. Molly nodded quickly. 'All right, all right, me love, calm down now. I'll

17

take yer baby – I promise.'

The girl let out a sigh of relief. 'Oh thank you, God bless you.' She gasped, and suddenly her grip on Molly's hand slackened and there was only silence, save for the swaying of the yew trees in the wind.

Molly scratched her head in consternation. She had no way of knowing if the girl had lapsed into unconsciousness or passed away. All she did know was that she had to get help – and quickly. Her mind sought about for the best thing to do. There was no way at all that she could carry the girl. That was out of the question. She would have to go and get people to help and bring them back here.

Afraid to waste another minute, she hoisted herself to her knees and then she suddenly remembered the tapestry bag and the girl's insistence that she should take it.

Reaching down, she grasped the handles and swung it as best she could on to her shoulder. Inside there might be some clue as to the girl's identity, and if there was, then she could let her next-of-kin know what had happened. With a last worried glance at the poor young woman, Molly stumbled from the shelter of the doorway and back out into the blinding snow.

Within the shelter of the snow-laden yew trees a silent observer drew further back into the shadows, scarcely daring to breathe in case Molly should see him. He had followed the girl for days and witnessed the whole sorry tragedy that had just taken place. But now all he had to do was

18

wait for Molly to leave and then his job would be almost done and he could report back to his master.

In the warmth of the back room in the small tavern, the servant stood twisting his cap in his hands as he faced his master.

'It is done then?'

'Yes, sir. Just as you said.'

'And the child – are you quite sure that it was dead?'

'Aye, sir. I am. She died trying to bring it.'

'Then go – and *never* breathe a word of what has happened this night or it will be the worse for both of us.'

'Yes, sir.' The master extended his hand displaying five gold sovereigns but the servant shook his head and backed away. Then turning about, he scuttled from the room like a thief in the night. He wondered how he was ever going to live with himself after what had passed this night. But it was too late for regrets now. What was done was done.

Once alone, the man turned and, leaning heavily against the mantelpiece, he stared down into the fire as tears trickled down his cheeks.

'May God forgive me for what I have done this night,' he murmured, but only the snapping of the logs on the fire answered him.

Chapter One

By the time the little row of terraced cottages in Attleborough Road where she lived came into sight, Molly was almost dropping with exhaustion. The added weight of the tapestry bag, and having to battle against the snow following a hard day's work, had taken their toll on her and she sighed with relief at the sight of her home. But it wasn't to her own door that she went first but to Bessie Bradley's.

Without pausing to knock she flung open the door unceremoniously and Bessie, who was kneeling before an old tin bath in front of a roaring fire, turned startled eyes to her. Bessie was in the process of bathing one of her brood who seemed to be dotted everywhere Molly looked.

'Bessie, come straight away,' gasped Molly, and Bessie's mouth dropped open at the bedraggled state of her.

'Good God, woman, whatever's wrong wi' yer? Yer look like the hounds of hell are pantin' at yer heels.'

'Just come *now.*' With no more words of explanation, Molly disappeared back into the snow, leaving the door swinging wide open to the elements. Already, Bessie was standing and drying her hands on her rough linen apron with a deep frown on her face.

'Mary, you see to this lot fer me, I'll be back as

soon as I can,' she told her oldest daughter as she rushed to the door, snatching up her huge old cloak and thrusting her feet into her boots. And with that she slammed it shut behind her and quickly picked her way through the thick white carpet to Molly's cottage.

Molly was pacing the floor agitatedly when Bessie entered; she turned to her immediately and said, 'Bessie, I don't know what to do. There's a young woman in the doorway of the Parish Church and she's in a bad way.'

Seeing that her friend was deeply distressed, Bessie patted her arm comfortingly.

'Calm down now then and tell me slowly what's happened.' Then, as the sorry tale was told: 'Poor soul, happen she's a street girl fallen on hard times.'

Molly shook her head in quick denial. 'She weren't a street girl, Bessie, I'd stake me life on it.' A picture of the girl's sweet face flashed before her eyes and again she heard the melodic ring of her voice. 'There was somethin' about her – some sort o' quality that seemed to shine from her, and I'm telling yer, she had the face of an angel.' She shook her head again. 'That girl is class, Bessie, believe me. I couldn't carry her nor do nothing for her, but she needs help – she's lying there all alone. What are we to do?'

Molly's eyes filled with tears as she thought of the plight of the poor girl, and in a second, Bessie's mind was made up. Molly was known as a bit of a loner but she had always been good to the Bradley family, helping them through many a hard time. Now Bessie could finally do something for her in return.

'Look,' she said kindly, noting Molly's pinched face, 'you're all in. I'll go back to the church, see what's happening, then I'll run fer the doctor, eh?'

Molly stared at her, gratitude lighting her face. 'Oh Bessie, you're a good 'un, but mind yer wrap up warm, it's bitter out there and no mistake.'

'Don't yer go worryin' about me now. You just make yourself a strong brew and get those wet clothes off, else it'll be you I'm fetchin' the doctor to.' Bessie looked at Molly's soaking wet skirt and flinched as she saw the blood on it, as well as the melted snow. Even more reason to make haste. 'I'll be back before yer know it,' she promised, and with that she quickly let herself out into the blizzard. Within minutes she was back in her own cottage pulling her shawl over her head. A hundred questions were being flung at her from the children but she didn't make time to answer them.

'Now, Mary, you and Toby are in charge till I get back, do yer hear me? Tell yer dad I've been called away on an errand fer Molly when he comes in.'

Mary nodded obediently as Bessie left the warmth of the kitchen to begin the journey back to the church. Within minutes she found herself up to her knees in snow, and more than once she lost her footing and almost went headlong, but still she pressed on. If the poor girl was as ill as Molly had said, then every second counted and she didn't even pause to catch her breath.

Attleborough Road was deserted and the odd cottages that she passed all had their curtains drawn tight against the freezing night. Now and again, the sound of families singing Christmas carols hung on the night air. Normally, Bessie would have found pleasure in the sound, but tonight all she could think of was reaching the church. At last it loomed into sight and for the first time, Bessie slowed her steps. She had never before in her life entered a graveyard at night. She was very superstitious, but after coming this far she didn't intend to let Molly down.

Battling up the path past the yew trees, she glanced this way and that at the tilting gravestones. Her heart was beating wildly but she was almost at the church doorway now. The snowfall had long since filled in Molly's earlier footsteps and appeared as a fluffy white carpet right up to the steps of the doorway.

'Hello?' Bessie called into the blackness. When no one answered, she cautiously stepped inside. Standing for some seconds, her teeth chattering with cold, she peered towards the heavy wooden doors. 'Hello!' Again there was no answer. She inched her way in further and further until at last her hand touched the cold brass handle of the door. There was no one there – no girl, nor anything to suggest that anyone had ever been there.

As Bessie plodded back to the lychgate, she had no idea that her old boots left red footprints in the snow.

Pulling aside the curtains, Molly peered up the lane yet again for a sign of her neighbour. The oil lamp was casting a warm glow about the room and the fire was blazing merrily now, but Molly couldn't settle, not till Bessie was back with news – and she knew that this could take some time if

Bessie had to run for the doctor. But then suddenly the door banged inwards and poor Bessie almost fell into the room. She was white all over, and Molly dragged her to the fireside.

'That was quick. I didn't expect you back so soon. How is she? Did yer get the doctor to her?' Molly bombarded Bessie with questions but the poor woman was so puffed out after her battle with the blizzard that for a few moments she could not answer. Molly pulled off her sodden boots and pressed her into a chair, and as Bessie held her blue feet out to the warmth of the fire, the hem of her skirt began to steam.

It was not until she had taken two great gulps from the mug of scalding hot tea that Molly had placed into her perished hands that she was able to answer. 'There were no one there,' she said gravely, looking her neighbour straight in the eye.

Molly's mouth stretched in disbelief. 'What do yer mean, woman? O' *course* she were there – the poor love were almost at death's door. What do yer think she did, just got up an' walked away?'

Bessie shrugged. 'I'm tellin' yer, love. There was no one there. As God's me witness, she were gone.'

Molly couldn't believe it and began to poke the fire in her agitation. 'Perhaps someone else found her after I left?' she suggested hopefully.

'That is a possibility,' her weary neighbour admitted. 'Unless ... you imagined it.'

Molly bristled with indignation. 'I *did not* imagine it, me gel. I ain't taken to fancy, as well yer should know.' Suddenly a thought occurred to her. 'Her bag!' she cried. 'Why, bugger me, I've got her bag. Yer know – the one I told yer she in-

24

sisted I take? Why, I'd forgotten all about it.'

She rushed to the side of the door where she had put down the bag when she first entered the room. Lifting it, she carried it to the hearth and placed it down on the brightly coloured peg rug. 'There,' she said triumphantly. *Now* tell me I imagined it.'

Bessie grinned at her sheepishly. 'Sorry, duck, but come on then – open it. It might give us some idea as to who she was.'

Molly bent and after fumbling with the catch, she opened the bag. As she peered inside, the colour suddenly drained from her face.

'What is it, love?' Bessie's voice was concerned.

Without answering, Molly reached into the bag and lifted out what appeared at first sight to be a bundle of clothes. Carefully she laid it on the hearth and as she did so, Bessie's face paled too.

'Why, God in heaven... *It's a baby.'* Bessie could hardly believe her eyes.

Solemn-faced, Molly nodded. 'So, the poor love weren't delirious after all.' Looking at Bessie with fear shining in her eyes, she whispered, 'But why is it so quiet?'

Dropping to her knees beside her, Bessie began to unwind the clothes that the baby was wrapped in. The outer layer consisted of a black skirt, worn but neatly wrapped around a tiny pair of blood-stained scissors, darned and obviously of a fine quality. Next was a white blouse, with tiny mother-of-pearl buttons, slightly frayed at the cuffs, and lastly a shawl of pure blue silk, the like of which neither woman had ever seen. However, it wasn't the shawl that held their attention but the tiny child wrapped inside it. It was a little girl and she was beautiful. A mop of tiny auburn curls framed a perfect heart-shaped face with long dark eyelashes that curled on to pale dimpled cheeks. But she was so still and silent that Molly gazed at Bessie in terror.

'Is ... is she dead?'

Pulling herself together with a great effort, Bessie took control of the situation. 'Right – get me some warm water,' she ordered briskly, and without a murmur Molly scuttled away to do as she was bid. She felt sick inside, for the sight of that little innocent had reawakened memories that she had thought were long gone.

In her mind's eyes she saw again three tiny graves all lying side by side in the churchyard – the graves of her own three stillborn babies – and the heartbreak of losing them one after the other all those years ago swept through her afresh. She and Wilf had lived in Atherstone, a neighbouring town, back then. Molly had not met and wed him until she was in her thirties, and they had dreamed of having a large family. But each pregnancy had resulted in a stillbirth, and even now never a day went by when she did not mourn her lost girls. Still, her consolation had been her beloved husband. It was he who had found the cottage she was living in now shortly after the birth of their third daughter, and they had moved here and lived happily ever since until his premature death.

'Please, God, don't let this little one go the same way as my babies,' Molly prayed silently as she stared down at the tiny form, and she went on praying as Bessie began to rub and coax life into the tiny infant. Once the water was ready, Bessie washed the little body inch by inch, forever rubbing and moving the little limbs to bring her back to life. But her efforts appeared to be all in vain, for the child remained motionless.

Molly's heart ached as she looked on helplessly. 'It's no good, Bessie.' Her voice was loaded with sadness as she reached out to still her neighbour's arm. Slowly, Bessie sat back on her heels to wipe the sweat from her brow with the back of her hand.

They gazed on the infant in silence for some moments, each lost in their own thoughts, until Bessie suddenly gasped and reached out to clutch Molly's arm.

'I'm sure I saw her fingers move just then...Yes, yes, I did. Look, she's alive!'

Without waiting for encouragement, Bessie immediately renewed her efforts, rubbing and moving the little limbs methodically. Suddenly the baby's eyes flew open and a thin wail pierced the air. Both women whooped with delight and by the time Molly had bent to lift the child into her arms, her lusty cries were echoing from the rafters.

'By God, Bessie, it's a miracle. Nothin' short of a miracle.' Molly laughed through her tears as Bessie looked on, beaming in agreement.

'Aye, it is that, but I reckon the next thing we need to do is feed the little mite. By, them cries are enough to waken the dead.'

Hastily she stood and dropped into the comfortable old rocking chair that stood at the side of the fire. Then, after fumbling with the buttons on her blouse, she pushed aside her warm woollen undershirt and bared her swollen breast.

'Here, give her to me,' she ordered, and within seconds the baby's cries stopped as if by magic as she fastened on to Bessie's nipple. As she sucked greedily, Bessie and Molly grinned at each other.

Bessie's own two-month-old baby, Beatrice, was tucked up in her crib fast asleep in Bessie's cottage, her little stomach full of her mother's milk. But it was obvious from the hungry slurping of this child that there was more than enough in Bessie's generous breasts to satisfy her too. After what seemed an age she gave a big hiccup of contentment and her lashes fluttered down on to her cheeks as she fell fast asleep in Bessie's arms.

'That's done the trick,' Bessie grinned. 'Now I'd best get round home and sort out some of our Beatrice's clothes fer her to use till yer decide what you're going to do wi' her.' As she spoke, she laid the baby in the corner of the old settee against a cushion.

'Right, Molly, now you sort out a nice deep drawer fer her to sleep in. Line it wi' a shawl or sommat nice an' soft, an' I'll be back in a minute.' And then she was gone, leaving Molly to do as she was told. After that she planned to soak the baby's wrappings in a bucket and then wash them through the next day, so they were as good as new. For they, too, belonged to the babe, since they had come from her mother.

Almost an hour later the two women sat tired but contented, in front of the fire, each gazing down on the baby as she slept soundly in one of Molly's deep dresser drawers.

'She's got the face of a little angel,' Bessie commented.

Molly nodded. 'Just as her mother had.'

They sat in companionable silence for some minutes until Bessie asked, 'Is there anythin' else in the bag, Molly?'

Drawing it on to her lap, Molly delved into its depths.

'I don't think so,' she mumbled, but then her fingers closed around something tucked deep in a corner. 'Hold on, there is somethin' in here.'

As she withdrew a small black velvet box, Bessie leaned forward to stare at it with interest. 'What's in it?' she asked curiously.

Molly shrugged. 'We'll soon find out, won't we?' So saying, she fumbled with a tiny clasp. As the lid sprang back, both women's mouths gaped with amazement at its contents. Nestling on a bed of silk was a beautiful golden locket attached to an ornate gold chain. A large emerald was set into its centre that sparkled and reflected the light of the fire.

'Well, stone the crows. It must be worth a king's ransom.' Bessie had never in her life seen anything like it. 'Look inside it,' she urged impatiently, and as Molly carefully opened it, two tiny portraits were revealed. On one side was a picture of a fair-haired young man with a kindly face, and on the other was a portrait of a strikingly attractive girl whom Molly instantly recognised as the young woman in the church doorway.

'That's *her*,' she exclaimed. 'The girl who was in trouble. I told yer she was beautiful, didn't I?'

'I won't argue with that,' Bessie agreed. 'Problem is, it don't tell us *who* she is, does it?'

Molly sighed as she shook her head.

'One thing's for sure, if you sold it you'd be set up for years,' Bessie commented.

Molly bristled at the very idea. 'This belongs to the little 'un, it's not mine to sell. It may be all she'll ever have of her mother.' Again they lapsed into silence until after some minutes Bessie dared to ask the question that was on both their minds.

'What yer goin' to do wi' her, Molly? Are yer goin' to keep her?'

Molly shrugged. 'Everything's happened so fast, I ain't had time to think, but happen we'll hear what's become of her mother.'

'That may well be, but what if we don't? Will yer keep her then?'

'How can I?' Molly's voice was sad. 'I'm no spring chicken, Bessie. What would happen to her while I was at work? An' I *do* have to work, yer know. There's no one to keep *me*.'

'Well, there's an easy way round that, woman. I could have her in the day for yer. Or there's another option: that loom upstairs is standing idle. Yer could always work from home again if yer decided that yer did want to keep her.'

Molly pondered on her words. The only other alternative for the poor little mite that she could think of was the workhouse, and the very thought of leaving her there made her shudder.

'In the meantime yer should think of giving her a name. We've got to call her somethin', haven't we?' Bessie went on.

Again Molly thought of her own three stillborn daughters and the names she had once so

30

lovingly chosen for them.

'We'll call her Amy Elizabeth Hannah,' she said softly.

Bessie grinned. 'By, that sounds posh,' she giggled. 'All o' my brood have but one name each.'

'But where would we tell everyone she came from?' mused Molly as her thoughts raced on ahead, and again both women lapsed into silence.

'I know,' said Bessie eventually. 'We could say she was yer daughter's child. That she lived away an' died giving birth. That she were a young widow, and you've taken your granddaughter in.'

Molly thought about it. 'I suppose that does sound believable,' she admitted, "cos by the time Wilf an' I got this cottage we were of an age that we could have had a daughter that had moved away to live. But that's only to be considered if we can't find her mother.'

Bessie nodded. 'Of course,' she agreed. 'I'd help yer all I could and it would be our secret, just yours and mine. No one else need ever know any different.'

Molly balked at the thought of the lies she would have to tell. But then the other option, the workhouse, was just too terrible to even contemplate. It was a dark forbidding place that the people of the town avoided whenever possible, and it was a well-known fact that many of the infants who were placed in there never came out again.

This had turned out to be a strange Christmas Eve and no mistake, both women thought as they sipped at their tea and sat admiring Amy Elizabeth Hannah who was sleeping peacefully in her makeshift crib.

31

Chapter Two

1835

As Bessie entered Molly's bright little cottage on a blistering hot day in 1835, she was as usual struck by the difference between her neighbour's home and her own. Molly's place was as spick and span as a new pin. Everything seemed to gleam – the copper pans suspended above the fireplace, the plates on the wooden dresser; even the stone floor with the brightly coloured peg rugs scattered here and there looked spotless.

Bessie sighed as she thought of her own cottage. She had yet another baby to care for now and her tiny home was bursting at the seams. Jeannie, her new baby, made her brood up to five children. There was Toby, the eldest at thirteen, followed by Mary, Beatrice, Henry and now little Jeannie, and there would have been seven of them, had she not lost two children the previous year to measles. Her husband, Jim, was a good man, a hard worker who tipped his wages up as regularly as clockwork every Friday. But even so, it was a continuous battle just to keep the wolf from the door. Even with Toby's wages it was still hard to cope with the demands of her ever-growing family.

Toby had recently joined his father at the Griff Hollows pit. Her firstborn was the apple of Bessie's eye and she had adored him since the moment he drew breath. She always laughingly told anyone who would listen that she had named him after the Toby jugs that were so popular at the time, because of his scrunched-up little face when he was born. He was a good lad, and although she was grateful for the extra money he earned, it hurt her to see him doing such a menial job, for her Toby was bright, with an unquenchable thirst for knowledge. Every day before beginning his shift at the pit he would study, and he never tired of telling his mother that one day he intended to be a teacher. Bessie did not doubt him: she felt her son was destined for better things and encouraged him in his ambition as much as she possibly could.

Bessie guessed that this was what had formed the bond between him and Amy, for already at just five years old she could say the alphabet and write her name, along with other words that even Bessie couldn't write. Toby would spend hours of an evening round at Molly's teaching Amy her letters and numbers, and Bessie had long since been forced to admit that Toby was closer to her than to any of his own sisters or brother Henry. He obviously doted on the little girl and she in turn doted on him. It had been like this ever since Molly took Amy in, and Bessie could see no sign of it changing now. In fact, she didn't mind it, for she was also extremely fond of her. Amy and her Beatrice had lain side by side in the same crib and fed from the same breasts, and Bessie loved the child almost as much as her own brood.

The sound of the children's laughter reached her now as they skipped past the cottage door. Amy and Beatrice were almost inseparable although they were as different as chalk from cheese. Beatrice was the taller of the two, with straight mousy hair and solemn grey eyes. She was a quiet little girl, content to follow Amy about whilst Amy, although more petite, had the more outgoing personality. She had huge dark brown eyes that could appear almost black if she were upset, and her hair, which defied any ribbon to hold it for long, cascaded down her back in thick auburn curls.

But it wasn't just the child's beauty and her dimpled smile that set her apart from Beatrice and the other children in the neighbourhood; it was the way that Molly dressed her. You would never see Amy in the dull browns and greys that were usual for the children thereabouts. Instead, Molly would sit for hours stitching her little dresses of all the colours of the rainbow from remnants of material that she had bought from the market. Sadly, Molly had never discovered what had happened to Amy's mother and sometimes Bessie suspected that Molly had forgotten that Amy wasn't really hers. In many ways Amy was spoiled, but even so she had such a bright and kindly little spirit that no one could fail to love her.

Molly absolutely adored her. Since taking Amy in, her life had completely changed. The child was her reason to live, and never a day went by when she didn't thank God for her. Molly also had a big soft spot for Toby, and since he had taken on the role of Amy's protector she loved him even more. Whenever she had a few pennies to spare she would buy him a book and he would read it from cover to cover again and again. He would sit at night and read stories to Amy as Molly sat in her rocking chair quietly sewing, and the old lady would smile at the expressions of wonder that flitted across the child's face as the stories unfolded. In truth, Molly could not confess to being much of a scholar herself, but that made her all the more determined that Amy should be educated. She was as proud of Amy as Bessie was of Toby, and this over the last years had strengthened the bond between them.

For some time now, Molly had taken to working at home again, using the loom in the attic. Once a week Amos Bennett would come and collect the ribbons she had weaved and pay her the wages that were due. Molly had soon discovered that she couldn't earn as much as she had when working in the factory, for her loom was merely a rude single handloom, which restricted the types of ribbons she could weave. It was, however, excellent for turning out tartan plaids and rich plain ribbons, and luckily these were still very much in demand. Amy would stand at the side of the loom for hours at a time, fascinated by the beautiful ribbons she produced as Molly smiled at her fondly. Although her savings jar was not quite as full as it had used to be, it suited Molly to have extra time to spend with Amy and she was more content than she had been for many years.

But today, Molly had no intention of working all day, for this was the day that Mary, Bessie's twelve year old, was going for an interview at Forrester's Folly for the position of laundrymaid. It was reputed to be a very grand house on the outskirts of the town, the home of a local factory-owner, and Mary had secured the interview after applying for the post she had seen advertised in a

35

local shop window. They were all very excited about it and could hardly wait for Mary to return to tell them all about it.

Glancing up at the skylight at the position of the sun in the cloudless blue sky, Molly realised that it was already mid-afternoon and that Bessie would probably already be downstairs waiting for her. Slowing the treadle, she leaned away from the rest and placed down the shuttle that she had been expertly throwing from hand to hand. Then stretching and flexing her aching fingers, she descended the stairs to find Bessie standing watching the children from the tiny kitchen window.

She smiled at Molly over her shoulder. 'Just come and look at these two little imps,' she urged as Molly joined her.

The two girls were running up and down the cobblestones that ran the length of the cottages laughing and giggling with not a care in the world, while Henry and little Jeannie watched them admiringly.

'It does your heart good to see them so carefree, don't it?' grinned Molly.

Bessie nodded. 'Aye, it does that, I just hope our Mary is smilin' when she comes back from her interview.' Her homely face suddenly clouded and Molly patted her arm.

'Mary is a good girl. She'll get the job, never you fear,' she said confidently. 'In the meantime, let's have a cup o' tea an' take the weight off our feet, eh?'

Shuffling away she pushed the kettle into the heart of the fire. She knew how much it would mean to Bessie if Mary got this job, although she

36

also knew that Bessie had very mixed feelings about it. Her daughter would have to live in the servants' quarters at Forrester's Folly, which would make a little more room in Bessie's cottage for the rest of her family, but Molly knew that Bessie would miss her dreadfully.

Bessie remained at the door. 'She surely can't be much longer now,' she sighed, gazing up the lane over the heads of the children.

Molly laughed. 'Come away in, woman. Yer know what they say – a watched pot never boils. Now come and drink this tea.'

Obediently, Bessie crossed to the large scrubbed table and plonked herself down while Molly made the tea. It was some minutes later when a shadow in the door blocked out the sunlight and Mary almost exploded into the room, her plain little face alight.

'I got the job, Mam – *I got it!*' She was almost beside herself with excitement.

Bessie threw her arms about her and hugged her in delight. 'You clever girl, you. When do yer start? What are yer hours? When's yer day off?'

Laughing, Mary held up her hand to stem the flow of questions, saying, 'Slow down, Mam, let me sit down an' get me breath back an' I'll answer as many questions as yer like.'

Once the girl was seated, both women stared at her intently.

'Now tell us *everythin'*, mind, right from the time yer got there,' ordered Bessie, and nodding, Mary began.

'Well, I got there and the gate man let me in, then it took me *ten whole minutes* to walk up the

37

drive – it seemed to go on forever. And the grounds ... eeh, you've never seen anythin' like 'em. There are flowerbeds everywhere and the grass is so green. Apparently there are two gardeners who work fulltime just to see to the grounds.'

Both women were already suitably impressed and stared at Mary in awe.

Aware of her captive audience the girl continued, 'Nearer to the house is trees all cut into the shapes of animals. A to ... topiarararay or sommat like that, I think it's called. Eeh, they're lovely, I'm tellin' yer. An' there are real marble steps that lead up to a front door that looks as big as the whole of the front of our cottages.'

Bessie gaped in amazement as Mary giggled and went on, 'To one side o' the house is a little wood, and inside it looks just like a carpet o' wild flowers. The other side o' the house, the lawns slope right down to the River Anker and there's a little boathouse where Mr Forrester has his very own boats.'

It was Molly's turn to gawp now and Mary, who was enjoying herself immensely, gabbled on, 'Well, as I'm approaching the front o' the house, the butler comes out to meet me. Yer should have seen his uniform; the buttons on his jacket were so shiny I could see me face in 'em. He told me to follow the path around the house to the back to the servants' entrance, so I did.' Here she stopped to catch her breath, but both women urged her on impatiently. 'Around the back is the stableblock, the laundry room an' the dairy, and by the time I got to the back door I can tell yer I was shakin' like a leaf.' She giggled again as she recalled her nervousness.

'Anyway, then the housekeeper appears and she takes me down this big long passage to the kitchen. I couldn't believe me eyes when I saw it. It must be as big as the one in Buckingham Palace!'

She nodded as if to confirm the truth of her words before hurrying on, 'The housekeeper, well at first she points to a chair and tells me to sit down, so I did, then she starts asking me all these questions. I was so scared by then that the words kept gettin' caught in me throat. After that she took me back out across the yard and showed me the laundry room – that's massive too. There's great dolly tubs and mangles everywhere, and there was a girl there washing who winked at me and made me feel a bit more at ease like. It's her job I'll be takin' as she's leavin' to have a baby. Anyway, the housekeeper asked me if I thought I could do the job and I said yes, so then she took me back to the big house and told me to sit down and sit still.' She paused again, trying to recall every single thing that had happened to her so as to leave nothing out. By now Amy and Beatrice had also joined her audience and were standing side-by-side, hands clasped, hanging on to her every word in the doorway.

Eventually, Mary continued, 'It seemed like I sat there for ages an' there were people scurryin' about everywhere. One of the maids was laying this little trolley on wheels for the master and the mistress's tea. I don't mind admittin', the things she were loading on to that trolley made me mouth water. There were tiny sandwiches all cut into dainty little triangles with the crusts trimmed off, an' homemade cakes and tarts with icing on the top and cream inside. And the teapot, well ... I'm tellin' yer it must have been made of solid silver, *and* the milk jug and the sugar dish. And the china tea cups and saucers and plates were so fine that you could see your hand through 'em.' She paused for effect and unconsciously licked her lips at the memory.

'Any road, once the trolley was fully loaded, this other girl comes in. Cook told me she was Lily the parlourmaid and she was really pretty. She had on a black dress with a little frilly apron and a starched white cap, an' off she goes to take the trolley to the master and mistress. Then when she'd gone, Cook gave me a cup of tea and a big wedge o' fruitcake. It were lovely and it melted in me mouth. I can still taste it now, mm!' She rubbed her stomach and grinned at the memory, and now it was Amy and Beatrice's turn to lick their lips.

'Cook's name is Mrs Gibbs but everyone just calls her Cook. She frightened me at first 'cos she were shouting out orders right, left and centre whilst she were gettin' the tea ready. But then once the parlourmaid had gone she calmed down and was really nice. She told me not to look so worried, that her bark was worse than her bite and that's when she gave me the tea and cake.'

By now Amy and Beatrice had sidled up to the table and were listening wide-eyed.

'After a time the housekeeper came back and told me to follow her. We seemed to walk for miles through all these corridors at the back of the house. She took me upstairs and showed me this bedroom, and it were then that I realised that I must have got the job because she told me that this would be the room I would be sharin' with the other laundrymaid, Lizzie, the one I had met earlier in the laundry.'

'What's the room like?' asked Bessie, and Mary frowned as she tried to recall every detail.

'I suppose it were fairly sparse. There was a wooden wardrobe that I'm to share with Lizzie, until she leaves that is, two beds an' a washstand.' In fact, although sparse, the room had appeared luxurious to Mary. She had never had a bed all to herself before, but she didn't like to say that for fear of hurting her mam's feelings.

'Next we went back downstairs and she told me that I will be issued with a uniform when I start. I can begin next Monday, and I'll have every Sunday afternoon off, then if I do all right after my first six months, I'll get to have two afternoons off. But I'm telling yer now, Mam, I *will* do all right, I promise, and one day I'll make me way up to be a parlourmaid, you just wait an' see.'

Her face was glowing with the excitement of it all, and in that moment her homely features could almost have been described as pretty. Standing, Bessie gathered her into her arms and gave her a big cuddle. She was delighted and yet also dreading Mary going, all at once. Mary would be the first of her brood to fly the nest, and the thought of losing her made Bessie's heart ache. She was a good girl, almost like a second little mother to her brothers and sisters. If truth be told, she was

41

Bessie's right arm – and she would miss her daughter sorely.

Noting the unshed tears in Bessie's eyes and guessing at her feelings, Molly rose noisily from the table. 'I think this calls for a celebration,' she said loudly, winking at Amy and Beatrice, and the two little girls clapped their hands with glee and went to fetch the others.

Within minutes they were all tucking into great wedges of Molly's own home-made sponge cake and the occasion took on a party atmosphere with much giggling and laughing. But all good things must come to an end and eventually Bessie rose, eyeing the mantel clock.

'Come on then, you lot,' she grinned. 'Let's be havin' yer back round home. Yer dad an' Toby will be home from work soon and expecting to find their meals on the table.'

With much merriment the little family departed and after clearing away the pots into the deep stone sink, Molly set about preparing their own meal of scrag end of lamb with a good handful of barley and carrots.

Amy hurried away upstairs and soon reappeared with her treasured pencils and papers, and within minutes was seated at the old oak table contentedly drawing. Molly never ceased to be amazed at Amy's sketches. She was obviously going to be a gifted artist, for already she could draw pictures that could put the work of most adults to shame. Were she to be given the choice between a new pencil or a sweetmeat, she would choose the pencil every time.

Lately she had taken to drawing hats, and when

she went into town with Molly she would always insist that they stopped before the hat-shop window so that she could admire the designs. Forrester's Millinery hadn't been open for long and was doing extremely well, as did most of Samuel Forrester's ventures. He already owned nearly all of the ribbon factories in Abbey Street and another hat shop in the nearby town of Atherstone as well as one in London.

But then Molly begrudged him none of his success. It was a well-known fact that Samuel Forrester was a selfmade man who had worked himself up from selling ribbons from a barrow in the town centre to being one of the wealthiest men in Nuneaton.

It was at his home that Mary would be going to work. Forrester's Folly had been the talk of the town when it was built almost twenty-five years before. It was a folly of Regency architecture with turrets and towers, built on the outskirts of Caldecote, a little hamlet approximately three miles outside of Nuneaton. Samuel had ordered it to be built after announcing his engagement, and it was even said that he himself had set to and helped the workmen to build it with bricks all made and fired in Nuneaton.

Samuel Forrester had married far above his class and it was to Forrester's Folly that he had taken his new bride once it was completed. The couple had lived there ever since, and it was known that Samuel Forrester still doted on his wife who was said to be a beautiful fragile creature. It was rumoured that he was a hard taskmaster but fair, and Molly had no doubt that Mary would be well cared for once she had entered his employ. She suspected that beneath his crusty exterior beat a heart of gold and had heard over the years of many kindnesses he had done for employees of his who had fallen prey to illness or hard times. It was actually he who paid her wages and those of the many other weavers hereabouts who worked at their own looms, for they all sold their ribbons to the factories in Abbey Street, many of which were owned by Samuel Forrester.

He was often to be seen about. A tall dark handsome man, he regularly walked about the town and visited the factories, although the same could not be said about his family. Of them he was extremely protective and private. It was thought that his wife had given him only two children, a son and a daughter, but no one was really sure, for he guarded them jealously. When he was young the son had been sent away to a private school, whilst his daughter had been educated at home by a governess until she was in her teens, when Samuel Forrester had employed a private tutor to further her education at The Folly and a further house that he owned in London where he spent part of each year.

Now that the time for her to leave was approaching, Molly was quite looking forward to Mary working at Forrester's Folly. No doubt she would come home and tell them tales of the happenings there, and Molly and Bessie enjoyed a good bit of gossip as much as the next person.

It was later that evening; the meal was over, the pots were washed and put away, and Molly was sitting at the side of the empty fireplace with the back door open enjoying the balmy summer night as she stitched yet another little petticoat for Amy. Every now and then a giggle from Amy or Toby, who were sitting at the table doing sums on a wooden abacus, made her look up and smile, and without thinking she offered up a silent prayer of gratitude. All in all, life was good and she had a lot to be thankful for. The youngsters' heads, bent close together at the table, made a pleasing contrast. Toby's fair hair, straight as a poker, and Amy's deep auburn curls seemed almost joined as they worked in harmony to do their sums. And it was as she gazed at them that, for the first time, Molly had a premonition of things to come. It was something in Toby's eyes as he looked at Amy. The youngsters looked for all the world as if they belonged together. Molly was a great believer in fate. What would be would be. And on that thought she returned to her sewing and left the children to themselves, with a smile playing at the corners of her mouth.

Chapter Three

Amy and Beatrice stared down the lane expectantly. It was Mary's first day off from Forrester's Folly since she had started her new job and they had been waiting for her for over an hour.

'She can't be much longer,' complained Amy, pushing her damp curls from her forehead. The sun was blazing down and both little girls were hot and sticky. Luckily they didn't have to wait much longer, for minutes later, Mary turned the corner in the lane and came into view. Delighted, both children flew to meet her and Beatrice hugged her sister tight. At sight of them, Mary's eyes filled with tears and a huge lump formed in her throat. The first week had not gone at all as she had imagined it would. The hours were long and hard; she missed her family and was suffering from a severe bout of homesickness. But not wishing to upset the children, she smiled at them as best she could and pointed to the basket on her arm.

'I've got some rare treats in here for yer,' she told them. 'Cakes left over from yesterday tea-time. Cook let me bring them for yer.'

'Cor, can I have one now?' asked Beatrice, her eyes shining greedily as she reached for the linen cloth covering the basket.

Mary laughed and gently slapped her hand away. 'No yer can't, yer little madam. You'll wait till we get home, so there.'

Beatrice pouted but then as Mary grinned at her she laughed and soon side-by-side they reached the little row of cottages.

As Mary passed, the neighbours called a greeting through their open doors and the girl waved back. Before she had even managed to get to her own door, Bessie flew out to meet her and caught her in a fierce embrace then, holding her at arm's length, she surveyed her quizzically.

'Are yer all right, love?' Her voice was loaded with concern as she noted Mary's pale face and red-rimmed eyes, but the girl smiled bravely.

46

'O' course I am, Mam, why wouldn't I be?' Arm-in-arm they entered the cottage. Within seconds the children were swarming around the basket like a plague of locusts and minutes later, every last crumb of the dainty tarts and pastries were gone.

'By, they made short work o' them,' laughed Bessie as Mary managed a weak smile. Now that all the goodies were gone, the children, apart from Amy and Beatrice, ran back outside, almost knocking Molly over in their haste as she entered the cottage.

'Steady on, you lot,' she scolded with a grin, but then as her eyes came to rest on Mary she frowned.

'Are yer all right, lass?' she asked, exactly as Bessie had done only minutes before. Suddenly Mary's lip trembled and her chin drooped to her chest.

Bessie was beside her instantly. 'Oh, there, there, lass, come on – tell me what's wrong now,' she pleaded, and the tears that had been threatening suddenly welled from her daughter's eyes to pour in torrents down her pale cheeks.

'I'm all right, Mam, honest – just a bit homesick, that's all. Take no notice o' me.'

Bessie's heart went out to her. 'Come on, now – tell me what's wrong, please. It can't be just that yer homesick. There must be sommat else.'

Catching Molly's eye, she shook her head slowly. This wasn't at all how she had imagined her daughter's first homecoming to be. By now Mary could no longer stem her feelings and, burying her face in her mother's ample bosom, she sobbed as if her heart would break. When

47

eventually she managed to calm down a little, Molly ushered Beatrice and Amy from the room, then going to Mary she said gently, 'Now then, darlin', come on. All the little 'uns are outside out o' the way now, so what's *really* the matter?'

Sniffing loudly, Mary slowly began to draw off the white cotton gloves she was wearing, and the sight of her poor hands made Molly and Bessie gasp. They were a mass of red weeping sores, the skin missing completely in places. At sight of them Bessie began to cry too.

'Oh, yer poor little love.' Guilt was flooding through her. 'You ain't going back there and that's a fact!'

Molly chewed on her lip. 'It's the washing soda that's done it,' she commented wisely. 'It's 'cos you ain't been used to having yer hands in water all day. But I promise yer, within an hour I can make 'em feel easier if you'll let me, though I'll have to be cruel to be kind.'

Looking Mary straight in the eye she waited for an answer and when the girl slowly nodded she crossed to Bessie's sink where she collected a tin bowl. 'Right, Bessie, get me a big block o' salt,' she ordered.

Bessie hurried away to the pantry and when she returned with it, Molly had the bowl half-full of hot water. She began to dissolve the salt in it before telling Mary in a voice that brooked no argument, 'Soak yer hands in there.'

Obediently the poor girl did as she was told but as her hands entered the water she cried out with pain.

Holding her wrists, Molly ordered, 'Keep 'em

48

in there now, I promise you'll benefit.'

Ten tearful minutes later, the trembling girl lifted her sore hands from the water and Molly tenderly dried them. Then, taking some salt, she began to rub it as gently as she could into Mary's chafed hands. Once that was done she hurried back to her own cottage and returned with a large jar of goose grease.

'There – now rub some o' that in, then put your gloves back on,' she said kindly. When everything had been done as she had asked, she smiled sympathetically at the solemn-faced girl.

'Now I know it hurts, but if you rub a bit o' salt in every night and then some goose grease, your skin'll harden up in no time. I know the goose grease has got a nasty smell, but I guarantee it'll work. Here, look – I'll tuck it in yer basket fer yer. There's sommat else as will help an' all if you've the stomach to try it.'

When Mary raised a questioning eyebrow, Molly grinned. 'Do yer have a chamber pot in yer room?'

Mary flushed, saying, 'Yes, we both have.'

'Good, then each mornin' wash yer hands in it afore yer empty it. Not the nicest o' things to do admittedly, but if it helps then it will be worth it.'

Mary wrinkled her nose in distaste at the thought but then gave a watery smile. 'Thanks, Molly, and don't worry, Mam – I *am* goin' back. Happen I was just feelin' a bit sorry for meself.'

From then on, the rest of the afternoon improved but when the girl left, Bessie was quiet.

'Do yer think she'll be all right, Molly?' she asked worriedly.

Molly smiled. 'O' course she'll be all right.

49

Mary is made o' stern stuff an' it'll take more than sore hands to make her walk away from such a good job,' she answered, but inside she was thinking, My Amy will *never* do a job like that so long as I draw breath.

The next Sunday saw a completely different Mary swinging down the lane. Her hands, although still red raw in places, were hardening up slowly just as Molly had promised, and she looked much more her usual cheerful self.

This week, besides her basket of goodies she had also brought them some gossip. 'I've been inside the main house,' she told them joyfully. 'And I'm telling yer, Mam, it's like nothing yer could ever imagine.'

It was slightly cooler this week and Beatrice and Amy stared at her with shining eyes, happy to stay in and listen.

'Why did you get to go in there then?' Amy asked curiously.

Mary patted the younger girl's springing curls affectionately. 'I'd fetched some dry towels in from the line and the housekeeper told me to take 'em up to the first floor to the mistress's rooms,' she told her. 'Oh, yer should see the carpet in the foyer – it's red and it goes right from wall to wall – and all the way up the stairs are great paintings all in heavy gold frames.' Amy's eyes were wide with wonder and as Mary went on they grew wider still.

She told them of huge crystal chandeliers that sparkled like diamonds in the sunlight, and solid mahogany sideboards that were polished till you could see your face in them, and every pair of eyes in the room were on her as she related her tale.

'Do yer ever get to see the master or the mistress?' asked Beatrice inquisitively.

'Occasionally,' Mary replied, 'and I *have* seen Master Adam, that's Mr Forrester's son, and his wife.'

'Ooh! What's she like?' Immediately Amy was interested again. 'Is she beautiful like a princess?'

Mary chuckled. 'I suppose she *is* pretty,' she admitted, 'but only in looks. No one seems to like her very much and she's...' She sought in her mind for the right words. 'Well, spoiled, I suppose. Her name is Eugenie and we often hear her shouting and throwing tantrums at Master Adam if something upsets her, yet he still seems to dote on her fer all that.'

'What about Master Adam's sister?' It was Molly asking now, but Mary could only shrug.

'All I know is that her name is Jessica. No one ever mentions her, but Cook told me on the quiet that she and the master had some big fall out some years ago and he ordered her from the house. They've seen neither hide nor hair of her since. And the mistress, well, from what I can make out, ever since then she's become some sort of an invalid, yer know? She stays in her room a lot, but I've never seen her either.'

'Who else is there then?' piped up Amy, and Mary screwed up her eyes as she tried to think of all the staff. After a time she began to count them off on her fingers.

'There's Lily the parlourmaid, an' Mrs Gibbs, the cook, then there's Ruby, the chambermaid, and o' course Alice, who works in the dairy.

There's Tom, he's the gardener but we don't get to see much of him 'cos he lives in a cottage in the grounds wi' his missus an' his kids and he has a young lad that works under him but I don't know his name yet. Apparently, the master took him from the workhouse an' he lives in wi' Tom an' his lot. Then there's Seth – Mr Turpin – he's head over all the stables an' he lives in the rooms above the stable-block wi' his missus, Winifred, an' their kids. There was a butler an' all when I first went there but he's left now an' it don't look like they're goin' to replace him. I heard Mrs Benn say sommat about him bein' surplus to requirements to the master when I passed 'em on me way to the laundry one day. And that's about all the people I've got to know yet. Oh, except for the house-keeper, Mrs Benn, who I just mentioned, but she tends to keep herself very much to herself. Oh, and o' course there's Joe, he's Seth's son an' one o' the stable-boys. He lives with his mam and dad above the stables.' As she mentioned Joe's name she flushed a dull brick-red and Beatrice giggled.

'Do yer fancy him then, our Mary? Is he hand-some?'

Mary flushed an even deeper red if that were possible. 'O' course I don't fancy him,' she denied much too quickly and Molly and Bessie ex-changed an amused grin. It sounded to them like Mary was developing her first crush, but neither of them wanted to embarrass her by pursuing it, so they quickly changed the subject.

The rest of the afternoon passed in happy chatter and when it was time to leave, Amy and Beatrice were allowed to walk Mary to the end of the lane with strict instructions to come straight back after seeing her off.

'Yer *will* come again next Sunday, won't yer?' implored Amy as they parted.

Dropping a kiss on her unruly curls, Mary grinned. ''Course I will,' she promised, and with a final wave she turned and hurried away.

'One day I'm going to go and work with our Mary,' Beatrice declared solemnly. 'Will you come too, Amy?'

Amy shook her head. 'No, I won't,' she replied without hesitation. '*I'm* going to work in the hat factory.' And on that note the two little girls made their way home.

The rest of the summer passed pleasantly enough, with Mary's visits one of the highlights of each week. Often, Molly would take Amy into town to shop. She had long since learned to avoid going in on Saturdays, for that was the day when the farmers brought their beasts into the cattle-market.

The butchers would be there, critically eyeing each animal as it arrived and once they had purchased the ones they wanted and struck a deal with the farmer, they would often slaughter them there and then, and sell off the joints of meat to the passers-by.

Amy had only witnessed this once and had become so hysterical that Molly had vowed never to let the child see it again. For months afterwards, Amy had suffered terrible nightmares and ever since, they had never gone into town on a Saturday again. More often than not, now they shopped on a Wednesday, which was also a market-day, and Amy looked forward to it. She loved the stalls and the hustle and bustle of the crowds and would drag Molly from one colourful display to another as the stallholders smiled at her indulgently and waved a cheery greeting.

Molly would swell with pride at the admiring glances. Amy was like a little ray of sunshine on a dark day and her mischievous but warm little nature made her shine all the more.

It was on one such day as they were walking along Abbey Street that Amy tugged on Molly's hand and pointed ahead excitedly. 'Look, Gran, look at the lovely horse and carriage.' She almost dragged Molly along in her haste as Molly smiled indulgently.

'Aye, I can see it, but slow down, love, or you'll have me over.'

The carriage was some way away, stood outside the hat shop. When they were still some yards from it, Samuel Forrester suddenly stepped from inside the shop and, walking round to the other side of the carriage, he climbed inside, nodding to the driver as he did so to move on.

Amy was still dragging Molly along, intent on catching a closer look at the beautiful dapple-grey mare before it pulled away.

It was as they passed the fine carriage that Molly caught a glimpse of the woman inside. She supposed that this must be Josephine, Samuel Forrester's wife, out on one of her rare outings, and instantly all the stories that Molly had ever heard of her were proven to be true. Josephine Forrester was indeed a beauty. Even as she was thinking it, the woman suddenly turned from saying something to her husband and glanced out of the window. What happened next shook Molly to her very core. As the woman's eyes latched on to Amy, every ounce of colour seemed to drain from her face and she leaned forward to stare at the child more closely.

At the same time the child looked up and for an instant their eyes locked. Amy flashed her a huge smile but then with a clatter of hooves on the cobblestones, the carriage pulled away.

'Eeh, Gran, did you see that lovely lady?' Amy said excitedly, her young imagination fired.

Molly nodded as the child rambled on, 'She were just like the princess in the fairy story Toby read to me last night, and did you see how she was dressed? By, her bonnet was lovely and that gown she was wearin' must have been real velvet.'

Amy sighed dreamily. To her, Josephine Forrester in her fine clothes was a world away from the rest of the women who were walking about in their drab dresses and dull shawls. But for some reason the joy had suddenly gone from the day for Molly, and tugging at the little girl's hand, she said, 'Come on, love, let's get away home, me feet are aching.'

'Aw, Gran – we haven't done all our shopping yet, nor even been to the pie stall.' Disappointment clouded her face but Molly was adamant. She was more than used to people looking at Amy, yet there was something in the way that Josephine Forrester had stared at her that had rung a warning bell in her mind.

'Never mind the rest o' the shopping, we'll do that tomorrow,' she said firmly.

'All right, Gran,' agreed the little girl, never one to sulk, and with her mind full of the beautiful lady she had just seen, she skipped merrily ahead longing to get home now so that she could tell Beatrice all about it.

Molly had told Amy when she was very small that she was her gran. She said that she had taken her in when her mother died after her father had been killed in an accident, and Amy never queried why she had the same last name as her gran. Every day the old women prayed to God for forgiveness for the lies she had told, but just as Bessie had once predicted, Amy and anyone else who knew her never doubted her word. But for some reason today, for the very first time in a long while, Molly found herself thinking back to that fateful Christmas Eve, and the lies she had told lay heavy on her heart.

Some time later, after throwing her coat across the back of a silk chaise-longue in the deep bay window at Forrester's Folly, Josephine Forrester crossed to a bell-pull and tugged it. Within seconds, a maid in a frilly white apron appeared as if by magic.

'Yes, ma'am?' The girl bobbed her knee respectfully and Josephine said, 'Tea, Lily, if you please.'

'Yes, ma'am – straight away.' The girl backed towards the door and scuttled away as if her life depended on it.

'Is anything wrong, Mother? You look pale.'

Looking across to her son, Adam, who was sitting on a settee with his wife, Josephine shook her head distractedly and replied, 'No, dear, I'm quite all right. It's just...'

As her voice trailed away and she gazed from the window across the lush green lawns, her husband exchanged a worried glance with their son.

'Your mother isn't feeling too well, Adam, despite what she says. I was hoping a ride out in the carriage and a little fresh air would do her good, but unfortunately we had got no further than the hat factory in the town when she decided she wanted to come home.'

Turning suddenly as if she hadn't heard a single word he had said, Josephine demanded, 'Samuel, you *must* have seen the child. She was...' She struggled to find the right words. 'She was standing outside the hat shop with an old woman. She smiled at me and it was almost like looking at Jessica when she was that age. She had the same red hair – the same dark eyes. She even had Jessica's smile.'

A deep frown creased Adam's brow and Eugenie pouted, as they silently watched Josephine pacing the floor.

'There must be *hundreds* of children about with red hair, Mother,' Adam patiently pointed out. 'And every time you see a young woman or a child who looks even remotely like Jessica we have this same thing.'

At that moment, there came a tap to the door and Lily reappeared pushing a laden tea-trolley.

'I'm going to my room for a rest before dinner. Are you coming?' Eugenie stared at her husband imperiously but for once she did not have Adam's undivided attention; his eyes remained on his mother.

'I'll be up shortly, darling,' he replied. 'You go ahead.'

Flouncing from the room in a swish of silk skirts, she closed the door resoundingly behind her.

Taking his wife's elbow, Samuel led her to a chair and pressed her gently into it as Lily poured out the tea.

'Look, darling, you're letting your imagination run away with you again.' His voice was heavy with sadness and regret. 'As Adam pointed out, it's the same every time you see anyone with red hair or dark eyes who looks anything at all like Jessica.'

Leaning forward in his chair, Adam asked, 'How old was this child anyway, Mother?'

Josephine sighed as a picture of the lovely faced flashed before her eyes. 'About five or six, I should say,' she replied eventually.

Waving aside the tea that Lily held out to him, Adam quickly rose from his seat and strode towards the door. 'I've just remembered I have something I need to do,' he said curtly, and without another word he too left the room, much as his wife had done only moments before him.

The kitchen door had barely closed behind Lily when she gabbled out, 'There's goin' to be ructions back there again. Miss Eugenie's just stormed out o' the room in a rare old strop an' fer once Mr Adam didn't go chasin' after her skirts.'

The staff were enjoying a well-earned tea break at the enormous scrubbed table and they all looked towards her, eager to hear whatever gossip she had to impart.

'What's goin' on now then?' Cook was the first

to give in to curiosity.

'Well...' Smoothing down her starched white apron and straightening her frilly mop cap, Lily approached the table. 'Seems like the mistress went out fer a ride wi' the master an' while they were out he called in at the hat shop in town. The mistress got herself all worked up 'cos she saw a little girl who put her in mind o' Miss Jessica standin' outside it. But soon as ever the mistress mentioned Miss Jessica's name, Miss Eugenie were off.'

'Hmph, that I can well believe,' the rosy-cheeked Cook grumbled. 'If it weren't fer that spoiled little madam then I've no doubt poor Miss Jessica would be here still. That little strumpet never could stand Miss Jessica – but then she never liked anyone who Master Adam paid any attention to.'

Mary's eyes were almost starting from her head as she listened. This had certainly put some spice into the day and she could hardly wait for Lily to go on. At this rate she'd have lots of gossip to take home to her mam and Molly this coming week-end. However, much to her disappointment, the untimely entrance of Mrs Benn, the house-keeper, stopped the gossip mid-flow.

'What's this then?' As she looked sternly from Lily to her rapt audience around the table, Lily stammered, 'I were just sayin' as how there's trouble back there in the drawin' room, Mrs Benn. The mistress had gone an' got herself into a state 'cos–'

'LILY – that is quite enough! I will *not* have you gossiping about the master and mistress's affairs, do you hear me?'

59

Lily flushed a dull brick-red and dropped her eyes guiltily from the housekeeper's furious face.

'Yes, Mrs Benn,' she mumbled, almost shaking in her shoes.

'As for the rest of you,' Mrs Benn's eyes swept the table, 'have none of you any work to do? I'm sure if you haven't, I could find you all some extra jobs.'

There was the sound of chairs scraping across the red quarry tiles as everyone rose hastily from their seats and scurried off in different directions. Muttering oaths beneath her breath, Mary made her way back to the laundry. Damn and blast Mrs Benn. She had just been starting to enjoy herself. Not only that, she'd made such a hasty exit that she'd left half of one of Cook's home-made scones on her plate. She pictured it, all dripping with butter and freshly made strawberry jam...

'That Mrs Benn's a bit of a tartar, ain't she?' she remarked to Alice, who was helping her with a particularly heavy batch of laundry. 'Makes me wonder who *is* the boss in this house, her or the mistress.'

Alice giggled. 'I reckon it's Mrs Benn every time. One word from her an' the lot of us jump. It's her that's responsible fer the hirin' and firin' so no one wants to upset her.'

'An' what about this here Miss Jessica?'

The smile slid from Alice's face as she quickly looked around the yard to make sure that they couldn't be overheard. 'Least said about her the better. If the master so much as hears her name mentioned he goes off into a mood an' the poor mistress falls into one o' her swoons.'

60

'But why?' The sound of the laundry-room door slamming behind Alice was Mary's only answer. Shrugging her shoulders she followed her.

Chapter Four

1845
Grabbing the handles of the old perambulator salvaged from Bessie's coalhouse, Amy gave it a mighty tug and dragged it across the step and into the kitchen. The rain was coming down in great blistering sheets and both she and Molly were soaked to the skin.

Molly looked totally worn out, so leading her to the old rocking chair at the side of the hearth, Amy took off her gran's outer clothing and then pressed her down on to it. She then took up the bellows and blew life into the fading embers before throwing a log on to the weak flames. Once she was sure that the flames had caught, she pushed the kettle into the heart of the fire.

'You know, Gran, you shouldn't have gone out in this weather. I'm quite capable of pickin' a few logs and a bit of coal by myself.' She was undoing the laces of Molly's well-worn boots as she spoke and Molly smiled at her gratefully as she pushed her frozen feet towards the warmth of the flames.

'Stop frettin'. There's nothing much wrong wi' me, lass. I'm just tired, that's all.'

Amy was not so sure, but she had no time to comment because just then Toby entered, slamming the door shut behind him.

'By, it's wicked out there!' he exclaimed, shivering. 'It's raining cats an' dogs.' Then, as he noted Amy's wet clothes, 'You've never been out in this, have yer?' he asked, eyeing the contents of the pram, then without waiting for an answer he said sternly, 'There was no need for you to go out an' get that. You know I'd have gone and got it for you.'

'I know you would, Toby, but I'm quite able to pick coal meself. I just wish Gran hadn't insisted on coming along, that's all. Besides, you already do enough for us as it is.'

Toby sighed. 'Stubborn as mules you both are, that's your trouble,' he grumbled, although he was smiling. He could never help but smile when he looked at Amy, for even with her hair soaked and flat to her head, she was beautiful. He still came as regular as clockwork every evening, and over the last months, Amy didn't know what she would have done without him – or Molly, for that matter.

Of late, Molly's hands had become twisted with arthritis and she was forced to sit longer and longer at her loom each day to make ends meet. It had happened gradually over the last two or three years, and Amy was gravely concerned about her. Even after she had finished the steaming hot tea that Amy placed in her hands, she still looked all in and the girl patted her arm lovingly.

'Why don't you turn in, Gran?' she suggested. 'I'll fill that stone bottle with nice hot water and bring it up to you, eh?'

Molly nodded; if she were honest with herself she was feeling far from well and wishing that she hadn't ventured out today. Amy had begged her not to go but she had been saving the money she usually gave to the coalman by coalpicking from the slagheaps. She had seen a lovely woollen coat in a pretty shade of burgundy in a shop in town and had been saving the money so that she could surprise Amy with the coat for a combined birthday and Christmas present.

'I'll warm that stew up before you go to bed so that you get something hot inside you, shall I?' Amy offered, but Molly shook her head as she struggled from the chair.

'No thanks, lass. To be honest I ain't hungry. Just me bed's all I need, you'll see. I'll be fit as a fiddle in the mornin' after a good night's sleep. I've just picked up a bit of a cold.'

Amy's troubled eyes caught Toby's as Molly hobbled off to the stairs. Her bed was upstairs in the tiny room next to the one that housed her loom.

'See yer lock up now when Toby's gone,' Molly ordered as she climbed the wooden staircase. 'Goodnight, me darlin's.' Every step was an effort. She felt as if she was climbing a mountain and ached in every bone in her body.

The two young people watched her slow progress, and when she was out of sight, Amy said worriedly, 'She does too much.' Pushing the plug into the large stone bottle she had just filled from the kettle, she wrapped it in an old pillowcase, saying, 'I'll just take this up to Gran and then I'll show you the sketches I did last night.'

Toby nodded and his eyes followed her as she skipped lightly up the steps. Then, turning, he placed one hand on the mantelpiece and stared down into the flames, his thoughts racing.

Amy would be fifteen soon and old enough to marry, and he would have plucked up the courage and asked her in a second, if he'd thought she'd accept. But in his heart he knew that she wouldn't, and it hurt him deeply. Oh, he had no doubt that she loved him, but as a brother, whilst his own feelings for her had been growing steadily with the years. Why else would he still be living at home at twenty-two years old with his mam and dad? Still, life had its consolations and as long as he could see her and be near her every day, then he was happy.

When Amy had tucked the stone bottle into the bottom of the bed she pulled the counterpane up to Molly's chin and planted a gentle kiss on the old woman's brow. The skin felt feverishly hot and Amy said, 'Look, Gran, if you need me in the night just call, eh? I'll be in straight away.'

Molly offered her a weak smile. 'Will yer just stop fussin'? I've told yer all I need is a good night's rest an' I'll be right as rain. Now be off with yer an' let me get some sleep.'

Amy grinned and within seconds was back in the kitchen with Toby where the grin slid from her face. 'I'm really worried about her,' she confided fretfully. 'Do you think I should fetch the doctor in?'

Toby shook his head. 'No, Molly's a tough old bird, happen she's just caught a chill as she said,' he reassured her, and soon they were sitting with their heads bent at the table, as Amy showed him her latest sketches.

Upstairs in her tiny room, Molly lay shivering beneath the heavy layers of blankets. She had on a warm flannel nightdress, a thick woollen shawl and knitted bedsocks. Yet even with all these and the hot stone bottle pressed to her feet she couldn't seem to get warm, and sleep evaded her. She was thinking of the two young people whom she loved most in the whole world, who were at this minute sat together at the kitchen table, no doubt poring over some book or sketch.

This winter was taking its toll on Molly and it wasn't even Christmas yet, which meant there were still months of cold weather to come. Lately it was becoming harder to get up in the mornings and even with Amy's help she always felt tired.

She could sense restlessness in Amy now. All of the other girls from the cottages and hereabouts had been working for some time, and occasionally Amy complained with a smile that she was being 'Molly'-coddled. In truth, she was right, but no job she had suggested as yet seemed good enough for her to Molly.

She had such high hopes for the girl. Amy could read and write, besides which she was also a very talented artist. All this, plus the fact that there was something about her that seemed to place her in a class far above the people hereabouts: some quality that seemed to shine from within. Placing her chilly feet on the stone bottle, Molly sighed. What opening was there around here for her granddaughter, as she always thought of her? The majority of girls of Amy's age had gone into service in the big houses, or into the factories that dotted the town. But Molly wanted better than that for Amy, and although she had wracked her brains, as yet she had come up with no solution.

Just once, last New Year's Eve, Molly had allowed her to go to the Forresters' house to help prepare for a big party that they were holding. Mary had begged Molly to allow it, knowing that Amy would enjoy it. She had now moved on from the laundry and joined Lily in the house, and Mr Forrester himself had asked her if she could recommend anyone suitable as a temporary kitchen help. The first person she had thought of was Amy, and the girl's eyes had shone with excitement when Lily asked her at the thought of being able to earn some money for her gran.

Molly had had grave reservations but Amy had pleaded so much that she eventually gave in and allowed her to go.

In actual fact, Amy had seen very little of Forrester's Folly apart from the kitchen, but even that had greatly impressed her. For months afterwards, Amy had talked of little else, and ever since then she had constantly pleaded with Molly to be allowed to go out to work and earn her keep, especially since Beatrice was working now; she had taken Mary's place at The Folly as a laundry-maid. Mary now held the enviable position of being the mistress's personal maid and was loving her new role, which was a huge step up from working in the laundry.

Molly knew that she couldn't hold out against the girl for much longer. But that at the moment wasn't her biggest worry. She fretted about what would become of Amy, should anything happen to her – as eventually it surely would. She had always hoped that she would live to see Amy grown up and settled, but recently she had felt so low that she wondered if it would come about. Shivering again, she pulled the blankets more tightly about her.

'Oh well,' she muttered, 'what will be, will be,' and soon after she slipped into an exhausted sleep.

Back downstairs, Toby examined Amy's latest sketches. They were all drawings of hats and dresses and all extremely good.

'You know, you have all the makings of a first-class designer,' he remarked.

Amy blushed at the compliment. 'And *you* have all the makings of a first-class teacher,' she teased, but then becoming serious she went on, 'I'd *really* like to work at the hat factory. I didn't mind missing the opportunity of becoming a laundrymaid at The Folly because I'd worry about leaving Gran on her own if I had to live in... But if I worked at the hat factory I could still come home each evening and look after her. But Gran won't hear of me trying to get a job yet.'

She looked so downhearted that Toby patted her hand sympathetically, thinking how pretty she looked with the firelight shining on her hair.

'It's only 'cos she loves you and she worries about you,' he pointed out gently.

Amy nodded in complete agreement. 'I know that, Toby, but I'm the only one of my age around here who isn't working yet, and I'd like to tip some wages up to Gran. She's kept me long enough and now I want to make life a little easier for her.'

'But you *do* make her life easier,' he argued. 'You wash, iron, cook and clean. In fact, you do more than your share.'

Sighing in exasperation, Amy stared into the fire. 'I know that – but it's not enough, is it? Gran works far too hard for a woman of her age but unfortunately I'm nowhere near as good as she is at weaving. I just don't seem to have the knack.'

Her head wagged miserably. 'I know lately, because she hasn't been feeling so grand, that she's been dipping into her savings jar to make ends meet and I just feel so useless.'

Toby sympathised. He could understand how Amy felt, but he could also see Molly's point too. 'Well, there's no sense in fretting,' he told her. 'Things will come right in the end, you'll see.'

But the very next morning Amy had cause to wonder, for when she took her gran a cup of tea, she found her burning up with fever and soaked to the skin with sweat. Even her blankets were damp and her eyes were unnaturally bright.

'Gran, Gran, what's wrong?' Amy's heart began to thud painfully against her ribs as she stared down at the woman she adored. Molly seemed incapable of answering and, panicking now, Amy put down the mug, slopping tea on to the chest of drawers at the side of the bed. She then flew down the stairs and along the row of cottages into Bessie's kitchen.

'Please come quickly,' she begged as tears rained down her cheeks. 'Gran's really bad and I don't know what to do!'

Bessie was in the act of clearing the breakfast

pots from the table but she immediately dumped them unceremoniously into the deep sink and hitching up her skirts followed Amy back along the fronts of the cottages at a trot.

When she saw Molly looking very old and frail in the great brass bed she wasted no time at all.

'Run for the doctor now,' she ordered sharply. 'And tell him to be quick about it, else he'll have me to answer to.'

Amy needed no second bidding, and without waiting to even snatch up her shawl she flew to do as she was told.

Luckily she caught the doctor just as he was leaving his house in Swan Lane and he followed her back to the cottage immediately. Once inside the tiny bedroom he ushered both Amy and Bessie into the next room. Then quickly he began to examine the old woman in the spotlessly clean bed. When he called them back in some minutes later, his face was grave. 'I'm afraid it's pneumonia,' he told them, and Amy began to cry. Molly was all she had in the world and the thought that she could lose her was terrifying. Bessie's arm snaked about her slim waist comfortingly. She felt like crying herself but knew that if she was to be of any help at all, then she must hold herself together.

'What can be done for her?' she asked as calmly as she could.

'Well, for a start-off I want her bed brought down into the kitchen; she *must* be kept warm. I want you to sponge her down regularly with cool water and you *must* get some fluids into her. Do you think you can manage that?'

Bessie nodded. 'We'll manage. Our Toby can

come and carry her downstairs, and the bed, and then me and Amy can see to the rest. I know that Jim will help too as much as he can, when he gets back from the pit.'

Satisfied that his orders would be obeyed, the doctor nodded then after fumbling about in his seemingly bottomless bag he produced a bottle of dark brown medicine. 'She must have one teaspoon of this four times a day,' he told her. 'And I'll call back again this evening on my way home.' Seeing their worried faces, he added kindly, 'Don't worry about payment tonight. We'll work something out.'

Bessie nodded as she took the medicine. 'Everything will be done just as you say,' she assured him and he smiled.

Amy was still crying but as soon as the doctor had gone, Bessie rounded on her. There were times when you had to be cruel to be kind and Bessie felt that this was one of them.

'Right then, Amy.' Her voice was cool. 'That'll be quite enough snivellin' fer now. If we're going to get your gran through this, then we've got to keep our wits about us, ain't we?'

Amy eyed her miserably, then slowly nodded.

'Good. Now run back to my place and tell our Toby that we need him straight away. That's if, God forbid, he ain't already left for his shift. Go on now, off yer go!'

Amy clattered down the stairs two at a time to fetch Toby. In no time at all he had Molly's bed set up in the kitchen at the side of a roaring fire, and had carried her in his arms down the narrow stairs. And then the really hard work began. All

70

day long, Amy and Bessie took turns in sponging Molly down with cool water and dripping liquid down her parched throat. But by teatime when the doctor called back as promised, the fever showed no sign of breaking.

'How long will she be like this?' Amy asked him, fear in her voice.

He could only shake his head. 'There's no way of knowing,' he admitted.

'You're doing all you can,' he assured her kindly. 'Just keep it up and I'll be back first thing in the morning.'

Amy thanked him as Bessie showed him to the door, her heart as heavy as lead within her chest.

Dr Sorrell wished that there was more that he could do, but the old woman's life hung in the balance now; it was just a matter of waiting. At eleven o'clock that night, Amy insisted that Bessie and Toby went home. Bessie protested, reluctant to leave them but Amy pointed out that Bessie had a husband and her own family to see to, and that she was quite capable of managing on her own till morning. Bessie eventually saw the sense of it and reluctantly slipped back to her own cottage, but Toby refused to go and nothing she said could persuade him otherwise.

'I'll sleep on the settee,' he told her, and although Amy objected, secretly she was glad that he was staying.

It was a seemingly endless night. Molly lay in a deep fever, so still sometimes that Amy feared that she had already gone from her. Tirelessly she sponged her down, talking to her softly all the while, praying that Molly could hear her.

'Don't leave me, Gran,' she begged a thousand times. 'I love you so much; you're all I've got.'

But through it all, Molly lay unmoving.

When Bessie arrived back at break of dawn, she found Amy red-eyed and exhausted. Toby was fast asleep on the settee and Molly was no better at all. As she scurried about making them all a bit of breakfast, a feeling of dread came on her. She was deeply fond of Molly and couldn't imagine life without her. She begged Amy to go to bed for a while and try to get some sleep, as the girl looked fit to drop. But Amy flatly refused and instead pulled a hard-backed chair close to the side of her gran's bed.

There eventually she slipped into an uneasy doze, her hand tightly clutching Molly's, and it was the doctor on his next visit that woke her. He looked down on the young girl and the old woman sadly. The longer the fever raged, the less chance the sick woman had of coming out of it, as well he knew.

'Is there nothing more we can do?' asked Bessie.

He solemnly shook his head. 'I'm afraid not. But take heart, it can't go on for much longer now. The fever should break soon and I'll call back again this evening.'

As the morning progressed, Molly appeared, if anything, to get even worse. The sweat ran down her face and she began to thrash about wildly. It took both of them now to bathe her, but not once did they cease in their efforts. Amy's face was the colour of bleached linen as she watched this beloved old woman slowly slipping away from her. Her eyes held such anguish that they tore at Bessie's heart.

'Please, please, Gran, don't leave me,' she begged over and over again, and suddenly – just when it seemed that things couldn't get any worse – Molly's eyes sprang open and rested on her face. Then, just as quickly, they fluttered shut again, her thrashing about ceased, and still now, she sank back into the pillows.

Amy was sobbing uncontrollably but to her amazement and disbelief she suddenly heard Bessie laugh.

'Don't cry, lass,' she said, pulling Amy into her arms. 'It's over. The fever's broken and she's come through it. Look – she's fast asleep!'

Hardly daring to look, Amy followed her gaze and saw Molly's old chest rise and fall regularly beneath her nightgown. A huge wave of relief swept through her and now she was laughing and crying and hugging Bessie all at the same time.

'She's alive,' she sobbed gleefully as Bessie beamed through her own tears.

'Aye she is, lass,' she agreed. 'Mind you, I don't know now why we was ever worried in the first place. She's as tough as old boots, is our Molly.'

By the time Dr Sorrell arrived back that evening, although still very weak, Molly was awake.

'What are you doin' here?' she demanded rudely, and they all began to laugh with delight.

'Now we *know* she's on the mend,' grinned Bessie. 'She's got her bloody cheek back.'

Chapter Five

The recovery was slow but sure, and after two weeks Molly was well enough to leave her sickbed and sit in her rocking chair for a while. Amy fussed over her, endlessly plying her with drinks and tempting her with tasty titbits to encourage her to eat. Usually an independent soul, Molly grew deeply frustrated and snappy. But Amy endured all her moods without complaint. As long as she could keep her gran, she would have put up with anything.

Every evening Toby came round and read to them, and Molly looked forward to his visits. Bessie was also a frequent visitor and once, when Amy was out of the room, Molly slipped some coins into her hand.

'Get Amy a birthday present fer me,' she whispered. 'I was hoping to buy her a new coat, but what wi' the doctor's bills an' me not bein' able to work fer a time, that's all I can manage.'

Bessie winked, and after shopping about a bit she did Molly proud. She found a slim silver chain bracelet hung with a little engraved heart at a bargain price.

When Molly gave it to her on Christmas Eve, Amy was absolutely enchanted with it and hugged her gran fiercely, although she scolded her at the same time.

'You shouldn't have done this, Gran,' she chided

her. 'You know we've got no money coming in at the minute.'

Molly was indignant. 'You don't think I'd let yer birthday pass wi'out even buyin' you a present, do yer?' she said, stubborn as ever.

Amy kissed her cheek tenderly. 'Oh Gran, I love you *so* much. I don't know what I'd ever do without you. But I didn't need a present. So long as I've still got you, I don't need anything else.'

A huge lump formed in Molly's throat, for Amy's words had touched her deeply.

Bessie had baked her a cake, covered with fluffy icing, and Amy was delighted with it.

'We'll save it until tonight when Toby gets here,' she declared, and sure enough, amidst a merry atmosphere that evening they all had a huge wedge of the delicious treat.

Toby presented her with a wonderfully bound book all about fashion designs that Amy absolutely loved. By now Molly's bed had been carried back upstairs, but although she was growing steadily stronger by the day, she still tired easily.

After they had all washed Bessie's cake down with a glass of Molly's home-made wine, Bessie went off home to her own brood, and Molly retired for the night. Amy tucked the blankets about her lovingly.

'Thank you for my bracelet, Gran,' she whispered, planting a gentle kiss on Molly's papery cheek. 'I'll treasure it always.'

Molly gazed up at her, pride shining in her eyes. Her girl was teetering on the brink of becoming a woman and it was a frightening thought. When Amy eventually descended the stairs again after

75

making sure that Molly had everything she needed, Toby pointed to the chair at the side of the fire.

'Sit there,' he smiled. 'I've got another surprise for you.'

'Oh, Toby, no, my book was more than enough,' she exclaimed, but all the same she sat down and did as she was told.

'Now close your eyes,' he commanded and giggling, Amy closed them.

Presently he dropped a bulky parcel into her outstretched arms, and she frowned as she felt it and tried to think what it could be.

'Well, go on then ... open your eyes and take a look. It won't bite you,' he teased.

Amy began to tear at the brown paper as excited as a child, with a radiant smile on her face. However, when she saw what the parcel contained, the smile vanished from her face and her huge velvety brown eyes filled with tears.

'Oh, Toby,' she whispered. 'This is just too much.' And to his dismay she began to weep. Inside the parcel was the beautiful woollen coat that Molly had hoped to buy for her. The old lady had shown it to him in the shop window weeks ago, and determined that Amy should have it, he had saved for weeks to buy it.

'Don't you like it?' His voice held such disappointment that her head snapped up.

'Not like it?' she cried. 'Oh, Toby – why, it's *lovely*. It's the most beautiful coat I've ever had; I just can't believe how kind you are. What with Gran pulling through and now this, it's just turning out to be the best Christmas and birthday ever. I can't believe how lucky I am.'

And with that she threw herself into his arms and gave him a resounding kiss on the lips, which made him blush to the very roots of his hair and caused Amy to burst out laughing again.

The coat fitted perfectly and Amy strutted up and down the kitchen in delight. Toby thought secretly that it set the colour of her hair off to perfection, but was too shy to tell her so.

She in turn looked at Toby as if for the very first time. Tall and broad-shouldered, with straight fair hair, his mouth was wide and his nose not quite straight – and yet his eyes, which were his best feature, more than made up for that. They were a lovely deep blue, almost sapphire, and when he smiled they lit up his whole face. Amy suddenly realised that he had grown into a very handsome young man and wondered why he wasn't courting or married. She knew that there was more than one girl who had set her cap at him, yet Toby had never seemed interested. Still, she supposed it was none of her business at the end of the day and they spent the next hour admiring the designs in her new book.

Later in the evening, however, her mood became more sombre and she decided to confide in him.

'Toby, I *have* to get a job now.' Her voice was heavy with anxiety. 'I know Gran doesn't want me to, but the savings are almost gone. It will be months before she's strong enough to start weaving again, and we can't live on fresh air, can we?'

Understanding her dilemma, Toby nodded his head, waiting for her to continue.

'As soon as she's well enough to be left on her

own I'm going job-hunting,' Amy declared with a defiant toss of her head. 'Beatrice has been working up at The Folly for ages now and here's me still stuck at home.' Amy missed her friend dreadfully.

'Then if that's your intention I'd say nothin' about what you're proposin' to do until after Christmas,' Toby advised. He could have said much more on the subject but wisely held his tongue. He knew Amy well enough to be aware that, once she had made up her mind to do something, nothing would change it. He also knew that once Molly learned of her decision, fireworks would go up and no mistake.

'I'd like to be a fly on the wall when you tell her,' he chuckled, and before they knew it they were both laughing naughtily at the thought.

Christmas came and went and Amy and Molly enjoyed it. Amy had decorated the cottage with holly branches and mistletoe, and they had a nice fat chicken for dinner. Wisely, Amy had followed Toby's advice not to mention her intentions of getting a job until the festivities were over, and the fact that she had almost lost her gran made them treasure their time together all the more.

December gave way to January 1846 and Amy became increasingly concerned about the dwindling money in the savings jar. But Molly still wasn't strong enough to be left alone yet, so she patiently bided her time.

Today was Mary and Beatrice's day to visit, and since she was still unable to get out and about, Molly looked forward to this treat immensely. Both girls always called in and had a cup of tea with them, and Molly never tired of hearing about the happenings at Forrester's Folly. Every few minutes Molly would glance at the mantel clock impatiently until at last Bessie entered with Mary and Beatrice close on her heels.

It was a dull overcast day with heavy rain-laden clouds dotting the sky, but Bessie's smile was brilliant as she entered.

'You'll never guess in a month o' Sundays what's happened,' she beamed, barely able to contain her excitement.

Amy and Molly stared at her expectantly.

'Our Mary is engaged,' she announced, and Mary flushed.

Amy hugged her delightedly. 'Congratulations,' she said, as Molly struggled stiffly from her chair to hug her too. 'I don't suppose the lucky chap would be Joe the stable lad you're allus on about, would it?' she teased.

Mary blushed and nodded.

'Well, that didn't take much working out, did it? Why, a blind man on a galloping donkey could see that you two were made fer each other. I just wonder why it took yer both so long to get round to it. I was startin' to fear you'd become an old maid.'

Mary laughed, before telling her excitedly, 'We had a word with the master yesterday and he's going to let us live in one of the cottages within the grounds.'

'That's grand then, lass.' Molly was genuinely pleased for her. 'I just hope Joe appreciates what a lucky chap he is.'

'Oh no, Molly, it's *me* that's lucky. I think I've loved Joe ever since the first day I set eyes on him, but I never thought he'd look at me.'

Amy sighed dreamily, her young heart alight at the romance of it all.

'Will you be having a white dress and a veil?' she asked.

Before Mary could answer, Bessie spoke for her. 'Yes, she will,' she said firmly and they all laughed. There was nothing quite like a wedding to lift everyone's spirits, and it had come just at the right time.

'How are things up at The Folly?' asked Molly curiously.

Mary frowned. 'To be honest, apart from me, the rest o' the staff rarely see the mistress at all now; she keeps to her own rooms much o' the time. I overheard Cook sayin' the other day that the master's sorely worried about her. As I once told you, it's been years now since the master ordered Jessica, the daughter, out o' the house, and the mistress has been going steadily downhill ever since, which is why he promoted me to fetch an' carry for her. She's a kindly lady though, an' I like workin' for her.'

'Poor soul,' said Molly. 'Have yer never found out why he threw the young mistress out?'

Mary shook her head. 'It's more than yer job's worth to even mention her name in front o' the master,' she confided. 'Mind you, there's the other madam, Miss Eugenie, Master Adam's wife – now *there's* one I'd like to see go. I reckon as even *he's* getting sick of her tantrums now. He stays away from the house more and more. He's either out riding on his horse, Pepperpot, or it's rumoured that he's taken to drinking – when he isn't working in his hat shop, that is. Not that you can blame him. That one could make a saint turn to drink from what I've seen of her.'

'Sounds to me like Mr Forrester's got his hands full and no mistake,' Molly said sadly. 'But then happen things wouldn't have turned out as they have if he hadn't thrown his daughter out.' And with that the women turned their talk back to the good news and the rest of the visit was spent discussing the wedding. Molly insisted that they should celebrate properly and ordered Amy to fetch a bottle of her homemade elderberry wine from the pantry.

'Ain't it a bit early in the day?' Amy questioned.

'It's never too early in the day to celebrate good news,' Molly told her. 'Besides – I've been keeping a few bottles o' me elderberry wine fer a special occasion an' it don't get much more special than this from where I'm standin', so just go and fetch it and do as you're told fer once.'

Thrilled to hear her gran sounding so much more like her old bossy self, Amy scurried away to the pantry. One bottle turned into two and two into three, and by teatime, when Mary and Beatrice finally made their unsteady way back to Forrester's Folly they were more than a little tiddly and in a merry mood, as indeed were they all.

With February came the snow. Molly had been expecting it for weeks, insisting that the skies were full of it, and when it did come it came with a vengeance.

They woke up one morning to a silent white world. When Amy pulled aside the pretty flowered curtains at her bedroom window, all she could see was a blanket of white. The windows were frozen over inside into intricate little patterns and she had to breathe on them and rub a little space to peep out. The sight that met her eyes made her shudder, and after washing as quickly as she could at the little pot bowl in her room, she got dressed and tied a warm woollen shawl about her. Then, hurrying downstairs, she skilfully banked up the fire and pushed the kettle into it. Molly was still in bed. Since her illness, Amy had insisted that she lie in until she had got the kitchen warm each morning, and today she almost envied her. It was so cold that her teeth were chattering, and after hastily brushing her unruly curls and tying them into a ponytail with a ribbon, she caught up the copper coal-scuttle and bracing herself, went out to the little coal shed in the yard. The snow had drifted halfway up the door by then and she began to shovel it aside with her hands. By the time she was done, her fingers were blue and she looked as if she were dressed all in white.

After finally managing to drag the door open she stared in dismay at the contents. There were still a few logs and odd bits of wood inside, but the remaining coal was little more than slack, and not much of it at that.

Filling the scuttle as fast as she could, she scurried back into the homely little kitchen and slammed the door shut behind her. Luckily the fire was burning brightly now and the room was getting warmer, so after she had mashed the tea, she poured out a cup for Molly and took it up to her room to her.

Later that afternoon, much against Molly's wishes, Amy took the old pram out to the slagheap to try and replenish their dwindling coal supply. Molly's troubled eyes kept going to the window.

'She should never have gone out on a day like this,' she fretted. 'Why, it ain't fit for a dog to be out.'

She and Bessie were huddled up by the fire, and reaching over, Bessie patted her hand comfortingly.

'She'll be all right, love,' she reassured her. 'She might not be very big but she's young and strong. Anyway, she's been gone well over an hour now; happen she'll be back soon.'

Molly hoped she was right. 'I need to get back to me weaving,' she told Bessie. 'The money I had put by has almost gone, but me damn hands don't seem to want to do what me head tells 'em!'

Bessie sighed at her dilemma until all of a sudden a solution to Molly's problems occurred to her.

'What about the locket?' She had never mentioned it once in all the years since Molly had brought Amy home.

But Molly discounted it immediately. In truth, she had almost forgotten about it herself. It was still hidden in the back of the attic in the tapestry bag where she had placed it so long ago.

'I know it seems wrong to sell it, but then desperate situations call for desperate measures, and were yer to sell it, it would probably fetch enough to keep yer both for years,' Bessie sensibly pointed out.

'That's Amy's legacy,' Molly said firmly. 'It's all I have to give her of her poor mother, apart from them clothes she were found in. I know you're only trying to help, Bessie, but if I sold that, I'd never be able to forgive myself.'

Bessie sighed, and the two women sat, trying to think of some other solution, but try as they might, nothing came to mind.

That evening, when supper was over, Amy plucked up her courage and dared to broach the subject that Molly had avoided for so long.

'Gran ... did you know that the money in the jar is almost gone now?'

'I know well enough,' snapped Molly, 'but don't go worritin' over that. I'm feeling better by the day now. Why, I've already decided that come tomorrow I'm going to get back to me loom.'

Amy sighed in despair. 'But you're not properly well yet, and anyway, it's freezing up in that room. If you go up there too soon, you'll be back to square one and in your sickbed again.'

They glared at each other for a moment, each as stubborn as the other until Molly's old shoulders suddenly slumped.

Amy's hand crept across the table and squeezed Molly's lovingly.

'You've been really ill,' she said tenderly. 'I can't let you start weaving again until you're properly better, and in the meantime we've got to live. You don't need me to tell you that, do you, Gran?'

Molly shook her head as tears welled in her eyes, and seizing her chance, Amy went on, 'It's high time I got a job.' She held up her hand as

Molly opened her mouth to protest. 'You know that all the other girls hereabouts have been working for years, so why should I be any different?'

'Because you *are* different, that's why! You're a cut above everyone around here, just as yer mother was before yer, and I want the best fer yer.'

'But you've *always* given me the best, Gran, and now it's my turn.' Amy's eyes were bright with tears too. '*Please* let me do this,' she begged, and Molly chewed on her lip as she sensed defeat. She could see that Amy was determined to have her own way this time and all the fight went out of her.

'I'll tell yer what, if yer can find a job somewhere respectable, where it's safe fer a well-brought-up girl to be, I'll consider it. How does that suit yer?'

Amy's whole face lit up. At least this was a step in the right direction.

'It's a bargain.' She laughed and they hugged each other fondly.

In actual fact, finding a job that suited them both proved to be a much more difficult task than Amy had anticipated. It was actually Mary on her next afternoon off who came up with a solution to their problem. They were all sitting around Molly's scrubbed oak table and Mary was filling them in with the goings-on at Forrester's Folly.

'The poor master's in a right old flap,' she told them. 'The influenza epidemic that has been going around has swept through the hat factory and the workers are dropping like flies. I heard the master tell the mistress when I was serving their tea that he's desperate for workers to fulfil a big order he's got.'

Amy's ears pricked up immediately. 'Do you think there'd be any chance of me being taken on?' she asked hopefully.

Mary shrugged. 'I don't see why not. Why don't yer go round there tomorrow and ask. You've nothing to lose, have yer? The very worst they can say is no.'

Amy hugged herself; she had always longed to work in the hat factory. 'Would that be all right with you, Gran?'

The old woman sighed in defeat. 'I suppose it would be safe there,' she admitted grudgingly.

'It's decided then,' Amy said. 'First thing in the morning, I'll go round there and try my luck.' And that's exactly what she did.

It was bitterly cold when she set off the next morning. The wind had dropped and for now it had stopped snowing, but the sky was grey and leaden. Molly saw her off from the door like an old mother hen.

'It's going to snow again, I can smell it,' she warned Amy. 'So just mind yer come straight home and don't go talkin' to no strangers.' All the time she was talking she was tucking the collar of Amy's woollen coat tighter under her chin.

Amy grinned. 'I'm not a baby, Gran.'

In that minute Molly had to admit to herself that indeed she wasn't. Besides her warm new coat she had a pretty warm shawl that she herself had decorated with burgundy velvet ribbons to match her coat, and it kept her head warm. Her hair, which only minutes before had been brushed, was already springing out, the shining auburn curls spilling down her back, and with her bright eyes and rosy dimpled cheeks she looked incredibly pretty.

As she went swinging off along the snow-covered cobbles, Molly watched her sadly. At the end of the lane, Amy turned and waved, and then she was gone. Suddenly Molly felt very old and alone. She had always known deep inside that she couldn't tie Amy to her apron strings for ever, and now it was time to start to let go.

Amy was bubbling with excitement. She knew all the short-cuts through the labyrinth of cobbled alleys in Nuneaton town centre, and despite the hindrance of the deep snow, she made the journey to the hat factory in record time. When she got there, her cheeks were glowing with the cold and her breath hung on the air, but suddenly the excitement waned and was replaced by nervousness. The factory was a large building with the hat shop that displayed its wares to the front and a door to the side of it which led to the factory. In the hat-shop window were hats of all shapes and sizes, some trimmed with artificial flowers, some with feathers or veils, and some with the locally woven ribbons all the colours of the rainbow. She stood for some minutes admiring them as she had ever since she was a child.

From the back of the shop in the factory she could hear the dull whirr of the machinery, so taking a deep breath, Amy drew herself up to her full height and made her way in, her head held high.

By the time she left it had begun to snow again, just as Molly had predicted, but Amy hardly noticed it, and flew down the alleys in a most unladylike manner. She was breathless by the time the familiar cottages came into sight but she never once slowed her steps and almost fell into the kitchen in her haste to tell Molly her news.

'I've got a job, Gran!' she shouted. 'Only as a runabout for now, but it's a start, ain't it?'

Molly couldn't help but be pleased for her. 'Well done, lass,' she said, and while Amy chattered on about the factory she hurried about getting her a warming mug of broth.

Amy was so full of her good news, it was hard to get a word in sideways but eventually Molly managed it. 'When do yer start?' she asked.

'Tomorrow ... *and* I'll get paid on Friday.'

It was going against the grain for Molly to think of Amy as the breadwinner. But the girl was so pleased with herself that Molly wisely held her tongue, not wanting to spoil it for her.

'It's only a temporary arrangement,' she warned. 'Just till I'm back in me stride.' But even as the words were uttered they both knew that it wasn't true, and that their life as they had known it was about to change.

Chapter Six

Right from when Amy had been a little girl, barely tall enough to gaze into the hat-shop window, she had imagined it as a very glamorous place. But within a very short time of working there she came

88

to realise that the only glamorous thing about it was the hats it produced. Her day began at 5.30 each morning when she would make her way there with some bread and cheese that would serve as her lunch wrapped in a clean piece of muslin.

All day she would sweep the floors, supply the weavers who worked the great looms with huge reels of silk and cotton, fetch, carry, and in general do anything that she was told. Sometimes if there was an order being prepared, it could be seven or eight o'clock at night before she finished, and then at last she would make her weary way home.

No matter what time she finished, Molly would always be watching from the kitchen window for her and would meet her at the door with a welcoming kiss and a hug. Sometimes Amy would be so tired that she would fall asleep over the meal that Molly had ready for her – but even so, never once did she complain. Often when in the large factory she would stand and admire the finished hats and imagine how she herself could decorate them.

Of all the women that worked there, she envied the designers most of all. They worked in a separate room right at the end of the factory floor, and occasionally Amy would glimpse them bent over their drawing boards or busily pinning together the unfinished hats. Unfortunately she was never allowed into that room. The women in there were highly respected and highly paid, unlike herself and the women who toiled long hours over the looms and machines.

Mr Forrester's office was at the other end of the factory on the first floor. To reach his office you had to climb a flight of steep metal stairs and occasionally on his visits, Amy would catch sight of him peering out of his office window as he surveyed his employees. Though now well into middle age, Mr Forrester was still a handsome man, but as yet Amy had never once seen him smile. Once a week he would walk amongst his workers with the supervisor, inspecting their work. He always had a word of praise for good quality work, but woe betide anyone whose work was not up to his standards. He himself had toiled long and hard to build up his little empire and he expected only the best. Anyone who couldn't meet his standards was swiftly shown the door and never given a second chance.

But on the other hand he was also known as a fair man. Recently a heavily pregnant woman had lost two of her fingers in one of the machines after working a thirteen-hour shift straight through to try and fulfil an order. It was a known fact that not only had Samuel Forrester paid all her medical expenses, but he had given her a very hefty bonus and a small pension too. All in all he was feared, yet at the same time respected as being a fair man to those who were loyal and hardworking. Amy had no regrets about going to work for him whatsoever. At the minute she was right at the bottom of the ladder, but she was also young and ambitious, and her deep love of design held her there.

Molly, however, who was growing stronger by the day, was still not too happy about the situation. 'It's bloody cheap labour, that what it is,' she would mutter when Amy came in at night tired to the bone. But Amy would only grin and let it go in one ear and out of the other.

It was satisfying being able to tip her wages on to the table each week. All of her life Molly had cared for her and now Amy felt that she was giving a little back. She was well aware of the sacrifices that Molly had made for her. To Amy's mind, Molly needn't have taken her in when her mother died. But she had, and for that alone, Amy would always be grateful. Molly had never really spoken too much about her daughter, except to tell Amy that she had been beautiful, and that her father had died before she was born. Amy didn't like to ask too many questions for fear of upsetting her, although at times she ached to. But sometimes when she was tucked up warm in bed at night, her imagination, which was lively at the best of times, would run riot.

Molly had told her that she looked very much like her mother, so Amy would lie there in the darkness trying to picture her mother in her mind and wishing she could have known her. Even so, she was more than happy with her lot and though she regretted never knowing her parents, she couldn't imagine ever loving anyone more than she loved her gran.

The evenings she spent with Toby were few and far between now, for most nights after her evening meal, all she wanted to do was fall into bed. Toby himself was very busy, too. As well as doing his shifts down the pit, he was also working for a few hours a week in the village school now, teaching the local children – and more than ever he now longed to make that job his career. On Sundays though, which was their day off, Amy would draw him sketches of some of the hats that were being produced, and then alter them to her own designs.

Toby was greatly impressed. Like Molly, he felt that Amy's talent was being wasted. But every time he voiced his opinion, Amy would simply smile. For now she was content.

'Everyone has to start somewhere, and patience is a virtue,' she would say and Toby would smile back, his face softening and his blue eyes proud.

As Mary's wedding day in mid-June approached, the cottages became a hive of activity. Bessie had scrimped and saved for months to buy the material to make the wedding dress. And then once it was purchased she and Molly sat long hours into the night stitching it. Molly's fingers were nowhere near as nimble as they had used to be, but even so the finished product was breathtaking.

Amy herself had designed it and supervised Molly and Bessie closely. She bought a plain poke bonnet and stitched a veil into it, and the few people who were allowed to see it before the big day swore that they had never seen anything quite like it. Once the veil was stitched to her satisfaction she then took scraps of ivory silk and made them into tiny flowers that she sewed all around the brim. And then at last it was finished and all they had to do was wait.

The big day finally dawned, and it was just as perfect a day as any bride could wish for. Amy intended to enjoy every minute of it.

The little church in Coton was bulging at the seams, and as all heads turned to watch the radiant bride walk down the aisle on her father Jim's arm, a gasp of admiration could be heard. Mary fairly floated and was everything a bride should be, and Bessie looked fit to burst with pride although her sniffs could be heard all through the ceremony.

When the happy couple finally left the church as man and wife, they were greeted with a shower of rose petals and rice. Mary's new husband Joe looked as proud as Punch and could barely take his eyes from her, and as they ran down the path of the Parish Church, the church bells pealed joyously. Once they were seated in the pony and trap, Mary threw her bouquet high into the air. It seemed to hang there for some seconds, its trailing ribbons fluttering in the warm breeze, and then suddenly it plummeted down and landed straight in Amy's arms. She giggled nervously as she looked up and caught Toby's eyes. He flushed and turned away and suddenly confused, Amy stared at him, but then a cheer went up as the pony and trap bore away the bride and groom, and the strange moment was gone.

Once they were all back at the Bradleys' cottage, the merrymaking began in earnest. Borrowed tables, which had all been pushed together, stretched the length of one wall, sagging beneath the weight of all the food that had been piled upon them. There were pies and pastries, whole cheeses, crusty new baked bread, cakes, tarts and great stone jugs full of homebrewed ale and cider, plus numerous bottles of home-made wine. The furniture had been pushed back against the walls in readiness for the party, and once the speeches had been made, the wedding cake was cut, and a toast was raised to the happy couple. Mary's father Jim then produced his flute and began to rattle out a tune as a good old kneesup got well under way. The sound of laughter and merriment was echoing along the little cobbled lane when suddenly the sound of a horse and carriage stopping outside the open doorway caused all eyes in the room to look towards the lane.

Mary's mouth gaped in amazement as Samuel Forrester and his son Adam alighted from the coach and strode towards her. Bessie herself was all afluster. She had never expected the likes of such a wealthy man to cross her humble doorstep and was momentarily struck dumb.

However, she needn't have worried, for Samuel Forrester was beaming as he grasped Joe's hand and shook it warmly.

'Congratulations, Joe.' He smiled. 'I have popped in because Mrs Forrester insisted that you should have your wedding present today.' Turning, he took a beautifully wrapped parcel from Adam who was standing behind him, and looking at Mary, who was blushing furiously, he placed it in her arms. 'Here you are, Mrs Turpin,' he said kindly. 'And may I say that you look absolutely beautiful?'

Totally lost for words, Mary bobbed her knee. 'Th ... thank you, sir,' she stuttered.

Amy, who was standing at the side of the open door next to Beatrice, was amazed at how different Samuel Forrester looked when he smiled, and watched with amusement as poor Mary squirmed with embarrassment.

'I must say, my dear, your dress and bonnet are most unusual,' Samuel Forrester commented as he eyed her up and down. 'Charming, in fact.'

'Amy designed them, sir,' Mary stated proudly.

He raised his eyebrows. 'Oh really? And who is this Amy then?' It was Amy's turn to blush as Mary pointed her out, saying shyly, 'That's Amy Ernshaw over there, sir.'

He turned, but then as his eyes fell on Amy, the smile slid from his face. After staring at her for what seemed an age but was in fact only a matter of seconds, he pulled himself together with an obvious effort, as Seth, the groom's father, and Adam exchanged a glance.

'Your designs are quite stunning, my dear.'

Amy smiled with delight.

Suddenly remembering her manners, Bessie bustled over to him. 'Would yer care fer a drink, sir?' Now that she had got over the initial shock of seeing him there, she was enjoying the fact that gentry had attended Mary's little reception and wanted to make sure that all the neighbours saw him.

Dragging his eyes away from Amy's face, he said hastily, 'Oh no, my dear Mrs Bradley, thank you, but as I said, I only called in to drop off the present and wish the couple well. I really must be going now. Do please carry on with your celebrations and accept my apologies for disturbing you.'

As he spoke he cast a last smile at Mary and Joe, then strode towards the door. The guests all followed him outside to the carriage, and as Adam climbed in before him, Mr Forrester turned briefly once more to the young couple.

'I almost forgot,' he was smiling again. 'The mistress said to tell you that you are both to take the next three days off work.'

'Oh, thank you, sir.' Mary flushed with pleasure. Then the door to the carriage slammed and it rattled away across the cobblestones.

'Well I'll be.' Bessie was almost beside herself and beaming from ear to ear. 'This is turning out to be a wedding to remember and no mistake. Who would ever have thought that the likes o' Samuel Forrester himself would ever darken my doorstep, eh?'

Everyone was slowly making their way back into the cottage and waiting excitedly for Mary to reveal what was in the beautifully wrapped parcel.

'Oh, it seems such a shame to rip it,' Mary declared, but she did all the same and gasped with delight when she saw its contents. Inside was a whole canteen of nickel-plated cutlery, and everyone admired it enviously. Everyone that is except Molly, who was seeing again and again in her mind the look that had crossed Samuel Forrester's face when his eyes lit on Amy.

By early evening Amy herself had long since forgotten the incident. The elderflower wine was flowing like water and she was more than a little tiddly and so was Beatrice, who had also been given the day off to attend her sister's wedding. Molly was watching both girls closely and when she saw them cross to the table to refill their glasses she stepped in smartly.

'I think you've both had quite enough o' that,

young ladies,' she said sternly.

'Molly's quite right,' Toby agreed. 'Now get yerself off to bed, our Beatrice, an' get some sleep – else you'll not be fit for work tomorrow. And how about if I take Amy for a stroll down the lane, Molly? Give her a breath o' fresh air, eh?'

Molly winked at him. 'I reckon that's a very good idea.'

Grabbing Amy by her elbow, Toby steered her over to the door. Beatrice lurched towards the stairs and they both laughed as she stumbled on the first step.

Once outside, Amy sighed happily and tucking her arm into Toby's they began to stroll along in companionable silence. The noise of the party gradually receded into the distance, and the little row of terraced cottages slipped away behind them. Eventually they reached the banks of the River Anker and contentedly they wandered along until they reached the fork in the midnight waters. The leaves on the overhanging willow trees gently kissed the water and the riverbed reeds swayed softly in the warm evening breeze. Through the evening twilight they could just make out the old water mill that stood in Mill Walk, and almost as one they sank down on to the velvety green grass of the riverbank. Nearby, a fat old water rat plopped into the water, leaving a trail of bubbles behind him, and the sound of nesting moorhens floated on the air. It was a glorious evening and high overhead the stars began to appear and twinkle down on them, casting their reflections like fairy dust on to the slow-moving current.

Amy hugged her knees and sighed dreamily.

'Eeh, Mary looked lovely, didn't she?' she said and Toby nodded, his eyes on her face as she stared into the water. But although he agreed with her, he was thinking at that moment that even Mary in her wedding finery couldn't hold a light to this girl sitting beside him now.

Luckily Amy was studying the progress of the old water rat that was swimming amongst the reeds and was oblivious to her friend's thoughts; her own locked tight on the wonderful day they had just spent.

There was nothing but the sounds of the night creatures scurrying about their business and the stars shining on the water, and there might have been no one else left in the whole world but the two of them. Suddenly the urge came on Toby to take her in his arms there and then, but using all of his self-restraint, he managed to stop himself as sadness crept over him.

Amy was beautiful, kind-hearted and talented, and somehow he felt that she was destined for better things. She was far too good for a simple man like him. Underneath he had always sensed it. There was a quality about her that set her far above the people in the cottages where she had grown up. Something about the way she carried herself. The way she spoke. Even the way she smiled made her a being apart and he knew that he would never be good enough for her even if he lived to be a hundred.

His thoughts made him sigh unconsciously and Amy immediately turned to him, her face full of concern. Her small hand came up to tenderly caress his cheek and again she saw him as the

98

young man he now was and not the boy she had grown up with. She looked at him in a different light, noticing the way his thick fair hair tumbled across his brow and the deep dark depths of his eyes. And she was instantly confused.

Their eyes met and locked, and suddenly she longed for him to kiss her. She had never been kissed before but her palm was tingling as it touched his face and her heart was pounding painfully in her chest. His large hand came up and gently covered hers and with not a word spoken they moved towards each other, lost in each other's eyes. But then suddenly Toby swung about – and the magical moment was gone.

Amy was deeply embarrassed. 'Oh, dear,' she giggled nervously, glad of the darkness that would hide her glowing cheeks. 'I'm afraid that the wine must have gone to my head.'

Toby, who was standing now, reached down and taking her hand, roughly pulled her to her feet. Then he began to stride back the way they had come, his hands thrust deep in his pockets.

'We'd best get back, else they'll think we've got lost,' he said shortly. Gathering up her skirts, Amy had to almost run to keep up with him.

The journey back was made in silence; they were both lost in their own thoughts, and once they had rejoined the party they spent the rest of the evening studiously avoiding each other. This was not lost on Molly and a sly little grin played about her lips. After Amy she loved Toby more than anyone else in the world and had long harboured hopes that one day they would come together. If this happened then she would die with an easy mind, safe in the knowledge that Amy would be loved and cared for. She had guessed long ago where Toby's affections lay. Still, Amy was little more than a girl at the minute and for now Molly was content to stand back and let nature take its course.

At ten o'clock a horse and trap sent especially by Mr Forrester arrived to carry the newlyweds away to their little cottage, and the wedding party spilled into the lane to see them on their way. There was more throwing of rose petals and rice, and good wishes floated on the night air as the horse and trap clip-clopped away down the lane, followed by Seth and his family who were returning to their rooms above the stable-block at Forrester's Folly.

Bessie beamed as she shouted her goodbyes, more than content with the day. 'Well, that's one settled,' she sighed happily. 'Only four more to go.' She looked pointedly at Toby.

The poor chap flushed. 'Give over, Mam.'

Seeing his embarrassment everyone chuckled, and with the departure of the happy couple the party began to disperse.

'I'll help you clear away a bit, shall I?' Molly offered.

Bessie shook her head adamantly. 'You'll do no such thing.' She was suddenly worn out. 'There's nothin' as won't keep till morning, so you get away to your bed.'

Needing no second telling, Molly bade her good night, and arm-in-arm she and Amy strolled back to their own cottage. Within minutes they were both tucked up in their beds. It had been a long

100

day and they were both pleasantly tired. Yet even so, sleep evaded Amy. Her mind was still full of the day that had just passed as she lay there reliving it.

It had been a lovely wedding and a grand party. She had enjoyed every single minute of it. Every minute that is, except for the time on the riverbank with Toby.

The effects of the wine she had drunk were wearing off now, and she squirmed with embarrassment as she remembered how, just for an instant, she had longed for him to kiss her. She screwed her eyes up tight in shame at the thought. He had looked so uncomfortable and she could only hope that by tomorrow he would have forgotten all about it.

Sunday morning dawned, another bright sunny day. Molly let Amy sleep in and it was the sunlight streaming through the chink in her curtains that woke her. She stretched luxuriously then sighed in contentment. Sunday was her favourite day of the week. In the kitchen she could hear Molly bustling about as she prepared breakfast and the smell of frying bacon wafted to her on the air.

Hopping lightly out of her comfortable feather bed, she hastily washed at the little jug and bowl on the washstand. Then after quickly dressing in her Sunday best for church, she made her way downstairs into the kitchen. Molly was humming softly to herself and when Amy appeared she smiled broadly. 'I've cooked yer bacon just as yer like it,' she greeted her.

Amy tutted. 'I would have done that, Gran,' she scolded.

Molly just laughed. 'Happen yer worth spoiling,' she said, and side-by-side they sat together at the table and tucked into a hearty breakfast.

When they were finished, Molly hurried away to help Bessie tidy up, and once their own table was cleared and the pots washed and dried, Amy went off to church.

An hour or so later, when Molly returned, the girl was back and had begun sketching. Peeping over her shoulder, Molly gazed at the drawings admiringly.

'Yer know, that dress and hat you designed for Mary is the talk o' the lane,' she commented. 'She almost looked like gentry. I don't mind bettin' there ain't no bride hereabouts worn a dress like that before.'

Amy grinned.

'Why, even Samuel Forrester himself was impressed,' Molly went on, still staring at the sketches spread out on the table. There were drawings of hats of all shapes and sizes and Amy had somehow seemed to make them stand out from the paper.

'Yer know, yer should never be sweepin' floors an' fetchin' an' carryin' wi' a talent like this. It's a crying shame,' she grumbled, but Amy only grinned.

'It's early days yet, Gran,' she told her confidently. 'Everything comes to those that wait.' And lowering her head again she returned to her sketching.

The long dry summer came and went pleasantly enough and so did Christmas. The coalhouse was full, the pantry was full, and with Amy tipping up the seven shillings that she earned each week, she and Molly had more than enough to meet their needs.

Amy's wage was in fact meagre compared to those of the women who worked the machines at the factory but for now, she was happy.

Molly herself was now doing a bit of weaving again, more to pass the lonely hours whilst Amy was at work than anything else. She found that she could only turn out a quarter of the ribbons that she had used to, but nevertheless the pennies in the savings jar were slowly rising again and Molly counted her blessings.

Mary still came to visit, though not as regularly now that she had her own home to see to, and it was on one of her visits that she had them rolling with laughter as she told them of the new addition at Forrester's Folly.

Samuel Forrester's mother had gone to live there and according to Mary she was a character to be reckoned with.

'I'll tell yer now, she puts that little madam, Miss Eugenie, in her place and no mistake,' she laughed. 'She don't dare throw no nonsense or tantrums in front o' *her*. In fact, everybody watches their Ps and Qs when she's about.'

'Is she horrible?' Amy asked, wide-eyed.

Mary shook her head. 'Ner, to tell the truth I quite like her. She don't suffer fools gladly, she says what she thinks but she's got no airs an' graces so you allus know where you stand wi' her.'

'Well, that's one blessin' then,' Molly remarked.

Mary nodded. 'From what I've heard it's her

that has made the master what he is today. Even now she still talks to him as if he's a little lad, an' the funny thing is, when she cracks the whip he bloody jumps.' She was dabbing at the tears of laughter in her eyes with a large white handkerchief and her amusement was so infectious that soon she had everyone else laughing too.

'I tell yer, the old dear is a tonic,' she giggled, and as she continued to recount the incidents she had witnessed they were all almost crying with laughter and holding their sides.

'The best thing to come out of her arrivin' is the fact that I've heard rumours that Miss Eugenie is naggin' young Master Adam to get their own house in London now,' Mary confided. 'Up until now they've spent their married life livin' between The Folly an' the master's house in London but now she's champin' at the bit to own her own place.'

'Do you think Master Adam will buy her one?' Molly asked.

Mary shrugged. 'I wouldn't doubt it; she usually gets her own way. An' if you were to ask me, I'd say the sooner the better. Master Adam is all right admittedly but she's a right hellcat. The poor bloke seems to be right under the thumb, though more fool him. Happen he should put his foot down with her.'

The topic of conversation then moved on to the famine that was sweeping Ireland, due to the potato blight that had destroyed the crops there, and the rest of the afternoon seemed to pass in the blink of an eye.

Chapter Seven

1847

As Amy entered the cobbled alleys of the town centre, a group of Irish navvies raised their hands in greeting, and Amy waved back. Almost every morning she saw them and they always made her smile. They made a comical sight, sauntering along in bare feet with their boots swinging about their necks from the tied laces. Once she had asked Mrs Davis, her supervisor, why they chose to walk barefoot, and Mrs Davis had explained to her.

'Well, it's like this, see, Amy. Back in Ireland where they come from, they're very, very poor. So when they get a job in our country their families all club together to buy them a pair of leather boots to work in.'

Intrigued, Amy had nodded as Mrs Davis went on, 'These lads don't want to wear out their boots just walkin' about – they're treasured, you see? So the only time they do wear them is when they're laying the tracks.'

Amy was saddened at the tale. She and Molly had known hard times, but they had always had boots, albeit worn ones.

The navvies had been in the town for months now, and their coming had caused great excitement. They had been brought in to build a railway station, the 'Trent Valley', and lay the tracks for the steam train that would make its maiden voyage to the town later in the year. The other thing that Amy found amusing about them was the hats that they wore, although in fact they were fairly common in Nuneaton. They were actually made in Samuel Forrester's other hat factory in Atherstone, of which Master Adam was in charge, and had been nicknamed Billycocks or Atherstone Cocks. Very cheap round felt hats, they were enormously popular with the working men. But somehow on the navvies with their boots strung around their necks they looked doubly comical and never failed to make her smile. Now that the tracks were almost finished, Amy guessed that the navvies would soon move on to some other town where they would be employed to dig out canals or again lay track, and she knew that she would miss their cheerful faces in the mornings.

'You be havin' a good day now, me beauty,' one of them shouted, raising his hand in a final salute as they rounded a corner and disappeared.

Smiling broadly, Amy hurried into the hat factory. As usual she was one of the first to arrive and as she crossed the shop floor, Mrs Davis appeared from the design department and stopped her in her tracks.

'Amy, love, how do you fancy a few extra hours' work? Please say you do, and save me life.'

Amy grinned at her. 'What doing?' she enquired and the answer she received made her eyes stretch wide with delight.

'It's like this. Milly who cleans in the design department is down with 'flu. Right poorly she is by all accounts, so how do you fancy taking her job, eh? It would mean you staying behind at night when the designers have gone an' starting a little earlier in the mornings. Just till Milly's better like, of course.' The scrawny woman eyed Amy hopefully; she had taken a shine to her and had always found her polite and respectful.

Amy's eyes lit up at the prospect. 'I'd love to do it,' she agreed immediately, and relieved, Mrs Davis nodded.

'Good girl. Well, start tonight when the designers have gone and when you've finished, the night watchman will let you out and lock up after you.' She had no qualms at all about leaving Amy alone in the factory. She had always found her trustworthy and hardworking, and now that the first problem of the day had been solved, she bustled away content.

That evening, when Amy arrived home late, she was almost beside herself with excitement and bursting to tell Molly her good news. But instead of being pleased for her, Molly's brow creased with concern.

'I were worried sick when you were late home. Don't yer think you already do enough hours as it is, lass?' she questioned worriedly.

Amy dropped a kiss on Molly's wrinkled brow. 'I'm sorry to worry you, Gran. I couldn't get word to you but I'd do a *double* shift to get into the design department even if it's only as a cleaner,' she declared, and from the animated look on her face Molly believed her.

'Well, all right then,' she agreed reluctantly. 'Give it a try just fer a few days if yer must. But if it's too much for yer, then yer must be sure to

107

say so.'

'I will, Gran,' Amy promised, and wisely she then let the subject drop and turned the conversation to other things.

That evening as she lay in bed, she hugged herself in the darkness. Her mind was full of the designs she had glimpsed in the design room and she could barely wait for the morning to come.

She had a good feeling inside her and for now sleep was the last thing on her mind. Eventually she went to the window and after drawing back the curtains, she sat with her chin on her hands staring out into the night. Somewhere she could hear a wise old owl hooting his greeting to the night. She sighed dreamily. At last she was allowed into the design department and although it was only as a cleaner, it was a start.

The next morning, Amy set off for work bright and early as usual. Apart from the navvies who shouted their usual cheery greeting the cobbled streets were deserted.

After collecting her mop and pail from the cupboard at the factory she set about her duties and soon the workforce began to arrive. They took their seats at the machines that dotted the factory floor and within an hour the whole place was a hive of activity, with people having to shout to be heard above the whirr of the machinery.

For the whole day Amy was run ragged, fetching and carrying and running to see to the workers' needs, and by the time the last one had left late that evening she was tired out. But even so as she entered the design room to begin her work in there, there was a little bubble of excitement in her stomach.

She set to with a vengeance and didn't stop once until the whole room was spick and span. Then she stood for some minutes enjoying the peace and quiet and gazed about with fascination. Large easels and drawing boards were stood here and there with designs from start to finish of hats of all shapes and sizes sketched upon them. Dotted about were wooden hatstands displaying hats of all kinds, from the very plainest of styles to elaborately decorated creations. Amy eyed each one critically, turning her head this way and that, looking at them from different angles and seeing them in her mind's eye as she would have dressed them.

Her mind was full of ideas and that evening when she arrived home she immediately began to draw sketches of the styles she had seen. Both Molly and Toby were deeply impressed but Amy impatiently waved aside their compliments.

'Look at this one here,' she ordered, pointing at a sketch of a very elaborate bonnet. 'I think it should have a long length of veil, very fine, tied round the brim and trailing down the back like this.'

With a few strokes of her pencil she demonstrated to them what she meant, and after patting his chin thoughtfully, Toby slowly nodded in agreement.

'I see what you mean,' he admitted. 'That does look much nicer than those flowers.'

Amy grinned at his approval before going on to show him some of her other ideas.

'Why don't you show some of these to the

designers?' he suggested after a while.

Amy shook her head. 'Can you just imagine what they'd say?' she frowned. 'A cleaning girl telling them their job?'

Toby's heart went out to her. Amy had such talent that it saddened him to see it going to waste. But still he was also a great optimist. He had always believed deep in his soul that Amy was destined for better things and had a feeling that somehow things would surely come right for her in the end.

By the end of the week, Amy was finding it hard to keep her hands off the unfinished hats in the design department. It was late on Saturday evening and everyone else had gone long since. Although she had finished her chores, still she lingered eyeing one particular hat. Next to it was a sketch of how it would look when it was finished and she felt that the design was totally wrong. Shaking her head, she sighed with frustration. It was a sophisticated style taken from a man's top hat with clean straight lines. Amy felt that the flowers planned to adorn it were too fussy. It needed something more elegant and clean cut. Her fingers were itching to dress it as she felt it should be dressed, and suddenly she could resist the temptation no longer.

Hurrying over to another table she carefully selected two tall brightly coloured peacock feathers. Then, crossing to another table, she selected a length of plain scarlet silk ribbon. After carefully cutting the feathers to the length she required, she fixed them firmly to the side of the hat at a jaunty angle. Then carefully she looped the ribbon around the crown in one simple length. When it was finished she stood back and viewed it with satisfaction.

It was stunning in its simplicity and she was pleased with her efforts. However, just then she spotted the nightwatchman, working his weary way across the shop floor towards her, and instantly her elation turned to panic. She had intended to put everything back as she had found it before she left, but now she would have no chance. Seconds later he pushed open the door and asked her worriedly, 'Is everything all right in here, love? I were beginning to think you'd got lost.'

Amy snatched up her broom guiltily. 'It's all right, Mr Stubbs, everything's fine ... I was just coming.'

As she reluctantly followed his retreating figure from the room, she looked back one last time at her handiwork and her stomach sank into her boots.

It was as she made her way home that a thought occurred to her and she began to relax. Tomorrow was Sunday. There would be nobody in the factory and if she went in early on Monday morning, before Mrs Davis arrived, she would have time to put everything back as it had been and no one would be any the wiser. Whistling with relief, she made the rest of the way home in a slightly easier frame of mind.

As planned on Monday morning, Amy arrived early and crept across the factory floor. As she had hoped, there was no sign of Mrs Davis – but when she pushed open the door to the design room, the sight that met her eyes made her stop dead in her tracks. Milly was busily mopping the floor and it was hard to say who was the most startled, she or Amy.

'Cor, yer didn't half give me a fright, gel.' Milly grinned. 'Thanks fer covering fer me while I've been ill. I bet you're glad to see me back, eh?' She coughed and blew her nose.

Amy returned her smile weakly; in truth, she was far from glad to see her back. Her eyes went to the hat she had dressed on Saturday night and her stomach churned.

As Milly's eyes followed hers, she grinned. 'It's lovely, ain't it? I'd do anything to have a hat like that, wouldn't you?'

Amy nodded miserably. There was no chance now of putting it back as it had been, and she didn't know what to do.

'Oh well, I'd best get on,' Milly said, although she still looked far from well. Amy turned and went to fetch her own mop and pail. Now that she was here she might as well go about her own duties, and as for the hat... Well, it was too late to worry about it now. What would be, would be. She could only hope that once her interference came to light, as it surely would, she wouldn't be dismissed.

Outside, a watery sun rose in the sky and inside Amy fetched and carried – one fearful eye on the door of the design room all the time, every minute expecting to be summoned. But the morning passed uneventfully and no one disturbed her. Just before lunch Samuel Forrester and his son arrived and after striding across the factory floor they made their way up the steep metal staircase at the far end of the room and disappeared into the office. Minutes later, Amy saw one of the designers mount the stairs to join them and when they descended together only moments later and entered the design room, Amy's stomach twisted into a knot.

They seemed to be in there for what appeared to be an eternity but eventually Mr Forrester reappeared in the doorway and beckoned to Mrs Davis. Just as Amy had feared, Mrs Davis, after exchanging words with him, raked the factory floor with her eyes until they came to rest on Amy. Then, picking her way through the whirring machines she approached her.

'Mr Forrester wants you in the design department right now.' She had to shout into Amy's ear to make herself heard. 'You'd best hurry; he doesn't like to be kept waiting.'

Amy was quaking in her boots but she obediently retraced Mrs Davis's steps and entered the door.

Mr Forrester was standing, legs slightly apart, arms behind his back, staring at the hat she had trimmed. Silently she went to stand before him, aware of the eyes of the designers tight on her.

When eventually he turned his head to look at her, a glimmer of recognition shone in his eyes. 'What's your name, girl?' His voice was curt.

'Amy, sir.'

'Amy *what?*'

'Amy Ernshaw ... sir.' She was staring back at him now, her head high. If he was going to sack her, then so be it. But why was he staring at her like that? After all, dressing a hat wasn't exactly a hanging offence, was it?

'Haven't we met before?' he asked uncertainly.

'Yes, sir, we 'ave, at Mary and Joe Turpin's wedding reception.' Her voice was clear, and suddenly recognition dawned in his eyes as he remembered her. It was the mob cap she was wearing that made her look so different.

After staring at her thoughtfully for some seconds he went on, 'I believe you were the last person to leave this room on Saturday evening?'

'Y ... yes, sir.' Her confidence suddenly flew straight out of the window.

'Are you responsible for this?' He pointed at the hat and without hesitation she replied, 'Yes, sir.'

Molly had taught her never to lie, and if she were to be dismissed then at least she would go with dignity.

He stared unnervingly at her again but she looked him straight back in the eye.

'I'm very sorry that I interfered with it. I know it was wrong o' me but I didn't like the sketch o' the finished product. I felt it was too fussy and thought the shape o' the hat lent itself to something a bit more stylish.'

Mr Forrester, Adam and the designers were obviously taken aback, and Amy felt herself flush at her own boldness. But still, it was said now and the way she saw it, she might as well be hanged for a sheep as a lamb. She waited for Mr Forrester to erupt but instead he studied her intently. Then, suddenly turning about on his heel, he strode from the room.

'Follow me,' he ordered, and Amy meekly did as she was told, with the young Master Forrester close on her heels.

'Aren't you the young woman who made Mary's wedding dress?' Mr Forrester asked eventually as they climbed the steps to his office.

Amy nodded. 'Yes, sir, I love designin' clothes, especially hats; I spend a lot of my spare time sketchin'.' Fumbling deep in her apron pocket, she withdrew half a dozen designs that she had drawn the night before. She boldly held them out to him and taking them, Samuel spread them out on the desk in front of him and he and Adam began to study them intently. When he finally raised his eyes, Samuel said, 'Do you have any more of these?'

'Yes, sir, hundreds back at home.' She explained swiftly, 'I carry a pencil and bits o' paper about with me so that I can jot down ideas – in my breaks, of course,' she added.

'Do you know where Forrester's Folly is?' Mr Forrester asked eventually.

Bemused, Amy replied, 'Yes, I do, sir.'

Mr Forrester glanced at his son, who nodded almost imperceptibly, before saying, 'Right then, I would like you to bring some of your designs there tomorrow – shall we say at four o'clock? I shall ask Mrs Davis to let you leave work early.'

Amy nodded dumbly.

'Very well. You may go about your duties now.'

On unsteady feet, Amy left the office and descended the staircase. The women's eyes followed her curiously but Amy's mind was in such turmoil that she didn't even notice. Why would Mr Forrester want to see her designs, and why hadn't he dismissed her? She had no answers as yet to her questions, but wild horses wouldn't have stopped her from keeping their appointment – and the excitement in the pit of her stomach began to grow.

When she told Molly of the morning's happenings later that evening, the old woman scratched her head in bewilderment. 'An' yer say you're to go to Forrester's Folly and he didn't sack yer? Well, I don't quite know what to make of it.' But all the same she hurried away to look through Amy's wardrobe, determined that she should look her best for her appointment.

It was a good walk to Forrester's Folly from the factory, and the next day, armed with a bag full of her best sketches, Amy set off in good time with Mrs Davis's consent. Her hair, which was confined in a mob cap at the factory, was hanging loose down her back and on her head was a pretty warm bonnet. She was wearing the woollen coat that Toby had bought her for her fifteenth birthday and beneath that a lovely blue gown embroidered with tiny pink rosebuds that set off her dark beauty to perfection. Molly had sat for hours and hours stitching that dress for her, and Amy treasured it so much that it was kept strictly for high days and holidays.

However, as she left the factory yard, Amy suddenly felt very small and insignificant and her legs felt as if they had turned to jelly. One half of her longed to turn and run straight back home to the safety of her gran's loving arms; the other half of her was curious as to why Mr Forrester wanted to see her. Nevertheless, even with a worried expression on her pretty face she drew more than a few admiring glances and slowly her spirits began to lift. It was wonderful to be out in the open air, after being confined to the factory, and eventually she found herself humming as she hurried along, clutching her precious sketches. After leaving the town behind her she struck off across the Weddington fields and headed for Caldecote. The fields appeared like a giant patchwork quilt laid out before her, and every now and then a little bobtailed rabbit, his whiskers twitching, would scurry out of her path causing her to smile.

In no time at all the tall chimneys of Forrester's Folly came into view. Pausing at the side of a babbling brook, she admired the sight. Smoke from the numerous chimneystacks curled lazily up into the sky, each seeming to try to touch the watery February sun. Even though it was not yet four o'clock, the brightness of the day was already waning and mist was beginning to gather along the river, making it appear almost fairy-like. Amy was entranced – and then suddenly nervous again as she proceeded on her journey. The walk down the drive to the house seemed endless and she wished now with all of her heart that she hadn't come. But now that she was this near her pride wouldn't allow her to turn back, even if it meant coming away with a flea in her ear.

When she finally rounded the bend and the house came into full view she stopped in her tracks and gazed in amazement.

The last time she had come to Forrester's Folly as a kitchen help it had been evening and pitch black. But today for the first time she saw it spread out before her in all its splendour and the sight almost took her breath away.

It was a beautiful house with turrets and towers and real marble steps leading up to the huge front doors, on each side of which were ornately carved stone pillars. The windows were all dressed in heavy curtains, and as the late sunlight caught the huge leaded windows they sparkled. Amy sighed deeply. What must it be like to live in a house like that and have servants to wait on you? And fine carriages to ride in? She could only guess, for this was like entering another world a million miles away from the little terraced cottage she had been brought up in.

A picture of her gran floated before her eyes, and Amy's chin thrust out as she drew herself up to her full height. What was she thinking of? Her gran had brought her up to believe that she was as good as anyone else! And as the thought gave courage to her shaking legs, she climbed the steps and rapped smartly on the great brass knocker.

The door was opened immediately by a young maid in a starched white apron and mob cap all trimmed with broderie anglaise.

'Miss Amy Ernshaw?' she enquired, and Amy suddenly lost her tongue and nodded dumbly, guessing from what Mary and Beatrice had told her that this must be Lily.

The door was held wide. 'Follow me, please,' the maid said primly. 'The master is expecting

118

you in his study.'

Amy gulped to swallow the great lump that had formed in her throat, and followed the girl along a huge hallway, her feet sinking into the Turkey carpet as she went.

Eventually they stopped before a large oak-panelled door, on which the maid tapped lightly.

'Come in.' When a voice came from the other side of the door, Amy's heart did a somersault.

'Miss Ernshaw, sir,' the maid announced, pushing the door wide, and Mr Forrester, who was standing behind a large mahogany desk, nodded impatiently. 'Well, show her in then!'

The maid quickly ushered Amy into the room, then bobbing her knee respectfully she quickly withdrew, drawing the door shut behind her.

Amy stared about her in awe, so taken with the huge bookshelves and luxurious furnishings that she temporarily forgot to be nervous. It was very much a gentleman's room, with great gold-framed oil paintings of hunting scenes dotted about the walls. There was an ornate marble fireplace with two leather deep-winged chairs to either side of it and a fringed Oriental rug on the floor between them.

'So ... you found us then, Miss Ernshaw?' Mr Forrester's deep voice pulled her back to the present.

'Yes, sir.' She was squirming beneath his gaze and feeling extremely uncomfortable, when suddenly she became aware of another presence in the room. An old lady was sitting almost hidden in one of the winged chairs to the side of the fireplace. She too was closely scrutinising her, and

119

Amy felt the sweat break out on her forehead. The old woman was so aged and wrinkled that she made Molly appear almost young in comparison. Yet for all that, her eyes were bright and alert. She was extravagantly dressed in so many frills and bows that they seemed to swamp her tiny figure. And her face with its white complexion, highly rouged cheeks and scarlet painted lips reminded Amy of a china-faced doll that she had seen in the toy-shop window in the town. The whole look was topped by what was obviously a very elaborately curled dark wig that only seemed to emphasise the pallor of her face. The old lady's eyes had narrowed to slits. In fact, she was staring at Amy so intently that they appeared to have almost disappeared into her wrinkles. Her hands were covered in rings that caught and reflected the weak fading light that shone through the windows, and one of them clutched a silver-topped walking stick that she suddenly tapped impatiently on the floor.

'Well, come 'ere then, lass, and let me 'ave a good look at you,' she ordered in a voice that brooked no argument. The walk across the room seemed endless but eventually Amy stood before her.

'Take off your 'at,' the old woman ordered shortly.

After fumbling with the ribbons beneath her chin, Amy did as she was told. Her long auburn curls spilled about her shoulders and the old woman's eyes went from Amy to Mr Forrester's. 'You were right,' she said. 'The resemblance is uncanny.'

Amy had no idea at all what the woman was talking about, so for now she wisely remained silent.

'Amy, this is my mother, Mrs Forrester senior.'

Amy bobbed her knee respectfully. 'How do you do, ma'am,' she said politely, and for the first time the old woman's face softened, her eyes still tight on her.

'Now then – I believe you have some sketches to show me.' Mr Forrester was impatient to get down to the business at hand, and relieved for an excuse to escape the old woman's scrutiny, Amy crossed to the desk and, hastily withdrawing the sketches from her bag, she placed them in a neat pile before him. Samuel began to lift them one by one and study them closely.

'Mother, come and look at these,' he said eventually, as if Amy were not even present, and stiffly the old woman rose from her seat and leaning heavily on her cane, she hobbled over to him.

As she began to leaf through the sketches, looking through an eyeglass that hung from her neck on a silver chain, Samuel pulled a bell-rope, and seconds later, the young maid who had shown Amy in reappeared at the door.

'Ah, Lily, show Miss Ernshaw to the kitchen and see to it that she has some refreshments.' He smiled for the first time at Amy. 'I'm sure you must be thirsty after your walk?'

Amy nodded, feeling totally out of her depth.

'Go with Lily, my dear, and my mother and I will look more closely at your sketches until you return.'

Obediently, Amy followed the maid from the room, and once the door had closed behind them she let out a great sigh of relief.

The maid grinned cheekily. 'Don't let old Mrs Forrester frighten yer. Her bark's far worse than her bite.' She was leading Amy to a green baize door that stood right at the far end of the long hallway, and after following her through a maze of corridors, they passed through another door and into the kitchen.

The cook was sitting with her feet propped up on a stool at the side of the large kitchen range and a young girl was standing at the sink washing a towering pile of dirty china.

'Hello, love, you're Mary and Beatrice's young neighbour, ain't yer? The one who helped us out one night a couple o' years or so back?' She smiled kindly and pointed to a chair. 'Sit yerself down, pet, and you, Lily, fetch that jug o' lemonade out o' the pantry.'

Lily hurried away to do as she was told and within minutes was back bearing a great stone jug and some heavy glasses.

Soon they were all seated at the great scrubbed table sipping their drinks and Amy felt herself beginning to relax a little.

'What brings yer here then?' asked the cook, who didn't like to miss anything, and quickly Amy told her of her interference at the hat factory and how she had been caught out. Both Cook and Lily were grinning by the time she had finished relating her tale and Amy found herself smiling too.

'An' yer say the master and the old mistress are in there right now lookin' at yer designs, eh?' Cook stroked her chin thoughtfully. 'Well, all I can say is whatever yer did to that hat must have pleased the master, 'cos I'll tell yer now he don't suffer fools gladly. An' what's more – if he's taking the trouble to show yer designs to the old mistress, well ... he must be impressed 'cos big as he is, he don't do nothin' without her say so. To tell the truth I sometimes think it's her as should be wearing the trousers in this house and not him.' She laughed, which set her double chins wobbling and then as she looked at Amy again she became more solemn. 'I'll tell yer something else an' all,' she commented. 'Yer don't 'alf remind me o' Miss Jessica. I don't mind admittin' yer give me quite a gliff the first time I saw yer.'

Amy stared back at her curiously. 'Isn't Miss Jessica Mr Forrester's daughter?'

But Cook never got a chance to answer her, for just then a bell sounded, summoning her back to the study.

'Hope to see yer again, love,' she told the girl good-naturedly, and quickly Lily ushered Amy back the way they had come. Within minutes Amy found herself back in the oak-panelled study.

As soon as the door was closed behind her, Samuel Forrester addressed her. 'I have to admit, Miss Ernshaw, that my mother and I are quite impressed with your sketches. Are they all your own ideas?'

'Oh yes, sir, they are, but I've only brought a fraction of them to show you. There are too many to carry all in one go.'

His eyebrows rose as he glanced at his mother who screwed up her eyes suspiciously.

'Who taught you to draw like this?' she snapped.

Amy shrugged. 'I taught myself, I suppose. I've loved to draw ever since I was a little girl.'

The old woman frowned. 'This one...' She stabbed a bony finger at a particular sketch. 'What weight would you expect that to be when it was finished?'

'Oh, no more than three or four ounces, I expect, for the actual body of the hat. Then o' course there'd be the added weight o' the trimmings, though for this particular design I would use a very fine lawn veiling, which would have very little weight at all.'

'An' this one.' The old woman pointed to another sketch, a much more elaborate design this time.

'Definitely silk, stiffened and trimmed with ostrich feathers for more formal occasions. I think that this style might be favoured for day visiting. It would obviously be heavier – possibly nine or ten ounces without the trimmings.'

'An' how do you know all this? I doubt you'd get the chance to wear such outfits.'

'I er ... my gran buys me books on the latest fashions when she can afford to,' Amy told her meekly.

Mrs Forrester nodded. 'Well, you seem to have a fair grasp o' fashion, but I could teach you a lot more,' she commented, and she then proceeded to listen to Amy intently as she fired yet more questions at her. Eventually, seemingly satisfied with the girl's answers and without excusing herself, she began to hobble towards the door.

'I'm going to have a lie-down before dinner,' she told her son over her shoulder, ignoring Amy completely. 'But I'll tell you something, Samuel; I think this young lass has a rare gift. Puts some o' those silly overpaid women you call designers to shame, she does. And if you take my advice you'll give 'er a chance!'

Then without so much as a backward glance she was gone, the door banging resoundingly behind her, leaving Amy to stare after her openmouthed.

Chapter Eight

1848

'Will you be late home, lass?' Molly asked as she walked Amy to the door.

'No, Gran, I should be home for about six tonight.' Amy planted a warm kiss on her cheek as the old woman nodded.

'Good, just see as yer get straight back, mind, and don't get talkin' to none of them damn weird folk that's hangin' about.'

Amy chuckled happily. The coming of the railway the year before had caused great excitement in the town. She had taken Molly to see the first steam engine chug into the newly built Trent Valley railway station, but Molly was not as impressed with the new form of transport as Amy was.

'Newfangled dirty things,' she had said scornfully. 'Chuckin' all that muck an' smoke out. Can't see what's wrong wi' a horse an' cart meself. They've always been good enough before but then happen this is progress.'

Amy had found her gran's attitude highly amusing. She was very set in her ways was Molly

125

Ernshaw, and not one for change.

The weird folk her gran referred to were actually a small group of people called Mormons who had travelled from America to preach their religion and eventually arrived by train in Nuneaton.

From the little she had seen of them, Amy found them to be extremely polite but she was in a minority and on the whole, the townfolk were not accepting the strangers at all. When it was discovered that the Mormons could and often did have more than one wife, the menfolk became angry and convinced that they had come to take their women. This was a view that was shared by Molly.

'It ain't natural,' she had spluttered. 'A man should keep 'imself to one woman. Why, it's *immoral*, so it is.'

Her indignation had caused Amy and Toby to fall about laughing. But nothing they said in the Mormons' defence would cause Molly to change her mind and eventually they stopped trying.

In truth, the Mormons were leaving the town already. Only last week two of them had been dragged from the Temperance Hotel whilst still in their beds by irate menfolk, claiming that the Americans had come to steal their daughters. The poor men had been severely beaten in full view in the marketplace, then tarred and feathered and donkeyed from the town.

Amy felt deeply sorry for them, but Molly was in full agreement of their treatment.

'Serves 'em bloody well right,' she had stated. 'Decent women won't rest easy in their beds till every last one of 'em is gone.'

Sighing deeply, Amy had let her rant on, knowing only too well that once Molly had made her mind up about something, nothing and no one would change it. Stubborn as a mule she was, but Amy loved her nonetheless.

As she set off for work there was a spring in her step. It was a beautiful March morning and from beneath the hedgerows the early flowering primroses peeped out at her. The birds were awakening and chirping their dawn chorus to the sun that was just beginning to rise from the gently moving clouds. It was the sort of morning that made her glad to be alive; the sort of morning when the problems of the past year slipped into the back of her mind, and she found herself humming as she hurried along.

It was over a year now since she had started work in the design department following her first eventful visit to Forrester's Folly, and what a year it had turned out to be.

It had been a long hard slog to become accepted in her new role. Not just by the other designers but by the people on the shop floor too. Her sudden promotion had caused a stir to say the very least, for after all, who had ever heard of a menial cleaner suddenly becoming a designer? It was a position that took most designers years to achieve and here was Amy, a humble cottage-dweller, suddenly promoted overnight.

Sometimes as she passed the workers on the shop floor a snide comment would reach her ears. 'Huh, look at little Miss High an' Mighty, thinks she's a cut above us now she does,' they would mutter, or, 'It'll all end in tears, you'll see. Yer can't make a silk purse out of a sow's ear.'

But she bore the whispers without complaint, her head held high, although inside her heart would be aching.

Sometimes at night when she arrived home, she would collapse into Molly's arms and sob inconsolably and Molly's heart would go out to her beloved girl's plight.

'They'll never accept me, Gran, *never*,' Amy would cry, and Molly would hold her close, stroking the auburn curls and muttering words of comfort.

'Oh yes they will lass. Rome weren't built in a day. You'll see! Things will get easier; just bide yer time and remember that everythin' comes to those that wait.'

And sure enough, by the time November came round, things had eased a little. It had long been a tradition in the factories to celebrate St Clement's Day on 23 November. Clement had been adopted as the Patron Saint of Hatters. Legend had it that in the first century, a footsore St Clement had placed a pad of wool in his sandal and found that it had turned to felt during his pilgrimages. The special day was celebrated at the factory with a tea-party in the workrooms. Great jugs of ale would be brought in and Mr Forrester and his son would always call in and supply the food. It was during the festivities that the older Mr Forrester noticed Amy sitting slightly apart from the rest of the workers, seemingly no part of the labourers nor yet the designers, and he had a hasty word with Adam, who had been an invaluable help to Amy during the preceding months, always at hand to offer help and encouragement.

When the party was over, Mr Forrester mounted the staircase to his office and standing halfway up, he addressed the workforce from there as he usually did when giving his annual speech.

Everyone was in fine spirits, chatting and laughing in small groups. However, as they noticed him the laughter and the chatter died away and within seconds silence reigned as the workers stared up at their master.

'Well!' His voice echoed across the factory. 'I think we'll all agree that all in all it's been a good year.' A ripple of agreement flowed through his audience. 'As you know, the coming of the railway has allowed much faster communication between here and London, hence the growing orders and the rise in your pay packets.' Again the workforce nodded and Mr Forrester went on, 'Now that we are able to transport the hats more quickly I envisage another good year ahead. Down at our hat shop in London, the gentry there are showing great interest in our designs.' He stared about the upturned faces before continuing, 'Which brings me to the next thing I wish to speak to you all about. As I am sure you are now all aware, some time ago I moved Miss Amy Ernshaw into the design department as an apprentice designer. It is some of her designs that my London connections are showing great interest in. However, we all know that there is much more to hatting than just designing them.'

Amy squirmed uncomfortably as sullen eyes glared her way, but the moment Mr Forrester continued, all eyes returned to him.

'Miss Ernshaw has expressed a wish to learn

everything there is to know about our business, from the raw products that are used to the finished products – and that is where you can all help her. Each and every one of you does an invaluable job. We work as a team, each reliant on the other, and I would like all of you to show her the part you play. The more she knows of hatting, the better her designs will become. And the better the designs we produce, the more hats we will sell, so we will all benefit from her talent.'

He paused to smile at some of the guilty, uncomfortable faces that were watching him. They had never looked at it this way before and they were now seeing Amy in a slightly different light.

Mr Forrester then continued with more mundane matters that needed to be addressed and finally bade them all farewell. The following day, as was usual, he was going to his townhouse in London where he would spend Christmas and the New Year with his wife as he did each year.

As he and Adam left the factory Mr Forrester happened to catch Amy's eye and to her amazement he gave her a crafty wink. There was something about this young woman that he had taken to. Like him she had come from humble beginnings but he truly believed that she had a genuine talent and he had every intention of giving her the chance to develop it. He sincerely hoped that his talk this afternoon would make things easier for her, and to Amy's relief it did. From then on the workers slowly began to accept her in her new role and she became a regular sight bent over some machine or other having the different jobs explained to her.

As Amy had learned at a very early age, Warwickshire was nothing short of a hatter's paradise. It boasted everything it needed to meet a hatter's demand in abundance. Blocks to shape the hats were fashioned from the leafy trees of the Warwickshire forests and woods. On the hillsides, outcrops of coal were easily accessible and used to fuel the felt-makers' kettles, and all along the banks of the River Anker, the sheep that would provide the wool for the hats grazed peacefully. Numerous streams, mostly of which poured into the River Anker, fed Nuneaton and this gave the hatters the supply of water that was so important to their trade.

On top of all this, Samuel Forrester was fortunate enough to have in his employ an excellent 'journeyman' who ruled his apprentices with a rod of iron. Richard Paggett was a very accomplished craftsman at his trade and he would accept nothing less than perfection from those he taught, which was why Samuel Forrester's hats were so highly regarded. It was this gentleman who was one of the first to accept Amy, following her promotion. She would often take one of her designs to him and ask his opinion on the way to shape it, discussing sizes and weights, and he soon recognised that she did indeed have an eye for design and respected her for it.

Things were looking up, Amy decided. It had been a difficult year in some ways, yet wonderful in others. Through it all, Molly remained Amy's mainstay, the port in the storm where she could take shelter. And on this wonderful early-spring morning, as she hurried along the leafy Warwickshire lanes, Amy's hopes were high. Mr Forrester and his wife had returned from their London townhouse almost three weeks before, and today he would be visiting the factory.

Amy had worked hard whilst the master had been gone and was looking forward to showing him some of the designs she had created while he had been away. She didn't have to wait too long, for at ten o'clock Samuel Forrester strode into the factory, and after spending some time in his office, he then made his way to the design room. After speaking for some time to the other women present, he eventually went over to Amy and gave her a friendly smile. Amy thought he looked tired. His hair was peppered with grey and his face lined; yet for all that Samuel Forrester was still a fine-looking man.

Amy smiled back at him as he bent his head to look at the drawing board. His eyes also took in the pile of sketches on her desk.

'It looks like you've been busy.'

Amy nodded. 'I have, sir, though I must admit I've been spending quite some time on designs for gentlemen, and I have one that I'd particularly like you and Master Adam to look at.'

As she spoke she drew a sketch from the bottom of the pile and placed it before him. She had drawn three different sketches of this particular hat, all from different angles, and Samuel Forrester stroked his chin thoughtfully as he studied it.

She then ventured, 'As you know, the menfolk – that is, the working class – tend to wear Billycocks for work and flat caps for high days and holidays.

132

I thought this might be a nice alternative – you know, for them to wear for church and suchlike?'

He gazed at the hat intently. It was a jaunty little creation and it appealed to him. It wasn't quite as dressy as the bowler hats and top hats favoured by the gentry, but eyecatching all the same. It had a narrow brim, a deeply indented crown and a pinch at the front.

'I've already spoken to Mr Paggett and the dyers,' she hurried on, her eyes brimming with excitement, 'and they've both assured me that it would not be difficult or too expensive to produce. Oh! And I've got some samples of material that I thought might be suitable for the hat coverings. Rabbit-hair felt would be perfect, but we could also make them in tweed or wool.'

Quickly withdrawing the materials from a drawer, she laid them out side by side next to the sketch. Samuel nodded slowly, his mind racing. The lass had a very valid point. The working-class men of the town were very restricted as to their choice of headgear and it would be nice to offer them an inexpensive option to the customary flat caps, particularly as hats were luckily becoming more and more of a status symbol.

Amy held her breath as she waited for his reaction and when it finally came she let out a sigh of relief.

'I like it.' He turned his head this way and that as he studied the sketches from different angles. 'In fact, I think you may have come up with an excellent idea. As you know, Adam tends to deal with the men's design side of the business but I'm sure he would be interested in this.'

She blushed at his praise, delighted.

'I'd like you to bring this sketch and the samples of material to Forrester's Folly to show to Adam and Mrs Forrester senior, and of course bring the other sketches you've done whilst I've been away and we'll spend some time looking at those too. Be there in the morning at, say ... eleven o'clock?'

Amy beamed, and nodding, Samuel Forrester turned on his heel and strode from the room.

Before leaving the factory he spent a further half-hour closeted in his office with Mrs Barradell, the head of the design department. Mrs Barradell had been in his employ for many, many years now. She herself was responsible for most of their more popular designs and he valued her opinion highly. She, like him, knew everything there was to know about their trade and now he asked her bluntly, 'So – how is Amy doing?'

Without hesitation she answered, 'She's doing extremely well. To tell you the truth, sir, some of her designs far outshine the other designers'. She's young and not afraid to try out different styles. On top of that, she seems to have a flair for choosing the right material for the right design. I've trained many a designer in my time, as well you know, but I'll tell you now I would have to say that Amy is better than the lot of 'em. She soaks up everything you tell her like a sponge, and added to that she's a hard worker. She often stays behind unasked, long after I've gone home, not content to finish a piece of work until she feels it's just right.'

Samuel nodded. The woman before him, now beginning to stoop with age, had become almost his right hand over the years, and he was pleased that she felt about Amy as he did.

'Thank you, Meg.'

She smiled and left him and Samuel sat for some time longer at his desk, quietly contemplating an idea that was forming in his mind.

That evening, Amy paced restlessly up and down the stone-flagged kitchen floor as Molly grinned at Toby who was seated at the table.

'Will yer *please* sit down an' take the weight off yer legs, lass?' she implored. 'You're struttin' up an' down like a caged animal an' wearin' out me good floor.'

Amy's face was animated. 'I can't help it, Gran, I'm just so excited! Mr Forrester really liked my new design, I'm *sure* he did. I'm going to talk to Adam about it tomorrow because he has more to do with the men's designs than Mr Forrester.'

Toby looked at her fondly. She had grown into a beautiful young woman and he knew that she could have had her pick of almost any young man she wanted from the cottages hereabouts. But luckily up to now, Amy seemed totally disinterested in anything but her career.

It was getting harder lately to keep the love he felt for her from showing in his eyes when he looked at her. Unknown to him though, both Molly and Bessie were more than aware of his feelings and had been for some time.

Often, her tired old bones aching, Molly would lie in bed at night praying that Amy would open her eyes and see him for the fine young man he had become. But up until now her prayers had gone unanswered and more and more, Molly

135

worried about what would become of her precious girl, should anything happen to her.

As the night wore on, Molly rose and stretched stiffly. Amy and Toby were sitting together now, their heads bent across a book. Amy was reading to him and Molly's heart swelled with pride. Many of the young people from the town could neither read nor write. Instead they would sign their name with a cross, but Amy could read and write as good as the next. Molly knew that a lot of that was due to Toby. Amy had also attended Sunday school for years as a child. That was the only form of education that was open to the children hereabouts unless they were lucky enough to have parents who could afford to pay for a tutor or for them to attend the tiny village school for a paltry few hours a week. That, plus Toby's many patient hours of coaxing, had made Amy into the learned young lady she was today.

'I'm off to me bed, it's callin' me.' Molly yawned as Amy hurried over to plant a kiss on her cheek.

'Night, Gran,' she smiled, and Toby yawned and rose too.

'Happen it's time I should be away as well,' he grinned, but Amy made to stop him.

'Oh, don't go yet, Toby, stay a while longer. I'm so excited about tomorrow; I'll never sleep if I go to bed just yet. Let's just read a bit more, eh?' she implored.

Willingly, Toby sank back into his seat and as Molly slowly climbed the stairs she sighed. Why couldn't Amy see that he loved her? And the answer came. *There are none so blind as those who do not wish to see.*

Chapter Nine

Samuel Forrester swirled the brandy in his glass. He was sitting to one side of a roaring fire in the sumptuous drawing room of Forrester's Folly. His mother, who sat to the other side of the hearth, sipped at her nightcap and watched him from hooded eyes. Josephine, as was her custom lately, had retired to her room following dinner, and the old woman's eyes crinkled in concern. Her son was obviously very worried about his wife, as indeed was she.

'She'll come out of it, Sammy,' she tried to comfort him. 'She can't go on grieving forever.'

Samuel wasn't so sure. 'But she's not getting any better, Mother, and well you know it. If anything, she's getting worse. Why, only last night she was wandering about the grounds in her nightshirt like a waif. All these years and yet still she expects Jessica to walk in through the door at any minute.' His chin sank to his chest. 'If I hadn't found her last night, it would be the talk of the servants' quarters by now – that is, of course, if it isn't already. They don't miss much, as you know. I really thought that our time in London would do her good, but it doesn't seem to have helped at all.'

The old woman chewed on her lip. Beneath her crusty exterior beat a heart that was as soft as butter and she hated to see her only son so distressed. Josephine had been the love of his life since the moment he had clapped eyes on her, and his adoration had not diminished with the years.

He looked up at her from tortured eyes. 'I'll never forgive myself if I live to be a hundred. A thousand times I've gone over in my mind the day. I ordered Jessica from the house. How *could* I have been so cruel?' His voice held such anguish that the old woman's heart went out to him.

Reaching over, she gently squeezed his hand with her ring-bedecked bony claw. 'There's no sense in whipping yerself, son. We none of us can turn back the clock.' Slamming his cut-glass brandy schooner on to the polished table at the side of his chair, Samuel put his head into his hands.

'I've no need for you to tell me that, Mother. I live with the consequences of my foolish actions every waking moment, and I can only pray that God will forgive me. For there's nothing so sure that, as long as I live, I shall never forgive myself.'

And as the old woman looked on helplessly, tears of regret began to course down his cheeks.

The four of them had been closeted in Samuel's study for almost two hours, when suddenly rapping her silver-capped cane on the floor, the old woman stretched her neck stiffly.

'Samuel, ring the bell an' order some tea, would you, dear? I'm as dry as a bone.'

He rose without question to do as he was told, while from her high-backed brocade chair, the old woman studied Amy closely. The girl she had last met over a year ago had turned into a very beautiful young woman, and her personality and nature seemed to match her looks. Over the last two hours as she explained the different sketches she had brought to them, her enthusiasm had deeply impressed the old woman. There was a freshness about her designs that set them apart. Some of the sketches were extremely plain, yet stunningly elegant in their simplicity. The old woman had put some of her particular favourites to one side, and as Lily wheeled in the tea-trolley it was of these that she spoke.

Ushering the maid away impatiently with a flap of her hand she ordered brusquely, 'Pour the tea, girl.'

Trembling, Amy did as she was told, her hand shaking beneath the weight of the ornate silver teapot. Once or twice a few drops of tea splashed on to the fine bone china saucers and she prayed that the master and the old mistress wouldn't notice. If they did, thankfully they didn't comment, and when they had been served she sat back uncomfortably, her own cup and saucer rattling in her hand as Adam grinned at her. She had never seen a tea service the like of this before in her whole life. Not even in the china-shop window in the town. Painted on it were delicate red and white roses, and it was so fine that she could see her hand through it. She suddenly wished with all her heart that Molly could see it too, for her gran was partial to a nice bit of china. Although her whole collection only amounted to a few plates, nowhere near as fine as this, she displayed them on her oak dresser in the kitchen with pride.

The old mistress's voice pulled Amy's thoughts

sharply back to the present and she started. She was addressing her son, and Adam and Amy listened quietly.

'If you go on my advice, Sammy,' she stated, 'you'll have a good number o' the designs I've put to one side made up and sent off to London as soon as possible. I reckon that they'll sell well.'

This was praise indeed from old Mrs Forrester, and furthermore, the man's hat design was amongst the ones she had singled out; it was one of Amy's own particular favourites too.

'And *you*, young lady.' She turned to Amy now, her voice stern but her eyes kindly. 'The very first time I met you I 'ad a feeling – call it intuition if you like – that you'd do well. I'm a great one, always 'ave been, for trusting to instincts, and all my instincts tell me that you'll go far. Though I don't want this bit of praise going to your head, mind.'

Amy couldn't help but giggle and it must have been infectious, for soon they were all laughing.

'I agree, Grandmama,' Adam told her with a wide smile as he looked at Amy. 'And I'm especially excited about the new design for the men's hats.'

'Then, Mother, if that is your advice, I shall take it, you have never been wrong before,' Samuel grinned, and it was in a merry mood that Amy eventually set off to tell her gran the good news.

The following weeks passed in a blur. Amy worked from early in the morning until late at night overseeing the making of her designs as they slowly took shape She fretted over every minute detail until she was quite satisfied that they were perfect, each and every one. But then at last they were ready and after being individually packed into large cardboard hat boxes, they were then placed into great wooden crates and loaded on to the horse and cart that would take them on the first leg of their journey to the train station.

Mr Forrester himself personally travelled with them on the train to London, and Amy could barely contain her excitement. It was hard to believe that in just five hours' time her hats would be in London. Before the coming of the train it would have taken at least a full day's journey by horse and cart. But tomorrow her very own designs would be displayed in Mr Forrester's smart London shop. It was like a dream come true, and now all she could do was wait to see how the public responded to them.

Just two weeks later, much to Amy's delight, the order came in for more of the same and the whole process began all over again. This time she changed the colours of the styles and sometimes the trimmings, not wishing the order to be identical to the last one.

Molly fussed over her endlessly when she arrived home worn out at night, sure that she was working too hard, but Amy just smiled. She might be tired but she was happy and with that, Molly had to be content.

Besides overseeing the orders for the hats that had already been approved, Amy continued to work on new designs, and these she took now on a weekly basis to Forrester's Folly for the old mistress's approval. Amy looked forward to these visits. There was something about the old lady, minus her many frills and furbelows, that reminded her of her gran. She was aware that they had come from the same beginnings and had they ever met, Amy felt that they would have gotten along famously. They were both stubborn and outspoken and both mentally alert and bright. Despite her fancy clothes and her many glittering jewels, the elderly Mrs Forrester was still proud of her roots and not ashamed to tell anyone that she had helped Samuel to build his empire from nothing, which Amy found touchingly endearing.

It was on one of these visits that Amy met Eugenie Forrester for the first time, and the meeting was far from pleasant.

She was armed as usual with her latest sketches and the spring sunshine was so warm that she took off her bonnet and swung it merrily by its ribbons. After entering the great gates that opened on to the drive of Forrester's Folly, she struck off it and made her way towards the woods. She had discovered this short-cut some time ago, and after the heat of the sun on her back, the woods with their overhanging canopy of leaves were cool and refreshing. It was like walking into a fairy glade, for the floor was a carpet of bluebells, each one offering up its blooms to the rays of sunlight that filtered here and there through the branches. Amy was reminded of the fairy stories that Toby used to tell her when she was a little girl. Here and there, little clumps of toadstools thrust their way through the blue carpet and Amy could almost imagine tiny winged fairies sitting upon them.

When she finally left the shelter of the woods she came upon a row of cottages, all with their own little gardens front and back. These had been built for some of Mr Forrester's staff who worked on the estate, and Amy was aware that the end one was occupied by Mary and Joe.

After passing these she continued to skirt the woods and eventually Forrester's Folly came into view. Stepping out smartly now across the emerald-green lawns, Amy was suddenly aware of a noise behind her and, turning quickly, she saw a white horse and woman, riding sidesaddle, bearing down on her at breakneck speed. Without even stopping to think, she threw herself to one side and landed painfully in a breathless heap. By now the horse and rider had passed her, and as she struggled up on to one elbow she saw the woman fighting to control the creature. Eventually the bucking horse slowed, and to her horror Amy saw the marks of a whip all across his flanks. His nostrils were flaring and he was rearing in distress, but still she whipped him unmercifully until eventually he came to a shuddering halt. Then dismounting heavily, the rider strode over to Amy in a towering rage, her cheeks an angry red.

'Who the hell are *you?*' she demanded. 'Don't you know that this is private land? Why – I've a good mind to set the dogs on you!'

Amy tried to answer but the woman was so furious that she couldn't get a word in edgeways. She stared in consternation at the designs that were scattered all about and the grass stains on her skirt, and as the woman's eyes lit on the drawings, a look of recognition passed over her features and her lips drew back from her teeth in a sneer.

'Why, let me guess ... I bet you're the new little brown-eyed designer we're all so *sick* of hearing about. Well, this little tumble will bring you down to earth, won't it? Why don't you keep to the servants' entrance as befits you?'

Her eyes were flashing fire but Amy wisely held her tongue although she stared back defiantly and unafraid.

The woman was impeccably dressed in a jade-green riding habit topped off with a matching velvet hat that sported an ostrich plume. On her feet were gold buckled leather riding boots and she slapped her crop against them threateningly as she continued to glare at Amy.

Amy had guessed that this was Eugenie, Master Adam's wife. At one time, the woman must have been very attractive, but time and too much good living had robbed her of her good looks, which was partly why she was gazing so jealously at Amy now.

Even with her auburn curls tumbled and her skirts spread about her, the girl was beautiful and Eugenie took an instant dislike to her. She was sick of hearing her name. Sick of hearing the praise that poured from the lips of her father-in-law, and Adam and his grandmother every time her name was mentioned. But more than anything, she was sick of no longer being the centre of attention. Her fury was such that she could barely contain it, and afraid of what she might do, she turned on her heel and mounted her horse none too gently.

'Just make sure you use the servants' entrance next time,' she said spitefully. 'If I ever come across you again, I'll mow you down like the common little guttersnipe that you are.'

And then with a crack of the whip to the terrified horse's rump, she galloped away. Amy could only stare after her indignantly. It had taken all her self-control not to answer the woman back, but now the confrontation was over she shuddered, wondering how anyone as nice as Adam could have saddled himself with such an unpleasant wife.

For the first time she entered the house from the rear, and when she was eventually shown into the study where old Mrs Forrester awaited her, the latter stared at her with concern. Amy had straightened her clothes and tidied her hair as best she could, but there was nothing she could do about the grass stains on her skirts.

'What's happened to you then?' The old woman missed nothing. 'You look as if you've been in a boxin' match.'

'Oh, it's nothing really.' Amy was trying to make light of things, not wishing to cause any trouble. 'I took a short-cut through the woods and as I was crossing the lawn I got in the path of a woman on a white horse.'

'Hmph, that'll be Eugenie, no doubt, galloping around the grounds like a mad thing as usual. She'll kill one o' them poor horses one o' these days, you just mark me words. Too fond o' the whip by far, that spoiled little madam is. Why, there's nothing I'd like more than to take a whip to her meself!'

Amy believed her and suddenly grinned, seeing the funny side of it. 'Well, there's no harm done,' she assured her. 'As Miss Eugenie said, I was the one in the wrong. I should have approached the house from the servants' entrance.'

Mrs Forrester's eyes stood out from her painted face with rage. 'She dared to say that to you, did she? Well, you listen to me, *I'm* saying you may approach the house any damn way you choose, and if that vicious little minx ever says otherwise again, she'll have me to answer to. Do you understand?'

Amy nodded dumbly. The old lady was obviously furious, and eager to turn her mind to other things, Amy quickly removed the sketches from her bag and began to discuss them. Luckily, after a time the old mistress calmed down and the rest of the afternoon passed uneventfully. In fact, Amy might even have said pleasantly.

That evening, for the first time in her whole life, Amy lied to Molly – about the grass stains on her skirt.

'I slipped on the lawns,' was all she'd say, although she was careful to keep her eyes averted from her gran's as she said it. She could well imagine the explosion that would have occurred had she told her the truth, and she could see nothing being gained by it. She knew that today she had made a formidable enemy in Eugenie Forrester, and were Molly ever to find out, she would only worry.

The following evening, Amy finished work at six o'clock. Lately she had often worked until much later but the last order had just been finished and sent off to London and she was looking forward to a quiet evening in with her gran and Toby. As she made her way through the cobbled alleys of the town centre, the stench was almost overpowering; it had been a warm day and the smell was always much worse then. The conditions that the weavers lived in were appalling. Their cottages consisted of only two rooms, one up and one down. The upstairs room housed their looms as well as serving as a sleeping space. The downstairs room was the kitchen-cum-scullery, as well as a sleeping space for those who couldn't fit in upstairs.

It was common for a whole family consisting of a mother, father and five, six or even more children to dwell in these humble abodes. Tiny communal courtyards contained an outside lavatory that sported two seats. The seat, in fact, was merely a plank with two holes cut into it and a bed of ash below. Once a week the dung cart would come and shovel out the waste and then fresh ash would be thrown in. In the middle of the courtyard was usually a pigsty. The pig that it housed was always owned by more than one family who would jointly feed it to fatten it up then once it was slaughtered the meat would be shared out; a piglet would replace it and the whole process would begin again. Next to the sty was a well, which would serve the families with water for washing, cooking and drinking. Needless to say, the water was usually tainted and illness and death were tragically common occurrences.

Amy always shuddered when she passed these dwellings, particularly on days such as this when the stench was almost unbearable.

Compared to the cottagers who dwelt here, she and Molly were fortunate indeed. With their own cottage being on the outskirts of Attleborough they had fresh air and rolling fields about them, and although in her life they had known hardships, she was aware that theirs were as nothing compared to those endured by these people on a daily basis.

It was rare for the townfolk to rear all of their offspring, and it was common practice for them to pay tuppence to an undertaker to place one of their little ones in with the body of the next person he buried whose family could afford a coffin. At least this way, although their child's grave would be unmarked and often unknown, the bereaved parents could rest easy knowing that their little ones were at least lying in consecrated ground.

Amy found this heartbreaking, but because it was a known fact she accepted it. Even now as she hurried by, little raggy-arsed urchins were playing in the streets, bare-footed yet surprisingly smiling, and she returned their smiles as she passed, pressing more than the odd penny into outstretched grubby little hands.

In the heart of the town were numerous public houses and inns. These were a favourite stopping place for the hatters and the miners on their way home following a hard day's labour. There were also various shops, including an ironmonger, baker's, butcher's and grocery shops. Amy had a particular fondness for Mr Armstrong the grocer. When she was small he had always slipped her a bull's-eye when she visited with her gran; he was also well-known for letting the locals run up a slate and settle it on payday.

Soon the church came into view and the smell began to recede as the town gave way to countryside. Amy slowed her pace and then in the distance she saw three people approaching. One of them was Toby, the other man was Mr Hickman, an Attleborough villager who worked with Toby down the mines. They were both in their work clothes and covered with soot. But it wasn't them that Amy's eyes fastened on but the pretty girl at Toby's side. Cathy was Mr Hickman's daughter. Amy recognised her from the Sunday school that they had both attended. She had fair hair tied back from her face with a blue ribbon and she was laughing up into Toby's face at something he had said.

The little group made a merry picture as they approached and for no reason that she could explain, Amy suddenly ducked behind a hedge and hid until they had passed. She watched them from her hiding-place as they made their way along the lane. Cathy appeared to be in fine spirits and suddenly she slipped her arm into Toby's, regardless of his sooty clothes, and almost on tiptoe whispered something into his ear. He laughed at whatever comment she had passed and as the sun slid behind a cloud the joy suddenly went from Amy's day.

She was in a sombre mood when she arrived back at the cottage and Molly was quick to pick up on it.

'What's up wi' you then – have yer lost a bob an' found a penny?'

'No, no, Gran, I'm just tired, that's all. I reckon the last few weeks have caught up with me.'

Molly placed her evening meal before her, but Amy moved the food about listlessly before finally pushing it aside and rising from the table.

Molly kept a close eye on her until eventually Amy joined her at the side of the low fire.

Dropping to her knees, she placed her head into her gran's lap and Molly gently began to stroke her hair.

'I saw Toby on his way home tonight,' Amy mumbled. 'He was walking with Cathy Hickman, you know the one? She lives in the village; I used to go to Sunday school with her.'

'Oh aye, I know the one,' Molly replied. 'Turnin' up on Bessie's doorstep regular as clockwork now, she is. I reckon she's set her cap at Toby.'

She waited for Amy's reaction but when none was forthcoming she went on, 'A nice girl, is Cathy. As I said to Bessie, Toby could do far worse fer himself. But then again I'm amazed he's escaped the net fer this long. Toby would make a fine catch for any girl and no mistake.'

Amy rose abruptly, confused by the feelings that were flowing through her. She had always imagined that Toby would always be there for her, solid and steadfast like her gran and their little cottage. The thought of life without him was unthinkable. But then as Molly had pointed out, Toby was well past the marrying age.

Heading for her bedroom, she said huffily, 'I'm off for an early night, Gran. If Toby comes round, tell him I was tired. Night.' And with that she was gone.

As Molly listened to her stamp away up the stairs, she raised her eyebrows. Could it be that Amy was finally realising what a good husband Toby would make? She could only hope so.

Chapter Ten

For the next week Amy barely had time to think of anything as the very next day Mrs Barradell was taken home from work suffering from severe pains in the spine. Her back had been troubling her for months until now it was almost unbearable. Mr Forrester had ordered her not to come back until she was fully recovered. It was whispered that she was lying in bed with a board beneath her mattress to help relieve her suffering, and that she could remain that way for weeks.

Surprisingly, although Amy was still as yet only classed as an apprentice, it was to her that the designers now came for advice, and she found herself almost rushed off her feet. She saw very little of Toby or even of her gran, for that matter. She would arrive home at night and fall exhausted into bed.

The following week, yet another order arrived from London and the factory was working overtime already. Word came that Mrs Barradell was slightly improved and Amy was pleased to hear it as she liked Meg Barradell. She had been so busy that she had had to forego her weekly visit to Forrester's Folly and she found that she missed it. She had become very fond of old Mrs Forrester and enjoyed their chats and lively discussions on designs. Underneath she felt it might be a long time before she could even think of going again, as they were all so busy trying to meet the latest order. She also guessed that although it was said that Mrs Barradell was on the mend, it would be some while before she was fit to return to work again. However, on that score she was very quickly proven to be wrong, for the very next morning, Meg Barradell hobbled into the factory leaning heavily on Mr Forrester's arm.

Mr Forrester quickly whispered something into Mrs Davis's ear and she began to hurry about, asking the workers to stop their machines. Slowly the factory ground to a halt and after sitting Mrs Barradell on a chair, Mr. Forrester took up his usual position on the staircase to address his workforce.

'I am sorry to pull you from your labours.' He grinned as a ripple of amusement went through the factory and he held up his hand to silence them. 'Before I begin what I have come to tell you, I would just like to say that I appreciate how hard you have all been working. Your efforts have not gone unnoticed, I assure you!'

He stared out at the sea of upturned faces; many of those there had worked for him for years. Then on a more solemn note he continued, 'As you will all be aware, Mrs Barradell here has recently been unwell with back pains. It is a recurring problem that has troubled her for many years, and I must say it is to her credit that she has never let me down.' His eyes were kindly as he looked down on his loyal employee's scarlet face.

'Yesterday I visited Mrs Barradell at her home and we both agreed that it is time she retired. She will be a great loss to us all, as I am sure you will agree, which is why I asked her to come here today to say goodbye to you all.' He paused and then went on softly, 'I have searched my mind for an appropriate leaving gift for this dear lady. A gift that would befit someone who over the years has become my right hand.'

He was now making his way down the staircase, and when he stopped before Mrs Barradell's chair he withdrew a long sealed brown envelope from his inside jacket pocket and placed it into her trembling hands.

'Please accept this,' he said humbly, 'with my heartfelt thanks for all your years of loyal service, and know that you will be sadly missed.'

Necks craned as Meg Barradell fumbled with the seal. When at last it was broken she tore her eyes from her master's and withdrew a stiff parchment. Then, as her eyes scanned the paper, her mouth suddenly gaped and tears sprang from her eyes.

'Why – it's the deeds to me cottage, and made out in my name.' Her voice was incredulous but Samuel Forrester only smiled.

'It's no more than you deserve,' he assured her, and pleased at her reaction, he again turned to his workers.

'Now to my next issue.' His voice was businesslike again. 'Obviously yesterday when Mrs Barradell and I met to discuss her retirement we were also obliged to discuss appointing her replacement. As we all know, the design department is the very heart of our business. No matter how well the hats are made, if the design is unpopular then we lose trade. On this decision I must admit

153

I was happy to be governed by Mrs Barradell's opinion. Lately, as you all know by the hours of overtime you have been forced to work, to meet our orders, we have been doing extremely well. In fact, I am already in the process of setting on more workers to meet the demands. Much of this success is due to a young lady whose new ideas and designs have been like a breath of fresh air. I am referring of course to Miss Amy Ernshaw.'

Amy's eyes almost started from their sockets.

'Therefore,' Samuel grinned, 'I am delighted to say that I am following Mrs Barradell's sound advice and appointing Miss Ernshaw as the new Head of Design.'

A murmur of approval rippled through the crowd and the next moment they were applauding and all smiling her way.

Amy wanted to pinch herself to make sure that she wasn't dreaming, but as the workers streamed across to shake her hand and clap her on the back, it slowly sank in. It was true; she was the new head of the design department. Her dream had come true.

Before Samuel Forrester left to take Mrs Barradell home he made his way across to Amy and shook her hand warmly.

'Congratulations, my dear.' He smiled at her. 'You deserve it, and may I tell you that my mother is delighted too. She has taken quite a shine to you, if you did but know it. Anyway, I would much appreciate your calling at The Folly tomorrow at two o'clock prompt. There are a few things that my mother and I need to discuss with you. And furthermore, I think I may have some more good news for you. At least, I hope you'll think it is. But then, I'm sure it can wait until tomorrow. I think you've had quite enough of a shock for one day.'

Amy nodded dumbly into his smiling face and turning about, Samuel Forrester hurried away.

She was bursting to share her good news by the time she got home that night. She nearly fell inside the cottage in her haste, but then wondered if her good news had somehow preceded her, for there seemed to be a party going on already. Molly, Bessie and Toby were all seated at the table, a half-empty jug of ale and a bottle of elderberry wine between them. They all seemed to be in good spirits and Amy beamed at them.

'Oh, so you've heard then,' she said.

Molly nodded. 'Oh aye, lass, we've heard all right. It's wonderful news, ain't it? Bessie here is as proud as a peacock.'

Toby raised his glass to her, more than a little tiddly. 'I reckon I'll enjoy being an uncle.'

'A what? What are you on about?' Amy was totally confused.

'Why – the *baby*, o' course. Our Mary is to have a baby. Me mam's goin' to be a gran just like yours.' He fell about laughing at his own joke as Bessie cuffed him playfully around the ear.

'Cheeky young bugger,' she grinned. 'I just hope that the little 'un has better manners than its uncle.'

As the meaning of their words sank in, Amy pulled up a chair to join them and her eyes shone.

'You mean Mary is expecting a baby?' She was

155

so delighted that she momentarily forgot her own good news.

'She is that. About seven more months, the doctor reckons, so you'd best get yer knittin' needles out, or better still, get designin' some baby bonnets.'

The mention of bonnets brought Amy's mind back to her own news.

'Well then, we'd better make this a double celebration as I've got some good news of my own to tell you.'

'Oh, God above, don't tell me you're wi' child an' all,' Molly cackled playfully.

Laughing, Amy slapped her hand. 'Now then, Gran, I reckon you've had enough of that wine, you know it always goes to your head.' Her voice was stern but her eyes were dancing, and now that she had their attention she hurriedly began to tell them of the day's events. She was so excited that her words ran one into the other, and every now and then she had to stop to draw breath.

'I'll tell you, you could have knocked me down with a feather,' she confided as they stared at her in awe.

Molly shook her head as if to clear it, then placing her hands firmly on the table, she stared into Amy's sparkling eyes.

'You mean to tell me, *you* are the new head o' the design department?'

When Amy nodded, Molly gaped incredulously.

'Well I'll be,' she muttered softly. 'Didn't I allus say my girl was destined fer better things?'

'Yer did that, Molly, yer surely did,' Bessie agreed. 'By, what wi' our Mary's news and now

156

this on top, well, it's turned out to be a day to remember an' no mistake.'

Toby, who had said not one word whilst Amy had been speaking, leaned across the table and squeezed her hand.

'I always told you you could do it, didn't I?' he said quietly. 'You were always meant for greater things.'

And inside his heart was saying, 'Yes – far greater things than I could ever offer you,' and although he smiled and offered his congratulations, inside he knew that she had gone yet one step even further away from him.

She arrived at Forrester's Folly promptly at two o'clock the next day, boldly going to the front door as the elderly mistress had told her to. Lily was sick and confined to bed in the servants' quarters, so it was Mary who opened the door to her and gave her a crafty wink. She looked smart in her frilled apron and mob cap, and as they walked along the huge hallway, she whispered, 'Well done, Amy.'

Amy grinned at her. 'You too,' she whispered back, and Mary proudly patted her stomach. Then she knocked sedately at the door, formally announced the visitor and showed her into the study before quietly withdrawing.

Mr Forrester and his mother were waiting for Amy and both immediately noted her glowing cheeks and bright eyes.

'So, how's our new Head of Design feeling today then?' asked the old woman.

Amy beamed at her. 'I'm feeling wonderful.'

'Good, good, well come and take the weight off

157

your feet. You know I'm not one for formalities and then, happen when we've had a cup of tea, I'll have something to tell you that will make you feel *even more* wonderful.'

Amy was intrigued and sat impatiently while another maid pushed the tea-trolley in. As was habit now, once the maid had gone, Amy began to set out the cups and saucers and pour out the tea, but it was not until Mrs Forrester was noisily sipping that she spoke again.

'Do you think that you can handle your new position?' she questioned bluntly.

Without hesitation, Amy said, 'Yes I do, ma'am, although I am very aware that I still have a lot to learn.'

'Good – that's exactly what I thought, which is why I've come up with an idea.'

Amy remained silent but stared at her curiously.

'As you may be aware, I lived for some years in London in Samuel's townhouse, until I came to Forrester's Folly,' the old lady went on. 'In actual fact, I was the one responsible for opening Samuel's shop there. And I also helped Adam to open his shop there too.'

Amy hadn't known that and she listened with interest.

'It was in London that I learned a lot. Now *there's* a place to learn. Puts this backwater to shame it does, for fashion. Anyway – I got to thinking and I reckon that a month in London would do you the power of good. Let you see how the other 'alf live. Samuel 'ere agrees wi' me, so what I'm proposing is we all go. It won't be a holiday,

158

mind – you'll spend a lot of time working there, getting some new ideas into your 'ead. What do you think?'

Amy was speechless and the cup she was holding began to rattle in its saucer.

'It will also give us a chance to get you some more fashionable clothes – not that yours ain't perfectly clean and respectable, o' course,' the old lady added hastily, not wishing to cause offence. 'But as the head o' the design department, part of your duties will be meeting with the buyers and suchlike, so we'll need you to look the part.' Her piercing blue eyes bore into her but Amy could only nod speechlessly.

'Good, good. That's settled then.' Taking Amy's silence for agreement the woman nodded with satisfaction. 'You get off 'ome now and clear it wi' your gran, and then we'll set a date, eh?'

Again, Amy could only nod soundlessly and Samuel, who had been listening to the interchange with amusement, quickly stepped in. 'All right, Mother, that's enough for now. I think you've made poor Amy quite lose her tongue.'

Turning his attention to the dumbstruck girl he said kindly, 'Off you go, Amy. Take the rest of the day off and talk it over with your gran as my mother has suggested. But do please assure her that you will be very well chaperoned and well taken care of. If she has no objections to you going, I thought we might take the train from Trent Valley station to Euston in London, and then we can go from there to our family house by pony and trap. My wife and mother will be accompanying us, and if you have never visited

London before I think I can safely predict that you will find it most interesting, as my mother has already said.'

'Y ... yes, sir.' Amy's voice came out as little more than a squeak. Everything was happening so fast that she could barely take it in, and suddenly she longed to escape so that she could put her thoughts into some sort of order before seeing her gran.

On legs that seemed to have developed a life of their own, she stood up and, after excusing herself, set off for home. Her mind was so full that she even forgot the formidable Eugenie as she almost floated across the well-tended lawns. It wasn't until she reached the shelter of the bluebell woods that her footsteps slowed and she hugged herself with excitement. Not only was she now the head of the design department but she was going to London too. *London!* To Amy, who had never been further than her hometown it seemed like a world away. Oh, she had seen pictures of it in books that Toby had shown her, but the thought of actually *being* there made her dizzy. Her lively imagination was running riot. Suddenly throwing back her head she laughed aloud and clasping her arms about the trunk of a great tree she hugged it fiercely as if it could share her joy. Then, gathering up her skirts in a most unladylike manner, she sped from the woods at breakneck speed, intent on getting home and sharing the news with her gran.

However, by the time the row of cottages came into sight, Amy's footsteps had slowed again and she was deep in thought. The first flush of elation had receded and all she could think of now was the fact that she would be leaving her gran all alone. Never for a single day in her whole life had the two been apart, and the thought of leaving her and being so far away was daunting. Her gran was no longer a young woman, although if asked, Amy could not have stated her actual age. Once or twice over the years she had ventured cheekily, 'So, exactly how old are you, Gran?' and Molly had playfully cuffed her ear and replied, 'I'm as old as me tongue, an' a little bit older than me teeth, an' that's all you need to know, me gel!'

Amy grinned at the memories but then became solemn again. *What would I do if anything happened to her while I was gone? Who would take care of her?* Her thoughts ran on as she weighed up the wonderful opportunity that had been offered to her against the prospect of abandoning her gran, and by the time she entered the cottage she was in a sombre mood, as Molly was quick to note.

She was sitting at the old scrubbed table with Bessie, with a great brown teapot between them, and they were both furiously knitting what looked like a tiny shawl and a bonnet that Amy rightly assumed would be for Mary's baby.

'Why, you're nice an' early fer a change,' Molly commented as she looked up. 'That were right good timin'. The tea's just brewed so fetch a cup an' join us, love.'

As she was pouring the tea, Molly asked her impatiently, 'So come on, then – don't keep us in suspense. How did the visit go?'

Amy shrugged. 'It went well. My wages have been raised to a guinea a week.'

Both Molly and Bessie's eyes stretched wide with amazement and Molly's chest swelled with pride. Yet knowing Amy as she did, Molly also guessed that there was more to come.

'*And?*' she persisted. 'I know there's sommat else, so don't just sit there as if the cat's got your tongue. Out with it.'

Amy sighed. She had never been able to keep anything from Molly; the woman could read her like a book.

'Well ... actually, the master *did* put a proposition to me.' She squirmed in her seat as both sets of knitting needles suddenly became still and the two women eyed her expectantly.

'The old mistress and Mr and Mrs Forrester have offered to take me to London for a month,' Amy gulped. 'They both feel it would stand me in good stead in my new position.'

There, it was said and now she sat back to wait for Molly's response. It was Bessie who reacted first when she beamed and said, 'Why, Amy, yer must be thrilled to bits. There's not many girls round 'ere as will ever be offered an opportunity like that, I'll be bound.'

As yet, Molly had said not a word and before she could, Amy announced, 'It's all right, Gran. I'm not going. I only told you because you'd asked.'

Molly's mind was working overtime and a feeling of dread had overcome her. London. Samuel Forrester had offered to take Amy to London. It sounded like the other side of the world to Molly, and what about the cholera outbreak they had suffered there the year before? But then she had read in the newspapers that it struck mainly in the slum areas, and she couldn't imagine Samuel Forrester having a residence anywhere like that. Even so, it had been a terrible epidemic, if what she had read was true. The poor souls had been dropping like flies. But then again, it *had* been over a year ago now, and Amy's eyes were so full of hope...

Pulling herself together with an enormous effort, Molly almost sputtered, 'What do you mean, you're not going? Why, it's the chance of a lifetime. *Of course* you're bloody well going! You'd have to be soft in the head to turn down an opportunity like this.'

Amy's chin jutted stubbornly as she crossed her arms and stared back at her.

'Come on then. Give me one good reason why you shouldn't go,' Molly demanded, and Amy's shoulders sagged.

'I'd worry about you being here all on your own,' she admitted miserably and at that, Molly roared with laughter.

'You soft young madam you. Is that all it is? Well, I won't be on me own, will I? I've got Bessie here, who's not a stone's throw away, as well you know. And besides, I'm not quite in me dotage just yet. I can still take care of meself, and happen it'll do me good not to have to run about after you for a few weeks.'

As Amy looked up into her gran's loving eyes they both smiled.

'There, that's sorted then,' Molly said firmly. 'You're goin', an' that's an end to it. Why, I'd never sleep easy in me bed if I thought you'd missed a chance like this over me.'

Amy suddenly rose and skirting the table, she

flung herself into Molly's arms.

'Oh Gran, I *do* love you,' she whispered.

Gently stroking the girl's soft hair, Molly nodded as she said chokily, 'Aye, darlin'. I know you do, an' I love you an' all.' And the words were spoken from the heart.

Chapter Eleven

On the morning of their departure, Molly chose not to go to the railway station to see Amy off. She couldn't walk as far now as she had used to and besides, she had chosen to say her goodbyes in the privacy of her own home. Toby had carried Amy's valise to the station the night before and left it in the ticket office for her, and now as Amy stood before her gran, her expression was anxious.

'Are you quite sure that you're going to be all right?' she asked for the hundredth time that morning.

Molly clucked her tongue impatiently. 'Just how many times do I have to tell yer? O' course I'll be all right. Now come here and let's tidy you up a bit.' She fussed with the ribbons of Amy's bonnet that were tied beneath her chin, then standing back she surveyed her with satisfaction. Amy was wearing the new dress Molly had hastily made for her, working long into the night to have it finished in time, and on the girl's head was a pretty poke bonnet trimmed with lace that was exactly the same shade of blue as her dress. Amy looked truly beautiful. She had brushed her hair till it shone and her dark eyes were bright. The flush of youth had lent a glow to her cheeks and as Molly surveyed her, her chest swelled with pride.

'There then, I dare say you'll do,' she said gruffly. There was a great lump swelling in her throat and her heart was aching but she was dry-eyed and outwardly calm. 'Let's be havin' yer then. If you don't get a move on you'll be missin' yer train.'

She ushered the girl towards the door and once they were both on the doorstep, Amy pulled her into a last embrace.

'Now remember what I've told you,' Molly told her. 'Don't get goin' out on your own. London is a big place an' full o' pick-pockets an' villains, from what I've heard of it. And *don't* get talkin' to no strangers.'

Amy's eyes were full of unshed tears and pushing her away seemingly impatiently, Molly flapped her hand at her. 'Now don't get startin' that,' she scolded. 'You're only goin' for a month. You'll be back in the blink of an eye, so just get yourself off an' enjoy yourself.'

'All right, Gran. I'll try.' Amy planted a last tender kiss on Molly's thinning hair and then with a final wave she was gone.

Molly watched her until she had disappeared round a bend in the lane, then turning slowly she re-entered the kitchen. Already, it seemed empty, and as she sank down into her old rocking chair, the tears that had been threatening to erupt all morning suddenly flooded from her eyes and made their way down her wrinkled old cheeks.

Deep inside she knew that her girl was on the verge of better things, just as she had always felt it was destined to be, and while one part of her heart rejoiced, the other part mourned the loss of the simple life they had shared. Somehow, Molly Ernshaw knew that from that day on, Amy was about to start another chapter of her life.

When Amy arrived at the station, she found a porter busily transferring numerous trunks, valises and hatboxes from the back of the horse and cart that the Forresters had sent ahead of them, into the rear compartment of the train. She stared at the mountain of luggage in wonder, wondering how anyone could need so much for just four weeks.

She had arrived in plenty of time and shortly afterwards, Samuel Forrester's smart horse and carriage drew to a halt at the entrance. The master was the first to alight and after acknowledging her with a cheery wave he then proceeded to help his mother down from the carriage. Amy had to bite her lip to stop herself from giggling when the old woman appeared. With her heavily painted face and overly frilled attire she made an amusing spectacle at the best of times, but today she had truly excelled herself. The hat that perched precariously on her wig was so wide and so heavily laden with silk flowers that it barely fitted through the carriage door, and she cursed irritably as her son struggled to assist her down the steps.

'Stop *pullin'*,' she scolded him, slapping peevishly at his hand. 'You'll 'ave me go me length, man.'

Samuel merely sighed. He was well-used to his mother's ways but eventually she stood in the road, straightening her hat and smoothing her voluminous skirts as she glared at him. When she spotted Amy standing patiently on the station platform she raised her hand in greeting and after waving back, Amy turned her attention back to the carriage. She had only ever seen Josephine Forrester from afar, and as yet had not been formally introduced.

As Mr Forrester helped her down from the carriage Amy saw that she was a very attractive woman. Although no longer young, her relatively unlined face was soft, and her auburn hair, although slightly faded in colour, was still thick and shining. But it was her eyes that were her best feature. They were a deep brown and, as Amy stared into them, she felt that she could almost have been staring into her own in a mirror.

The woman was dressed in a superbly cut velvet day costume in a rich ruby shade, and on her head was perched a jaunty little hat that Amy instantly recognised as one of her own designs. It was common knowledge in the town that Samuel Forrester had married far above his class, and from the way Josephine held her head high and her proud bearing, Amy could well believe it. Mary and Beatrice had told her that Mr Forrester obviously still adored his wife even after many years of marriage, and now that Amy had seen her she could understand why.

When they finally approached her, Samuel introduced his wife with pride. 'Amy, this is my wife, Mrs Forrester.'

Amy bobbed her knee respectfully as Mrs Forrester smiled at her kindly and said, 'How do you do, my dear. It's so nice to meet you at last. I've heard so much about you, and I know my husband and my mother-in-law have very high hopes for you.'

Unbeknown to Amy, Josephine Forrester had in fact been watching her comings and goings at The Folly for some time, unobserved from her upstairs apartments. The first time she had glimpsed her she had thought she must be seeing a ghost, for Amy bore a striking resemblance to the daughter who she still grieved for daily. Now, face to face with the girl, she was more than ever reminded of her beloved Jessica and her heart ached afresh. Up close, Samuel's protégée was very pretty, and Josephine warmed to her immediately. Unbidden, her thoughts slipped back to happier times but they were disturbed when the stationmaster blew his whistle.

'All aboard!' he shouted, and for the next few minutes they were all kept busy assisting the elderly Mrs Forrester into her carriage and settling her into her seat, which proved to be no easy task.

Amy finally stared out of the window, everything except the excitement of riding on a train for the very first time momentarily forgotten. She felt like a little girl again, all happy and bubbly inside, and it was all she could do to stop herself from laughing aloud with sheer delight.

Her excitement was not lost on the old woman, who winked at her son in private amusement. He grinned back, and as the last carriage door was slammed there was a final shrill whistle and with a jerk the train began to pull away from the station in a cloud of thick black smoke.

Just for a second, as all the old familiar places began to slip past the window, Amy's face clouded as she thought of her gran all alone back at the cottage. But then excitement took over again and she gazed in awe at the fields as they sped along.

It took some five hours and three stops before they drew into Euston station, and by then Amy was in fine high spirits again. Euston was enormous compared to the small station back at home, and as they alighted, she stared about her in awe. There were porters pushing luggage and people rushing here and there, everywhere she looked. Compared to her relatively quiet home town this was truly like another world.

Once all their luggage had been placed aboard a horse and carriage she watched Mr Forrester give the porter a generous tip before ushering them all into another carriage, and they then began their journey to Sloane Street. The old lady was tired by then and kept dropping into a doze, but Amy was wide-awake and as they drove through the streets she gaped in amazement at the size of the buildings. Everything here in London seemed larger than life, and hordes of people thronged the streets. She tried hard to absorb every single thing so that she could tell her gran all about it when she got home. Here and there on the street corners were flower-sellers with barrows full of colourful blooms, and all along the rooftops she saw fat pigeons perched high in the eaves of the buildings. Smart men in sombre suits and top hats scurried to and fro, and fashionable ladies in elegantly cut costumes meandered up and down the numerous shopfronts. Amy was sure that there were more shops in just one street here than there were in the whole of Nuneaton and as she continued to stare from the carriage window she was totally enthralled.

Old Mrs Forrester was fast asleep now, worn out from the long journey. She was snoring loudly, her chin drooped to her chest, but Amy didn't even notice, she was too intent on the sights that they passed.

After some considerable time they turned into what appeared to be yet another very smart neighbourhood. On either side of the wide streets were rows of huge terraced houses. They were all four storeys high, and to Amy's mind they almost seemed to touch the sky. Set into the brickwork here and there was fancy terracotta work carved expertly into the shapes of birds and flowers, and each house appeared to be trying to outdo its neighbour with the quality of the curtains and the heavy lace drapes.

It was in front of one of these houses that the carriage eventually drew to a halt. Amy peered out at it. It had a lovely, brightly painted front door and a great brass doorknocker in the shape of a lion's head. Steps led up to the door and an ornate iron railing ran all along the frontage. To one side of this were steps leading down to what Amy correctly guessed was the basement kitchen. The frontage of the house was nowhere near as big as Forrester's Folly but impressive all the same, and as Samuel helped them down from the carriage, the front door suddenly opened and an elderly lady dressed in a severe black dress appeared on the steps. This, Amy soon discovered, was Mrs Wilcox, the housekeeper. She greeted her master and mistress politely, and then after helping old Mrs Forrester up the steps she beckoned Amy to follow her.

Amy's heart was in her mouth. She felt totally out of her depth and was suddenly so nervous that she almost tripped as she hurried to do as she was told. Once inside the hallway, where the porter had deposited their luggage, Mrs Wilcox helped Mrs Forrester into the drawing room and Amy stood quietly taking in her surroundings. It was an extremely spacious hallway with a beautifully carved balustrade stairway leading up to the first floor. From the ceiling was suspended a beautiful chandelier, and on the wall above a highly polished hall table hung an enormous gilt-framed mirror.

She had no more time to gaze at her surroundings, for just then, Josephine Forrester entered, closely followed by her husband who was carrying two of her large valises, one in either hand. At almost the same time, another doorway opened at the far end of the hall and a young maid, whom Amy judged to be about her own age, appeared.

She smiled widely at the sight of her master and mistress and Mrs Forrester beckoned her over. 'Nancy,' she smiled, 'this is Miss Ernshaw, the young lady I informed you would be staying with us. Have you prepared a room for her?'

'Oh yes, ma'am, I 'ave.' Nancy bobbed her knee as Mrs Forrester nodded her approval.

171

'Excellent. Then may I ask you to show Miss Ernshaw to her room?'

'O' course, ma'am.'

Nancy turned to Amy with a timid smile as Mrs Forrester told her gently, 'Go along with Nancy, dear. She'll show you where everything is and then you can tidy up and have a short rest before dinner. I'm sure you must be tired after your journey.'

Amy nodded obediently, though in truth she was far too excited to be feeling tired. As they mounted the stairs, Amy noticed that Nancy's uniform was identical to the one that Lily wore, and she guessed that Nancy was probably therefore the parlourmaid here.

Nancy led her up three steep flights of stairs and Amy noticed that the higher they climbed, the less elaborate the furnishings and carpets became, although everything was still spick and span. Once Nancy was quite sure that they were out of earshot of the mistress she grinned at Amy tentatively.

'I'm afraid you're up in the gods wiv me, miss.'

'Oh please, Amy will do just fine,' Amy told her quickly. 'I'm simply a servant, the same as you.'

Nancy seemed to relax somewhat then as she led her along the final landing and pointed at a door. 'That's your room and this is mine 'ere. I 'ope I won't disturb yer when I get up in the mornin's.'

She threw open a door and Amy stepped past her into a surprisingly large room. 'Oh, this is lovely!' she exclaimed, crossing to a big brass bed as Nancy looked on and smiled.

'Well, it ain't as posh as the rest o' the 'ouse downstairs, an' it does yer in sometimes, climbin' all them apples an' pears, but I dare say yer'll find it comfortable.'

Amy looked curiously around the room, but then more interested in Nancy for now she asked, 'Are you the parlourmaid here?'

Nancy laughed merrily. 'Nah. I'm more of a general dogsbody, to tell you the truth,' she chuckled. 'There's only three staff 'ere an' that's Cook, Mrs Wilcox an' meself, so I suppose yer could say I were sort o' the laundrymaid, the parlourmaid an' general maid all rolled into one – not that I'm complainin'.' Her eyes were sparkling with mischief and Amy knew at once that she would like her. When Nancy then plonked herself down on to the quilted counterpane, Amy sat down beside her and began to undo the ribbons of her bonnet.

'You ain't exactly what I were expectin',' Nancy informed her cheekily. 'I thought you'd be much older.'

Amy laughed. 'Sorry to disappoint you.'

Nancy quickly shook her head, setting her brown curls bobbing. 'Oh no, I ain't disappointed,' she hastily assured her. 'It will be nice to 'ave someone me own age about the place fer a change, especially now I know you ain't all la di da.' Then suddenly remembering the time she rose guiltily and scurried towards the door. 'Good 'eavens! Mrs Wilcox will 'ave me guts fer garters if I don't get a move on, but per'aps we'll have time fer a proper natter later on, eh?'

'Yes, I'd like that,' Amy told her. 'And by the way, don't get worrying about disturbing me in the mornings. I'll probably be awake anyway; I'm here to work too so I get up early myself.'

Nancy nodded and after flashing her a final friendly grin she disappeared through the door.

Amy now looked about the room that was to serve as her home for the next month. It was a nice room with a huge mahogany wardrobe standing against one wall. Next to that stood a matching chest-of-drawers and on the wall to one side of the door was a wash-stand with a pretty flowered jug and bowl and a small pile of fluffy towels folded neatly on top of it. Compared to the little shaky-down featherbed that Amy had at home, the brass bed appeared enormous, and she bounced glee-fully up and down on the side of it until the springs squealed in protest. Smiling, she hopped off it and, crossing to the big window, she drew aside the cretonne curtains. The sight almost took her breath away, for she felt as if she was on top of the world. The rooftops of London stretched away before her, reflecting all the colours of the rainbow as the late-afternoon sun played upon them, and Amy tried to lock away every little detail of the wonderful sight in her memory.

By the time she went down to dinner later that evening she hadn't managed to sleep so much as a wink although she had washed and tidied herself and put her clothes away. She dined in the kitchen with Mrs Wilcox, Nancy and the cook and they all went out of their way to make her feel welcome. Cook, who was a round ruddy-faced woman, wrapped in a voluminous snow-white apron, had roasted a joint of lean beef for the master and mistress, but for them she had baked a large steak and kidney pie. The pastry melted in Amy's mouth. 'It's as tasty as my gran's,' she

174

praised and from then on, in Cook's eyes she could do no wrong. The main meal was followed by Cook's special jam tart, which again was so delicious that Amy had a second helping.

'Dear me, I shall be as fat as a pig by the time I go home,' she complained as she rubbed her full stomach.

Cook beamed with delight. 'There's nowt wrong wi' havin' a good appetite,' she assured her cheerily. 'An' nowt worse than seein' someone pick at their food.' She then went on to tell Amy that she too originated from Nuneaton and had worked at Forrester's Folly until the master had offered her a full-time position here.

'I nearly snapped his 'and off,' she admitted with a grin. 'I like London an' I'm settled 'ere now.'

Much later, when Amy had helped Nancy to wash and dry the pots and put them all away, she was summoned to the drawing room, where the family had retired to, following their meal.

Old Mrs Forrester had gone to her bed, worn out after the long journey, but the master and mistress were enjoying a glass of sherry as Amy nervously entered.

'So, my dear, has Cook fed you?' Mr Forrester enquired kindly.

Amy began to relax a little as she answered, 'Oh yes, sir. In fact, I don't think I could manage another single mouthful. It was delicious.'

'And your room – is it to your satisfaction? Have you everything you need?'

'Yes, thank you. It's lovely. In fact, everything's lovely. I can hardly believe I'm really here.'

'That's excellent then. I just hope you will still

feel as enthusiastic in a month's time.' He chuckled mischievously. 'But I warn you – I intend to keep you very busy indeed, young lady.'

Josephine, who had been listening with amusement to this interchange, now patted the seat beside her. 'Come and sit down, Amy, and tell me about some of the designs you have in mind,' she invited.

Amy did just that and the next hour passed pleasantly as she eagerly told Mrs Forrester of some of her ideas. The woman listened with interest, and when Amy finally climbed the seemingly endless stairs to her room she was in a happy mood. Undressing and hanging up her clothes, she then took up a pen and paper and began to write her gran a letter, telling her of as many of the day's events as she could remember. She could just imagine Toby reading it aloud to Molly in the cosy little kitchen at the cottage, and a wave of homesickness washed over her. It should be with them within a couple of days if it went on the mail train, but she would still be here, seemingly a million miles away. After putting it into one of the envelopes Josephine Forrester had thoughtfully provided, she addressed it neatly before curling up into a ball on the comfortable bed where Nancy found her almost half an hour later.

'What's up wiv you then?' she demanded.

Amy sniffed tearfully. 'I reckon I'm just missing my gran a bit,' she confessed.

'Well, I suppose that's to be expected. I missed me ma an' all when I first came 'ere but yer get used to it after a while.' The other girl was wearing a long white cotton nightdress with a warm

176

woollen shawl wrapped about her shoulders, and without waiting for an invitation she clambered on to the big brass bed and began to tell Amy about her family.

'Me da's a bit of a bugger,' she began suppressing a giggle. 'There ain't a finer man walkin' the earth when he's sober, but by God, when he's had a skinful, woe betide you. Not that he ever raised his hand to us or nuffink like that. He was just silly when he was in drink and couldn't hold on to a penny piece.'

She frowned now at the memory before going on, 'Me ma used to chase him about the kitchen wiv the rollin'-pin, which was no mean feat if yer try an' imagine that we all lived in a cottage not much bigger than this room. Eight of us altogether there were. Me mum and dad, me, three sisters and two brothers. There used to be ten of us but me youngest brother and sister died from the sickness two years ago. Not that it was surprisin', if you saw where we lived,' she said sombrely. 'There's a ditch dug between the cottages where the sewage runs away, an' some of the rats are that tame the cheeky bleeders don't so much as blink even when yer try to shoo 'em off. When I came here it was the first time I'd ever got to sleep in a clean bed all to meself in me whole life.'

Nancy grinned apologetically. 'Hark at me ramblin' on, eh? I'd better get off an' let yer get some rest. Yer must be weary after the long day you've had, an' you're out wiv the master to-morrow, ain't yer?'

Amy nodded as Nancy slid from the bed before padding barefoot to the door.

'Night, night, sleep tight,' she whispered, and Amy smiled sleepily as the girl slipped out on to the landing and closed the door softly behind her.

Just as Nancy had said, it had been a very long day, so Amy quickly slipped between the cold cotton sheets of the bed. And there she lay in the darkness listening to the noises in the street outside. Everything felt so strange and she was convinced that she wouldn't be able to sleep a wink, so it was a shock when her eyes flew open to find Nancy standing at the side of the bed with a steaming cup of tea in her hand. She was once again dressed in her maid's outfit and she grinned as Amy's tousled head appeared from beneath the warm blankets.

'Come on, Sleepy'ead, rise and shine. It's already 'alf past seven in the mornin' an' yer supposed to be meetin' the master in the foyer at nine. If yer don't get a shufty on you'll not 'ave any time fer yer breakfast.'

Amy blinked as she knuckled the sleep from her eyes, for a moment forgetting where she was. Then she pulled herself up on to the pillow and gratefully took the cup that Nancy held out to her.

'I must have slept like a log,' she yawned as Nancy headed back towards the door.

'Yer can say that again,' Nancy agreed. 'I reckon yer'd 'ave slept the clock round if I hadn't woken yer. Still, there's no harm done. Yer must 'ave needed it, so drink yer tea then come down to the kitchen. Cook's got some breakfast all ready for yer.'

Once Nancy had left, Amy quickly drained her cup before scrambling out of bed and selecting a

178

plain black skirt and a white high-necked cotton blouse from her meagre wardrobe. She then poured some water into the bowl and hastily washed and dressed. Finally she brushed her hair till it shone and tied it back with a fancy red ribbon that her gran had made with her own hands. Now she was ready to face the world but first she crossed to the window and drew aside the curtains. Although it was midsummer a thick smog hung in the air and Amy was amazed to find that she couldn't even see the houses on the other side of the street.

She commented on it to Cook while she was tucking into freshly fried bacon and eggs, and the big woman laughed, setting her double chins wobbling.

'Oh, you'll soon get used to London,' she assured her as she poured more tea into her cup. 'Come mid-morning it will be as clear as a bell. It's the winter smog you have to worry about. I'll tell yer now, I've known it to be that thick yer can't even see yer hand in front of yer, an' that's the 'onest truth.'

Amy shuddered at the thought but by nine o'clock she was standing in the hallway waiting for Mr Forrester, all ready to go. When he appeared minutes later from the dining room he smiled at her as he adjusted his hat in the hall mirror.

'Did you have a good night's sleep, my dear?' he enquired pleasantly.

'Yes sir, I did,' Amy told him. 'In fact, I think I'd still be in bed if Nancy hadn't woken me.'

'Good, good. Well then, it's time we got down to business now. I'm going to take you to my

179

shop here in Kensington today. I think you will find it very different to the shop we have back at home and I hope you will find it interesting.'

Crossing to the front door, he opened it and gazed up and down the foggy street then taking a solid gold fob watch from his waistcoat pocket he tutted impatiently. 'I ordered a horse and carriage to be here for nine o'clock prompt,' he grumbled, but at that moment the sound of horses' hooves clattering on the cobbled street reached them and seconds later a carriage drew to a halt outside.

'Ah, here we are.' He quickly tucked away the heavy gold watch and chain and politely stepped aside for Amy to precede him. They then descended the steps and boarded the carriage. Amy had to pinch her wrist to make herself believe that this was really happening, for somehow she knew that this would be a day she would never forget.

Chapter Twelve

The journey through the labyrinth of streets was nowhere near as interesting as the one of the day before, for the smog restricted their vision to a few yards. Every now and again, pedestrians appeared out of the mist like ghosts, but slowly the air began to clear. Eventually they stopped outside a smart shopfront, and after helping Amy down from the carriage, Mr Forrester paid the cabbie and she watched the carriage immediately rattle away.

Her employer pointed to the shop window with

pride. 'This is *Josephine's Millinery*,' he told her. 'And if you look in the window you will find a number of your designs displayed there.'

A shiver of pleasure rippled through her as Amy saw some of her hats proudly perched on fine hat-stands that showed them off to their best advantage. The window display was by far the finest she had ever seen, and she studied it carefully, determined to take some of the ideas home with her. A length of blue silk was attractively draped down the back of the display, making it impossible to see beyond the hats into the actual shop. Amy liked the idea instantly, for she realised that it lent privacy to the customers as they tried on the different styles. The silk continued all along the bottom of the window, and here and there were colourful silk flowers, all reflecting the shades of the hats, laid in loose bunches and tied with brightly coloured ribbons. All in all, it was an extremely eye-catching display, and Amy was deeply impressed. Taking her elbow, Mr Forrester led her inside and as they entered a bell tinkled merrily above the door. Immediately, a pretty young woman came to greet them, introducing herself as Miss Drake, the manageress. While she bustled away to fetch them tea, a portly little gentleman with a pair of gold pince-nez spectacles perched on the end of his nose appeared from behind a rich brocade curtain that disguised a doorway to the rear of the shop. Hand outstretched, he quickly made his way to Mr Forrester and shook his hand, and then as his eyes came to rest on Amy, he greeted her warmly. 'You must be Miss Ernshaw,' he said. 'The young lady I have heard so much about who is responsible for our recent rise in sales.'

Amy flushed with pleasure.

'Yes, George, this is indeed the young lady I told you about,' Mr Forrester nodded. 'Amy, I am pleased to introduce you to Mr George Harvey. This gentleman keeps my London businesses running like clockwork for me and I'm sure that you two will get along famously. During our stay you will be spending a lot of time here and I'm sure that you will learn from the experience. I am happy to say that many very fashionable ladies favour this particular establishment. In fact, Mr Harvey and the lady manageresses we have employed have built up a very elite clientèle over the years. I feel that if you actually see first-hand the styles that are favoured, and listen to the requests of the ladies, it will stand you in very good stead.'

'Yes, sir.' Amy bobbed her knee and then whilst Mr Forrester and Mr Harvey disappeared into the back room to look at the account books, she was left to study the shop. It was a luxurious room decorated mainly in rich shades of burgundy and gold. The walls were covered in velvet flocked paper, and hung upon them almost everywhere she looked were heavy gilt-framed mirrors so that the clients could see the designs they were trying on from all angles.

Standing against one wall was a beautiful French-style sofa with delicate gilt legs. It was covered in cream velvet draped with gold tassels, and on the floor was a heavily patterned Turkey carpet that reflected the colours of the room. The long narrow counter was a far cry from the counter in the shop back at home. This one was made from a dark mahogany, inlaid with rosewood – and the top of it was so highly polished that it appeared almost mirrorlike. All along it stood hatstands of varying heights displaying yet more hats of all shapes and sizes. Once again, some of them were Amy's very own designs, and she thought how much Molly would have loved to see them so cleverly displayed.

Eventually Mr Forrester departed, promising Amy that he would send a carriage for her at four o'clock. And so began Amy's first day in *Josephine's Millinery*. Mr Harvey was a very well-spoken gentleman, but pleasant and smart as a new pin, and Amy had a feeling that she was going to enjoy herself. Miss Drake too was utterly efficient and charming, eager to explain the way things were run and the customers' likes and dislikes. Beneath the counter were piles of magazines, the like of which Amy had never seen before, and the ladies who frequented the shop were always greatly taken with them. Amy could well understand why. They were full of hand-coloured engravings and lithographs which had been copied from plates in French magazines, and the pages were crammed with advice on refined manners and literature as well as the very most up-to-date fashions in gowns and hats. *Godey's Lady's Book* was the title of the American magazine considered to be the leading authority on fashion and art, and Amy was sure that she could have flicked through the pages all day. While there were no customers in the shop, Mr Harvey was more than happy for Amy to browse through them. It was the Paris designs that most impressed her, and when she commented on this, he nodded in agreement.

'Paris is the hat capital of the world,' he told her knowledgeably. 'I have the magazines ordered and delivered each month, and they are always popular with my clientèle. You will discover that the London ladies are extremely fashion conscious, and one is always looking to outdo another as hats here are considered to be marks of rank.'

Amy listened to him intently, eager to learn as always, and by lunchtime she was well into the swing of things. The ladies who entered the shop were all dressed in the height of fashion but Amy considered some of them to be extremely rude. They would try on the hats, one after another, preening this way and that, whilst their maids stood meekly behind them, and then eventually they would usually select the one that they had tried on in the first place. She could only marvel at Miss Drake's patience, which seemed to be endless, as she ran to and fro fetching first one design and then another.

'Don't you ever get annoyed with them when they order you about?' she asked innocently after one particularly difficult customer had left the shop. They were sitting together in the little room behind the curtain sharing some sandwiches for lunch.

'The first thing a high-class milliner must learn is that the customer is always right, no matter how difficult they are,' the manageress told her patiently. 'The ladies who frequent this shop are mostly very wealthy women, and if they go away happy with the service they have received then there is every chance that they will come back and recommend us to their friends.'

Amy sighed. She had noticed that all of the hats sold here were at least four times as expensive as the same ones that were sold back in Nuneaton. She supposed that he was right. If the women were paying top prices then it was reasonable that they should expect good service. But even so, she doubted that she would ever be as patient as Augusta Drake or Mr Harvey. Some of the women who had come into the shop during the course of the morning had looked Amy up and down as if they had a bad smell under their noses, and Amy, who had always considered herself to be better dressed than most back home, was now suddenly very aware of her simple clothes.

When the carriage drew up outside at four o'clock, she could hardly believe it was that time already, for the day had passed so quickly.

Back at the house in Sloane Street, Nancy opened the door and winked at her cheekily.

'The old mistress is waitin' fer yer in the drawin' room,' she informed her, and after removing her bonnet and tidying her hair as best she could in the mirror, Amy quickly made her way there.

'Ah, so you're back then,' the old lady greeted her as she entered the room, then she pointed to a laden tea-trolley. 'Come and pour the tea. I've been waiting for you, and then you can tell me all about your day.' She was now fully recovered from her journey of the day before and eager to hear Amy's news.

Amy was only too happy to oblige and whilst she

was pouring the tea, Josephine Forrester joined them to listen to her. The girl was so full of the smart ladies that she had met and the wonderful shop that her eyes sparkled and Josephine found herself smiling. She was like a little ray of sunshine in a dark world – young and fresh and enthusiastic – and as Josephine listened to her she began to understand why her mother-in-law Maude and her husband Samuel thought so highly of her. It was almost more than she could do to stop herself from reaching out and stroking the girl's shining curls, so very like her own sweet Jessica's, but she curbed the desire and instead listened intently.

Eventually, Amy excused herself. Her head was bursting with ideas and she wanted to go to her room and get them all down on paper before dinner, which is exactly what she did.

Dinner proved to be a merry affair. Amy had them all in stitches in the kitchen as she sashayed up and down mimicking some of the ladies that Miss Drake had served, and when she finally retired to bed she was tired but happy. Nancy eventually joined her in her room for what was to become their regular bedtime chat and the two girls gossiped well into the early hours of the morning. Already a friendship was springing up between them that was to last for the rest of their lives.

Almost before she knew it, Amy's first week in London had passed. Most of it had been spent at the exclusive Kensington shop, but Mr Forrester had also taken her to visit his other two establishments.

On her first Saturday in London she awoke late and stretched lazily. Samuel had informed her that there would be no work today. He wanted her to have a rest and so apart from doing some sketching, Amy had no idea of how she was going to fill in her time. However, if she had no plans someone else certainly had, as she was to discover after leaving the kitchen following a late breakfast. Amy had just entered the hallway on her way back to her room when she saw Josephine Forrester descending the stairs, and as she spotted Amy she raised her hand.

'Ah, you're just the person I wanted to see. Would you come into the drawing room, dear?' she asked pleasantly. She was obviously in fine spirits. 'My mother-in-law and I have a little idea that we would like to put to you.'

Intrigued, Amy followed her into the drawing room where the elderly mistress was reclining on a sofa with a magazine spread out in front of her.

She patted the seat at the side of her, and Amy took her place at the old woman's side without hesitation.

'Now then, shall I tell her or will you?' The old lady cocked an eyebrow at her daughter-in-law and after Josephine inclined her head she went on, 'Now then, lass, Josephine and I have had our heads together and we've decided that all work an' no play is good for neither man nor beast.' Unsure of what she meant, Amy frowned as the old woman wagged a ring-bedecked finger in her face. 'You're going on a shopping trip, me gel,' she informed her gleefully. 'We've decided it's time you had a few new outfits.'

Amy immediately opened her mouth to protest but the old woman held up her hand to silence her. 'Now don't go getting on your 'igh horse,' she warned. 'It ain't charity we're offering. We need you looking smart in the shops. It's all part and parcel of your new role. Besides, if truth be told, you'll be doing Josephine a favour. She loves shoppin' and spending my son's money. I'd come with you meself but I ain't as nifty on me feet as I used to be. So what do you say, eh?'

Amy thought about it for a moment. 'I'd say that would be lovely if you're quite sure,' she told her shyly.

Josephine beamed with satisfaction. 'Very well then. Get yourself upstairs and put your bonnet on and we'll be off. There's no time like the present.'

Amy needed no second bidding and after respectfully bobbing her knee she flew from the room and took the stairs two at a time. She was back in the hallway in record time, her hair brushed and her eyes gleaming. When Josephine joined her a few moments later, looking beautiful in an elegant day suit and matching hat, it would have been hard to say who was the more excited of the two. It had been many years since Josephine had been able to spend time with a young woman, and she was looking forward to the shopping trip immensely. She had hoped to find a daughter in Eugenie when Adam had first married, but had soon discovered that this would never happen. Eugenie showed no interest whatsoever in spending time with her mother-in-law, and this had been a huge disappointment for Josephine.

In no time at all a carriage arrived to take them to Piccadilly Circus, the heart of London, and as the horse clipclopped along the cobbled streets, Josephine pointed out places of interest. Amy stared in awe, leaning out of the carriage window as far as she dare.

The magnificent store of Swan & Edgar was situated on the corner of Piccadilly Circus – mere minutes away from Buckingham Palace, Josephine informed the awestruck girl. The store was very exclusive, and an immaculately dressed assistant hurried over to them. There was a bubble of excitement in Amy's stomach but as she began to look through the rails of beautifully presented clothes she bit her lip in consternation. Everything looked so expensive! Noting her reaction, Josephine began to draw out different garments.

'What about this?' she asked, holding up a smart grey skirt, then before Amy could protest she selected a pretty white blouse with lace ruffles all around the neckline and cuffs, and tiny gold buttons all down the front.

'Do try them on,' she urged, and obediently, Amy followed the hovering assistant to a private dressing room. She was dreading revealing her plain cotton underthings, but they were sewn by herself and had pretty flounces, so in the end she was not too ashamed.

When she reappeared, Josephine clapped her hands in delight

'Oh, my dear, you look absolutely charming,' she said.

Amy blushed. She had never worn clothes of this quality in the whole of her life and felt a little out

189

of her depth. But Josephine's mind was made up.

'We'll take them,' she told the smiling assistant. She gave the woman her address and asked for the items to be delivered along with the bill, before dragging Amy off to the next shop, enjoying herself immensely. By lunchtime, Amy's head was spinning; Mrs Forrester had bought her outfits that she had only ever dreamed of owning. Apart from the skirt and blouse there was a smart day gown, petticoats, shoes and stockings, not to mention a large amount of new underwear. Mrs Forrester then took her to a very upper-class tea room in Regent Street for lunch, and there they were served with soup, tiny wafer-thin sandwiches and cream pastries, all washed down with tea.

When they had both eaten their fill, Josephine dabbed daintily at her mouth with a linen serviette before saying to Amy, 'Now, my dear, I'm afraid I have a confession to make. I've already spoken to Samuel about this and he is in full agreement with me, although I do have to admit that it was my mother-in-law's idea in the first place.' Suddenly realising that she was rambling on a little she giggled self-consciously and Amy was highly amused. This was a side of her mistress she had never seen before. The girl had always thought that Josephine was attractive, but when she laughed she was positively beautiful.

'You'll have to excuse me, but I haven't enjoyed myself so much for a long time,' she said. 'Which brings me back to what I was about to tell you.'

Amy was all ears and stared at her expectantly.

'The thing is, we felt it wouldn't be right for you to come to London without visiting the theatre, and so Samuel is going to get us all some tickets to see a play at the Theatre Royal in Drury Lane next Wednesday evening. You *will* accompany us, won't you?'

Amy stared back at her blankly. Surely she must be hearing things? Her gran would never believe it and she was so thrilled at the prospect that she was momentarily struck dumb.

'Come along, dear,' Mrs Forrester ordered, taking her silence as an agreement. 'I've saved the best bit until last. We're going to go and get you an evening gown now. As I'm sure you are aware, London society dresses for the theatre and we do want you looking the part. I might even have a new one too if something catches my eye. And of course we must also find you a nice new cloak to go over your other new clothes.'

Rising, she waited for Amy, who was suddenly all fingers and thumbs, then she gaily tripped away with the girl following in hot pursuit. They took a carriage through the teeming streets of what Josephine called 'the West End' and Amy was soon hopelessly lost. However, Josephine seemed to know exactly where she was going and eventually they came to a halt outside a very ornately decorated shop called *Isabelle Modes*. Amy could only gape open-mouthed at the colourful array of gowns displayed in the window.

'This is one of my very favourite shops,' Mrs Forrester confided as she paid the cabbie and alighted from the carriage. 'I'm sure you won't be disappointed.' And without further ado she led Amy inside.

The next hour would remain in Amy's memory

191

for the rest of her life. She tried on one beautiful gown after another and paraded up and down in them for her mistress's approval. She herself thought every single one was lovely, but Mrs Forrester kept shaking her head until she finally emerged from the dressing room in a dark green silk evening gown. An off-the-shoulder design with a low neckline, it was tucked in tight to the waist then the skirt billowed out in shimmering folds. It was without doubt one of the simplest gowns that Amy had tried on, but it made her look elegant and sophisticated, and emphasised the colour of her hair and her tiny waist.

Mrs Forrester drew her to a full-length mirror and pointed at the reflection there, and Amy could scarcely believe that the person staring back at her was herself. She looked so totally different that she suddenly wished with all her heart that Molly were there to see her.

Mrs Forrester's mind was made up. 'It might have been made for you!' she cried. 'We couldn't have found one more perfect if we had scoured the whole of London. And now ... we must find you a pretty evening shawl to go with it, and some evening slippers, of course.'

Within minutes she had the shop assistants scurrying to and fro with various articles until she had selected the ones that she felt were just right. The shawl she chose was pure silk and almost exactly the same shade as the dress, with a deep shimmering fringe that complemented the gown to perfection. Josephine placed it about Amy's shoulders personally and stood back to study the effect. She then chose silk evening shoes and a small matching bag and beamed with satisfaction.

'That's excellent,' she said. 'And now I'm going to choose a new gown for myself.'

So for the next hour, roles were reversed as Josephine tried on various gowns and sashayed up and down in them, asking Amy for her opinion. They eventually both agreed on one in a rich, sapphire-blue velvet, and as their purchases were being carefully wrapped they then chose a new day coat for Amy and smiled at each other like two schoolgirls.

It was late afternoon by the time they left the shop, and once out on the pavement, Josephine sighed with contentment.

'Do you know,' she said regretfully, 'I would love to go on, but unfortunately I'm still rather weak after my illness, so I'm afraid it's time that we headed for home or Samuel will be getting concerned.'

She hailed a passing carriage and when the driver drew the horse to a halt, Amy helped Mrs Forrester inside, where she sank back gratefully against the seat. They arrived home tired but happy to find Mr Forrester waiting in the hallway for them.

Samuel's eyebrows rose as he noted the parcels in the hall that had already been delivered. 'Mm, been spending all my hard-earned money, have you?' The words were stern but Amy was relieved to see that his blue eyes were shining with affection as he looked at his wife. He couldn't remember when he had last seen her looking so happy, and decided that whatever her little shopping expedition had cost him it was worth every penny.

Old Maude Forrester had been impatiently waiting for the shoppers' return too and now her voice carried to them along the hallway, 'Well, get yourselves in here then an' let's have a look at your purchases.'

They hastily joined her in the drawing room but Josephine stubbornly refused to let them see either of the gowns.

'You'll just have to wait until we wear them to the theatre,' she told them determinedly and no amount of persuasion would make her change her mind.

It didn't stop Amy from showing Nancy her dress though, last thing at night in the privacy of her room. 'Cor, you ain't 'alf lucky,' Nancy sighed dreamily as Amy held the gown to her. 'I know,' Amy said. 'I just can't believe how kind the Forresters have been. I never thought that things like this would happen to me.' She hung the dress on the wardrobe door and joined Nancy on the bed where they sat admiring it.

'The Forresters are kind people,' Nancy said pensively as she tucked her knees beneath her chin and wrapped her arms around them. 'When I first come 'ere I felt as if I'd died an' gone to 'eaven – a clean warm bed to sleep in, food on the table an' not having to worry about me da rollin' in blind drunk all the time. 'Sides that, me wages have helped me ma out no end. I still missed 'er though, even if she were a bit rough an' ready.'

Amy's kind heart went out to her. At least she had always had Molly's unconditional love and a stable home-life.

The girls lapsed into silence. The rest of the

household had long since retired to bed and now all they could hear were the night sounds of London through the slightly open window.

'I'd never really met Mrs Forrester properly until we set off to come here,' Amy confided to her new friend eventually. 'But I do think that she's a lovely lady. I used to dream that my mother would be just like her...' Her voice held such a wealth of sorrow that Nancy peeped at her from the corner of her eye.

'Did yer never know yer ma then?'

'No,' Amy admitted sorrowfully. 'She died just after I was born and my gran brought me up.' She had never told anyone that before but she found Nancy remarkably easy to confide in.

'An' what about yer da?' Nancy probed gently as she hugged her knees.

'He died too in an accident before I was born.'

'Cor, that's really sad,' Nancy sympathised. 'But what about yer gran? Is she kind?'

'Oh, yes,' Amy was quick to answer. 'She's been my whole world and I don't know what I would do without her.' She began to tell Nancy all about the little cottage they lived in and her friend listened, enthralled. She had never stepped outside of London and the sound of the cottage where Amy lived, skirting rolling green fields, sounded idyllic. She had been brought up in the back streets with only cobbled alleyways as her playground, yet still she begrudged Amy nothing. It was not in Nancy's make-up to be envious. She had an optimistic cheery nature and instead of dwelling on what might have been she tended to count her blessings.

'Well, I reckon yer've done wonders fer the mistress,' she now told Amy. 'I've ain't never seen her so happy as she has been this visit an' I reckon yer've got somethin' to do wiv that.'

When Amy cocked a curious eye at her, Nancy grinned. 'I reckon it's because yer remind her of Miss Jessica, her daughter. I 'eard Cook sayin' yer was the spittin' image of her.'

'And do you think I am?'

Nancy shrugged. 'I couldn't rightly say. I've ain't been 'ere that long but Cook can remember both Master Adam an' Miss Jessica when they was nippers, and she says they were as close as two peas in a pod. Apparently, Miss Jessica thought the world of 'er little bruvver an' there weren't an 'appier family walkin'. But then, as yer probably know, when Miss Jessica was nearly grown, she 'ad an almighty ruckus wiv the master an' he ordered 'er from the house. Nobody seems to know what it was about though, an' Cook reckons he regretted it almost immediately. But as far as I know she ain't been seen from that day to this, which I suppose accounts fer the mistress usually bein' so low.'

Amy's heart ached for her kindly mistress as she listened to the sorry tale.

'Master Adam ain't been quite the same since Miss Jessica left home neither, accordin' to Cook,' Nancy went on. 'Apparently he married Miss Eugenie wivin months of 'er bein' gone. Eugenie is from a very well-to-do family an' they reckoned 'e worshipped the very ground she walked on. But that didn't last fer long. She's given him an 'ell of a life, poor sod. I 'ate it when she comes here, dishin' orders out left right an' centre. Cook says

196

she wanted a family an' when no babies were forthcomin' she blamed poor Master Adam. Plus, she never lets 'im live down the fact that she's 'igh above 'im in class, because her father is Sir Something-or-other. She reckons she married below 'erself an' she treats 'im an' the rest of us like dirt now. Still, Cook reckons he's lookin' to get a house of 'is own soon in London, so wiv a bit o' luck when he finds one we won't 'ave to see *her* again.'

Amy nodded in the darkness. Having sampled a taste of Eugenie's temper herself, she could well believe what Nancy was saying.

When Nancy finally retired to her own room, Amy lay in bed gazing at the gown that was catching the light of the moon as it shone through the window.

One way or another it had been a long day and soon she slipped into a contented sleep.

Chapter Thirteen

The following Monday, Mr Harvey allowed Amy to serve a customer for the first time. She was looking very smart in her new skirt and blouse, and when the customer had finally gone he congratulated her on her efforts. The woman had wanted a hat to wear for her daughter's wedding and had not been easy to please. But Amy remembered what she had been taught – 'The customer is always right' – and patiently brought one hat after another for the woman to try on until she had

197

tried almost every hat in the shop. Eventually, to Amy's delight, she chose one of Amy's own designs and went away with it in a smart hatbox, very pleased with her purchase. Amy was amazed at how many women did come in wanting hats to wear for weddings and as she pondered on this, an idea began to form in her mind.

Immediately after dinner that evening, Amy retired to her room and set about sketching. By the time she arrived at the shop the next morning she was eager to share her idea with Mr Harvey, but they were all kept extremely busy and it was mid-afternoon, when Miss Drake had left, before she got the chance. At last she fetched her sketches and laid them out on the counter before him. Besides being an expert salesman, Mr Harvey also had a very good eye for detail and she would value his opinion as he had a knack of seeming to know what would appeal to the customers.

Slowly thumbing through the sketches, he listened to what Amy had to say. The designs were extremely good and he had to admit that he was impressed with them.

'I'm sure there'd be a market for these,' she told him earnestly. 'I've been amazed at how many of your customers come in looking for wedding hats, and if we could offer a range for the bride as well as for the bride's mother... Well, we might make a double sale, particularly when word got around.'

He stroked his chin thoughtfully, peering through his pince-nez at the drawings. Amy could just have a point and he had never been one to dismiss a good idea without giving it a chance.

'Leave these with me,' he told her eventually,

not wishing as yet to commit himself. 'Mr Forrester will be calling round this evening and I will talk it over with him.'

Amy thanked him warmly. That night, she could hardly sleep. Tomorrow she might have a decision about her designs. But better yet, tomorrow she was going to the theatre. She would get to wear her beautiful evening gown and she tingled with pleasure at the thought.

She had barely set foot in the shop the next morning when Mr Harvey drew her towards the counter. 'I had a word with Mr Forrester about your idea and showed him your designs,' he told her without preamble. 'And without wishing to raise your hopes, I think I can truthfully say that he thought it was a very good idea. I have to admit that I do too, but obviously there are certain things to be considered. Mr Forrester is actually visiting his London hat factory today and he is going to roughly price up the cost of making up such designs as these. Personally I can't see that it will work out too expensive, but just be patient and I'm sure he will get back to you in due course.'

Amy clapped her hands with delight. 'Oh, thank you, Mr Harvey, that's wonderful!' She darted to a far corner of the shop. 'If he does decide to go ahead with this, I thought here would be a good place for the bridal display.' She spread her arms wide. 'This corner catches the light from the window. We could have all the hat-stands set at different heights to show the different styles, and perhaps we could drape a length of white satin down the wall behind them to show them off to their best advantage. What do you think?'

'Yes, that could look very effective,' he admitted. 'But let's wait and see what Mr Forrester has to say about it first, eh? And Miss Drake may well have some ideas to put forward.'

Content for now, Amy nodded, and as her mind now filled with thoughts of the imminent theatre trip again her excitement began to mount.

She had barely set foot in the house that afternoon when Nancy waylaid her. 'Cook's got yer meal ready early fer yer so that yer'll 'ave more time to go and prink and preen,' she informed her gleefully.

Amy shook her head. 'Tell her thank you for me, would you, Nancy, but I couldn't eat a thing! I'm so excited my stomach is in a knot.'

Nancy giggled; Amy's excitement was infectious. 'Well, go on up then and have yer wash. I'll be up as soon as I can to help yer wiv yer 'air.'

Amy smiled gratefully at her before tripping away up the stairs. She had a long leisurely wash in the steaming hot water that Nancy had prepared for her and then washed her hair until it was so clean that it squeaked when she dried it on the towel. She then sat by the open window where she brushed it as it dried until it shone.

When Nancy appeared, she helped Amy into her dress, and after placing a box of hairpins on the dressing-table, she began to style her hair for her. 'But don't get peekin' in the mirror until I've finished it,' she warned with a chuckle. 'I know exactly how I'm gonna do it and I want it to be a surprise.'

200

Amy obediently closed her eyes as Nancy began. It seemed to take forever but at last Nancy stood back to survey her work and, satisfied with the results, she told her, 'All right, yer can look now.'

When Amy tentatively opened her eyes and looked in the mirror she hardly recognised the sophisticated young woman who stared back at her. Nancy had piled her hair high on top of her head then teased it to fall into shining fat ringlets that framed her heart-shaped face.

'Oh, Nancy!' Amy's voice was incredulous. 'You've done absolute wonders. I feel like a princess.'

'Yer look like one an' all,' Nancy said proudly with a catch in her voice. 'But come on now. Let's be gettin' yer downstairs otherwise they'll be goin' wivout yer.' Snatching Amy's shawl from the end of the bed she draped it about her slender shoulders before handing her the little silk bag.

As Amy stared at her newfound friend she wished with all her heart that she was coming too. But Nancy ushered her towards the door and with a little wave, she disappeared off into her own room.

Amy slowly descended the stairs, afraid of tripping on her voluminous skirts, and after taking a final disbelieving glance in the hall mirror she made her way to the drawing room. She had expected to find it empty as she was a little early, but to her surprise she found her elderly mistress waiting for her. Maude Forrester's eyes softened at the sight of her. 'Why, yer look absolutely lovely, pet,' she said.

Amy flushed prettily. 'Thank you ... but why

aren't you ready too? The carriage will be here to pick us up soon.'

'To tell yer the truth I'm not feeling too grand, so I've decided not to go. All I really want right now is me bed, but I wanted to see you in this mysterious gown before I went up. The only damn thing I'd managed to find out about it up until now is that it was green, but I do admit it was worth waiting for. Oh, and I wanted to catch you on your own because I have something for you.'

When Amy eyed her curiously the old woman lifted a black velvet box from a small table to the side of her. 'I'd like you to wear these tonight,' she said, and when she snapped the lid Amy gasped at the contents. Nestling against a bed of silk was an emerald and diamond necklace the like of which the girl had never seen before.

'Oh no ... I couldn't,' she protested, but the old woman flapped her hand at her, her usual no-nonsense self.

'Of course yer can,' she said decisively. 'I want you to. It's laid in its box for years. I always intended it to go to my granddaughter, Jessica. Emeralds were her favourite, yer see...' Her voice trailed away and her eyes grew moist as she was swamped with memories, but then she pulled herself together again and ordered brusquely, 'Come over here to me now, before I change me mind.'

And on shaking legs, Amy did as she was told.

'That's better, now bend down.'

Amy's skirts billowed around her like a silken pool as she did as she was bid and now the old woman's gnarled fingers fumbled with the clasp until she had secured the sparkling necklace about Amy's slender throat.

'There, that's it. Now get up before yer crease your dress up.'

Too full to speak, Amy rose and stared down at her then, suddenly unable to control herself for a moment longer, she flung her arms about the old woman's neck and hugged her fiercely as unshed tears trembled on her lashes.

'Thank you,' she whispered brokenly, overcome at her generosity. 'I promise I shall guard it with my life.'

Mrs Forrester blew her nose noisily on a silk handkerchief. 'Oh, just get yerself away before you have me going all soft on yer,' she scolded, but her eyes were gentle.

Amy backed towards the door. 'I wish you were coming.' Disappointment was clear in her voice and the older woman smiled.

'You'll have so many admirers tonight yer won't have time to miss me,' she assured her. 'Now go on ... go and enjoy yerself.'

Amy slipped from the room just in time to see the master and mistress descending the stairs. Josephine Forrester looked radiant. About her neck was a glittering sapphire necklace that exactly matched the colour of her gown, and Mr Forrester looked resplendent in a full evening suit. They both smiled at her, pride shining in their eyes as Amy unconsciously fingered the necklace about her own throat. She felt as if she was floating, and when the sound of a carriage drawing up outside came to her ears she followed them silently, feeling like one of the princesses in Toby's fairy stories.

The theatre proved to be everything she had dreamed of. After entertaining the ladies with an account of the recent scandal – for a walled-in skeleton of a stabbed gentleman had been discovered during building works – Mr Forrester helped them to alight from the carriage and escorted them, one on each arm, up the steps to the magnificent foyer. All around them were boards advertising the forthcoming attractions, and ladies drifted here and there like multicoloured butterflies on the arms of immaculately dressed gentlemen. Amy was attracting more than a few admiring glances, and these were not lost on her master and mistress, who exchanged amused looks with each other.

Mr Forrester had reserved a box, and once they had been shown to it, Amy gazed down enthralled at the sea of faces below. The stage for now was curtained off with huge, heavily tasselled velvet drapes. People were milling about as they searched for their seats and occasionally, Mr Forrester would point out one of his acquaintances to his wife, who was surveying the audience through a small pair of opera glasses.

Eventually, everyone was seated and a hush fell on the crowd as the lights began to dim. The drapes slowly parted revealing the actors all in position, ready to begin Act I, Scene I of Shakespeare's *Romeo and Juliet*. The smell of gas lamps and greasepaint hung heavy on the air and Amy leaned forward in her seat, eager not to miss a single word. By the time the curtains swished together again for the interval, she could hardly contain herself. She applauded loudly then turned to the Forresters, her cheeks glowing. They were served with glasses of sparkling wine from a silver tray right there in their private box, and Amy felt like royalty.

Attractive young men glanced appreciatively her way, wishing that they had an excuse to approach her, but their interest was lost on her because she was too wrapped up in the pleasure of the moment to notice.

As soon as the second half of the play commenced she was once again lost in the story, and when it finally reached its tragic conclusion tears were shimmering on her lashes and she applauded until her hands ached.

Their carriage was waiting outside when they left the theatre but the magical night was not quite over yet, as Amy was soon to discover. Mr Forrester helped both ladies into their seats and after a muttered conversation with the driver he then climbed in to join them.

'We are going on a little detour on the way home,' he informed Amy. 'I thought you might like to see Buckingham Palace, my dear.'

Amy gasped as her hand flew to the precious necklace about her throat. This was truly turning into a night that she would never forget. In what seemed like no time at all they were trotting along The Mall, and then there was the Palace sprawled out before them in all its splendour. She stared past the enormous gates and the guards in dumbfounded amazement. It was absolutely magnificent – and to think that Queen Victoria and Prince Albert might be within those very walls even now! It was almost more than she could comprehend as she was dazzled by the many gas lamps that illuminated the palace. The scene was like something out of a fairytale.

On the way home she could speak of nothing but the wondrous evening they had just spent and the Forresters looked on fondly as they listened to her excited chatter. They too had enjoyed the evening almost as much as Amy had, for her unspoiled nature made her a charming companion. When they arrived back at the house they invited her into the drawing room for a nightcap but Amy politely refused. She had already drunk far more than she was used to at the theatre and was feeling light-headed and gay. She was also eager to visit the old mistress in her suite of rooms and return the beautiful necklace that she had so kindly entrusted to her. So, after bidding them both good night and thanking them profusely for such a treat, she sped up the stairs to the first floor, where Maude Forrester slept. She tapped at the door lightly, not wishing to disturb her should she be asleep, but almost immediately the old woman's voice answered, 'Come in.'

After slipping through the door, Amy crossed to the enormous brass bed where the woman lay propped up on a mound of lace-trimmed pillows. Amy had never seen her before without her face being heavily made-up, and now as she saw her stripped of her paint and powder and her flamboyant wig, she was shocked at how fragile the old woman looked. Her scalp showed through her sparse grey hair and she seemed to be lost in the sheets. She looked incredibly frail and ancient, but her face softened at the sight of Amy and laying aside a book that she had been reading she tapped the side of the bed.

'Did you enjoy it then?' she asked, although she already knew the answer from the look on Amy's face.

'Oh, Mrs Forrester ... it was *so* amazing! But I wish that you had come.' Amy was fumbling with the clasp of the necklace and after managing to undo it she placed it gently into the woman's hands.

'Thank you so much for allowing me to wear this,' she said gratefully, and before the old woman could reply she began to tell her all about the play and the unforgettable evening she had just spent.

When she eventually crept from the room and went upstairs to her own, she found Nancy waiting for her, so as Nancy helped her out of her dress she related the whole tale all over again.

'Cor blimey.' Nancy was flabbergasted.

Amy giggled as she stepped out of her petticoats, saying, 'Oh Nancy, you do talk funny.'

'Huh! Yer cheeky bugger. I could say the same about you,' Nancy retaliated. 'There's nuffink wrong wiv the way I speak. I'm a true Cockney, born wivin the sound o' Bow Bells an' proud of it.'

Happy to be alive, Amy impulsively hugged her and Nancy hugged her back.

'I shall *never* be able to sleep tonight,' Amy trilled. 'I'm far too excited.' But only minutes later, when Nancy had left the room, she laid her head on the pillow and went out like a light.

On the following Saturday, Nancy had the

afternoon off and so she and Amy decided that they would go shopping. Amy wanted to buy some presents, one for her gran and one for Toby, so Nancy offered to take her to the Leather Lane market, off Holborn in the City, ten minutes' walk from St Paul's Cathedral.

'Don't go wearin' none of yer new fancy clothes though,' she warned. 'The pickpockets round 'ere are rife, an' if they have an inklin' that yer well to do, they'll stick to yer tail like glue.'

Amy sensibly did as Nancy had suggested and went out in the shabby clothes in which she had arrived. She enjoyed the teeming market immensely, although it was a very different world from the shops she had visited with Josephine Forrester. The friends went from stall to stall trying to choose suitable presents. Eventually Amy found a warm woollen shawl for her gran. It had been handknitted by the stallholder and was a lovely shade of blue, not too bright nor yet too dark. But Toby's present was another matter entirely and she just couldn't decide what to buy him.

'I know,' Nancy suggested, trying to be helpful, 'wharrabout a book? Yer said he loves readin' an' I know where there's a good bookshop.'

Amy nodded. It was a brilliant idea, so arm-in-arm they strolled through the busy marketplace and as they went a thousand smells assailed her. There was a stall with fish of all shapes and sizes laid out on large stone slabs amidst heaps of ice. Another stall displayed colourful arrays of fruit and fresh and some not so fresh vegetables. A butcher's stall had salted joints of meat with flies buzzing around them, and here and there were crates containing live birds – chickens, cockerels and geese all cackling indignantly at their treatment. Underfoot, the cobbles were strewn with straw, and flowersellers held their bright posies out to the girls as they passed by. Another stall boasted bottles and jars of potions, claimed to cure all ills. Amy screwed up her nose as they passed. Here and there were barrows selling hot chestnuts and others selling mushy peas. Amy scarcely knew where to look first and stayed close to Nancy's side as they wended their way through the thronging crowds. Eventually, Nancy struck off down a narrow cobbled alley that stank of urine and something Amy couldn't distinguish until they came to a grimy shop window.

'This is it,' Nancy declared. 'It might not look much from the outside, but if yer able to read, which I ain't, more's the pity, then I'm told it's a treasure trove.'

Amy wasn't so sure. The windows were so dirty that she could barely see inside and paint was peeling from the doors and sills. Still, she followed Nancy trustingly inside and the smells of ink and leather immediately greeted her. She saw at once that the inside was not much cleaner than the outside. On one side of the shop new books were displayed in neat regimental rows, at complete variance to the other side of the shop which was piled with second-hand ones. It was to these that she headed. Everywhere she looked were dusty bookshelves sagging beneath the weight of the numerous volumes piled upon them. Books were strewn everywhere in untidy piles all over the floor, but soon she forgot the smell as she began to lift them one by one and browse through them.

At last she found just what she was looking for. It was an atlas, with maps of various parts of the world on every page and she knew instantly that Toby would love it.

It was two shillings, which Amy considered to be quite expensive, but also in very good condition, and so she paid for it without a qualm, happy with her choice and trying to imagine Toby's face when she gave it to him.

Nancy was horrified and berated her as they left the shop. 'Yer must be soft in the bloody 'ead!' she scolded. 'Fancy payin' two whole bob just fer a bleedin' book.'

Amy just laughed at her, highly amused at her reaction. Once they had retraced their steps and were back in the market, Nancy asked, 'Have yer ever tried jellied eels?'

Amy shook her head.

'Well, we'll 'ave to put that right. Yer can't come to London wivout tryin' jellied eels. Lovely they are, caught fresh from the Thames each day.' So saying, she took Amy's hand and almost dragged her along until they came to the stall she had been seeking.

As Amy stared down at the glutinous mass Nancy placed in her hand a few minutes later, she wrinkled her nose in disgust. 'Ugh, you don't really expect me to eat *this*, do you?' She shuddered.

Nancy laughed. 'Just shut yer eyes an' try it,' she urged. 'You'll love it,' she promised with her own mouth full.

Gingerly, Amy lifted a small piece of the slimy slippery fish and raised it to her mouth. 'Ugh!' She spat it out in horror, oblivious to manners, and Nancy almost choked with laughter. Amy looked suspiciously as if she was going to be sick and had turned a very unbecoming shade of grey.

'What's up, mate? Don't yer like 'em?' the other girl quipped.

Wiping her mouth on her handkerchief, Amy managed to mutter, 'I've never tasted anything quite so revolting in the whole of my life.'

'Well, give 'em 'ere then,' Nancy told her. 'Yer know what they say, waste not want not.' Snatching the offending delicacy from Amy's hand she began to cram the contents into her mouth, causing Amy to turn even greyer if that was possible. Her poor stomach rebelled all the way home, much to Nancy's amusement.

'Yer don't know what's good fer yer, that's the trouble wiv you,' she giggled, but just this once, Amy had to disagree with her. One thing she was sure of, a jellied eel would never pass her lips again for as long as she lived.

The rest of Amy's stay in London passed all too quickly, and just five days before she was due to leave, Mr Forrester, returning late one evening, asked her to join him in his study.

'I wanted to talk to you about the bridal bonnet sketches,' he told her almost immediately. Amy listened with her hands folded demurely in her lap and her heart thudding with anticipation.

'I've given this idea a great deal of thought and I've also made extensive enquiries about the costing, et cetera, of producing these designs. I have to say I think it's an extremely good idea – but I also wondered if perhaps we couldn't take it a stage further?' He was pacing up and down the room with his hands joined behind his back, and after a moment he went on, 'Mr Harvey and I both feel that a shop offering such bonnets could become very popular. Even more so if we could offer bridal gowns to wear with them, which got me to thinking ... didn't you design young Mary Turpin's wedding gown?'

Flustered, Amy nodded as he stopped his pacing to stare at her.

'Then do you think you might be capable of turning out designs to complement the hats?'

With her mind racing, Amy gulped deep in her throat before looking him straight in the eye. 'Yes, sir. I think I could.'

'I thought you would say that,' he smiled. 'So tomorrow, please take advantage of this room and see if you can come up with a few ideas, then in the evening we will look at them together.'

'Yes, sir.' Amy rose and after bobbing her knee she retreated from the room. She could barely take in what Mr Forrester had just suggested but her chin set. She *could* do it, she *knew* she could: all she had to do now was prove it – and that was exactly what she set out to do.

Following the evening meal the next night, Amy and Mr Forrester once again retired to his study and she spread out several designs on the desk before him. She had worked until the early hours of the morning on them and was so tired that she was sure she could fall asleep at the drop of a hat, but she was also very excited and nervous about what he might think of them. He studied them intensely for some time, picking up first one then another until finally he raised his head and smiled at her.

'It seems to me that I'd better be on the look-out for some seamstresses,' he said, and Amy's heart leaped.

Grasping her small hand in his large one, her employer shook it gently up and down. 'I think that Forrester's Bridal Wear has just been born, my dear, and I also think that in the future I'm going to be keeping you very busy indeed.'

Amy could only gaze at him with a large lump in her throat as all her plans and dreams began to become a reality.

Chapter Fourteen

As Nancy closed the lid of Amy's case and snapped down the clasp, she sniffed noisily. 'I'm really going to miss yer.' The words were said from the heart and Amy hurried over and placed her arm about her friend's shoulders.

'I shall be coming back,' Amy promised. 'Mr Forrester says that I'll need to be staying here regularly once the new Bridal Shop is open. I'll be back before you've even had time to realise I've gone, you'll see.'

She was wearing the flattering day gown that

Mrs Forrester had bought her on their shopping trip, and a jaunty little hat was perched on top of her head. Her hair had been swept up and she looked every inch the sophisticated young woman. It was hard to believe that she was the same girl who had arrived with her hair loose about her shoulders in her country clothes just four weeks ago. There was now a quiet air of confidence about her, yet her gentle nature remained unchanged, and although their friendship was still only blossoming, Nancy knew somehow that it never would. They hugged each other before beginning to cart Amy's now considerable luggage down the stairs. In no time at all they were off and Nancy waved from the steps of the house until the carriage turned a corner and Amy was lost to sight.

Once they were on the train the journey home passed quickly. Old Mrs Forrester dozed for most of the way, whilst Josephine sat quietly enjoying the views from the carriage window. Amy and Samuel, meanwhile, spent most of the journey discussing different styles and materials. Samuel had already made discreet enquiries about a vacant shop in an exclusive area in Knightsbridge that he felt would suit their needs very well, and he had left the negotiations on it in Mr Harvey's capable hands, content that the man would secure a favourable deal. He had also employed, on the recommendation of a colleague, two very experienced seamstresses who, even now as the train chugged towards Nuneaton, were working on the first two sample bridal gowns of Amy's designs. All in all it had proved to be a very worthwhile visit.

He was also pleased to note that his wife looked more relaxed than he had seen her for years, and if his new venture succeeded as he felt sure it would, then who could know where it might lead?

When they arrived back at Trent Valley railway station, the Forresters' carriage was waiting for them. Samuel insisted on dropping Amy off right outside her gran's cottage door. He was amused to note that the curtains of the neighbouring cottages were twitching as if they had been caught in a strong breeze when the carriage drew to a halt, but was too much of a gentleman to comment on it as he helped Amy alight before lifting her luggage down for her.

Molly had been like a cat on hot bricks all day, endlessly checking the lane for a sign of her beloved girl, and now she hastily drew back into the shadows of the kitchen, reluctant to run out and greet Amy until the fancy carriage had gone. It was early evening by now and she watched Mr Forrester speaking to Amy before picking up her valise and carrying it personally to the door for her. Amy looked wonderful, yet somehow different, more grown-up and elegant. Just for a moment, Molly was apprehensive but then as the carriage rolled away, the door suddenly burst open and Amy spilled into the room and straight into her waiting arms.

'Oh, Gran, I've missed you *so* much!' Amy was laughing and crying all at the same time and as her smooth cheek pressed against Molly's old wrinkled one, their tears mingled and fell together. She gazed at her gran as if she could never see enough of her, noting with alarm that Molly seemed to have lost weight.

'Have you been eating properly?' she questioned sternly.

Flapping her hands at her, Molly smiled through her tears. 'O' course I have. But I don't want to talk about me. I want to hear about everythin' you've done an' seen. And that means *everythin'*, mind!'

Hands joined, they crossed to the fire and Molly pointed at the neat stack of letters that Amy had written to her and that were piled on one side of the mantelshelf.

'Poor Toby, I've made him read every last one of 'em to me time after time. The poor lad must know 'em all off by heart by now.' She chuckled as she pressed Amy down into the chair at the side of the hearth. 'Now I've got some nice hot soup all ready fer you, an' when you've had it yer can start to tell me about all you've been up to. Toby's due home any minute an' happen he'll want to hear all your news an' all. He's been like a bear with a sore head while you've been gone, so he has.'

Amy smiled indulgently and while Molly pottered about getting the soup she carefully removed her hatpin and placed her hat on the table, gazing affectionately about the little room. Every single thing was just as she had left it, spick and span as a new pin. When she had felt homesick in London, all she had needed to do was close her eyes and she could see in her mind every single detail. The range black-leaded and polished until it shone; the kettle swinging on its hook above a cheery fire, and the copper pans gleaming where they hung above the hearth. She knew now that neither of Mr Forrester's grand residences could ever mean to her what this little cottage did. This was her home, and as Molly was fond of saying, 'Be it ever so humble there's no place like home.' Now she understood exactly what her gran meant and she was truly happy to be back.

She had so much to tell that she barely knew where to begin, but once Toby had joined them she prattled on merrily, holding them both enthralled as they listened to her adventure. Halfway through the evening she suddenly remembered the presents in her valise and she skipped away to fetch them, as excited as a child.

She gave Molly her shawl first and the old woman was thrilled with it.

'Lord above! This must have cost an arm an' a leg. Yer shouldn't have gone spendin' yer money on me, lass,' she scolded, but her pleasure was plain to see.

Next, Amy presented Toby with the smoothly bound leather atlas. It was by far the most expensive book he had ever owned, and although he was delighted with Amy's gift he also felt that it somehow emphasised the distance that was appearing like a chasm between them. As he looked across at her it struck him like a blow that she looked every inch the capable young businesswoman. Her eyes were shining and her hair was gleaming like burnished copper in the glow from the fire, but the girl he had known and adored for so long was gone. Everything about her seemed different now. Her back was upright, her chin firm, and there was a quiet dignity about her that

217

he had never noticed before. He felt in that instant that he had lost her forever, and it was almost more than he could bear. The urge came on him to cry as he had never cried since he was a child, but instead he rose brusquely and dragged his eyes away from hers in case she should see the pain there.

'Thanks, Amy, I shall treasure this always.' He nodded to Molly, then to their amazement he turned and strode to the door without so much as another word.

Once inside the privacy of his own home he crossed to the scrubbed oak table in the middle of the room and throwing the book on to its well-worn surface he gripped the edge of it until his knuckles turned white. A solitary candle burning bright and the low embers of the banked-down fire were the only light in the room and he thought himself to be alone, but suddenly his mother's voice came to him from the depths of a chair to the side of the hearth.

'What's wrong, lad?' Like many others she had seen Amy arrive home that evening and she had known, as only a mother could, that tonight her lad might have need of her.

For a moment he remained silent then, as she quietly approached him in her cotton nightgown with a shawl pulled tight about her shoulders, he looked at her from tortured eyes.

'I ... I've lost her, Mam.' His voice was broken and she quickly did what she had never done since he was a child, she gathered him into her arms and held him close to her heart.

'There, there, lad,' she soothed as sobs wracked

his body. He was crying as if his heart would break and she, who had known of his deep love for Amy, cried inside for him.

'Let it all out now. That's it ... then leave it in the lap o' the angels, for what will be will be, an' there ain't nowt neither you nor I can do about it.'

Chapter Fifteen

The client twirled in front of the full-length mirror as she surveyed her bridal gown from every angle. Amy stood respectfully with her hands clasped tightly at her waist until eventually the young woman turned to her and smiled.

'It's perfect,' she breathed, unable to conceal her delight.

It was all Amy could do to stop herself from sighing with relief. This was the final fitting, and most definitely one of the most elaborate gowns that she had ever designed, but as she looked at the end result she felt that all her efforts had been well worth it. The bride-to-be was from a very upper-class family – in fact, Mr Harvey had hinted that she was distantly related to royalty – so the cost of the gown had been irrelevant. She looked absolutely stunning in Amy's creation and on her wedding day she would have the satisfaction of knowing that nowhere else was there another gown like it.

Amy reminded herself that she must congratulate the seamstresses. They had followed her instructions to the letter and she knew that the embroidery detail on the bodice and the train must have taken them hours and hours of painstaking work. The bonnet that would match the dress had been finished weeks ago and lay ready in an elaborate hatbox designed exclusively for the bridal shop. And now all that remained was to make a few very minor alterations to the length of the gown, and then it would be carefully wrapped and delivered to the family home in readiness for the wedding.

Amy's reputation was spreading and she was becoming very much in demand. Molly complained that she seemed to be constantly rushing between the shop in Nuneaton, Forrester's Bridal Wear in London and The Folly.

The success of the new bridal range had far exceeded any of their wildest dreams and showed no signs of waning. On the contrary, it was going from strength to strength, and although it was only just over a year since the shop had opened, Samuel Forrester had already had to employ two more seamstresses to meet the growing demand for the gowns. Now, once the manageress, Miss Jane Mellor, had seen the latest satisfied customer from the shop, Amy looked around her little empire with satisfaction.

Although much larger than the hat shop that Miss Drake managed in Kensington, it had been very similarly decorated; the walls and carpets were in shades of ivory and cream that complemented the colour of the gowns. All around were mannequins displaying wedding dresses of all styles, from very simple satins to heavily embroidered taffetas, each and every one of them Amy's own designs. The majority of the brides-to-be who frequented the shop with their mamas would choose one of the gowns on display and a copy of it would then be made to fit their own measurements. But if, like the bride who had just left the premises, someone came in requesting an individual design, Amy would be sent for and she would make one of her now frequent visits to London, to meet the client and discuss her needs. The brides were usually happy to follow Amy's advice, for she seemed to have a knack for knowing what sort of style would suit them and what sort of bonnet or veil would best go with their final choice.

Now she made her way upstairs to the room above the shop where the seamstresses were hard at work, and after speaking to them for some minutes about various gowns that were in the process of being made, she then donned her bonnet and warm woollen coat. Bidding Jane Mellor goodbye, she went out on to the fashionable Knightsbridge street and hailed a passing carriage. She would be staying at the Forresters' abode as she always did, and as the carriage rolled across the cobbles she sank back in the seat looking forward to seeing Nancy. The girls were firm friends by now and enjoyed nothing more than their nightly get-together which still took place whenever Amy stayed at the smart townhouse.

When the carriage pulled up, Amy saw Nancy peeping out of the hall window, and within seconds she was on the steps with a broad smile on her face.

'The kettle's on,' she chirped brightly as she ushered Amy into the hall and helped her off with her coat. 'An' Cook says to go straight through to the kitchen. She's made yer one o' yer favourite fruitcakes, an' seein' as Mrs Wilcox is out fer the day the 'ouse is empty except fer us so we can 'ave a chat an' a nice cup of rosie lee together.'

Amy almost felt as if she was coming home, and the two girls continued to chatter as they hurried through to the kitchen where Cook gave Amy a hug and a welcoming kiss. In no time at all they were all sitting at the table with a good hot cup of tea and a wedge of Cook's famous fruitcake in front of them.

Cook had a big soft spot for Amy – always had, in fact – although she was also just a little in awe of her. It was common knowledge that Amy was becoming extremely well-known in London society, for women would go to her with vague ideas of how they would like a gown to be made and Amy, with her gift for design and a few strokes of a pencil, would make their ideas become a reality. She had long since learned the gift of patience from Mr Harvey, and how to deal with customer needs, and all this, plus her stunning good looks and the fact that she was not yet even twenty-one years old, made her a remarkable young woman in Cook's eyes.

The lovely girl they had known when she first came to them had now matured into an even lovelier young woman, but her gentle, bubbly personality remained unchanged and she was still quite content to chatter away to the others for hours about her beloved gran and her home town.

Nancy had also changed over the last year. She was now walking out with a young man. His name was Billy and he worked on one of the numerous wharfs that were studded along the banks of the River Thames. Whenever she spoke of him, which was increasingly often, her face would soften and she would become all starry-eyed. Cook teased her unmercifully about him but Nancy took it all good-naturedly and Amy had high hopes of a romantic wedding for her friend in the not-too-distant future.

'So how's your gran doin' then, luv?' Cook now asked conversationally as she slurped at her tea.

A small frown creased Amy's brow. 'She's not too bad,' she confided, 'although this cold weather plays havoc with her poor hands.'

Cook tutted sympathetically. She knew that Amy had been concerned about her gran's arthritis for some time, which was why, when she came to London, she rarely stayed longer than one or two nights at a time unless it was absolutely essential.

'You'll be off home in the mornin' then?' she said.

Amy nodded. 'Yes, I'll be up bright and early. I need to go and see Master Adam at his shop and talk to him about the men's hats I designed. Apparently they're going like hot cakes and he wants to discuss another material he has in mind for them, to vary the look. He and his father have decided to call them Forrester hats, which I'm really pleased about. But then I hope to be catching the ten o' clock train, so I'll be home by teatime.'

'In that case I'll make sure as your breakfast is on the table fer seven o'clock sharp,' Cook promised and Amy smiled at her gratefully.

Nancy sipped her tea. 'It must be nice to see blokes walkin' about in hats you've designed yerself,' she commented and then, laughing, she went on, 'An' it's *so* much nicer 'ere since Master Adam an' that snotty-nosed wife o' his got their own place in Holland Park, even though it's a bit too close for comfort. She used to have me runnin' around after 'er like a mad thing, an' even *then* nothin' I did fer her was ever right, silly mare.'

Cook nodded in agreement. 'Yer right there, luv. All I can say is, God help the poor buggers she's got workin' fer her now. I doubt she'll keep staff fer long, the way she carries on.'

'I feel sorry fer Master Adam,' Nancy said. 'They reckon she's spendin' money on their house left right an' centre. It'll be a smaller version o' Buck Palace at the rate she's goin' on.'

'Then happen it's time Adam put his foot down wi' her,' Cook said wisely, but none of them really thought that would happen, knowing Eugenie as they did.

That evening, when they had retired to bed, Amy and Nancy had their usual late-night chat.

Amy no longer shared the top landing with Nancy but at the old mistress's insistence now had a room on the second floor, which was kept ready for her frequent visits at all times. For the past hour she had been listening with amusement to Nancy going on about Billy's seemingly endless virtues, and now she was feeling sleepy and warm.

The fire in the ornately tiled grate was burning brightly as the two young women chattered on, content in each other's company.

'When will yer be comin' back again?' Nancy asked eventually when they had caught up on all their gossip and she had run out of things to say about Billy.

'Next week. The seamstresses have almost completed that new design I was telling you about and I have to come back for the client to have her final fitting. That's why I'm calling into the shop on my way home tomorrow.' She chuckled as she went on, 'To be honest, I think the seamstresses will be glad when this one is finished. They've spent hours and hours working on it. Up to now they've stitched on five thousand pearls and sequins. I reckon the gown will be worthy of Queen Victoria herself, by the time it's done.'

Nancy sighed dreamily as a picture of the beautiful dress Amy had described floated in front of her eyes.

'If I ever 'ad a dress like that I don't think I'd ever want to take it off,' she stated, and the two girls then fell together laughing as they pictured Nancy cleaning out the grates and doing her household chores in it.

Amy was up with the lark the next morning and after eating one of Cook's hearty breakfasts she kissed Cook and Nancy soundly and stepped out into the foggy London streets. As she climbed into the waiting carriage, she shuddered and pulled her coat more closely about her. For weeks, Molly had been saying that snow was on the way, and Amy could well believe it.

After her visits to the two shops she made it to Euston station in good time and settled comfortably into the train carriage, tucking her hands into the pretty fur muff that matched her bonnet. She had promised to visit the Forresters that evening, but first she wanted to go home and see her gran.

When she alighted at Trent Valley, Amy called into the grocer shop in the town to buy some treats for Molly for her tea then set off on her chilly walk home. It was almost four o'clock in the afternoon by now, and already the brightness had gone from the day. Frost was forming on the grass and little tufts of it stood erect like tiny sentinels as her feet crunched across it. Her breath was hanging on the air in front of her and by the time she entered the warmth of the cosy little kitchen her nose was red and her cheeks rosy.

'My goodness, you look frozen through,' Molly fussed as she heaved herself out of her old rocking chair. 'Come over here and warm yourself by the fire while I get you a dish o' nice hot stew. I've been waitin' for you to get back afore I had mine. There ain't much fun in eatin' alone.'

After shrugging her arms out of her coat, Amy did as she was told and held her hands out to the welcoming blaze of the fire. Once she was warmed through, they sat together at the table to eat their meal while Amy told her gran all about her latest trip. Molly listened with interest; she was very proud of Amy but she also worried that the girl was doing too much. She seemed to be constantly flitting from Forrester's Folly to London, and when she wasn't doing that her nose was always stuck in a sketchpad. To Molly's mind it wasn't healthy at all. Amy was only a young woman and she should be out having fun in her free time like other girls her age, instead of working all the while. Not that Amy seemed to mind hard work – in fact, she seemed to be thriving on it – and when Molly aired her concerns she would just laugh them off and tell her that she was perfectly content with her life just the way it was.

Once the meal was out of the way, Molly carried the dirty dishes to the deep stone sink as Amy watched her with concern.

'Are your legs hurting you again, Gran?' she asked.

Studiously avoiding her eyes, Molly shrugged. 'No more than usual. They're always worse in cold weather, as well you know. Come the summer they'll ease off again, so don't get frettin'.'

Amy sighed as she looked at her gran's gnarled old hands. Her days of ribbon weaving were long since over, and the loom had not been used for years now, but stood idle gathering dust. Amy had begged Molly to let her and Toby move it into one of the small outbuildings, but it had been her beloved husband's loom and Molly was adamant that it should stay where it was. This had posed a problem for Amy, although she could understand how her gran felt. Molly had been struggling with the stairs and the small room under the eaves she slept in for some time and so Amy came up with a solution.

'Very well, if you won't let me move the loom then you and I can exchange rooms,' she told Molly sensibly. 'My room is much bigger than

227

yours and I don't need much space. You'd be so much more comfortable in my room.'

'I'll do no such thing,' Molly had protested, but on this point Amy would not be swayed and so she and Toby had spent the whole of one Sunday transferring Molly's bed and possessions into Amy's room. Amy then made sure that her gran's new bedroom was warm and comfortable, with new curtains at the window and soft thick blankets to keep out the cold on the bed as well as thick rugs on the floor. In truth, there was no longer any need for Molly to weave. The money that she had once earned, each bronze penny so important back then, was no longer necessary. Mr Forrester was a more than generous master and Amy was now earning more money than they could spend.

Amy had also ensured that the rest of the cottage was made more comfortable too with some of her earnings, and although Molly grumbled Amy knew that she was secretly pleased with the things she had bought. Her old rocking chair, which she would not hear of being done away with, was now padded with thick cushions, and Amy had bought her a stool to put her feet up on. Bright rugs were scattered all across the floor and good thick curtains hung at the windows. The coal house was full to brimming, as was the pantry, and Molly felt as if she had never had it so good. She was a good girl, was her Amy.

'Are you in for the night now?' she asked hopefully as she returned the washed crocks to the dresser a short while later.

Amy was lying in the fireside chair with her stockinged feet stretched out to the warmth of the fire.

She stretched lazily. 'No. I've promised the old mistress I'd take some of my new sketches to The Folly tonight for her to look at. In fact, I ought to be getting off soon or I'll get so comfy that I won't want to go.' As she pulled herself out of the chair with an effort, Molly clucked her tongue disapprovingly.

'You should never be going back out in weather like this,' she scolded. 'It's fit for neither man nor beast, an' I was hopin' Toby might come round an' have a glass o' me special home-made wine wi' us tonight.'

'You two go ahead,' Amy told her as she pulled her soft high-buttoned leather boots on. 'And don't worry, Gran, I'll wrap up warmly. I shouldn't be gone for too long anyway.'

'Well, if you must go just get back soon as you can.'

Amy looked at the two little pink bonnets that Molly had placed on the table. They had taken the old woman weeks to knit, for her hands were not as nifty with the knitting needles now as they had used to be. She guessed that they would be for Mary, who was the very proud mother of twins, little girls who were as alike as two peas in a pod. They were toddling about on their sturdy little legs now and into all sorts of mischief, but both Molly and Bessie utterly adored them and the knitting gave Molly something to do when Amy was away from home.

Bending, she placed a gentle kiss on Molly's papery cheek. 'You just stay by the fire now and keep warm,' she warned.

229

Molly grunted. 'Huh! I ain't hardly goin' to be out gallivantin', am I? Now get yourself off. The sooner you're gone the sooner you'll be back, an' take care.'

Amy smiled as she stepped out into the lane, just in time to see Annie Hayden entering Bessie's cottage – and the sight instantly swiped the smile from her face. Annie lived in one of the little ribbon-weaver's cottages in Abbey Street and was the latest in a long line of girls to set her cap at Toby. Cathy Hickman had long since given up on him and had married a local lad the year before. Annie was probably visiting on some pretext or another to see Toby, although Amy doubted that he would mind. Her gran had informed her that he seemed to be warming towards Annie lately, and as Amy set off on her journey her steps were heavy. The relationship between herself and Toby had changed noticeably since her very first visit to London. She had wondered at first if perhaps he could be jealous of the fact that she was trying to make something of herself, but had dismissed that idea almost immediately. It wasn't in Toby's nature to be jealous of anyone. Then she had thought that perhaps it was because he was having more to do with Annie, who had, as Bessie had bluntly put it, gone all out to woo him. But then again, no matter how she tried, she couldn't see why that should have affected their friendship. She and Toby had been close for as far back as she could remember. Eventually, she could only assume that the cooling was due to her hectic way of life and the fact that they had simply grown up and grown apart.

Whatever the reason, she found that his cool

230

attitude hurt her and she missed him far more than she could have imagined. Oh, he still came round to Molly's occasionally, and he still showed interest in Amy's designs when she showed them to him, but the closeness they had once shared seemed to be a thing of the past.

For a time she shuffled along the lane, her steps dragging. She was deeply lost in thought but then as the bitterly cold wind began to find its way through her many layers of clothes she quickened her pace. The wind was whistling eerily through the trees, which bent their barren branches towards her as if they were trying to snatch at her. But Amy hurried on regardless. The night held no fear for her and she knew every step of the way to Forrester's Folly like the back of her hand. Soon the chimneys belching their black smoke into the dark skies came into view and she cut across the white frosted lawns to the door of the big house, keen to be out of the cold.

Lily admitted her. As usual, she was immaculately dressed in a grey serge gown and a heavily starched apron and mob cap. She took Amy's outer things and hung them on a mahogany hat-stand. Amy thanked her and hurried towards the study, passing Beatrice, who had her arms full of Mrs Forrester's clean laundry, in the hall. Beatrice had taken Mary's position as lady's maid to Mrs Forrester after the birth of Mary's children, and loved her new role. Now she winked at Amy cheekily and Amy beamed back at her. They rarely got to see each other now, apart from the odd Sunday afternoon when Beatrice had time off and Amy was at home, but even so they had remained firm friends.

Both the master and mistress were waiting for Amy and they smiled at her warmly as she entered. Crossing to a heavy cut-glass decanter, Mr Forrester poured some of its amber contents into a glass and after placing it in Amy's hand he drew her towards the roaring fire.

'Get some of that down you,' he encouraged. 'It will warm you inside and out.'

Amy obediently sipped at the drink and as the fiery liquid made its way down her throat her eyes began to run and she coughed.

Patting her on the back, Mr Forrester chuckled. 'There you are, you see – didn't I tell you it was warming?'

'Burning' was the term Amy would have preferred to use as her insides felt as if they were on fire but she politely said nothing as she tried to compose herself. Once she was seated, she began to tell them about her latest trip to London. Mr Forrester was more than pleased with the pile of orders she placed in front of him, and leaning back in his chair he praised her. 'Well done, Amy. At this rate we're going to have to start to think about moving to larger premises to meet demand.'

Amy flushed at the compliment, and all the time Josephine Forrester, who as yet had said not a word, was watching her closely. 'You're not finding all this too much for you, are you, dear?' she asked now. To her mind, Amy looked tired.

'Not at all, ma'am. I love what I'm doing,' Amy assured her quickly.

'All the same, I don't want you making yourself ill. I'm quite aware of all the travelling you are having to do, so Samuel and I have come up with an idea that just might make things slightly easier for you.'

When Amy looked at her curiously, Josephine hurried on, 'The thing is, there is an empty cottage within the grounds of Forrester's Folly. If you were to come and live in it – with your grandmother too, of course, it could save you a lot of time, running to and fro. You could have the use of the horse and carriage and travel into Nuneaton with Samuel whenever necessary, to save you having to walk everywhere. And it could also take you to the station whenever you needed to go to London. It would be nice to have you near, now that Adam and Eugenie have moved into their own property in London.'

Amy's eyes stretched wide with shock, but then the more she thought about it, the more sense it made.

'I'd have to talk to my gran about it,' she told her mistress.

'Of course you must,' Josephine agreed, and she prayed that Molly would see the sense in her suggestion. She herself liked the thought of having Amy close at hand, as she had become very fond of her and looked forward to her visits enormously. She was a little lonely since Adam had moved out, although she could not say that she missed his wife. In fact, The Folly was a much happier place without Eugenie's tantrums, if truth be told. She now rose in a billow of silk skirts.

'Right then, that's agreed.' She smiled. 'You speak to your gran and if she's happy with the idea, we shall have the cottage made ready for you in no time at all.' Josephine sailed towards the door. 'Will you be looking in on Mother-in-law before you leave?' she asked, as she paused with her hand on the door handle.

Amy nodded.

'Very well. I shall excuse myself now then and look forward to hearing your decision. Good night, my dear.' She cast one last radiant smile at Amy and then she was gone.

Later that evening, when she was perched on the edge of the elderly mistress's huge brass bed, Amy told her of Josephine's offer.

'I 'ave to agree it would make sense,' Maude said thoughtfully. 'But what do yer think your gran will make of it?'

Amy shrugged. 'I'm not too sure,' she confessed, chewing on her lip. 'Gran is a bit set in her ways and not really one for change.'

'Well, I suppose yer could always come and live in the cottage on your own if yer gran wanted to stay put.'

Amy shook her head vehemently. 'My place is with her. I'd never even *consider* leaving her on her own.'

As the girl's eyes flashed, Mrs Forrester said gently, 'Then that's to your credit, my dear. But why don't yer just put the offer to her and see how she feels about it?'

'I will,' Amy promised, and soon she was on her way home with her mind in a spin.

Much later that evening, when Amy and Molly were sitting either side of the fireplace, dozing over a cup of hot milk, Amy plucked up her courage and asked cautiously, 'Gran, how would you feel about moving?'

'Where would I be thinkin' o' movin' to at my age?' Molly raised her eyebrows.

Amy peeped at her out of the corner of her eye. 'Well ... the thing is, Mr and Mrs Forrester have offered us a cottage in the grounds of Forrester's Folly and I wondered what you thought of the idea.'

Molly's shrunken old frame seemed to grow in stature as she almost choked with indignation. 'What? Leave here, yer mean? The place that's been me home fer nearly 'alf o' me life?'

As Amy nodded timidly, Molly's eyes roved around the familiar room. 'No, never!' she declared firmly. 'This is all I've ever wanted. I'm too old to be thinkin' o' pickin' up sticks an' movin' on now. The only time I'll ever leave here is feet first in a wooden box.'

Her answer was exactly what Amy had expected and she stared gloomily into the fire. Molly reached over, and her indignation gone now, she gently squeezed her hand.

'I'm sorry, lass. I know it would mean a lot less rushin' about fer you, but I'm too set in me ways. Why, I'd wither away if I had to move to somewhere strange now.'

When Amy nodded in understanding, Molly felt guilty. There was nothing in the world she wouldn't have done for this girl. Nothing, that is, apart from what she was now suggesting.

'You ... you could always go on your own,' she said, and now it was Amy's turn to be indignant.

235

'That's a silly thing to say, Gran. You should know I would *never* leave you, not even if they were to offer me a mansion.' Reaching out, she wrapped her arms around Molly and whispered, 'I promise I'll never mention it again. It was selfish of me to even consider it. I know that you're settled here, and anyway, if we were to go I'd miss Bessie and Toby.'

'Shush then, darlin'. Let's just leave it at that, eh? The least said on the matter the soonest mended.' And the old lady returned Amy's hug and stroked her shining hair, knowing that the subject would never be raised again.

The Forresters were disappointed at Amy's decision but they also respected it. Loyalty like hers was hard to find. And so the offer was shelved and life went on very much as it had before.

Chapter Sixteen

As Christmas 1851 approached, the snow finally came and Molly, who now never ventured very far anyway, found herself totally housebound. Before setting off for work each morning, Amy would fill the coal-scuttle to its brim and make sure that her gran had everything she needed. If she was going to London, Toby would come round and get in the coal for her before he went to work and then do the same again in the evening.

It was on one such evening, when Molly was

sitting at the table with him and Bessie that she brought up a subject that was much on her mind.

'I don't know what to get our Amy for her twenty-first birthday,' she confessed.

Bessie pointed to a jar that was almost full of coins on the shelf. 'I can't really see what you're frettin' about,' she said reasonably. 'All you have to do is tell me what you'd like for her and I'll go into town and fetch it for you. There's enough money in there to buy her a lovely present.'

'No!' Molly said adamantly. 'I don't want to buy her anything with that money. It's money that *she* earned. I want to get her something from me personally.'

They sat pondering on the dilemma for some time until Toby drained the tea in his mug and stood up. 'I'm afraid I'm going to have to leave you ladies to come up with a solution by yourselves,' he told them, suppressing a yawn. 'I'm off to my bed.'

Bessie nodded; he did look tired. 'Go on, lad,' she urged. 'You get yourself away an' tell yer dad I'll be round shortly.'

He nodded and for some minutes, the two women sat staring into the dancing flames. It was then that Bessie had her idea, and turning to Molly, her face became animated. 'I know what yer could give her. Why ... the answer's starin' us right in the face if yer did but know it.'

When Molly frowned, Bessie gabbled on, 'What about the locket? The one that yer found in the bag with her on the night yer brought her home? It's been hidden away all these years and you always intended to give it to her one day, so why not for her comin' of age? I meself can't think of a better present, an' I don't mind bettin', Amy would treasure it.'

Molly sat silent, thinking deeply on Bessie's words, and then slowly a smile spread across her wrinkled old face. 'Do yer know, Bessie, I think you could just be right,' she agreed.

When Bessie left a short while later, Molly hoisted herself up the stairs and going to the far side of the attic, she reached into the dark corner of the sloping roof and withdrew the tapestry bag that held so many memories for her. Her hand sought about inside until it came to rest on a small velvet box.

With unsteady fingers she snapped open the lid and instantly the emerald set in the centre of the locket flashed like fire in the glow from the candle. Molly turned it this way and that for a while as she admired it, then fumbling with the tiny clasp, she sprang the locket open to reveal the two small portraits, one either side. Molly's breath caught in her throat. The young woman was so like Amy that it might have been the girl herself smiling up at her. The other side of the locket revealed a gentle-faced young man. She squeezed her eyes tight shut as memories of that fateful night when she had found Amy in the church doorway came flooding back. Since then, the girl had been her whole life, and now Molly could not envisage living without her, although she still worried about the poor girl who had obviously been Amy's mother, and who had disappeared from the doorway without trace – never to be heard of again.

As a sob caught in her throat she closed the

locket and put it back into the tiny box then, after dropping it deep into her pinnie pocket, she returned the faded bag to the shadows. Bessie was right. There could surely be no other present that Amy would cherish more than this. With a sad smile, the old woman lifted the candle and creaked her way back down the stairs to wait for Amy to come home.

With only three weeks to go until Christmas, Amy's heart was light and she was humming cheerfully as she hurried through the woods on her way to Forrester's Folly. The snow lay deep on the ground and everywhere looked clean and bright. As Mary's cottage came into view she smiled at the sight of the twins who were in the garden, warmly wrapped in bright little scarves and hats, busily building, or attempting to build, a snowman. They were so enthralled with what they were doing that they didn't even see Amy as she emerged from the woods, but Mary and Beatrice did and they raised their hands in greeting.

'This is damn hard work, this is,' Mary called merrily. 'I think it was easier when I was workin' up at the house.'

'I've no doubt it was,' Amy grinned. 'But I know you wouldn't swap the job you're doing now.'

Beatrice came to the gate in the little picket fence that Joe had erected around the garden to try and keep the children in.

Amy returned her smile before asking pleasantly, 'What are you doing here?' The girls rarely got to see each other any more but they were still close.

'It's my day off,' Beatrice informed her. 'So I was up an' out o' the house at the crack o' dawn an' thought I'd spend a little time wi' Mary and the nippers before goin' home to see me mam.'

'You're looking very well,' Amy commented. There seemed to be a glow about her friend and there was a twinkle in her soft grey eyes.

'Well...' Beatrice wondered if she should confide in her but then rushed on, 'I'm walkin' out wi' Jake now, the young gardener that works under Tom, but I ain't told me mam yet, so you'll not say anythin' fer a while, will yer?'

'Of course I won't, and I'm really pleased for you.' Amy assured her. 'I'm sure your mam will be too when you tell her.'

'Hm. The trouble is, she'll be plannin' the weddin' afore I know it,' Beatrice chuckled. 'Which is why I decided to wait a while before I told her.'

Amy was just about to answer when a snowball caught Beatrice full in the face and she gasped before turning towards the children.

'I think I'd better try an' help our Mary get these imps under control,' she said, and so Amy shouted her goodbyes and went on her way, leaving Mary and Beatrice to play snowballs with the excited children. She was pleased to see her friend looking so happy and hoped that Jake would be good to her.

She was halfway across the rolling lawns when the house came into view. There was a pony and trap at the bottom of the marble steps that led up to the front door and Amy instantly recognised it as the doctor's. Someone must be ill. Gathering up her skirts, she flew across the frozen grass, her heart pounding in her chest. When she drew level with the pony she saw that he was pawing restlessly at the ground but she barely noticed his distress as she raced up the steps to the front door and banged on it impatiently.

Lily opened it, and Amy saw that the girl's eyes were red-rimmed from crying.

'Who is ill?' she demanded as she struggled to remove her coat.

Lily sniffed noisily. 'It's the old mistress.' There was a catch in her voice. 'She took poorly in the night. The doctor an' the mistress are upstairs with her now, but the master is in the library.'

Amy nodded, then almost threw her hat and coat in Lily's direction before hurrying along the hallway. Without stopping to knock, she opened the library door. Mr Forrester was standing in front of the fireplace, staring down into the flames, and when he turned she could see the raw pain in his eyes.

Completely forgetting her place, Amy hurried to his side and asked bluntly, 'What's happened?'

He sighed. 'It's Mother. She had a bad turn in the night and she's in a very serious way. I blame myself, Amy. She hasn't been quite herself for some time, as you are probably aware, and I *begged* her to let me get the doctor in to have a look at her, but she wouldn't have a bar of it. She snapped my head off every time I suggested it, but I should have gone ahead and asked him to call anyway. Anyway, he's here now. He's been upstairs with her for over an hour and I hope that when he comes down, he will be able to tell us what's wrong.'

Mr Forrester's face was ashen. Taking control of the situation, Amy crossed to the bell-pull and tugged on it. When Lily appeared moments later, Amy might have been mistaken as the mistress of the house as she told her, 'Lily, fetch Mr Forrester some tea please.'

Lily scurried away like a frightened rabbit to do as she was told, and she returned in a remarkably short time with a tray. Amy quickly poured out a cup of hot sweet tea and placed it into Mr Forrester's trembling hand.

'Drink this, my gran says it's good for shock,' she ordered, and they then sat together in silence, each lost in their own thoughts until at last, Josephine and the doctor appeared in the doorway.

Amy was quick to note that Josephine was even paler than the master. She had been up with her mother-in-law for most of the night and now she looked worn out and drawn.

'Well?' Samuel demanded abruptly as the doctor strode into the room and placed his black bag on the table.

The man chose his words carefully. 'I think your mother may have suffered a seizure,' he said eventually. 'It appears to have affected her all down her left side.' He wished that there was some gentler way to impart his news and watched with sympathy as Samuel's chin drooped to his chest and he screwed his eyes tight shut.

After a time he raised his head and looking the doctor straight in the eye he asked, 'Will she survive?'

'It is possible,' the doctor said cautiously. 'I have known people make a full recovery from this condition, but I'm afraid we must take into account your mother's age. She is going to need constant care and I have a feeling that she isn't going to be the easiest of patients. I cannot say in truth if she will ever completely recover as yet. That is something that only time will tell. For now we will have to take each day as it comes.'

Grateful at least for the doctor's honesty, Samuel nodded. Amy had crossed to Josephine's side and now the woman clung to her hand as if it was a lifeline as Amy patted it comfortingly. The doctor then went on to give them instructions on how the patient should be cared for before departing, promising that he would return later that evening.

Josephine turned to Amy almost as soon as the door had closed behind him. 'Would you mind going up to her, my dear?' she asked wearily. 'I think she would appreciate seeing a friendly face, and I would like to speak to my husband.'

'Of course, ma'am.' And on feet that felt as if they were weighted with lead, Amy left the room and climbed the splendid staircase that led to the old mistress's room. She found her propped high on a mound of lace-trimmed pillows, her face as white as the cotton sheets that covered her. Her left hand lay limply on the satin eiderdown and the left side of her mouth was pulled unnaturally down.

The old woman's maid retreated to a corner of the room to allow them to talk. Maude's eyes, when she turned them to Amy, were as bright and alert as ever, although they were filled with pain.

With her right hand she beckoned Amy to her

and without hesitation the girl approached the bed and grasped her limp hand gently.

'D-d ... do-don't y-you ... dare cry!' Speech was obviously difficult for her and not wishing to distress her more, Amy blinked back her tears and summoned a weak smile.

'Well then,' she said as cheerfully as she could, 'if you're going to be lying there idle for a time I shall have to find something for us to do. I tell you what – I'll read to you, shall I?'

The faint smile she received in answer was more of a grimace, and crossing to a small table on which a number of books were piled, she hastily sifted through them.

'I know,' she said suddenly. 'It just so happens that I have a new book in my bag that I'm reading at the moment. I bought it the last time I was in London. It's by an author called Ellis Bell and it's called *Wuthering Heights*. I'm sure you will enjoy it so I'll read you some of that and you can tell me what you think of it. Personally, I love it.' She lifted the book from her bag and pulled her chair closer to the side of the old woman's bed. Then, bending her head over the pages, she began to read, her voice quiet but clear. She was still there an hour later when Josephine entered the room and squeezed her arm gently.

'I think you can stop now, my dear. She is fast asleep,' she whispered.

As Amy quickly glanced up at the face on the pillow her heart ached. The old woman looked so ancient and fragile that it was hard to imagine her ever recovering. But then again, Maude Forrester was a fighter, and stranger things had happened, so Amy determined to try and stay positive.

Not wishing to disturb her, the two women crept from the room as the maid resumed her position at the side of the bed, and once out on the landing they stared at each other, their mutual love of the sick woman bonding them together.

'Samuel has gone to arrange for a nurse to come,' Josephine told Amy in a hushed voice. 'And he says I'm to tell you to take a few days off work. Mother-in-law so enjoys your company that we felt if you could call in here for a few hours each day instead, it would be beneficial to her. You could perhaps bring some sketches for her to look at, or read to her as you just have done. Do anything that you think may amuse her and take her mind off her illness.'

Amy nodded immediately, glad to be of help, and arm-in-arm, the two women made their way downstairs.

Eugenie, who had been watching from the drawing-room door, sneered at the sight. Adam had forced her to come back from London to The Folly with him for a few days as he had business to attend to at his shop in Nuneaton. It was bad enough, being stuck here in this godforsaken place, but what was even worse was the fact that that damn girl seemed to have the run of the house. Why, even Adam was greatly taken with her, and never seemed to tire of poring over designs of gentlemen's hats with her. The spoiled young woman's mind began to work overtime: perhaps that accounted for why he never seemed to want to spend any time with her any more?

And now all this fuss over that old harridan! She grimaced; there had never been any love lost between herself and Mrs Forrester senior, and she personally would be glad if the old witch died. Taking another long swig from the glass of brandy in her hand she then swung about in a flurry of satin skirts and strode back into the room where she refilled her glass to the brim.

For the next week, Amy visited Forrester's Folly daily, never tiring in her efforts to cheer the old mistress up. She read to her, chattered on about her gran and the sketches she was working on, and in general did anything she could to raise the old woman's spirits. Samuel Forrester had now employed two full-time nurses who administered round-the-clock care, and when Amy was not there, her devoted son and daughter-in-law kept up a constant vigil at her bedside. But all their efforts seemed to be in vain; the old woman was fading away in front of their very eyes.

Much to Eugenie's disgust, Adam delayed their return to London and stayed to oversee the running of his father's businesses as well as his own, but when he was at The Folly he walked about the house grim-faced and fearful. Not once had the old lady asked to see Eugenie, and by the time her husband arrived home one evening, she was in a towering rage.

'Oh, so you've decided to come back, have you?' she spat at him, her eyes flashing fire. 'Was it to see the old witch or your whore?'

He gazed at her disbelievingly. 'Just what are you talking about, woman?'

'Why, your brown-eyed girl, of course!' she sneered. 'You must think I'm a fool. All this time she's been coming here and I've only just realised what's been going on under my very nose.'

He stared aghast at her portly frame, hardly able to believe his ears.

'I can't even *begin* to think what has put this ridiculous notion into your head,' he ground out. 'But I'll tell you now – you are *wrong*, and behaving like this doesn't become you. I can't understand what has got into you lately, Eugenie. If you don't curb your spending habits soon, I shall be forced to sell the house in London and you will find yourself living here again. And to even *suggest* such a thing at a time like this...' he cocked his finger towards the ceiling. 'My grandmother is *dying* up there and I don't need anything else to worry about at present, so for goodness sake get these foolish notions out of your head.'

Eugenie gaped at him as for once he stood up to her.

'Now, if you will excuse me I am going to see my grandmother. I've no doubt you will have objections to that too. But frankly, I am beginning to be past caring.' And without a backward glance he strode from the room, leaving her to stare after him.

When he entered his grandmother's room, Amy and his mother were at the side of the bed. 'How is she?' he whispered.

Before either of them could answer, the old lady slowly turned her head and recognition shone in her faded eyes. She beckoned to him and as he leaned across her she tried to speak.

'Where is Jessica?'

The sound of his sister's name caused him to screw his eyes up tight and his mother's hand to fly to her mouth in distress. But pulling himself together with an enormous effort he told her softly, 'You will be seeing her very soon, Grandmother.' All of them knew that the chances of that were highly unlikely now, but Adam would have said anything if it gave her comfort.

The old mistress visibly relaxed and her hand fell back to the bed. Adam took a seat at the side of her and there he remained until her eyelids eventually drooped and she found relief from her pain in sleep.

Leaving her in the capable hands of the nurse, the trio then crept from the room, and as Amy made her weary way home her heart was aching and she feared the worst.

She slept little that night and despite all of Molly's pleas, was unable to eat a thing. The next morning she set off back to The Folly bright and early, and the first thing she saw as she approached the house was the familiar sight of the doctor's pony and trap. When she entered the hallway she found him there talking to the master, whose face was grave.

'I'm afraid my mother has suffered another seizure,' he told her gently. 'Mrs Forrester and Adam are with her now, but do go up. She has been asking for you.'

Amy silently nodded and when she entered the old woman's room minutes later, Josephine and Adam rose quietly and tiptoed away, closing the door softly behind them. Amy sat down gingerly on the side of the bed as the nurse looked on and as the old woman's eyes flickered open and came to rest on her, she smiled with her crooked mouth and squeezed her hand with her good right one.

'I'm so glad you came.' Her voice was weak and indistinct and Amy had to bend low to hear her. 'There's been too much sorrow in this house but you have brought joy back into it and I thank yer for that.' The woman's breath was coming in quick short gasps now, and the tears that had been trying to choke Amy suddenly gushed from her eyes and coursed unbidden down her cheeks. Willing the old woman to live, she gripped her hand tightly.

Now, as the pain subsided, Mrs Forrester's eyes, that had always seemed so bright and alert, were clouded and she seemed to be looking beyond her.

'Jessica... I knew you would come!' A look of incredible joy played across her face, and perplexed, Amy looked towards the nurse for help. The woman ran from the room, her starched white apron rustling, and seconds later she returned with the old woman's family, who crowded around her bed. Amy left the room, not wishing to invade their privacy, and once out on the landing she buried her face in her hands and sank on to the windowseat. And there she waited. Occasionally maids flitted by as they went sombrely about their duties, the only sound they made being the swish of their skirts as they passed. Below in the hallway she could faintly hear the tick-tock-tick-tock of the grand-father clock, and the urge came on her to rush down and stay its hands, for she was aware that it could be measuring the beloved old mistress's last minutes on earth.

The minutes stretched into an hour and then two, but the bedroom door finally opened and Samuel Forrester appeared, his face deathly pale and his arm tight about his sobbing wife's shoulders. Seemingly oblivious to Amy's presence, he led her gently away and seconds later, Adam followed them from the room. As his eyes found Amy's he slowly shook his head and rising without a word being spoken she made her way downstairs, her steps heavy. Lifting her bonnet and coat she soundlessly slipped from the grieving house. Inside, her heart was crying but she was dry-eyed and pale, for the pain she was experiencing went beyond tears. After leaving the grounds she walked blindly across the fields that would lead her home. The River Anker, its surface frozen to ice, stretched away into the distance like a silver ribbon, but Amy walked numbly on, heedless of her surroundings, and by the time the familiar cottages came into sight, still not a single tear had she shed. For no reason that she could explain, her steps led her not to her own door, but to Bessie's, and as she approached it, the one person she had need of at that moment came into sight.

Toby had just stepped into the lane and immediately he saw her, the closed look she had come to dread dropped like a curtain across his eyes. But then as he noted her ashen face and obvious distress, he stepped quickly towards her, his indifference forgotten and his face a mask of concern.

'What is it, Amy?'

'Oh, Toby,' she sobbed, and suddenly the tears

that had been locked in her heart gushed out of her, threatening to choke her. 'Sh ... she's gone. The old mistress has gone.' Her voice held such a wealth of sorrow that he instantly pulled her into his arms and soothingly held her to him, stroking her hair whilst she sobbed as if her heart would break. Just as she had broken his.

The old mistress's coffin was placed on a table in the magnificent drawing room at Forrester's Folly, where she lay in state for three days, with the curtains tightly drawn and candles in heavy silver candlesticks shining down on her day and night.

On the day of the funeral, six perfectly matched black stallions with enormous feather plumes rising from their manes attached to the glass hearse that would take Mrs Forrester on her final journey, stood outside impatiently pawing at the ground. Inside, the mourners who wished to pay their final respects filed silently past her casket, their faces wreathed in sorrow, for despite the fact that Maude Forrester had been an abrupt kind of woman, she had also been loved by many. Finally it only remained for the close family to say their goodbyes. Amy was allowed to enter the room with them and as she looked down on the old woman she had come to love, a huge lump formed in her throat. At each corner of the beautiful mahogany coffin stood men in tall black silk hats encircled with purple ribbons, their hands encased in black gloves crossed respectfully in front of them, their heads bowed. This was the first time that Amy had seen the old woman since the night of her death and she knew that it would

251

be the last. Just as she would have wished, Mrs Forrester had been dressed in her most flamboyant gown and she looked so peaceful that Amy could almost believe that she was simply fast asleep. Without their numerous rings, her hands were criss-crossed with veins, and death had kissed her lips with a faint tinge of purple.

They each said their goodbyes in their own way. Josephine bent and kissed the wrinkled cheek. Samuel and Adam stood with bowed heads offering up silent prayers. Eugenie chose to stand in a corner of the room looking totally disinterested in the whole proceedings, whilst Amy reached into the coffin and squeezed the hand that the woman had extended to her in friendship in life. It was as cold as marble but she hardly had time to think of it when a fifth man, who had been standing a respectful distance away, stepped forward. It was time and the family silently filed from the room whilst the coffin lid was nailed into place.

It was a silent procession that wended its way to Caldecote Church. It was some distance from The Folly, but the old woman had loved it there; Samuel's father – her late husband Charlie – was buried there, and it had been her wish that she should be interred next to him. The snow had begun to fall softly and as each white flake settled on the cheeks of the mourners they mingled with their tears. The white carpet blanketed the sound of the horses' hooves and the carriage wheels. The tiny church had never seen so many mourners, for the Forresters' friends and colleagues had travelled from far and wide to attend the funeral.

When the pallbearers finally placed the coffin in front of the altar, the church doors had to be left open so that the mourners who were forced to stand outside when the church was full could hear the service.

The vicar's voice rang from the rafters and out into the snowy churchyard, and once it was over the pallbearers again lifted the heavy coffin on to their shoulders. Each perfectly in step, they bore it to the grave that had taken two gravediggers a whole day to dig in the hard ground of the peaceful little churchyard. There the coffin was lowered into the yawning hole, and by the time the guiding ropes had been removed and the men had respectfully stood aside for the final part of the commitment, the gleaming mahogany lid and the shining brass nameplate were already white over with snow. Loud and clear, the vicar's voice echoed to every corner of the churchyard as he solemnly intoned the last words of the burial service, his heavily embroidered stole standing out in stark contrast to his crisp white surplice and his black clerical robes.

Amy's eyes sought Josephine Forrester's but they were hidden behind a heavy black veil. Samuel Forrester stood beside her, his eyes bottomless pools of pain, but he held himself erect, his shoulders straight and his head high, determined that his mother should enter heaven with the dignity that she deserved. It was unusual for the womenfolk of gentry to attend a funeral, but mindful of his roots Samuel Forrester had decided to ignore propriety so that the whole family could be there to say their goodbyes.

And then at last the mourners slowly turned from the graveside and began to make their way back to Forrester's Folly, where a meal befitting a queen awaited them. Amy had been invited but had chosen not to attend. However, as she turned away, Adam's hand gently settled on her arm and momentarily drew her to a halt.

'Amy, could you come to the house this evening at about seven o'clock, please?' he asked. 'The solicitor should have read Grandmother's Will and left by then and my mother and father wish to speak to you.'

Incensed that her husband should be seen speaking to someone whom she considered to be low class in public, Eugenie's hand dragged on his arm and she began to haul him away, her once-pretty face set in grim lines. As she watched them go, Amy sighed before turning to make her way home alone.

Chapter Seventeen

Knowing how much the elderly mistress had come to mean to Amy, it hurt Molly to see the girl so low, and she fussed and fretted over her all afternoon. The wisdom of age had taught Molly that for now, no words of comfort she could offer would ease Amy's pain; for now all she could do was be there for her. But it had also taught her that time was a great healer.

Amy sat staring morosely into the fire until the

late afternoon gave way to evening and it was time to return to The Folly. For once, Molly raised no objections as Amy put on her warm outdoor clothes, although she did think it strange that the Forresters would want to see her on the evening of the funeral. Amy herself felt that no amount of warm clothes could warm her, for her heart was chilled.

Molly saw her off at the door with a kiss and then hurried back to the warmth of the fireside and settled down to wait for her return, her heart heavy for the girl.

As Amy approached The Folly it was ablaze with lights and seemed to shine like a beacon into the darkness. In the hallway she found the house-keeper and the maids rushing to and fro as they put the house back to rights following the endless stream of visitors. Lily stopped to divest Amy of her hat and coat and the thick shawl that Molly had insisted she should wear across her head and shoulders, and Amy then hurried towards the drawing room.

Mr and Mrs Forrester were sitting either side of a blazing fire both dressed in mourning, and Amy was relieved to see that there was no sign of the obnoxious Eugenie. Although Josephine's eyes were red and swollen from weeping she gave Amy a smile and held her hand out to her.

'Thank you for attending the service today, my dear,' she told her once Amy was seated sedately on the chaise longue between them. 'I am sure Mother-in-law would have wanted you to be there. She had come to think a great deal of you.'

255

Unsure of how to answer, Amy simply inclined her head, deeply touched at the kindness of these two dear people.

'It was a fine service, don't you think?' the master enquired.

Amy nodded quickly in agreement. 'Yes, sir. Indeed it was.'

'Well, perhaps now we should think of getting back to some sort of normality. My mother would not have wished us all to sink into the doldrums. She had very high hopes for your designs, as she was fond of telling you, and yesterday I received a letter from Mr Harvey asking if we could both visit him in London at our earliest convenience. Now that the funeral is over I thought perhaps the day after tomorrow might be a good time to go. Would that be convenient for you, Amy?'

'Yes, sir,' Amy replied without hesitation. She would be glad to get back to work because then she would have something else to think about, other than what she considered to be their mutual loss. Even so, she was curious as to why Mr Harvey should wish to see them both together, as for some time now she had been travelling to and from London alone, if and when she was needed. She also wondered if this was why Mr and Mrs Forrester had wished to see her this evening, but as she was soon to discover, they had sent for her for a totally different reason.

The stresses and strains of the previous week and the warmth of the room had taken their toll on Amy, and suddenly to her horror she had to suppress a yawn, which did not go unnoticed by the mistress.

'Are you tired, my dear?' Mrs Forrester asked solicitously.

Amy flushed. 'I am a little,' she admitted.

Josephine was immediately contrite. 'It was thoughtless of us to ask you to call this evening,' she apologised. 'I should have realised how tired you must be, with all the rushing backwards and forwards you've been doing.'

'It's quite all right, really,' Amy insisted. 'But I ought to be getting home now.'

Josephine stared out of the window at the snowy night. 'Why don't you sleep here tonight, to save you going out into the cold again? Lily could prepare you a room in no time at all.'

'No, thank you all the same,' Amy said. 'I really do appreciate the offer, but if I don't go home my gran will be up all night worrying about me. She never settles until I am back safe and sound.'

'Of course – but at least let me have the carriage prepared for you. It really is the most appalling night.'

Again, Amy shook her head, smiling gratefully at the mistress. 'I'd rather walk, really. I am used to walking.'

Josephine sighed. She could well see why her mother-in-law had thought so highly of this young woman, which brought her thoughts back to the reason why she had asked Amy to call.

'The reason I asked you to come is because I have something for you,' she said as she looked towards her husband. When he nodded, she crossed to a highly polished sideboard standing to the side of one of the long sash-cord windows. Opening one of the drawers, she withdrew a long slim velvet box and returning to where Amy still sat, she placed it in her hands.

'Some days ago, following one of your visits, my mother-in-law gave this to me with explicit instructions that I was to pass it on to you, should anything happen to her.'

Amy was puzzled and more than a little embarrassed as she turned the box over in her hands until the master ordered, 'Open it, my dear. I assure you it isn't going to bite you.'

Obediently, Amy opened the lid and her mouth fell open as the colour drained from her face. 'I ... I don't understand,' she murmured as her questioning eyes sought theirs.

'Mother wanted you to have it.' Samuel's voice was gentle as she stared down at the sparkling emerald and diamond necklace. It was the same one that the old lady had once allowed her to wear for the theatre trip in London.

'I ... I really can't accept this,' Amy said, but Mr Forrester wagged his finger at her sternly.

'Oh yes, you can, young lady. I don't know if you are aware of this but our daughter, Jessica, left home many years ago. My mother always intended her to have this one day, but unfortunately despite all our attempts to find Jessica we have never succeeded.' His eyes clouded as his mind slipped away into the past but then he composed himself. Coughing to clear the lump that had formed in his throat he went on huskily, 'My mother doted on Jessica and I know that, like my wife and me, she never got over her leaving us as she did. But then you came into her life and brightened her days again. This gift was left for you with all her love. So

258

... are you going to refuse one of her last wishes?'

Amy stared at him speechlessly. She had declared to Molly only hours before that she was sure that there was not another single tear left in her but now they came, fast and furious, flooding down her cheeks. She had never thought to own an item of jewellery like this in her whole life-time, and yet had it been a cheap trinket she would have treasured it equally as much.

'Th ... thank you.' The words seemed so in-adequate for such a gift but they were all she could think of to say.

When Amy showed the necklace to Molly later that evening the old woman's eyes almost popped out of her head.

'Good God above!' she choked. 'Why ... it's *beautiful*.'

The pair sat in silence admiring the glittering jewels as Molly's mind raced.

Poor Amy had had a rare old week of it, there was no mistake about it. And just before her birth-day too! Her thoughts moved on to the other little velvet box that was now tucked beneath her mattress. Somehow it didn't seem the right time now to give Amy her mother's locket. It was bound to stir her emotions more than they already were, and Molly felt that the poor girl had far more than her fair share of them to deal with right now.

She had waited this long to give it to her, so happen it wouldn't hurt to wait for just a while longer. And so with her mind made up, Molly sought in her head for what to buy her as an alternative.

As the carriage that would take her to the station rattled down the lane towards them, Molly pulled Amy into a warm hug and smiled at her tenderly. 'I'll see you tomorrow night then, darlin' – an' don't forget, keep your chin up. Every cloud has a silver linin', you'll see.'

Amy nodded as disentangling herself from her gran's arms she lifted her small valise and pecked Molly on the cheek.

'Take care, Gran,' she said. 'I'll be home before you know it and then we can have a nice quiet Christmas together, eh?'

Molly stood in the cottage doorway, her shawl pulled tightly about her as she watched Amy climb into the coach and watched it rumble away.

Mr Forrester took her valise from her and as Amy settled back in her seat, she saw that Adam was accompanying them too. But at least there was no sign of Eugenie, which made her wonder if the rumours that Nancy had told her on her last visit to London were true. According to the maid, Adam was being forced to sell the smart town-house in Holland Park because of his wife's extravagant spending. Now that Amy came to think about it, he had certainly been staying at Mr Forrester's London residence a lot lately, leaving Eugenie at Forrester's Folly, not that his wife seemed at all happy with the arrangement. Still, Amy supposed that their domestic life was nothing to do with her at the end of the day and she stared through the carriage window, wondering what Mr Harvey had summoned her and the master for.

Heavy snow on the train lines delayed their

260

journey by almost two hours, and by the time they arrived in London it was already well into the afternoon. The light was quickly fading from the day, so they headed straight for *Josephine's Millinery*, instructing the coachman to wait for them outside.

As they entered the warm interior, Mr Harvey hurried forward and shook Mr Forrester's hand as he offered his sincere condolences on the master's bereavement.

'Your mother was a most remarkable lady, sir,' he told him solemnly and Mr Forrester's face stiffened as he nodded in agreement, the pain of her loss still very raw.

'You are quite right, George. She certainly was and I appreciate your kind words. But I have to tell you, Amy and I have just had an intolerably long journey due to the atrocious weather conditions and as I am sure you haven't asked us to come all this way just to tell me that, perhaps you could inform me what was so important that you requested both our presences?'

Mr Harvey was instantly apologetic. 'Of course, sir. But first let me put the Closed sign on the door and then we can speak without interruption.' He bustled away to lock the door and turn the sign, then, crossing back to them he cleared his throat noisily, wondering where to begin. Eventually he eyed them both nervously and wrung his hands together as he began, 'As you are aware, I have long been interested in the Paris designs – and I have even been able to get some of our own designs in a couple of the smaller shops there. It is common knowledge that some of the most favoured hat designs in the world originate from the larger Paris fashion houses. That is why I always ensure that I have the very latest magazines available for my clients to browse through, should they so wish. Anyway, many months ago, our late mistress visited me and put to me an idea that had long been forming in her mind.'

Mr Harvey cleared his throat and went on: 'As we are all aware, she had great faith in Amy's designs and felt that in Amy we had found our jewel in the crown, so to speak. Mrs Forrester firmly believed in following her instincts – which were that some of Amy's designs by far outshone the Paris ones. And so, some time ago, she took it upon herself to contact one of the most famous fashion houses in Paris. The House of Laroque. She personally wrote to Monsieur Laroque himself and forwarded to him a small selection of Amy's sketches, asking for his opinion of them. Some time later, Monsieur Laroque replied to Mrs Forrester expressing his interest in the designs and requesting that she send more of the same, plus some of the finished articles, at her earliest opportunity.'

Here, Mr Harvey paused to catch his breath before going on, 'At this particular time, the dear lady's health was failing and so she left the matter in my hands. I was only too delighted to follow her instructions to the letter and sent Monsieur Laroque a further selection of Amy's best-selling designs, both bonnets and gowns as he had requested. And the outcome of this latest correspondence is what I have here.'

Barely able to contain his excitement now he

quickly delved into the pocket of his exquisitely embroidered waistcoat and withdrew an envelope of the finest quality, heavily covered in foreign stamps.

By now, both Mr Forrester and Amy were watching his every move raptly and Mr Harvey beamed at his captive audience. 'I apologise if up to now my actions have appeared rather under-handed, but I always had great faith in the late Mrs Forrester when she felt something, as she always referred to it, "in her water". I believe in this instance you will both agree that her reactions have paid off. She has left to you, my dear Miss Ernshaw, a rare legacy indeed, for I have here a personal invitation from Monsieur Laroque himself, requesting that you both visit him in Paris to discuss the designs as soon as you can.'

At that moment it would have been hard to decide who was the more shocked of the two people standing in front of him. Mr Forrester's mouth gaped slackly open and his eyes bulged, whilst the colour drained from Amy's face. They both stood there in dumbfounded silence for some minutes and then slowly a large smile spread across Mr Forrester's face, while Amy's eyes filled with tears at this last act of kindness from her late mistress. Just as Mr Harvey had said; this was a rare legacy indeed, for the old woman's faith in her was about to make her wild-est dream come true. She was going to Paris, the most fashionable city in the world.

Chapter Eighteen

The last few weeks had been hectic, with Amy rushed off her feet preparing for the trip, sometimes sketching late into the night. She had spent her twenty-first birthday quietly at home with Molly. But now in less than an hour Mr Forrester's coach would be coming to collect her and she would be gone on the first stage of the long journey ahead of her.

Josephine Forrester had thoughtfully provided a large trunk, and it was this that Amy was fussing over now.

'Oh, I'm sure I will have forgotten something,' she fretted.

Molly sighed loudly. 'You've got everything in there except the kitchen sink, so for God's sake close it up and be done with it, else you'll still be here this time next week.'

Amy strapped it up obediently. She was so excited that she had hardly slept a wink the night before, but no one would have known it, for she was positively glowing. Molly looked back at her with pride. Amy was wearing a fine cord day suit, cinched in at the waist, with billowing skirts and a tight-fitted jacket trimmed with black velvet buttons and braid. The outfit showed off her trim figure to perfection. She had brushed her hair until it shone and now it was secured neatly on the back of her head in an elegant chignon. The soft brown suit matched the colour of her eyes exactly and Molly thought that she could easily have been taken for gentry, for she looked sophisticated and graceful.

So much had happened in such a short time that Molly had barely had time to take it all in, and now a mixture of emotions were rushing through her. First and foremost was excitement at the adventure that Amy was about to embark upon because to Molly, who had never set foot outside her hometown, Paris sounded like the other side of the world. But there was also a measure of apprehension. The thought of Amy sailing across the sea was terrifying and she had lain in bed night after night for weeks with pictures of sinking ships flashing in front of her eyes.

Could Molly have known it, Amy was apprehensive too at the thought of leaving her gran alone for so long, although she had done everything within her power to ensure that Molly had everything she needed. The coalhouse was full to bursting, the larder was stocked with as much food as she could cram into it and the money jar on the mantelpiece was full to overflowing. Yet still she was anxious.

'Now are you quite, quite sure that there's nothing I've forgotten to get for you, Gran?' she asked for the umpteenth time that morning.

Molly raised her eyes to the rafters that crisscrossed the low ceiling. 'Yes, love, I'm quite sure,' she said, biting back a hasty retort. They had so little time left now that she did not want them to spend their last few minutes fratching.

'Now don't forget, Mary will be bringing the

twins to see you tomorrow,' Amy told her yet again. 'And Toby's going to call in at least twice a day to fill the coal scuttle. If you should need anything at all in between, Bessie is there for you day or night.'

As she stared into Molly's eyes, which were dangerously shiny with unshed tears, she realised that she was rambling on and stopped abruptly.

'Sorry, Gran ... I think I must be a bit nervous.' Suddenly they were in each other's arms. 'Oh Gran, I'm going to miss you *so* much,' Amy choked. *'Please* promise me that you'll take good care of yourself. I don't know how I would bear it if I didn't have you.'

'Shush now,' Molly soothed as she held the girl to her. 'It should be me worrying about you, madam, gallivantin' off halfway across the world. But I know Mr and Mrs Forrester will take good care of you, and this is the chance of a lifetime. You must grasp it with both hands and make the most of it. This is what the old mistress wanted for you, God bless her soul, and if she's where I think she is, then you can bet there will be a very happy, proud angel smiling down on you today, and make no mistake.'

It was at that moment that the door opened and Bessie, with Toby close on her heels, appeared. They had come to say their goodbyes.

'Now don't you get worrying about your gran,' Bessie told Amy kindly. 'We'll keep a very close eye on her, I promise. You just go and enjoy every minute.'

'I'll try, Bessie.' Amy sniffed loudly as she now looked towards Toby. His hair was windswept and his large frame seemed to fill the doorway, but his eyes had that closed look about them and Amy's heart sank. Following Mrs Forrester's death, they had seemed to regain some of their old closeness but immediately he had heard of the proposed Paris trip the shutters had come down again and it hurt her more than she could say. The urge was on her to throw her arms about him and hug him as she had used to do, but she didn't dare. So instead she politely held out her hand and as their palms joined she noticed that his was sweating, despite the bitterly cold day.

'I hope you enjoy your visit, Amy.' As he studiously avoided her eyes, Amy felt as if she was addressing a stranger. It was then that they heard the sound of the horse's hooves in the lane outside and pandemonium broke out as Molly flew into a flap.

'Eeh, you've not even got your bonnet on yet,' she scolded and Amy laughed. Seconds later the carriage drew to a halt and whilst Molly fiddled with the ribbons on Amy's bonnet, Toby lifted the heavy trunk as if it weighed no more than a feather and carried it outside without a word.

Seconds later, Bessie and Molly ushered Amy outside to join him and watched as Mr Forrester helped her into the carriage.

'I promise I shall take very good care of her and return her to you all in one piece,' he told them all, 'and I won't let her do anything that you wouldn't let her do either.' When he winked at Molly mischievously, she found herself smiling back at him as she thought to herself, Eeh, he's all right, he is! And then almost before she knew it

267

they were gone, with Amy leaning out of the carriage window waving until they were out of sight.

'I have to say, I do like that Mr Forrester,' Molly admitted. 'He might have enough money to buy and sell us all but he ain't got no airs and graces and he obviously still remembers his own humble beginnings.'

Bessie nodded in agreement and, hoping to delay the time when she would find herself alone, Molly promptly invited both her and Toby in for a brew.

Bessie accepted the invitation instantly but Toby said, 'Thanks all the same, Molly, but I reckon I'll go for a walk. I could do with a bit of fresh air to blow the cobwebs away.' And so saying he strode away up the lane with his hands thrust deep in his pockets and his shoulders slumped.

The two women watched him go, their faces sad.

'He loves her, don't he?' sighed Molly.

'Always has,' Bessie admitted without hesitation. 'But your Amy is on the way up in the world now and well he knows it.'

Arms linked, the two women turned and entered the cottage, each lost in their own thoughts.

It had been agreed that Amy and the Forresters would spend the first night of their journey in London, as Mr Forrester had some business to attend to before they left for Paris. Adam was already there and it had been agreed that he would oversee the running of all the establishments whilst they were gone.

Amy was only too happy with the arrangement

as it meant that she would get to see Nancy. The thought of it made her spirits lift as the train sped along on its way. The last time she had seen her, just a couple of weeks before, Nancy had been radiant because Billy had asked her to become his wife. Needless to say, she had readily accepted. The only dark cloud on the horizon was that the wedding was planned for whilst Amy was in Paris. The young couple were so besotted with each other that they saw no reason to postpone it for a day longer than was necessary. Nancy was all starry-eyed and dreamy. Amy had spent a lot of time with her recently, for once Josephine Forrester had been informed of the impending trip to Paris, she had insisted that she and Amy should have a complete new wardrobe. They had spent hours together shopping for every conceivable thing that Josephine felt they might possibly need, and the trips had gone a long way towards helping to lift the veil of sadness that had cloaked them after the old mistress's death. Following one such trip, Amy had visited the grave in the little church-yard in Caldecote. The grave was unmarked as yet, as the fine marble headstone that Mr Forrester had ordered had not yet been delivered. It had been a day much like the day of the funeral, bitterly cold with the snow falling thick and fast. She had stood there for some time with her head bowed and the tears she had shed had fallen on to the grave making small pit holes in the snow.

'Thank you for the opportunity you have given me,' she had whispered, hoping that wherever the old lady was she would hear her, and then she had finally walked away as peace of a kind began to seep through her and her heart began to heal.

And now here they were, on their way at last. For most of the journey, Mr Forrester had been reading *The Times* but now as he glanced up and saw the radiant smile on Amy's face, he found her excitement infectious and he too began to smile. Sitting there in her fine velvet suit and her plumed hat with her head erect, looking so pretty and petite, she could well have been mistaken for a young lady of class. In many ways, Samuel recognised some of the traits in Amy that were apparent in himself. She had the same straightforward nature. She still respected her humble roots and he had a feeling that were she ever to drip in gold and jewels and become rich beyond her wildest dreams, nothing would change her. In the comparatively short time since he had known her she had touched many lives. Because of her interest in Amy, his wife was happier than he had seen her for years. The staff in both of his homes adored her. His son held a great respect for her, and before her death, he was well aware that his mother Maude had come to love her. He himself had become extremely fond of her and he knew that all this was down to Molly. The wizened-up old woman whom Amy idolised had brought the girl up all on her own to have respect for others, and the end result sitting in front of him now was a credit to her.

By the time they arrived at the house in London they were all in fine spirits and as usual, Nancy hurried to meet them, her face alight.

She bobbed her knee. 'Master Adam is waitin'

fer you in the study, sir, madam,' she informed Samuel cheerily as she took his hat and coat and hung them up. 'Shall I bring yer some tea in?'

'That would be lovely, Nancy, thank you. Would you care to join us, Amy?'

'No sir, thank you very much but I have to go straight back out. I want to go to the *Bridal Wear* shop.'

'Very well, my dear. We shall see you later then.' Mr Forrester inclined his head before heading towards the study.

Meantime, Nancy's face was a picture of disappointment. 'Oh, do yer really 'ave to rush back out?' she asked. 'I was 'oping to see yer for a chinwag before yer left in the mornin'.'

'And you will, I promise,' Amy assured her as she headed back towards the front door. 'But first I have some important business that I need to attend to. I shan't be gone for long, and then we can chat all night if you want to.'

Completely unaware of what Amy was up to, Nancy grinned: 'Go on then, get yer arse movin' an' be off wiv yer. I dare say the sooner yer gone the sooner you'll be back.'

Recognising one of her gran's favourite sayings, Amy chuckled as she set off for the shop in a light-hearted mood.

It was well after nine o'clock that evening before Nancy joined her in her room, and by then, Amy was almost bursting with excitement and it was not all on account of the forthcoming trip.

'How are the plans coming along for the wedding?' she asked within seconds of Nancy entering the room.

271

The girl's eyes shone with happiness. 'Oh, every-fink's fallin' into place. The church is booked an' after the weddin' we're goin' to live wiv Billy's ma fer a while, just till we can afford to rent some-where of our own. Billy's dad's bin dead fer some years past now an' his bruvvers an' sisters have all left home. Billy was the youngest of eight, so I think his mam will be glad o' the company. She's really nice, she is – the salt o' the earth, an' I reckon we're goin' to get along like an 'ouse on fire.'

She paused for breath before hurrying on, 'Cook is makin' us a weddin' cake. Real fruit, wiv icin' on top it is. It's only goin' to be a very small weddin', o' course, but that don't bovver me. Just so long as me an' my Billy are wed, that's all I care about. The only sad bit to all this is the fact that I won't be livin' here any more, so I won't get to see so much of yer in future.'

Delighted to see her friend so happy, Amy reassured her, 'Oh, I'm quite sure we'll still get to see each other. But have you decided on your wedding outfit yet?' she now asked innocently.

Nancy shrugged. 'To tell the truth, I thought I might wear that dress yer gave me. Yer know – the cotton one wiv the little flowers on it. An' I thought perhaps I could get a bonnet to wear wiv it down at the market. What do yer think?'

'I think you look absolutely lovely in that dress,' Amy told her sincerely. 'But don't you think you should perhaps have something a little grander? After all, it *is* your wedding day and every bride should look her best.'

'To tell the truth, I can't really afford a brand

new outfit,' Nancy admitted quietly, and Amy suddenly laughed out loud, unable to keep her secret for a single moment longer.

As she padded across to her wardrobe with her hair flying loose about her shoulders, Nancy looked on in bewilderment. Then, after withdrawing a large cardboard box, Amy carried it back to where her friend was sitting and placed it on the bed between them.

'What's this then?' Nancy frowned.

'Open it and find out,' Amy ordered her.

Nancy hesitated for just a fraction of a second before cautiously lifting the lid to be confronted by a thick layer of fine white tissue paper.

'Go on, go on,' Amy demanded impatiently and as Nancy drew aside the paper her frown deepened.

'I ... I don't understand.' She drew back and suddenly Amy could stand the suspense no longer.

Delving into the box she quickly withdrew an ivory satin gown and holding it up by its shoulders she displayed it to her friend.

'It's your wedding dress, Nancy,' she told her breathlessly. 'I designed it myself and the seamstresses have been working all hours to finish it for me so that I could give it to you before I left for Paris. I have to admit, I sneaked into your room and measured your clothes to be sure I got the size just right. This is what I shot off to collect earlier on. You *do* like it, don't you?'

Nancy was speechless and sat there openmouthed as the smile slowly slid from Amy's face.

'You *don't* like it, do you?' she muttered miserably. 'It's my fault; I should have asked you what sort of styles you liked.'

To her horror, Nancy began to sob uncontrollably.

In the blink of an eye, Amy had laid the dress over the end of the bed and snatched the girl into her arms.

'I'm so sorry, Nancy,' she muttered, deeply distressed. 'I didn't mean to offend you, really I didn't.'

'Offend me, yer silly bugger!' Nancy exclaimed as she pushed her roughly away. 'Why, I can't believe me bloody eyes. I've never seen a dress like it an' I can't believe that yer've done this fer me.'

Relief flooded across Amy's face as she visibly relaxed. 'So, you *do* like it then?'

'Like it? *Like it?* Why, it's the most beautiful dress I've ever seen in the whole o' me life. It would suit a bloody toff, that would. Not a guttersnipe like me.'

'Rubbish!' Amy retorted. 'Now come along, I want to make sure that it fits. Let's try it on, eh?'

Needing no second bidding, Nancy threw aside her shawl and dragged her cotton nightgown over her head. Amy helped her get into the garment and once she had fastened the row of tiny pearl buttons that ran from the neckline to the waist she adjusted the skirts and drew Nancy towards the full-length cheval mirror.

Nancy gazed astounded at her reflection. The gown fitted tight into the waist then ballooned out into a billowing skirt with a short, pearl-encrusted train trailing behind. The same heavy beading was all around the neckline and carried on to the leg of mutton sleeves.

'Why, it fits like a glove!' Amy exclaimed joyfully. 'Now you'd better see the bonnet that I had made especially to go with it.' Rushing again to the wardrobe, she withdrew another smaller box and carefully lifted out a bonnet in the same material as the dress.

She then placed it gently on Nancy's head and tied the ribbons beneath her chin. It was a beautiful bonnet with pearls to match the ones on the gown sewn all around the brim. A short veil had been cleverly attached to its crown and now it floated around Nancy's shoulders like filmy butterflies' wings.

'There,' Amy said approvingly. 'Your Billy will fall in love with you all over again when he sees you looking like this. I just know that you're going to have a wonderful wedding!'

Tears suddenly slid again from Nancy's eyes and her face became sad.

'Oh Amy, I wish yer were goin' to be there,' she sobbed.

Taking her hands, Amy smiled. 'But I *will* be there, every single second in my mind. You'll think of me when you wear this and when I come back you'll be able to tell me all about it. And all day I shall imagine you looking just as beautiful as you do now. So stop crying now, otherwise you'll set me off too and you'll get tear-stains all down your dress.'

Nancy giggled then hiccuped and within seconds they were both giggling.

The tears started again the next morning when Amy and Nancy said goodbye on the steps.

'You just be careful now,' Nancy warned. 'I've

'eard tell what some o' them Frenchies can be like. Remember Old Boney and what he got up to, eh?'

'I'll be fine,' Amy told her as she hugged her. 'You just worry about your wedding. Just think, by the time I see you again you'll be an old married woman.'

''Ere, less of the old,' Nancy grinned, and then the Forresters emerged from the house and Mr Forrester was ushering Amy towards the carriage.

Amy waved from the window as Nancy waved back, and then they were off. The adventure was about to really begin now, and Amy could hardly believe it.

Chapter Nineteen

When the carriage had dropped them off at the station, they then caught a train to Dover, and the Forresters watched Amy with amusement. She was so excited that she could scarcely sit still. Amy's first sight of the docks was nothing at all as she had expected it to be. The smell of rotting fish hung heavy on the air and rats scurried fearlessly here and there. Women whom Molly would have termed as 'blowsy' stood here and there in low-cut dresses, trying to get the attention of any matelot who happened to pass them by.

Averting her eyes from them, Amy turned her attention to the ships that were docked, and again her eyes stretched in amazement. They were so much bigger than she had pictured them, and a ripple of apprehension passed through her. How could anything so bulky and heavy ever stay afloat?

Burly seamen with ruddy faces were dragging huge trunks up the gangplank, and as one of them caught Amy looking at him he winked at her cheekily, causing her to blush with embarrassment. Overhead, seagulls dipped and dived as they searched the quay for morsels of food.

It was already late afternoon and Mr Forrester had booked them all a night passage for the twelve-hour crossing to Calais. Taking her elbow he led her towards one of the ships that towered over them and she saw the name of it – the *Dolphin* – painted crudely on its side. Amy glanced down at the water slapping against the quay. In the books she had looked at with Toby, the sea had always been a beautiful clear blue, but here it was a murky brown colour with litter floating upon it.

Mr Forrester assisted his wife and Amy up the gangplank as Amy studiously avoided looking at the sailors who were scurrying around, and once aboard she was shown down numerous flights of metal steps to her cabin. It was very small, boasting little more than a narrow bed, a washstand and a small porthole. Even so she was relieved to find that it was clean and comfortable. Mr and Mrs Forrester had accompanied her to make sure that she had everything she needed, but now they excused themselves and went off in search of their own cabin to have a rest.

Amy gave the cabin boy who had carried her trunk for her a generous tip, and once she was alone she crossed to the porthole and peered out.

There was very little to see except the grimy side of the dock, and eager to explore now she hastily turned about and, lifting her skirts, made her way back through the bowels of the ship and climbed back up the many metal stairs, the heels on her small leather buttoned boots making a clanging noise as she went. Once she reached the deck she made straight for the rail, drawing many admiring glances from sailors and passengers alike, but she was so excited that she didn't even notice them as she moved through the people who were milling about.

Eventually the heavy gangplank was pulled aboard and she watched as the sailors winched a great anchor from the seabed. Then, with a sickening jolt, the ship shuddered and began to pull away from the port. Slowly the white cliffs dropped away into the distance and the lights on the quay became mere specks that resembled flickering fireflies along the shoreline. The enormous craft began to rise and fall with the swell of the waves, and that was when Amy first began to feel unwell. The further the ship got out to sea the more it swayed, and by the time there was nothing but ocean to see, Amy felt as if her legs no longer belonged to her. The contents of her last meal seemed to be rising and falling in time with the ship and she was still clutching the rails as if her very life depended upon it when Mr Forrester found her there some time later.

Instantly concerned when he saw her pale face he asked, 'Are you feeling unwell, my dear?'

Amy had no need to answer him; her face told its own story. She looked almost green in the

278

fading light and suddenly unable to hold it back a second longer, she leaned across the rail and began to vomit in a most unladylike manner.

'Oh, dear me,' Mr Forrester fussed as she clung limply to the rails. As soon as he was able he escorted her back to her cabin personally then hurried away to fetch the ship's doctor, who told him in no uncertain terms that there was nothing to be done.

'The young lady is suffering from a severe bout of sea-sickness,' he informed him flatly then turning on his heel he left the cabin.

Samuel and Josephine eventually left her in the care of one of the cabin crew with a large bowl at hand, and by the time the ship arrived in Calais early the next morning, Amy was convinced that she was dying.

Mr Forrester helped her from the ship on unsteady legs, and as soon as they were ashore, Amy thanked God that she was back on solid ground. Josephine too had been very queasy.

'Perhaps we should delay the next stage of our journey until you are both feeling better?' Samuel suggested thoughtfully. 'We could always book into an hotel and continue tomorrow.'

After the ship the long coach ride to Paris that lay ahead of them seemed as nothing, and both women were determined to go on. Mr Forrester was silently impressed with their courage, especially Amy's. As he had discovered, Amy might not be very big in stature but what she lacked in size she more than made up for with spirit. And so they boarded the coach and continued with their journey.

After three hours the coach stopped at a quaint coaching inn for refreshments. Amy refused food – her stomach rebelled at the very thought of it – but she did drink two glasses of lemonade made with freshly squeezed lemons, and by the time they resumed the journey she was beginning to feel slightly better. As they passed the French fields and villages, Amy stared from the carriage window with interest. Dotted here and there were enormous fields in which French peasants were busy toiling. They waved gaily in greeting as the carriage rumbled past on the uneven roads, and beginning to enjoy herself again, Amy waved back.

Set up in the hills were the châteaux of the wealthy. With their turrets and towers and the sunshine reflecting off their windows, they reminded Amy a little of Forrester's Folly and she pointed them out to Mr Forrester, who smiled indulgently.

It was pleasant rolling along with the spring sunshine pouring in on them. Amy had not slept a wink the night before on the ship and now the warmth of the sun and the gentle rolling of the carriage lulled her off to sleep.

The next thing she knew, Mr Forrester was shaking her arm and as she started awake she realised with a little shock that they had stopped.

'Come along, Sleepyhead. We're here,' he told her.

Amy gaped as she straightened her bonnet. 'What ... you mean we're in Paris?'

'We most certainly are. This is our hotel.'

'But why didn't you wake me?' she asked sleepily.

'Judging from the snores that were bouncing around the coach I think I might have had quite a job trying that. And anyway, you were worn out and we thought the rest would do you good.'

Peering from the window, Amy saw that they had drawn up outside a palatial building called the Hôtel Meurice. Beneath the colonnades was a doorman in scarlet and gold livery, his highly polished brass buttons reflecting the lights in the Tuileries Gardens.

As Mr Forrester climbed from the carriage, the man came to unload the luggage.

He said something in French and Amy noticed that when Mr Forrester answered him in the same language he sounded almost as French as he did. He then handed him a coin and bowing deeply, the doorman thanked him, *'Merci, monsieur.'*

Within minutes Amy had been shown to a luxurious suite of rooms that was to be hers for the duration of their visit. The young maid who escorted her there could speak nothing but French, and as Amy could only speak her own native tongue, conversation between the two of them consisted mainly of sign language and smiles.

When her luggage had been delivered and she was alone at last, Amy yawned and stretched, too tired for now to even explore her rooms. After taking off her suit she crawled into an enormous mahogany bed in her undergarments and there she slept soundly until the following morning.

Once she was up and dressed, yet another young maid showed her down to breakfast, and she found Mr Forrester waiting for her in the dining room... He was seated at a table in the window but the minute he saw her he stood up and drew out a chair for her. 'Well, if you don't mind me saying, you're certainly looking better this morning, my dear,' he told her. 'I trust you slept well?'

'Like a log,' Amy grinned as she joined him.

She was feeling so much better, in fact, that she tucked into a hearty breakfast that would have satisfied someone double her size. There were hot croissants and baguettes served with butter and various jams, and a huge steaming pot of coffee. Amy enjoyed every bit of it.

Between mouthfuls, Mr Forrester told her of the plans for the day and she listened intently.

'Monsieur Laroque will be sending a carriage for us at ten o'clock and we will be meeting him at one of his largest fashion houses. I must say I'm looking forward to it tremendously. It might give us some ideas for the shops back in London. My wife will be resting but we will see her later on.'

Amy nodded and at ten o'clock sharp she was waiting in the foyer, looking as smart as a new pin, with Mr Forrester.

Monsieur Laroque's stylish carriage arrived promptly on time and as it rattled down the rue de Rivoli, round the Place de la Concorde and up the Champs Elysées towards the Arc de Triomphe, Amy gazed in awe from the window. Dotted here and there were colourful little cafés and bistros with tables and chairs standing outside on the pavements. Even at such an early hour of the morning, Amy was fascinated to see that people were already seated at them, sipping at glasses of wine.

'Isn't it a little early in the day to be drinking

wine?' she asked.

'Oh, you'll find that the French drink wine like we English drink tea,' Mr Forrester chuckled, and Amy wondered what her gran would have made of it all.

Ladies and gentlemen, all dressed in smart attire, were streaming up and down the busy pavements, and horses and carriages filled the streets.

They eventually drew to a halt before what appeared to be a very grand shop in a busy part of the city. Above the door was a large sign with LAROQUE emblazoned on it in large gold letters, and on either side of the door were two enormous windows displaying gowns of all shades and colours. Amy was suitably impressed and suddenly more than a little nervous.

After climbing down from the coach, Mr Forrester took her elbow reassuringly and together they entered the shop. They found themselves in a small but luxuriously decorated foyer. Two women in identical day dresses were standing on either side of the door and the elder of the two immediately approached them.

'Monsieur Forrester?' she enquired in a heavy French accent.

He took off his hat and inclined his head politely. *'Oui, madame.'*

She beckoned them to follow her through a door concealed by a heavy velvet drape and into a small hallway. In comparison to the room they had just left the hallway was stark but spotlessly clean, and smiling at them pleasantly, their guide then took them up a metal staircase. They soon found themselves on a long landing. Rooms led off either side of it: Amy peeped in as they passed and could see large windows, and women busily sewing. There seemed to be dressmaker's dummies with gowns all at various stages of completion on them everywhere she looked. Amy would have loved to pause and study them, but instead she continued to follow the woman until she came to the end of the landing, where she paused to knock at a door. She then held it open for them so that they could pass her, and once they were inside she inclined her head politely and withdrew.

They found themselves in what appeared to be a large office, and almost immediately a man rose from behind a vast desk. He was nearly as tall as Mr Forrester and he smiled at them welcomingly. He was immaculately dressed in a smart black tail-suit, and beneath the suit he was wearing a bright satin waistcoat with a heavy gold chain attached to a fob watch that was tucked into a pocket. Beneath that was a stiffly starched white shirt and an elegant blue silk cravat. His greying hair was heavily greased and lay fiat to his head, and he had bushy sideburns and a little waxed moustache. Amy felt somewhat intimidated by him, but when he approached Mr Forrester with his hand outstretched, he was smiling.

'Monsieur Forrester,' he beamed as the two men shook hands warmly. 'You are most welcome.'

Amy was relieved to hear that although he too had a heavy French accent, he spoke in English.

'And you must be Mademoiselle Ernshaw,' he said, turning his attention to Amy.

Amy nodded and to her embarrassment he clicked his heels together and bowing from the waist he then took her hand and kissed it, his eyes openly admiring. *'Enchanté*. I am ... how do you say? Most charmed to meet you.'

Amy stifled the urge to giggle as he ushered them to the far side of the room where he opened a large cabinet that contained numerous bottles of wine and a number of elegant cut-glass wine goblets.

'Voudriez-vous quelque chose à boire?' he asked, and then remembering who his visitors were, he quickly repeated in English, 'You would like a drink?'

Amy shook her head, feeling totally out of her depth, and once Monsieur Laroque had poured a generous measure of red wine for himself and Mr Forrester, he then ushered them to a sofa.

'I am most delighted that you have come,' he told them sincerely. 'I am intrigued with the designs that I have seen so far. They are very impressive. But do forgive me ... I am forgetting my manners. Before we go on to that I must enquire, is the hotel that I booked for you to your satisfaction?'

Amy and Mr Forrester nodded in unison.

'Yes, thank you, Monsieur Laroque,' Mr Forrester assured him as he placed his glass on a small table. 'Indeed it is. In fact, it is very comfortable indeed.'

The Frenchman nodded with satisfaction. 'Good, good. I always book Le Meurice for business colleagues who are visiting my establishments. I have never as yet been disappointed with the service they receive, but please, if there is anything that you require, do not hesitate to ask.

I wish your stay to be as enjoyable as possible and, I hope, mutually beneficial.' There was a twinkle in his eye as he smiled at Amy and she felt herself begin to relax a little.

'Anyway, let us now get to the purpose of your visit, Mademoiselle Ernshaw. As I have already expressed, I have been most impressed with the designs for hats and clothing that I have already seen. You have, I hope, brought me some more to look at?'

Amy nodded and immediately withdrew a pile of sketches from the large leather bag at her side. Monsieur Laroque took them to his desk and began to study them and before they knew it two hours had passed as they sat discussing the different styles and fashions.

When Monsieur Laroque finally raised his head from the sketches he was smiling broadly. 'I think, Monsieur Forrester, you have in Mademoiselle Ernshaw what you English call a star?'

Amy blushed furiously as Samuel smiled in agreement.

'But now, enough!' the Frenchman declared. '*Assez!* It is time to eat and then after lunch you shall see one of my salons. Come!'

Obediently they followed him from the room, back along the landing and down the metal stairs, and in no time at all they were sitting outside one of the colourful little cafés that lined the grand avenue. They ate freshly baked rolls, split down the middle and filled with a delicious variety of cheeses, and then they had tiny little choux pastries all covered in mouthwatering fruits and topped with freshly whipped cream. Amy had not

286

felt hungry at all after eating such a large breakfast, but she tucked into every mouthful, wondering if it tasted so much better because they
were outside in the open air. The meal was washed
down with a large carafe of white wine for the men
and delicate cups of hot chocolate for her, and
when it was finally over, Monsieur Laroque sat
back in his chair and patted his protruding belly
contentedly.

'Ah, that was good, no?'

Enjoying herself immensely, Amy caught his
eye and grinned, sure that she would never want
to eat again.

After Monsieur Laroque had paid the bill he
led them back through the crowded streets of
Paris to his fashion house, chatting to them amic-
ably as he went.

'As I promised earlier, this afternoon you shall
see one of my salons,' he stated. 'I think you will
find it most interesting, *n'est-ce pas?* Here we do
not have the same sales techniques as you have in
England, but we shall see, eh?'

When they got back to the salon, he spoke for
some moments to one of the women, then turned
back to his guests.

'My assistant informs me that there is presently
a customer in the salon, so you shall please come
with me and see how we sell gowns in Paris.'

Leading them to a second, velvet-draped
doorway, he stood politely aside and ushered
them into what he referred to as 'the salon'.

Amy stared around in awe. A raised platform
ran along one wall, and in front of it were dotted
elegant little settees with dainty gilded legs.

287

On one of them was seated an immaculately dressed elderly lady, with a large plumed hat on her head, and a much younger, but equally beautifully dressed woman at her side.

The older woman raised her eyes imperiously at their entrance, but then as the heavy curtains at the end of the platform parted she turned her attention back to the show. A very attractive young woman appeared, dressed in a stunning sapphire-blue ballgown, and walked slowly up and down the platform with her hand on her hip, twirling this way and that so that the gown was shown to its best advantage. The moment she disappeared, another equally confident young woman swept through the curtains in a totally different style of gown.

'In Paris, this is how we display our gowns to our customers,' whispered Monsieur Laroque. 'Two models parade in the gowns until the customer sees one that they like. Only then do they order a copy and give their measurements.'

Amy sat entranced as the two models, with smiles seemingly painted on their faces, came and went.

'You approve of our designs, yes?' Monsieur Laroque enquired. He leaned forward and went on in a hushed voice, 'My salons are frequented by the very elite of Paris society, so they expect to be how do you say ... pampered?'

The rest of the afternoon passed pleasantly as Monsieur Laroque gave them a tour of his fashion house. He took them upstairs to meet the seamstresses and some of his designers who worked in a separate room.

That evening, as Amy and the Forresters enjoyed a leisurely dinner together in the hotel dining room, she could talk of little else. She and Josephine retired, tired but content, leaving Mr Forrester to partake of a nightcap with some other gentlemen in the bar.

After hastily washing, Amy pulled on her nightgown and took the pins from her hair. She then brushed it until it shone before leaping into the huge comfortable bed where she snuggled down and slept like a baby.

The following day passed much as the first. Monsieur Laroque took them to visit another, if possible even grander one of his salons, situated on the other side of the River Seine – known as the Left Bank – near the Palais du Luxembourg. While they were there, he left some of Amy's designs with his head designer to peruse.

During the afternoon, as they rattled back to the hotel over the Pont Neuf, heading once more for the rue de Rivoli, he enquired politely, 'Please to tell me. Have you made any arrangements for this evening?'

Still struggling to understand his deep accent, Amy was relieved when Mr Forrester answered for them. 'No, *monsieur*, I think we were intending to stay in at the hotel.'

'Ah, good, good. Then may I ask if you would care to join my family and myself for dinner at our home – the Château de Chêne. *Le chêne* is an oak tree – I believe you British have the hearts of oak, *n'est-ce pas?*' He beamed at them. 'My wife, Edwige, and my son and daughter, François and

289

Adeline, are most eager to meet you.'

Amy's eyes danced with excitement at the prospect as she glanced towards Mr Forrester to see what his reply would be.

'That is most kind of you, monsieur. My wife and Miss Ernshaw and I would be delighted to accept your invitation.'

'Then that is settled,' said their host. 'My carriage shall call for you at seven o'clock. I trust that will give you both time to prepare?'

Amy hugged herself in anticipation. Oh, what a lot she was going to have to tell Molly and Toby when she got home. They were never going to believe her, not in a million years.

Chapter Twenty

With her hands on her hips and her head to one side, Amy stood eyeing the three evening dresses that she had hung on the wardrobe doors, wondering which one she should wear. Although the family was still officially in mourning, they were away from home and knew that Maude would have scoffed at the convention of dressing all in black.

As well as the green satin gown that she had worn to the theatre in London, Amy now possessed a further two. Mrs Forrester had insisted that she should have them, convinced that she would need at least three during her stay in Paris. So now she was spoiled for choice. The first of her newest gowns was a rich cornflower-blue colour. The second was a warm deep burgundy with a full skirt in a stiff taffeta, trimmed all around the neckline and the hem with fine silk ribbon.

If she wore the green she knew that she could wear the beautiful emerald and diamond necklace that the elderly mistress had bequeathed to her, but she dismissed that idea almost immediately, wishing to save it for a very special occasion. Eventually she decided on the taffeta. It was elegant in its simplicity, and once she was dressed and had pinned up her hair in a simple style, she eyed her image in the mirror with satisfaction, pleased with her choice. Even if she had not been, she was fully aware that it was too late to change her mind now, and so snatching up her shawl she tripped down the stairs to join the Forresters in the foyer. Josephine was standing at the bottom looking pretty in grey silk and pearls, and Samuel was looking extremely handsome in a dark dinner suit and a colourful cravat. He eyed Amy admiringly as she approached them.

'Why, you look lovely, my dear,' he complimented her, and Amy blushed happily. She was looking forward to the evening tremendously and could hardly wait for Monsieur Laroque's carriage to arrive and take them to the château which lay, she had been told, beyond the north-west corner of Paris, in an idyllic small town called Neuilly-sur-Seine. Once it came, they swayed along the boulevards and through winding streets until eventually they began to leave the city behind. Some time later they drove through decorative wrought-iron gates and turned into the drive that led to Monsieur Laroque's château. As they approached it, Amy was shocked to see that it was even larger than Forrester's Folly. When the horses drew to a halt and the coachman assisted them down from the carriage, she stood open-mouthed at the sight before her. The sprawling château, lit by flaming torches set high on the portico, nestled into a deep oak wood, the stars twinkling in the night sky far above.

They were greeted at the door by a manservant, and found themselves in a magnificent vestibule. On either side of it an elegant staircase twisted up-wards to a fine galleried landing, all lit by candles.

It was all too much. Amy's excitement vanished and she gulped nervously, feeling like a fish out of water. It was at that moment that Monsieur Laroque appeared from one of the many door-ways leading off from the hall. He hurried for-ward and greeted them in his usual way, with a firm handshake for Mr Forrester and a kiss on the hand for Josephine and Amy. Smiling broadly he then invited them to follow him and they entered an elaborately decorated drawing room. Two women immediately rose to greet them and Monsieur Laroque proudly drew the older of the two forward.

'Monsieur Forrester, Mademoiselle Ernshaw, please to meet my wife, Edwige.'

Mr Forrester bowed politely as Amy bobbed her knee respectfully. Although Edwige Laroque was well past the first flush of youth she was still an extremely attractive woman. She was taller than Amy and slender with thick brunette hair that was piled high on her head, and the way she

292

held herself suggested that she was from the upper class. But her dark eyes shone kindly as she flashed them a brilliant smile displaying a set of straight white teeth.

'And this is my daughter, Adeline,' Monsieur Laroque now told them as he introduced his daughter who had come to stand beside her mother. Amy found herself looking at a young woman who appeared to be about the same age as her. But there any similarity between them ended, for in looks they were as different as chalk from cheese. Adeline Laroque towered over Amy, and her hair was as black as a raven's wing; she had just missed being beautiful, for her nose was a little too straight and her chin a little too prominent. Even so, her dark eyes, which were her best feature, sparkled with fun and as they smiled at each other, Amy instantly took a liking to her.

'My son François has been delayed in Paris on business today, but I am expecting him to join us for dinner at any moment,' Monsieur Laroque told them. 'So we shall have a glass of wine whilst we wait for him – *oui?*'

They were soon all seated and the next half an hour passed pleasantly as they chatted about all manner of topics.

The manservant who had admitted them eventually appeared at the door and muttered something to his master. Monsieur Laroque smiled apologetically.

'Pierre informs me that dinner is about to be served. We can delay no longer, or the meal will be ruined. I am sure that François will join us as soon as he can, so come, let us eat.' He took his wife and daughter, one on each arm, and sailed towards the door.

'Please to follow me,' he told his guests solemnly, and Mr Forrester copied his host and put his wife on one arm and Amy on the other.

Amy had to bite on her lip to stop herself laughing at the ceremony of it all as a picture of herself and her gran sitting at the kitchen table in the cottage eating a bowl of rabbit stew flashed into her mind. Everything was so grand here and she felt like pinching herself to check that this was really happening.

They had just entered the hallway when the enormous front doors burst open and a man whom Amy judged to be in his late twenties, almost tripped into the house. As she watched a servant take his outer garments and hand him a bowl in which to rinse his hands, time seemed to stand still and Amy's mind was clear of anything but his face as she felt hot colour flood into her cheeks.

Monsieur Laroque turned to them.

'Monsieur et Madame Forrester, Mademoiselle Ernshaw, I am proud to introduce you to my son, François. He apologises for being delayed in Paris but he has made a great effort to join us.'

François formally shook hands with them, but then as he turned to Amy and smiled down at her, their eyes locked.

He was without question the most handsome man she had ever set eyes on and her heart began to race.

He bent and kissed her hand, squeezing it gently before releasing it.

'Please allow me to escort you to dinner, *made-*

294

moiselle,' he whispered, and taking her arm he tucked it firmly into his, leaving Amy with no other choice but to follow him.

The little procession then made its way into a beautiful dining room. The long table that stood in the centre of the room was laid with the finest silver and china, and in the centre of it stood a huge candelabra, its many candles casting dancing lights upon the tiny cut-glass vases full of flowers that were dotted here and there along its length. For now it was all lost on Amy and she had to concentrate very hard to stop herself from staring at François. Could she have known it, she was having the same effect upon him, and as he pushed the exquisitely served food about his plate he found that his appetite had completely vanished.

Maids in frilled snow-white aprons served the first course, which Amy eyed suspiciously. Seeing the look on her face, Monsieur Laroque said, 'You must try this, *chère mademoiselle*. You cannot come to Paris without trying our two most famous delicacies. There, on that dish, are *les cuisses de grenouilles*, dipped in flour and fried in olive oil and crushed garlic. On the other dish are *les escargots à la Bourguignonne*, again lightly fried, but this time with parsley, garlic, butter and spices. Mmm.' He kissed his fingers to add emphasis to his statement. 'You have not lived until you have tried them,' he assured her.

Amy was still not convinced and asked quietly, 'What are these dishes in English?'

A titter rippled around the table as her host smiled at her mischievously.

'In your language, my dear, they are frogs' legs

and snails.'

Amy quickly waved them away. 'Thank you all the same but I think I will miss this course,' she told the maid hurriedly, and everyone roared with laughter at the look of horror on her face.

There followed several courses, each more to Amy's taste than the first. The next was *brandade canapés*, which Amy soon discovered was salt cod and potatoes puréed and served with crème fraiche and garnished with caviar. The main meal was *poulet à la crème*, chicken which had been infused with thyme and wine, served with caramelised mushrooms, onions and shallots. For dessert there was a delicious and refreshing raspberry *eau de vie* sorbet that melted in the mouth but Amy, who was used to much simpler food, found it all a little rich and could scarcely swallow a morsel. She was afraid that her hosts would think her ungrateful, so it was a relief when the meal was finally over and Monsieur Laroque rose from the table to lead them all back to the sitting room.

They were offered coffee and yet more wine by a young French maid and once they had all been served they sat informally *en famille* as the two men discussed the political situation as well as the latest fashions with their wives. After a time Adeline rose, her long black hair gleaming in the moonlight that was spilling through the open French doors.

She said something in French to her parents before turning to their guests. 'You will please be forgiving me,' she said in clipped English. 'But I had already made arrangements that could not be broken for the rest of this evening, and I must be leaving you. But I hope to be seeing you again very soon, yes?'

They smiled up at her so after saying their goodbyes she flashed them one last friendly smile and gathering up her skirts, she left the room.

Seizing his chance, François immediately turned to Amy and smiled charmingly, asking, 'Would you care to take a walk around the grounds with me, Mademoiselle Ernshaw? The paths are well-lit and I think you would enjoy some fresh air.'

Amy looked at Josephine, who nodded. Madame Laroque told her, 'Be sure to take your wrap, my dear. Although it is spring time the nights can still be chilly and I would not wish you to be catching the cold.'

Flustered, Amy joined François at the open doors. He draped her shawl about her shoulders and after then gallantly offering her his arm, they strolled from the house into the velvety blackness of the night.

He led her first towards the woods at the rear of the house and then, skirting the trees that stood motionless as if watching their progress, they gently strolled along. The moon was sailing high and the inky sky was scattered with stars that seemed to be winking down at them. Amy was ridiculously aware of the strong muscled arm beneath her small hand and grateful for the darkness that would disguise her blushes.

Eventually they came to a small plateau that jutted out from the hillside, and there they paused as she stared down at the city of Paris spread out far below them. Running through the centre of it, the River Seine caught and reflected the moonlight and Amy gasped in wonder at the wonderful sight. She felt as if she was floating on air and her eyes were as bright as the stars above them.

François silently surveyed the young woman at his side. She was so incredibly beautiful that she made his pulses race, and it was all he could do to stop himself from snatching her into his arms there and then.

'Will you be staying in Paris for long, *mademoiselle?*' he asked instead.

'For four weeks,' Amy informed him and he sighed with satisfaction.

'That is good then. With your permission, I shall ask your Monsieur Forrester if he will permit me to show you the sights of Paris. There is much to be seen in the city and it would be sad if you were to return home without visiting them.'

Amy smiled shyly up into his handsome face. 'I'd like that very much indeed. Thank you.'

Gently squeezing the hand that was tucked into his arm he returned her smile and they continued their stroll, each content in the other's company.

By the time they rejoined their elders in the sitting room some time later, they were both starry-eyed and breathless, and Madame Laroque watched them with her lovely dark eyes alight with mischief.

François seemed relaxed and totally at ease in this charming young woman's company, and for the rest of the evening his mother observed them tactfully, her woman's instincts sensing an impending romance.

The following two weeks passed in a pleasurable

blur for Amy. During the day she visited Monsieur Laroque's salons, where with the help of an interpreter she talked to his designers, and gradually she gained enough confidence to put suggestions to Monsieur Laroque himself.

But the nights ... oh, the *wonderful* nights. Amy was quite sure that she would never forget a single second of them for as long as she lived.

François would arrive at the Hotel Le Meurice, looking handsome and dashing, before whisking her away like a knight on a white charger accompanied by Adeline's lady's maid who would act as their chaperone at Madame Laroque's insistence. It would not have been correct for a young woman to be escorted by a gentleman without a chaperone. However, Anaïs Babineux always stayed discreetly in the background and for most of the time Amy and François could almost forget she was there. He escorted her to the theatre, took her on a trip in a private boat along the River Seine, and gradually taught her to enjoy French cuisine. They fed the pigeons that were as common in Paris as the sparrows were back in her hometown, and in the middle of the third week, she and the Forresters were again invited to dine at the château.

It turned out to be another enjoyable evening and this time, Adeline stayed in and chatted to Amy.

As they were being driven home in Monsieur Laroque's fine carriage, Mr Forrester observed Amy's shining eyes and smiled.

'Are you enjoying your stay in Paris, my dear?' he asked kindly.

'Oh *yes*, sir,' Amy said without hesitation. 'I

wouldn't have missed a single minute of it. I have so much to tell my gran when we get home that I shall scarcely know where to begin.'

He nodded, then on a slightly more serious note he continued, 'You seem to be getting on extremely well with François.' Josephine sat looking at Amy, waiting for her to reply as they bowled along.

Amy looked through the carriage window, unable to meet his eyes. 'I do find him very good company,' she admitted. 'But I assure you he has always acted as a perfect gentleman and–'

Mr Forrester held up his hand to stop her flow of words. 'You misunderstand me, Amy. I never meant to insinuate for a single moment that he would ever be anything less. Had I believed that, I would never have allowed him to be your escort. But you do realise, don't you, that we will soon be returning home ... and I would hate to see you get hurt.'

Her face dropped and she stared out of the carriage window miserably, all the joy suddenly gone from the evening.

The following day, as she sat at Monsieur Laroque's desk with him in one of his salons, he suddenly sat back and steepling his fingers, he stared at her across the top of them. They had spent the last hour discussing aspects of her designs, and the more he saw of her ideas, the more impressed he was with the young Englishwoman sitting beside him.

'I think, *mademoiselle*, that should you so wish it, you could go far in the fashion empire.'

Delighted with his compliment she flushed with pleasure.

'Should you ever think of moving to Paris I would take you on as one of my personal designers in the blink of an eye.' He was testing the ground but her answer when it came disappointed him.

'I could never leave England, *monsieur*,' she told him soberly. 'Mr Forrester and his wife have been extremely kind to me and Mr Forrester is a good master. But I also have an elderly grandmother who I live with, and I could never leave her, ever.'

'I see.' Monsieur Laroque tapped his chin thoughtfully. 'Your loyalty to your master and your grandmother do you justice. But if that is your final decision and I cannot tempt you away from them all, then I am sure that Mr Forrester and I can come to some suitable arrangement about your designs that will be beneficial to us all.'

That evening, when François arrived at the hotel to collect her, he found Amy in a sombre mood and instantly decided that he must try and shake her out of it.

'Come, *ma petite*,' he urged. 'Tell me what you would like to do this evening. I am yours to command.'

Amy sighed. 'To be honest, François, I am feeling a little tired tonight.' She blushed as she looked towards Anaïs Babineux, who was standing a discreet distance away. 'I am so sorry that you have had a wasted journey but I think I should retire and have an early night.'

He looked crestfallen and she felt a little stab of guilt.

'I really am sorry, François. Perhaps we could go out tomorrow evening? That is, if you have no other plans.'

'Of course, of course,' he assured her all too quickly. 'I shall be here at the same time tomorrow then.' Lifting her hand he kissed it tenderly. 'Until tomorrow.' He then turned and walked away with his shoulders slumped, and Anaïs followed him as Amy miserably made her way to her room.

Once there, she sat quietly staring from the window over the rue de Rivoli as Paris by night slowly came to life. So much had happened in such a short time that she was glad of some time alone so that she could think. It seemed that she rarely had time for thinking any more as she seemed to be constantly rushing from one place to another.

Since Mr Harvey had told them of Monsieur Laroque's invitation back in London, her life had changed almost beyond belief. But then as she sat there it came to her that it had actually changed long before that – almost from the day Mr Forrester had promoted her to the status of designer. The life she lived now was a far cry indeed from the life she had lived with her gran and Toby before then, for who would ever have thought that she, little Amy Ernshaw, would ever be sitting here in a grand hotel room, dressed in clothes fit for a princess in the heart of Paris?

And then, of course, there was François. Just the thought of him made her heart beat faster, and again, Mr Forrester's warning sounded in her ears. *I would hate to see you get hurt.*

What had he meant by that statement? Even as

302

she asked herself the question the answer came to her loud and clear: she was falling in love with Francois, for no other man had ever made her feel as he did.

But then, her mind reasoned, what *is* love? If it was enjoying every second of a man's company and missing him every second they were apart; if it was the strange tingling sensation that she got every time he was near and the longing she felt to kiss him, then yes, this was love.

Had Mr Forrester recognised how she felt even before she had, and tried to warn her gently that this love could only ever cause pain?

It was her kindly master's words that had brought her back down to earth with a bump, and now as she analysed her feelings, she knew, just as Mr Forrester had known, that nothing could ever come of them.

Mr Forrester treated her as an equal, but even so he was still her master, albeit a generous one, and he always would be.

François Laroque was the heir to one of the wealthiest men in Paris, whilst she was the granddaughter of a lowly cottage-dwelling ribbon weaver. Amy knew that she owed everything to her gran. The woman had taught her values and to hold her head high and be proud of who she was. But even so, Amy now saw that she and François were socially poles apart.

The knowledge caused hot stinging tears to blind her. She had been a fool, allowing herself to be swept along on a tide of emotion and to have dreams far above her station. And now she must pay the price.

When François arrived at the hotel the next evening he found Amy waiting for him in the ground foyer and instantly noticed that she looked a little pale.

'Are you unwell, *ma petite?*' Concern was sharp in his voice as he took Amy's hands in his own.

She smiled. 'No, Francois, I am still just a little tired.'

'Then what would you like to do this evening? I thought perhaps we could go to the theatre, or perhaps you would prefer to have dinner in a restaurant?'

Amy shook her head. 'I thought it might be nice if we could just walk a little,' she told him quietly.

He nodded. 'Of course, if that is what you wish then it shall be so. And I think I know exactly where I shall take you. My uncle has a vineyard on the Ile de France. My carriage shall take us there and then we may walk to your heart's content, *nest-ce pas?*'

Despite herself, Amy smiled. The idea of seeing the vineyard was appealing so she allowed him to escort her out to his carriage, where Anaïs was waiting for them.

They rattled away through the busy city streets towards Notre Dame, and Amy felt herself beginning to relax. After all, what harm could there be in simply enjoying his company? she asked herself. Just as she had told Mr Forrester, François had never behaved as anything less than the perfect gentleman. He obviously thought of her as nothing more than a friend and as he could have no idea of her feelings for him, then where was the harm in spending some time together?

The carriage eventually pulled off the road and Amy peeped through the window with interest. She had never visited a vineyard before and was looking forward to it. They stopped outside a rambling villa, which looked far grander than she had expected it to be. It was a long low building with ivy climbing profusely up the walls and bright spring blooms in the flowerbeds beneath its many windows.

François helped her down from the carriage, saying, 'Would you care to come in and meet my aunt and uncle?'

'Not this evening, if you don't mind,' Amy said gently. 'Let's just walk. It's such a beautiful evening.'

'Very well, I shall just tell the coachman to inform them that we are here, and he can go to the kitchen to take some refreshments until we return. Anaïs might like to go with him.'

She smiled gratefully, and as he hurried away to the front of the coach she turned around and gazed about her. Here it felt as if she were a million miles away from the streets of Paris, for there was nothing to be heard but the sound of the night creatures and tall, dark vines stretching away into the darkness for as far as her eyes could see.

She saw the coachman climb down from his seat and, after a hurried word with François, he led the horses away to the stables at the rear of the villa, with Anaïs following close behind. François hurried back to her side.

'Come.' He pulled her arm gently through his. 'I think you will enjoy it here. It is very peaceful.

When I was a child I loved it here and would come whenever my *maman* would allow it.' He laughed at his childhood memories. 'I think sometimes I have been a great problem to my poor uncle, for I found the whole business of wine-making fascinating from start to finish, and I always insisted on helping, though in truth I was probably far more of a hindrance. I have tried everything – picking the grapes, treading them, and once I almost fell into one of the great vats where the crude wine ferments. I should not have been near it and my papa, as you English say, "tanned my behind".'

As they strolled on, the towering grape vines closed around them.

'The grapes, when they grow a little more, are of many different sizes and colours.' He pointed them out, and when Amy nodded he went on, 'This is how we are able to make the very dry to the very sweet wines. The stage of ripeness they are picked at decides the quality of the wine.'

Amy was impressed at his knowledge.

'Once I thought I would own my own vineyards,' he confided. 'But then as I grew up I became interested in fashion and so, after all, I joined my papa in his business. Now I am very glad that I did, for had I not, I would never have met you.'

Amy felt her cheeks grow hot as they came to a little clearing in the vines. A wide stream ran through it and a small wooden bridge led to the vines on the other side.

'You will always find vineyards built near running water,' François explained to her as he led her on to the bridge. 'As you will now be aware after your stay, we can often go for weeks here without rain, and when this happens the peasants who pick and tread the grapes water the vines with buckets from this stream. It is very back-breaking work but *très nécessaire*.'

When he drew her to a halt in the middle of the bridge they stared down into the water. The moonlight was dancing on its surface and they were enveloped in the warm balmy air. From somewhere far away they heard a nightingale serenading the moon and as François stared at her, Amy's hair, which tonight was cascading loosely about her shoulders, was caught in the moonlight, which changed it from deepest auburn to molten gold.

'I cannot believe that in less than a week you will be gone,' he said sadly, and something in his voice made her turn and look directly into his eyes.

'It is probably for the best,' she replied. 'I fear you have wasted far too much of your time on me and I am very grateful for it. I shall always remember your kindness.'

'Kindness!' His voice was heavy with annoyance. 'Kindness – is that why you think I have escorted you? Because I am *kind*?'

'Why, y ... yes. Of course – why else?'

'*Why else?* But surely you must know I am in love with you, Aimée. I have never been able to tell you before because Anaïs has always been present. I think I have been since the very first second I saw you. I was beginning to hope that you felt something for me too, but perhaps I was wrong?' There was such anguish in his voice that her heart twisted in her chest.

'You were not wrong, François,' she admitted on a sob. 'I do care about you a great deal. More than you could ever know. But it is better if we do not speak of our feelings, for nothing could come of this ... ever.'

Her voice was flat and so full of finality that he took her by the shoulders and swung her about to face him. As she stared up at him he saw the tears glistening on her cheeks and a frown distorted his handsome face.

'What is this you are saying? You tell me in one breath that you care for me and in the next that nothing can ever come of it. Why is this?'

'Because we are worlds apart in class, that's why,' she said shakily. 'Don't you see? You have been brought up totally differently to me. You have had servants to wait on you hand and foot and the best education that money could buy. I have been brought up in a tiny cottage with two rooms up and two rooms down. The whole of my home would fit into the drawing room at your château and give you room to spare. Whilst you were with your private tutors and attending your fine private schools, I went one day a week to Sunday school and a few hours at the village school. The rest of my education came from Toby, our neighbour's son, who works by day deep in the earth as a miner. He is very clever and wants to be a teacher one day. He used to come round to our cottage in the evenings to teach me my letters and my numbers. So there, do I really need to go on? That is why there can never be anything more than friendship between

308

us. We are from different social classes, François. You are from what we call "the gentry" in England, the heir to a great fortune, whilst I am merely a servant.'

He stared at her dumbfounded.

'B ... but *ma petite*, love knows no class,' he said. 'We are all equal in this world. I love you for *who* you are, for *what* you are. Do you not see?'

As she stared into the depths of his eyes she felt herself weakening and quickly looked away.

'François, if it were not for my gran, I would probably have spent the early part of my life in an orphanage or the workhouse. I could *never* leave her. Don't you understand?'

'Yes, yes, of course I understand, but there are ways around this. If you would not leave her then I would come to you. No problem is insurmountable.'

He suddenly pulled her to him and his lips pressed down hard on hers, and despite all her misgivings, Amy gave herself up to the joy of the moment. They clung together as if this was the only moment they would ever share, and when they finally drew apart, Amy was breathless and her heart was racing.

'*There*,' he said with a satisfied smile. 'Now we shall have no more of this foolish talk. We shall take things slowly. But do not think that when you return to England, you will have seen the last of me. For I warn you, *ma petite*, when I want something I do not give up easily.' His eyes were alive with mischief and Amy laughed aloud.

'Well, we shall see. As my gran would say, "what will be, will be".' And then with their arms linked, the two lovers made their way back through the vines to the villa, to pay their compliments to their hosts.

Chapter Twenty-One

The remaining days of Amy's stay passed all too quickly. She and François spent every single second they could in each other's company and the day before she was due to leave he arrived at the hotel with a large box in his hands.

'Open it,' he urged her, as excited as a child.

Amy obediently did as she was told and gasped with delight. Inside, concealed in layers of fine paper, was an evening cloak in a rich emerald-green that would match her favourite gown.

'Why, this is one of the new designs that I showed to your father,' she said wonderingly.

'That is correct, *ma petite*. I have had our *couturières*, how do you say, work around the clock to get it finished for you, and one day soon I shall come to England to see you wear it.'

As she clung to him fiercely, her heart was aching. Their last evening together was bittersweet and she locked every precious moment away in her memory to sustain her through the long lonely days until they could be together again.

The next morning, Amy said goodbye to Monsieur Laroque at the Hotel Meurice and then she and François slipped outside to wait by the carriage until the Forresters joined them. The two gentlemen had struck a business deal that suited them both very well, and now as the two young people stared bereft into each other's eyes they sought for words to say. François held her hand gently as unshed tears trembled on Amy's eyelashes.

'This is only the beginning, you shall see,' he told her wistfully, and then his lips brushed hers before Mr and Mrs Forrester and Monsieur Laroque exited the hotel and came to join them.

Amy waved at him from the carriage window until he was gone from sight and then shrank back deep into her seat to begin the long journey to Calais. The Gare du Nord was being rebuilt, which meant a long and tiring journey by road to the port of Calais. Amy was dreading sailing home, but thankfully the sea was slightly calmer on the way back and although she felt queasy she managed the return journey without being seasick.

If the Forresters noticed that Amy was somewhat quiet, they put it down to tiredness. She did not seem overly upset at leaving François and Samuel could only hope that she had taken his advice and had not become attached to the young man.

Amy was experiencing a mixture of emotions. Her designs had gone down far better in Paris than she had ever dared to hope, and she could see from the broad smile on Samuel's face that he was more than pleased with the business deal that he and Monsieur Laroque had arrived at. The trip to Paris had been a wonderful tonic after the death of his mother. Amy was missing François and yet she was also longing to see her gran and Toby. She had so very much to tell them.

Already the romantic city she had just left behind seemed a million miles away and she wondered if she would wake up the next morning and find that she had dreamed the whole trip. But then a picture of François' handsome face flashed in front of her eyes and she knew that every second of it had been real. She realised now that he had reminded her of Toby in many ways, for although they were nothing alike in looks, they had surprisingly similar natures. They were both kind and generous to a fault, and as she thought of Toby now, she suddenly began to realise just how much she had missed him.

A huge tide of homesickness suddenly washed over her as she stared from the window, eager for a glimpse of her hometown.

By the time their luggage had been carefully loaded into a carriage at Trent Valley station, Amy was beside herself with impatience to be home, and Mr Forrester regarded her with high amusement. The young woman never ceased to amaze him. She had come a very long way in a comparatively short time, and yet he was aware that no position he could offer her would ever change her love for her grandmother or make her forget her humble beginnings. These were some of the qualities that he most admired about her.

He was eager to see his own home so when the carriage pulled up outside Molly's cottage, he hastily lifted down Amy's trunk, and after assurances from her that she could manage, he climbed back into the carriage and it rattled away.

Leaving the luggage exactly where it was for now, Amy lifted her skirts and flew into the cottage like a whirling dervish.

Molly was standing at the sink when the door was flung open and when she turned and saw Amy, her mouth gaped open. She had not expected her until the following day at the earliest, and now she had to blink to convince herself that she wasn't seeing things as tears started to her eyes and slid down her wrinkled old cheeks.

'Eeh – pet!'

Amy hugged her so fiercely that she almost knocked the wind from her gran's frail old body. When the first joy of their reunion was satisfied she then held her gran at arm's length and studied her critically.

Molly seemed smaller somehow, as if she had shrunk in her absence. Her clothes were hanging loosely on her and Amy was concerned to see that she looked frail and unwell. Even as Amy continued to stare at her, Molly began to cough and the girl's face creased with concern.

Seeing her expression, Molly flapped her hand at her, banging her chest with the other until the coughing bout had subsided.

'Now don't get frettin' over this,' she told her sternly. 'It's nothin'. I come down wi' a bit of a cold shortly after yer went an' it's left me wi' this chesty cough. But I'm on the mend again now. So come on, I'll put the kettle on an' then yer can tell me all about your trip, eh?'

Amy silently nodded and while Molly made the tea she went back out into the lane and began to drag her trunk into the kitchen. Whilst she was in the process of doing this, Toby appeared further down the lane with Annie Hayden close on his heels. Cathy Hickman had long since given up on him and had married a lad from the village. Annie was the latest girl to set her cap at Toby and Amy felt a stab of disappointment. She had hoped he would come straight round to welcome her, but he obviously had better things to do.

After ushering Annie through the doorway of his own cottage he smiled and raised his hand in greeting. His pulses were racing at the sight of Amy and he was finding it hard to conceal his joy, but he raised his hand and told her casually, 'I'll be round later this evenin' after I've walked Annie home.'

Amy nodded, far more unsettled than she would have cared to admit.

He kept his promise and that evening as they were clustered around the kitchen table she told him all about her trip and the places she had seen. Molly had already heard it, but she smiled indulgently as she listened all over again.

Toby couldn't help but notice how often François' name cropped up and the way Amy's face softened whenever she spoke of him. It caused a feeling of jealousy the like of which he had never known, and it rose like burning bile in his throat.

'I'm glad that everythin' went so well,' he said, straight-lipped. 'It sounds like this is only the beginnin' fer you an' yer fancy Frenchman.'

Amy lowered her eyes at the peevish tone that had crept into his voice despite his very best efforts to disguise it.

'It's perhaps time yer were thinkin' o' settlin' down,' he went on. 'I know I certainly am. An' I reckon I shan't have to look much further than Annie. I've kept her danglin' fer far too long, so happen I should start to think o' makin' an honest woman of her.'

'If that's what you want then perhaps you should, Toby,' Amy told him, her chin in the air. 'And all I can say is – I wish you well. There's no one I know who deserves to be happy more than you do.'

As Toby slowly rose from the table their eyes momentarily met. 'Right, well ... thanks. Happen I'd better get off now; you'll be wantin' to get to your bed no doubt after your long journey. Night, Molly. Night, Amy.'

Molly, who had been listening to the pair of them sparring, sighed heavily as Toby slipped away without another word.

Here were the two young people she cared about most in the world facing each other as if they were saying their last goodbyes. She had the urge to rush around the table and bang their two bloody silly heads together but she wisely stifled it.

Oh, Toby could marry his Annie and Amy could well end up marrying her Frenchman, although she felt the chances of that happening were slim. But would either of them ever know true happiness if they did? She very much doubted it, but if they were unable to see what was staring them in the face, then what could she do about it?

After silently lighting her candle from the lamp that was sputtering on the table, she placed a gentle kiss on Amy's cheeks and went to bed,

315

leaving the girl staring quietly into the empty fire-grate.

Molly glanced at the envelope with its foreign stamps propped up against the clock on the mantelpiece and sighed. They had been coming as fast as the post would allow for months now, and she knew that Amy often sat up late into the night replying to them. She had secretly hoped that Amy's affair with François would fizzle out, but as the months wore on and the letters kept coming, her hopes of that had begun to fade.

She supposed that it was selfish of her to feel as she did. More than anything she wanted to see Amy happy and settled. But try as she might, she just could not imagine her married to a Frenchman. In fairness, there had been no mention of marriage as yet but even so, Molly had a feeling that it would only be a matter of time before there was. Her greatest wish now was to see Amy settled before she died, but sometimes of late she wondered if her wish would be fulfilled.

She was having to rise later in the mornings and retire to bed earlier at night, and sometimes her old body ached so much that all she wanted to do was close her eyes and never wake up again.

Since returning from her trip to Paris, Amy had been forced to spend more and more of her time in London. Mr Forrester had opened another two shops, or salons, as he now referred to them, and Amy had asked that they be designed along the same lines as the ones she had worked at in Paris. These new, Parisian-style businesses were thriving, and were extremely popular with the high-society ladies of London. So much so that Mr Forrester now employed many new staff in order to meet demand. It was the same story in Paris, as Amy knew from the letters that she received from François; he assured her that her designs were selling as fast as they could be made.

Just as he had always been, Mr Forrester was a more than generous master and Amy was now a young woman of considerable means. Yet still she spent as much time at the cottage with Molly as she could, and Molly began to worry that she was holding her back. She also worried about the amount of money Amy spent ensuring that the cottage was now as comfortable as it possibly could be. Amongst other things, her bedroom now boasted a fine marble-topped wash-stand on which stood a pretty china jug and bowl, and downstairs a brass fender that had Bessie sighing with envy every time she set eyes on it, skirted the hearth.

Molly had once expressed her misgivings and Amy had nearly bitten her head off. 'I like you to have nice things, Gran. You deserve them. And also, if you don't want me here, and think I should be living somewhere else, then just say.' Her eyes had been deep wells of hurt.

Molly had been instantly contrite. 'O' *course* I want yer here! You know that, lass, but I want yer to get on in the world as well.'

'But I *am* getting on, Gran – although I don't know if it would be the same story if I didn't have you to come home to. You're the one that keeps my feet on the ground. You're my port in a storm when I need someone to turn to. Don't you know

317

that by now?'

More touched at her words than she cared to show, Molly had hugged her and she knew then that behind the fine clothes and the confident manner was still the same girl she loved. The subject of Amy leaving home was never mentioned again.

Now with a last glance at the letter on the shelf, Molly dragged herself from her comfy chair. Amy would be home soon and the old woman had no doubt that she would be ready for a good strong brew. It was bitterly cold outside and although it was only five o'clock in the afternoon the lane outside was already as dark as pitch. After pushing the sooty kettle into the heart of the fire, Molly measured some spoonfuls of tea into the well-used brown teapot and shuffled away to check the shepherd's pie that was cooking in the oven of the black-leaded range. Happy now that all was as it should be, she returned to her chair and settled back to wait for Amy's return.

Meanwhile, Amy was hurrying through the cobbled streets of the town centre, gripping the smart overnight valise that she had treated herself to for her stays in London. She had left the house in Kensington that morning in a happy frame of mind following a most enjoyable early-morning gossip with Nancy. Married life was obviously suiting her and Amy had never seen her friend so happy. Nancy was getting along famously with Billy's mother, so much so that their plans to start searching for a home of their own had been temporarily shelved. Even now, months after the wedding, all she could talk about was her wonderful Billy and what a lovely wedding they had had. After leaving the house, Amy's day had continued on a good note. Each of the shops she visited was doing extremely well and she knew that Mr Forrester would be pleased when she passed on the news to him tomorrow.

Humming to herself, she hurried along and soon was passing the Parish Church on the last leg of her journey home. She thought how pretty it looked with the frost on the roof sparkling in the glow of the new gas lamps that had recently been installed, but then her thoughts turned to François as they so often did and she wondered if there would be a letter from him waiting for her when she got home. She smiled at the thought. She now had a whole pile of letters from him all tied with a ribbon and tucked beneath her mattress. But sometimes lately she had to screw her eyes up tight and concentrate with all her might to remember his face in detail. Still, she supposed that this was to be expected. After all, it had been some long months now since she had returned from Paris, and she had been so busy that many things about the trip were slowly fading in her memory.

When she entered the warmth of the kitchen, the smell of the shepherd's pie greeted her and she said, 'By, Gran, that smells good enough to make my mouth water.'

Molly chuckled. 'Well, sit yourself down at the table then an' get some of it inside yer. Then you can tell me all about what's been goin' on in London.'

319

Amy obediently took off her coat and bonnet and after hanging them on the smart new coat-stand and having a good wash to get rid of the grime of the journey, she gratefully tucked into the plateful of steaming food that Molly placed in front of her.

Between mouthfuls she told her gran of all the news from London and as always, Molly listened avidly. She now heard so much about Nancy and the staff in the shops that she felt as if she knew them personally, for Amy could almost bring them to life with her tales.

'Has anything interesting happened here while I've been away?' Amy asked casually,

Knowing exactly what she meant, Molly nodded towards the mantelpiece. 'Well, there's another letter from Paris arrived if yer could call that interestin',' she said.

Amy's eyes lit up as she hurried to the shelf and popped the letter into the pocket of her dress. 'Oh, thanks. I'll read it later.'

Molly's eyebrows rose but she'd no time to comment because at that moment, Toby ambled in.

Seeing Amy, he smiled. 'Ah, so you're back again then. I was just callin' in to see if yer gran needed her coal-scuttle fillin'. But seein' as you're here I'll do it and be on me way.'

'Can't you stay for a drink?' Amy asked him when he had brought more coal in and was washing his hands. 'There's fresh tea in the pot. I was just about to have one.'

Toby shook his head. 'No, thanks all the same but Annie's round at me mam's, an' if I'm not needed here I'd best be off an' see her home.'

Swallowing her disappointment, Amy forced a smile. Molly would be off to bed soon and she would have enjoyed Toby's company. It seemed such a long time since they had had a good chat. But still, she consoled herself, I have my letter to read, and the thought cheered her.

'Very well then, Toby. Good night, and thank you for calling round.'

He stared at her for a moment, then nodding at them both, he stepped back out into the bitterly cold night.

'He's a good lad, make no mistake,' muttered Molly as the door closed behind him. 'He looks after me like a mother hen, so he does, when you ain't here. I reckon they broke the mould when they made that 'un.'

Amy nodded in agreement. She knew that she had a lot to thank Toby for. But shortly afterwards, when Molly went to bed and as she settled down by the fire to read her letter from Paris, all else was forgotten.

The next morning, Amy set off for Forrester's Folly bright and early. Lily let her in with a cheery smile, and for the next few hours she was kept busy going over the account books in the study with Mr Forrester. This was another side of the business that he had lately involved her in. Amy was actually very good with figures as he had quickly discovered, and when all the ledgers were up to date he sat back in his chair and sighed with satisfaction. Every single one of the shops and factories that he owned were doing well, and he was aware that a lot of this was due to Amy.

'Well, I think that's quite enough of that for now, young lady, don't you?' Rising from the desk, he smiled at her. 'It's time we joined Mrs Forrester in the drawing room while Cook rustles us up some lunch.'

It was usual for Amy to dine with her employer now, and once the lunch was served they all sat around the dining table tucking into one of Cook's delicious steak and kidney puddings. Amy noticed that Mrs Forrester seemed to be in an exceptionally good mood and she soon discovered the reason why.

'Has Mr Forrester spoken to you about the party yet?' she asked.

'No, I haven't,' her husband replied indulgently as he dabbed at his mouth with a starched white linen napkin. 'I thought I would leave that up to you, my dear.'

Josephine instantly turned her attention back to Amy.

'The thing is,' she confided, 'I got to thinking that it's been many years since we had a party at Forrester's Folly. It's almost a year now since Samuel's mother died and it's also coming up to Christmas. On top of that, I believe it is also your birthday on Christmas Eve, Amy, so what better time for a party could there be? Samuel and I are both aware that you have worked very hard this year, and this house has known enough sadness to last an entire lifetime. So, I have decided, on Christmas Eve we shall throw a party and you must come and bring your grandmother. What do you think of the idea?' She was as excited as a girl and Amy found her good mood infectious.

'I think it's a wonderful idea,' she told her. 'And thank you very much for inviting us both.'

'That is settled then.' Josephine's mind was already on the invitations and the menus and so the rest of their lunch was spent on planning the forthcoming event.

When Amy got home later that afternoon, she could hardly wait to tell Molly the good news. Molly was a little dubious about going but Amy assured her, 'I shall design a new dress and bonnet for you and you'll be the belle of the ball, you'll see. I know that you'll get on well with Mr and Mrs Forrester and it's going to be lovely!'

Molly had not seen Amy so excited since her trip to Paris, and although the thought of the party held no appeal whatsoever for her, she said nothing for Amy's sake, unwilling to upset her.

During the next few days, Amy brought home numerous samples of material for her gran to look at but Molly turned her nose up at all of them.

'Oh, Gran, *please!*' Amy scolded. 'You'll have to make a decision soon otherwise I won't have time to get them made up for you. Please look again. What about this lovely dark green? It's not too bright and you've always liked green.'

More than a little uncomfortable, Molly sniffed, feeling as if she had been backed into a corner. She had been putting off the inevitable but now it must be said and done with.

'Look, lass,' she began tentatively, 'I've no wish to hurt yer, you know I'd cut me right hand off rather than do that ... but the truth is, I ain't goin' to the party.'

'What do you mean, you're not coming?' Amy

was appalled. 'But, Gran, you *must* come. Mr and Mrs Forrester will so disappointed if you don't. And so shall I!'

The loose skin that had once formed Molly's double chin quivered as her head shook slowly from side to side.

'Disappointed or not, I ain't goin'. Yer know I've never been one fer parties. An' anyway, I'd just stick out like a sore thumb, as yer well aware. Truth is, Amy, I'm past gallivantin' about at my age. All I want is a peaceful life an' me own fireside. I wouldn't fit in wi' the sort o' folks as you're mixin' wi' now. In your case it's different. I always knew you were destined for better things.'

Amy's eyes flashed with disappointment as she asked, 'Oh yes? Then tell me, Gran, just how do you know that?'

Molly shrugged her rounded shoulders. 'That's like askin' how do I know night will follow day. I've just always known it, that's all, an' right proud I am o' you an' all, make no bones about it. But I still ain't goin' to no party so yer may as well stop yer naggin' an' get used to the idea. I ain't comin', an' that's that. I'm too old an' set in me ways to start rubbin' shoulders wi' the gentry now.'

As Amy recognised the note of finality in her gran's voice, her shoulders slumped and she sat down heavily on a chair. Once her gran had made her mind up on something she was as stubborn as an old mule and Amy knew better than to try and change it. It would just be a complete waste of time.

'If that's how you feel, then I won't go either,' she declared petulantly.

Molly bristled. 'Oh yes, you *will* go, my girl– If I have to drag yer there meself kickin' an' screamin'. An' don't go givin' me any o' yer lip now, 'cos you ain't too big to go across me lap an' have a slapped arse, so just think on it.'

Amy had to bite her lip to stop herself from laughing aloud. Molly had never so much as raised a finger to her, let alone put her across her lap in her whole life. The same thought must have occurred to Molly, for suddenly her eyes were bright and she pulled Amy into her arms. 'Now then, that's enough,' she whispered. 'That's about the closest we've come to a row in many a long day. But yer know, darlin', on this one yer have to accept me decision. Yer wouldn't want me to come an' feel miserable, now would yer?'

Amy shook her head. 'No, I wouldn't,' she admitted. 'But I was so looking forward to showing you off, Gran, because you know, I'm just as proud of you as you are of me.'

The words were spoken from the heart and as Molly held Amy tightly to her she was deeply touched. Closing her eyes, she thanked God for bringing this lovely girl into her life.

Chapter Twenty-Two

'Ah, please say yer'll come, Amy!' Nancy's eyes were imploring. 'I know yer'd enjoy it an' my Billy 'ud make sure as yer didn't fall.'

Amy had grave misgivings and pursed her lips.

325

'But I've never been ice skating in my whole life, Nancy,' she pointed out truthfully.

Nancy giggled. 'Well, then it's about time yer did. Yer know what they say, there's a first time for everyfink. Now come on an' stop bein' such a spoilsport. What do yer say?'

'Oh, very well then, I suppose it wouldn't hurt to give it a go. But don't get blaming me if I pull you over,' Amy said sullenly.

Nancy threw back her head and laughed aloud. '*You* pull *me* over? Huh, there's about as much chance o' that as a snowball's chance in 'ell! Yer don't weigh as much as a bag o' spuds wet through. But I'd best be off now. Billy's ma will 'ave the tea on the table an' she'll skin me alive if it's ruined. We'll meet yer at the Serpentine Bridge in Hyde Park at seven, an' make sure yer wrap up warm. I'll bring yer a pair of skates, so don't go worryin' about that.'

'I will,' Amy promised, still wondering if she had done the right thing in agreeing to go. Nancy gave her a final wave and disappeared through the door humming merrily.

Amy wondered what she had let herself in for. This would be her final night in London this year, and she was looking forward to going home to her gran and having a whole week off before Christmas. Now that Nancy no longer lived in, she missed their late-night chats and usually ended up going to bed early to sketch or read a book. But tonight she was going skating, and hoped she wouldn't end up breaking her ankle or something equally as painful.

Still, there was no getting out of it now. She had

326

promised Nancy she would go, so she would do the best she could and hope that she didn't make too much of a fool of herself.

Despite her misgivings, Amy had an exhilarating evening and when it was over, she moved through the throng with her friends and kissed them both soundly at the park gates. It would be the last time she would see them before Christmas and they all hugged each other fondly before parting on a happy note. As Amy watched the couple walk away with their arms entwined, she sighed happily. They were obviously very deeply in love, and seeing them so wrapped up in each other made her thoughts turn to François. She wished that he could have been here tonight to share in all the fun. But then, even as the thought crossed her mind she realised that she somehow just couldn't picture him larking about as Billy had. Blinking the snow from her eyelashes as Nancy and Billy disappeared around a corner, she herself turned about and headed for home.

As she hurried along Kensington Gore, she wondered what Nancy would make of the Christmas present she had bought for her and Billy. She wanted it to be a surprise and had left it with Cook, with strict instructions that she wasn't to give it to them until Christmas Eve. It was a fine china teaset that would have graced the table of any lady, and Amy had known the moment she spotted it in an expensive china shop in Piccadilly that Nancy would love it. However, whether it would ever be used or not was a different matter entirely, as Nancy would probably say it was far too lovely to risk it getting broken. The happy thoughts speeded her footsteps and soon Amy was back in the warmth of the big house in Sloane Street, frozen through but happily content.

Before leaving the next day she also left prettily wrapped presents for Mrs Wilcox, the house-keeper, and Cook, and they both thanked her sincerely.

'Now you're not to open them until Christmas Day,' Amy warned them with a teasing smile.

'We won't, luv,' Cook assured her. 'An' God bless yer. You're a good girl, Amy, an' this has been a happier house since you came into it, there's no doubt about it. But now you get yerself off 'ome an' 'ave a lovely Christmas. Oh, an' give me love to that gran o' yours, 'cos I ain't afraid to say it, yer a credit to her.'

Amy left in a happy mood, her only concern that the train might be delayed because of the atrocious weather conditions. Thankfully it was on time and once she was back in Nuneaton she took a carriage to the end of the lane where the coachman told her regretfully, 'Sorry, miss, but I ain't goin' to be able to get up there with the snowdrifts. Will yer manage yer luggage?'

'I'll be fine, I don't have that far to go,' she assured him, and after paying him she began to struggle up the lane with her heavy valise and a large box containing the rest of the Christmas presents that she had bought in London. She was almost halfway along when Toby appeared out of the darkness, his face covered in coal dust and his hands grimy, fresh from his shift at the mine.

Laughing, he took the large box from her and exclaimed, 'Good grief, woman! What have you

328

got in 'ere? Is it full o' lead off the church roof or somethin'?'

Amy blinked the snow from her eyes as she moved her valise from one hand to the other. 'Actually it's full of Christmas presents for you, my gran and your mam,' she told him, and with their heads bent they battled on, contently silent in each other's company. Suddenly, she was very glad to be home.

By the time Amy opened the door of the cottage, her feet were so cold that she had lost all feeling in them and her nose was glowing. She was so tired that she was sure she could have slept for a month, but the sight that met her eyes made her forget all about her tiredness, and she stopped so abruptly that Toby almost ran into the back of her. She never failed to experience a sense of homecoming whenever she entered the cottage, but tonight she felt as if she was walking into a Christmas grotto. Holly and mistletoe were everywhere she looked, and in pride of place next to Molly's dresser stood a little Christmas tree that Molly had decorated with remnants of ribbons all the colours of the rainbow, left over from her ribbon-weaving days.

Molly smiled at the look of pleasure on Amy's face as she asked eagerly, 'Do yer like it, lass?'

'Like it? Why, it looks absolutely beautiful, Gran,' Amy answered truthfully as she dropped her valise on to the floor and flexed her frozen fingers.

'I can't take all the credit for it,' Molly admitted. 'Most of it is down to our Toby 'ere. He nearly ripped his hands to ribbons, God bless him, collectin' all this holly an' mistletoe. But we thought yer'd like it.'

As Amy's appreciative eyes swept the room, Toby looked embarrassed, and hurriedly crossing to the table, he deposited the large box on it.

As Amy's eyes settled on a big bunch of mistletoe hanging from one of the beams she had the urge to kiss him there and then, but she wisely stemmed it, not wishing to embarrass him any more than he already was.

Holly was strewn all along the mantelpiece, its scarlet berries glowing in the firelight, and candles standing erect in little pot saucers were dotted here and there adding to the enchantment of the cosy scene.

'I've brought you something that might make the tree look even prettier if that's possible,' Amy bubbled as she hurried to the box that Toby had placed on the table.

'But it ain't Christmas Day yet. Yer shouldn't be givin' out presents just now,' Molly objected.

'It doesn't matter. This is something that you can have right away.' Amy rummaged about in the box as excited as a child and eventually withdrew an ornate gold box. Carrying it to the hearth, she beckoned Molly to join her and once the old lady was seated in her old rocking chair, Amy placed it into her twisted hands.

'Go on, Gran, open it,' she urged expectantly.

'Well, I'll be!' Molly exclaimed when she had done as she was told and withdrawn the first of its contents. 'I don't think I've ever seen anythin' quite so fine in the whole o' me life.' In the palm of her hand was a small blown-glass ornament suspended from a fine silver cord in the shape of a little reindeer. Eager to see the rest now she delved into the box again and this time she came up with a snowman. One by one she unwrapped the contents to reveal an angel and a bell, and so it went on until she had twelve items in all spread out across the coarse calico apron that covered her lap.

'They're for the Christmas tree.' Amy's eyes were dancing as much as the flames that were licking up the sooty chimney, but Molly was so taken with her gifts that she could only stare at them in awe.

'By the gods, it's just amazin' what they can do nowadays,' she muttered as she turned the baubles over one by one. 'But I reckon you an' Toby had best put 'em on the tree. Wi' my old butter fingers I'd likely drop 'em.'

Amy and Toby spent a pleasant few minutes doing just that before sitting back on their heels to admire them.

After a while Toby stood up and told her, 'I'd better get off now. I ain't even washed the muck off me yet an' me mam will be thinkin' I've got lost.'

'Thanks for helping with all this,' Amy told him as she spread her hands.

'It were nothin'.' He flushed self-consciously and then with a nod towards Molly he hurried away.

Soon Amy and Molly were seated at the table enjoying the leg of pork and crispy roast potatoes that Molly had cooked that afternoon. This was followed by a steaming hot dish of apple dumplings all dripping in sugary syrup. When Amy had scraped the last of the syrup from her bowl she leaned back and patted her full stomach contentedly.

'There's no one can make dumplings like you, Gran,' she sighed. 'But let's leave the dirty pots until the morning, eh?'

Just this once, Molly agreed. 'I dare say they'll keep.'

They retired to the sofa where Amy tucked her legs up beneath her and rested her head on her gran's bony old shoulder. They were both shrouded in an air of well-being and contentment, and as Amy stared into the fire she whispered, sleepily suppressing a yawn, 'Do you know what, Gran? I think this is going to be the *best* Christmas ever.'

Stroking the girl's hair, Molly smiled down at her, happy with her lot. 'Let's hope so, pet,' she sighed contentedly. 'Let's hope so.'

Chapter Twenty-Three

When Christmas Eve dawned, the cottage became a hive of activity. Amy dragged the old snow-covered tin bath in from the outside yard into the kitchen and Molly then filled it with kettlefuls of hot water from the copper boiler. Amy climbed in and washed her hair and every inch of herself until her skin took on a rosy hue, then she sat by the fire wrapped in a large towel while Molly brushed her hair as it steamed in the heat of the flames.

Her beautiful green gown was pressed and

hanging on her wardrobe door all ready to step into, and as she thought of the evening ahead a bubble of excitement formed in her stomach.

'Are you quite sure that you won't change your mind and come to the party, Gran?' she asked hopefully yet again. Earlier, she had helped the old woman to have a thorough wash from the head down, while seated on a stout wooden chair covered with a towel, and Molly looked as clean as a new pin. Amy had bought her a very smart dress and bonnet for Christmas, which would have been perfect for the party, but Molly would still not be swayed.

'But you look so lovely in your new outfit,' Amy protested one last time. 'It's such a shame for it not to be worn.'

'It will be worn, but not tonight,' Molly told her firmly. 'Me dress an' bonnet are the grandest I've ever owned, love, but me answer is still no. If I were to go out in this weather it would set me cough off again an' well yer know it. Besides, Toby is comin' round to read to me, so I'll be perfectly happy wi' me own fireside.'

Sighing, Amy finally gave up with her persuasions and they went about their day-to-day business.

Later in the day, as the afternoon light slowly gave way to twilight, Amy went to her room to get ready. She had barely closed her bedroom door behind her when Molly tapped and came in behind her; then sank down on to the side of the bed. She seemed a little subdued and nervy as she beckoned Amy over to her.

'Just come an' sit down by me for a second,

would yer, love?' she requested, still out of breath. 'I have somethin' that I want yer to have an' I reckon now is the right time for me to give it to yer.'

Curious, Amy sat down next to her as she searched her eyes and asked, 'What is it then, Gran?'

Delving into the pocket of her pinnie, Molly withdrew a small faded velvet box and told her, 'This was yer mother's.' She pressed the box into Amy's hand. 'It's all I have of her 'cept for a few clothes that I have upstairs in a bag.'

Amy opened the lid and blinked as the emerald in the centre of the locket winked at her in the glow from the oil lamp.

'Why, Gran, it's really lovely,' she breathed. 'And you say this belonged to my mother?'

'Aye, it did, love. Look inside it.'

Amy carefully withdrew the locket from its bed of silk, then gently pressed the clasp on its side, as it sprang open, two faces stared up at her. For a moment she was lost for words.

'That were your mam an' dad,' Molly told her softly.

Tears began to slide down Amy's cheeks. As she gazed at the woman's face she felt as if she was looking in a mirror, for there was the same auburn hair and eyes staring back at her. She then turned her attention to the tiny portrait in the other side of the locket and gazed upon the face of a man with gentle features, her father.

'Th ... they made a lovely couple, didn't they, Gran?' she sighed wistfully.

Placing her arm comfortingly about her

shoulders, the old woman nodded. 'They did that, love. So wear your mother's legacy wi' pride an' be proud of who you are. I know it ain't as grand as the necklace the old mistress left you, but I hope you'll treasure it all the same.'

Dragging her eyes away from the locket, Amy looked tenderly at her gran. Could the old woman have known it, there was nothing in the world that she could have given her that she could treasure more. A million times over the years, she had lain in bed at night wondering what her mother and father had been like and wishing that she could have known them. Her one consolation had been her gran, who had never shown her anything but love and kindness.

'I promise you that I shall treasure this until my dying day,' she told her, and taking the wrinkled old cheeks into her hands she kissed her soundly. 'But I shall never treasure anything as much as I treasure you, for you have been my guardian angel. Without you, I would have been nothing.'

Suddenly her old brusque self again, Molly pushed her away and flapping her hands at her as she struggled to climb from the bed, she told her, 'Pah! Now that's enough o' that soppy talk fer one night. Unless me mind is playin' tricks on me you have a party to go to, an' yer won't get ready sittin' there blartin'. So look lively, me girl, else it will all be over before yer even get there.' Then without another word she hobbled from the room as the lump in her throat threatened to choke her.

When Toby arrived some time later he found Amy standing in the kitchen in all her finery and

335

for a moment he was struck dumb. She looked totally out of place in such a humble dwelling. Her hair was tumbling about her shoulders in thick cascading curls, and she was wearing the beautiful cloak that François had given to her in Paris. Her mother's locket gleamed at her throat, the emerald in it complementing the colour of her gown.

Unable to help himself, he stared at her totally mesmerised. He had always considered her to be pretty but this evening she looked absolutely stunning.

'Happy Birthday, Amy,' he said, when he had finally found his tongue again. 'Yer look more like the gentry than they do 'emselves.'

She flushed at what she took to be a compliment. 'Why, thank you, kind sir.' She bobbed her knee just as they heard the Forresters' carriage rattling along the snow-covered cobbles outside.

Quickly planting a kiss on her gran's grey hair, she then moved towards Toby – and then paused. They were standing directly beneath the bunch of mistletoe that was dangling above the door, and without stopping to think, she raised herself on tiptoe and kissed him soundly on the mouth. Then laughing, she lifted her skirts and was gone, her cloak billowing out behind her like a sail.

As the coach trundled down the drive, Amy gazed from the window in awe at Forrester's Folly. It was ablaze with lights that shone from every single window, and all around the steps leading up to the front door, grand carriages were parked. Liveried coachmen were hastily throwing blankets across the horses to protect them from the snow and guiding them round to the stables. When the coachman assisted her down from the carriage, the whole situation began to take on an air of unreality, for she recalled that, not so very long ago, she had been nothing more than a cleaner in a hat factory – and now here she was attending a party at the home of her employer, dressed like a princess. Smiling, she shook out her skirts and held her head high, just as Molly would have wished her to.

The door was opened by a straight-backed butler who had been hired for the evening. 'Miss Amy Ernshaw,' he announced imperiously.

Amy suppressed the urge to giggle as she stepped forward.

Mr and Mrs Forrester, Adam and Eugenie, were standing in the line waiting to greet their guests, and the master and mistress stepped forward and shook her hand warmly.

Mrs Forrester was wearing a gown that was one of Amy's very latest designs, made of scarlet satin and with a large bustle at the back of it; a ruby necklace sparkled about her throat. She looked absolutely stunning, as did Mr Forrester who stood at her side looking strikingly handsome in a formal black dinner suit.

'Give Lily your cloak, my dear,' Mrs Forrester told her, 'and then go into the drawing room. Mr Harvey has already arrived and I'm sure he will be pleased to see you.'

They then turned to welcome the next guests who were waiting to be announced as Amy moved past them. Adam nodded at her politely, but

337

Eugenie refused to acknowledge her presence, a sullen frown on her face. Amy didn't care. She was determined that nothing should spoil this evening. Even Eugenie.

She found Mr Harvey standing next to a table on which stood many bottles of the very finest champagne sent as a Christmas present to the Forresters from Monsieur Laroque. She was soon sipping at a glass and laughing as the bubbles tickled her nose. The house was teeming with people and some time later she and Mr Harvey made their way to the dining room. The enormous table that usually stood in the centre of the room had been placed back against the wall and it was weighed down with a buffet that was fit to serve to the Queen herself. A whole roasted pig with an apple in its mouth lay on a bed of greens. There were roast chickens, ducks, pheasants, great hams and joints of meat cooked to perfection as well as every kind of pie and pastry imaginable. Amy was sure that there must be enough food there to feed a whole army.

A platform had been erected at the far end of the room and a four-man orchestra, dressed in smart, white-winged collars, matching cravats and black suits, were busily tuning their instruments on it. Women in multi-coloured gowns, each seeming to outdo the other, flitted about on the arms of smart gentlemen, with little elaborate fans in their gloved hands. Glad of Mr Harvey's company, Amy watched it all enthralled.

Eventually, when the last of the guests had arrived, Mr and Mrs Forrester entered the room and after declaring the buffet to be open they began to mingle with their guests as the orchestra struck up a merry tune.

Across the room, Amy saw Master Adam speaking to a man whom she recognised as the manager of one of the new London shops. Eugenie was at his side, being very loud with a large glass of wine in her hand. Although it was early, the way she was swaying suggested that she had already had more than enough to drink, and as their eyes met she cast Amy a scathing glance. Amy quickly averted her eyes and turned her attention to the middle of the room that was to serve as the dance floor, as gentlemen took their partners for the first dance. She found her foot tapping gaily in time to the music as the dancers swayed past, their bright skirts swirling and the gentlemen's tailcoats flicking.

Soon Mr and Mrs Forrester had worked their way around to them and Mr Forrester and Mr Harvey immediately became engrossed in conversation. Mrs Forrester smiled at Amy, but then as her eyes rested on the locket that hung about the girl's throat she reached out blindly and grasped her husband's arm; afraid that she was going to fall in a faint, Amy quickly moved towards her – but the woman flinched away and she pointed a trembling finger towards Amy's throat.

'Where did you get that locket?' she demanded in a voice that Amy had never heard her use before.

Baffled, and acutely aware that people were beginning to stare at them, Amy defensively raised her hand to her precious legacy.

Mr Forrester's eyes followed his wife's pointing

finger, and to Amy's horror he paled too. By now, Mrs Forrester was trembling like a leaf, and pulling himself together with what was obviously an enormous effort, Mr Forrester suddenly grasped Amy's elbow and began to propel her from the room. His wife followed close behind, looking for all the world as if she had seen a ghost. Across the room, Amy saw Eugenie watching what was going on and felt herself flush with embarrassment as she was hustled away.

Eugenie waited until they had left the room then slipping away from Adam's side unnoticed she followed them stealthily.

Once Mr Forrester had herded Amy into his study he led his trembling wife to a chair and helped her into it before turning back to Amy and asking her sharply, 'Amy – tell me the truth, now. Where did you get that locket?'

She stared back at him in total confusion, her heart racing. 'It ... it was my mother's,' she managed to stutter.

He shook his head in denial, his eyes harsh. 'That is quite impossible,' he stated bluntly, and now tears started to Amy's eyes and her chin jutted defiantly.

'I am sorry to argue with you, sir, but I assure you it was. She left it with my gran for me just before she died.'

For a second he lowered his head and screwed his eyes up tight, but then taking a deep breath he stared back at her and something in the depth of his eyes tore at her heart, for he looked like a man in torment.

'Please may I have a closer look at it?'

With fumbling fingers, Amy undid the clasp on the chain and silently passed it into his outstretched hand.

He stared down at it for some time as if it was burning him, then seeming to forget that Amy was there he turned on his heel and carried it across to his wife. She took the locket from him with shaking fingers. The couple looked deep into each other's eyes for what seemed like an eternity and then Josephine undid the clasp on the side and stared down at the two faces within smiling up at her.

Her face suddenly crumpled. 'Oh, my dear God,' she sobbed as if her heart would break. 'Samuel, look. It *is* Jessica's locket, I knew it the moment I saw it. It even has the portrait of herself she painted to place in it.'

As he paced the room like a caged animal, Amy noted with mounting horror that Mr Forrester was openly crying too. But what could all this mean? she asked herself. The evening had got off to such a wonderful start and now it was all ruined.

'How could this be?' Josephine was totally distraught, but for now her husband had no answer to her question and was as confused as she was.

'There must be some reasonable explanation,' he muttered as he continued to pace up and down. Then, stopping abruptly in front of Amy as if he had only just remembered her presence, he stared at her as if he had never seen her before.

Turning, he yanked on the bell-pull and when the maid appeared seconds later he barked at her, 'Lily, run around to the stable-block and tell them I want the carriage brought to the front of the house immediately.'

Lucy bobbed her knee. 'Yes, sir.' Realising that something was badly wrong, she scuttled away to do as she was told.

Meanwhile, Mr Forrester returned to his wife and squeezed her hand lovingly as he told her, 'Try not to upset yourself, my dear. We shall go and see Mrs Ernshaw right now and try to get to the bottom of this.'

Amy was totally at a loss. The evening was fast turning into a nightmare, and she had no idea why.

Lily reappeared shortly afterwards to tell them that the carriage was ready. Grim-faced, Mr Forrester ushered the two women outside without a word, pausing only long enough for the ladies to collect their cloaks.

Some of their guests stared in amazement as they watched their host and hostess disappear into the snowy night without so much as a civil word as they strode past them. Across the hallway, Eugenie raised her glass to her lips and smiled tipsily. Amy, the in-laws' brown-eyed girl was suddenly very much out of favour. And, she thought spitefully, long may it last! Let this be the last she would see of the common little guttersnipe.

When the sound of the carriage pulling up outside carried to them, Molly and Toby stared at each other in amazement. Glancing at the clock on the mantelpiece, Molly frowned. 'Why, it's barely nine o'clock,' she muttered. 'This surely can't be Amy back already, can it?'

Her question was answered when Amy burst into the room seconds later with the Forresters close behind her, their faces drawn and tense.

'Eeh, whatever's happened?' Guessing that something was badly amiss, she pulled herself painfully from the chair as Amy flung herself into her arms, sobbing uncontrollably.

'It's my locket, Gran,' she choked out. 'Mr and Mrs Forrester say it wasn't my mother's.'

Molly bristled. 'Oh yes it was, as God's me witness,' she told them boldly.

Mr Forrester drew himself up to his full height and stared at her disdainfully. 'I am afraid that is quite impossible, Mrs Ernshaw. You see, that locket belonged to my daughter. We had it commissioned and made for her in London for her eighteenth birthday. The picture of the young woman inside the locket is actually our daughter, Jessica. She was a very talented artist and she painted the portrait inside herself.'

It was Molly's turn to pale now. She had never been one for fainting, but as she stared into the master's cold eyes the room began to swim around her and an icy hand closed around her heart.

Back at The Folly, Adam searched the room for his parents and when he couldn't find them he made his way into the hallway and beckoned the butler to his side.

'Have you seen the master and mistress?' he asked.

The man nodded solemnly. 'Yes, Master Adam, sir. The master ordered the carriage to be brought around to the front some half an hour since, and he and the mistress went off with Miss Ernshaw.'

'But where did they go?' Adam was deeply puzzled. His parents' manners were impeccable, and he could think of nothing that would make them leave a houseful of guests unattended for no good reason.

'I am afraid I have no idea, sir. The master did not say.' Bowing stiffly, the butler quietly walked away to resume his duties.

Adam stroked his chin thoughtfully. Something was amiss. His mind sought for some plausible explanation to the puzzle but try as he might, he could find none. Even if Amy had been taken ill, it was highly unlikely that both of his parents would have escorted her home on tonight of all nights. But then he had seen Amy earlier in the evening and she had looked radiant and the very picture of good health.

As he stood there pondering, his eyes lit on his wife, who was standing at the far end of the hallway with a sly little smile dancing about her lips. She was obviously very much the worse for drink and was looking decidedly dishevelled.

'Do you know where my mother and father have gone?' he asked her coldly.

She grinned and leaned towards him, causing some of her whisky to splash over the rim of her crystal glass, down the front of her dress and on to the fine Persian carpet beneath them.

'Oh *yesh*, I know where they've gone all right.' Her voice was full of spite and her words slurred. Not wishing to make a spectacle of themselves in front of their guests, Adam took her arm and none too gently led her into the library, closing the door firmly behind them.

'Well?' he demanded impatiently. 'You say that you know where my parents and Amy have gone, so perhaps you would care to enlighten me.'

Enjoying his obvious concern she took another long slow swig of her drink before replying, 'Gladly.' She leaned towards him, sneering maliciously, 'It appears that their little country bumpkin isn't quite the angel they thought. She came to the party this evening wearing your precious sister's locket. You must remember the one? They had it made for her especially for her eighteenth birthday.'

He stepped away from her and gripped the edge of the desk as her whisky-smelling breath fanned his face. But the look of distress only seemed to enrage her more and now she spat, 'So come on then. How do you think the likes of her would have acquired that, eh? A common little ribbon-weaver's trollop? I think the answer is as clear as day, don't you? She must have stolen it! And now she will be getting her comeuppance – and not before time, that's what I say.'

As his chin sank to his chest she smiled with satisfaction. But then slowly he raised his head, and the look he gave her seemed to have a sobering effect on her, for never in her life had she seen such hatred, raw and burning.

'You'd like it if she was a thief, wouldn't you?' he said through gritted teeth. 'For you seem to have developed the same jealousy for Amy that you did for Jessica – though neither of them ever did you an injustice. But I'll tell you now: if that girl has my sister's locket I will stake my life that

345

there is a reasonable explanation for it, for I will not believe that she is a thief.'

'Oh *yes*, I thought you would defend the little whore,' she retaliated. 'Don't think I don't know what has been going on. She's your mistress, isn't she? That's why you have moved into the bed in the dressing room and why you won't allow me to come to the house in London any more with you, isn't it? *Isn't it?*' she screamed.

'Don't be so ridiculous, woman,' Adam stormed, with his fists clenched tightly at the sides of him. 'Amy is a mere girl and has never been anything to me other than a very talented designer. You have a mind like a cesspit because I tell you now, she is more of a lady than you will *ever* be, no matter where her roots are. And as for moving from your bed because of her ... I'll tell you now, I need no other woman as an excuse to move from your bed. If you must know, I moved out of our room because I can no longer stand anything about you. Not your looks, your nature, nor even the smell of you. So how do you like *that?* There was a time when I worshipped the very ground you walked on, Eugenie. But you soon put paid to that, with your tantrums and your airs and graces. Why, even tonight you have made a complete spectacle of yourself. I almost sank into a pit of despair with your treatment, and you would have ruined me had I not put a stop to your frivolous spending.'

She stepped back from him as if he had slapped her in the face, for she'd never seen him so angry.

'H ... how *dare* you speak to me like this,' she sputtered indignantly. 'Why, if I were to tell my father how you were treating me, he would–'

'Stop right there,' he growled. 'For that is *exactly* what I wish you would do. Please – go and tell your father. Although I doubt he would want to hear. Looking back, I am sure he must have been glad to be rid of you, just as I would be.'

Her mouth gaped, giving her the look of a simpleton as she stared back at him incredulously.

'What do you mean?' A note of fear had crept into her voice but his heart had finally hardened against her.

'I mean just this. I have had a bellyful of your spoiled, unpleasant, jealous nature. I cannot believe that I *ever* loved you – or indeed ever saw anything in you that was worthy of love. You have done your best over the years to make me bankrupt and miserable. Nothing was ever good enough for you, not even when I bought you the house of your choice in London, which was way beyond my means – as well you knew. Even that was not good enough for you, was it? You then went on a spending spree, filling it with every single stick of furniture that took your fancy until in the end I was forced to sell the whole lot at a loss. But it is done now. I shall instruct the coachman to take you to your father's house, and on Boxing Day I will have all your belongings packed up and sent on to you. You will, never, *ever* darken my door again. And if you do, I should tell you that I shall not be responsible for the consequences.'

Realising that she had gone too far, she held her hand out to him pleadingly, but he slapped it away in disgust.

'Our marriage is over, Eugenie.' His voice was colder than the snow that lay on the ground out-

347

side. 'My lawyer will be contacting you in due course at your father's address.'

'No, Adam ... *please.* You can't do this to me.'

It was his turn to sneer now as he turned away from her and headed towards the door. 'I think you will find that I *can* – and will. My only regret now is that I did not do it long ago.'

As he turned to look back at her florid face just one last time he could see nothing at all of the girl he had once fallen in love with.

'Goodbye,' he said quietly. 'I cannot say that it has been a pleasure to know you. It seems to me now that your only attribute was the fact that you were born with a silver spoon in your mouth, the only daughter of a titled family. But unfortunately it did not serve to make you a better person. On the contrary, perhaps that is why you lack one single ounce of love or compassion, because you were spoiled shamelessly. At this moment I can feel nothing but pity for you, for I see a long lonely life stretching before you. Unless, of course, you are fortunate enough to snare another man who is as big a fool as I was – but that I very much doubt.'

She began to weep noisily but her tears could no longer reach him and he stepped into the hallway, closing the door between them, praying as he did so that he would never have to look upon her face again for as long as he lived. He stood for some seconds with his head bowed gripping tight to the ornate brass door handle as her muffled sobs reached him through the heavy oak door.

It was there that the butler found him some minutes later. He had been serving the guests with glasses of sparkling champagne from a silver tray that was balanced expertly on one hand, but noting the young master's obvious distress he approached him tentatively.

'Is there anything I can get for you, sir?' he asked respectfully.

As Adam raised his head the torment in his eyes was terrible to behold.

'No, Mason, there is nothing you can get for me – unless you can give me a clear conscience,' he answered, and then before the confused eyes of the other man he pulled himself heavily from the door and marched out into the snow, without a word of explanation.

Once outside, he picked his way round to the rear of the house and slipped into the stable-block. The smell of hay and horseflesh met him, and the horses whinnied a greeting as he passed. But tonight, instead of stopping to stroke them as he normally did, he stumbled by them all, even Pepperpot his beloved mount, and made his way to a hay bale, on to which he collapsed before placing his head in his hands. Everything was such a mess and he could not envisage life ever returning to normal again. The sound of movement from above went unnoticed by him until Seth appeared on a rickety staircase that led up to his living quarters above. His braces were dangling about his knees and he held aloft an oil lamp as he shouted into the gloom, 'Hello, who's there?'

'It ... it's me, Seth.'

Hearing his master's voice, the man snapped his braces into place and climbed down the rest of the stairs to join him.

'Master Adam – why, whatever are you doin'

out here? An' why did the master an' mistress go harin' off earlier on? We got a message that they wanted the carriage made ready straight away, an' Bobby drove 'em off somewhere.'

'It's a long story, Seth,' Adam choked out, and when he offered no further explanation, Seth shuffled from foot to foot uncomfortably. There was a bad feeling in the pit of his stomach but seeing that the master was in no mood to expand on his explanation he said quietly, 'Well, I'll get away back up to me missus then, sir. Should I be able to get you anythin', just give me a shout, eh?'

'Can you give me a clear conscience, Seth?'

Adam raised his head to look into the man's perplexed face and then laughed softly. A cold bitter laugh that made the hairs on Seth's arms stand to attention. 'No, I thought not – so get away to your family and thank the Lord that you have them.'

Seth hovered for a moment, staring into the man's strained face before turning slowly and making his way back upstairs. Something was afoot this evening and he had an awful premonition that whatever it was, it was going to have repercussions on all of them.

Chapter Twenty-Four

With her old heart pounding, Molly stood for some time with her arm tightly about Amy's shoulders. Then, after taking a deep breath and composing herself as best she could, she nodded towards the old horsehair sofa and told Mr and Mrs Forrester, 'You'd better sit yerselves down.'

For a second, it appeared that Mr Forrester was not going to follow her wishes, but then he flicked aside the tails of his coat and sat down next to his wife, his eyes still firmly fixed on Molly.

She herself gently pressed Amy from her before settling into her rocking chair, and Toby instantly took Amy's hand protectively.

Molly had always feared that this day would come, and now that it had she did not quite know where to start.

A terrible silence settled on the room for some moments broken by Samuel when he said quietly, 'There is something amiss here.'

He had come prepared to be angry, but strangely now that he was here his anger had faded at the sight of the old woman who obviously adored Amy more than life itself. The dwelling he was in was humble to say the very least, and yet he could not help but be impressed, for everywhere he looked was as neat and tidy as a new pin. It was also very comfortable, with touches of Amy's impeccable taste evident in the drape of the curtains and the finishing touches about the room. And try as he might, he could not imagine Molly being a thief. She might be working-class but she had an air of quiet dignity and honesty about her. In fact, he realised with a little shock that in many ways she reminded him of his late mother, who had begun her life in a cottage no better than this one.

'Perhaps if we are honest with each other we may be able to get to the bottom of this,' he said quietly. 'And seeing as it was I that barged into your home, perhaps I should be the one to start?'

Molly nodded numbly and after glancing at his wife's tear-stained face, Mr Forrester sighed and began, 'Many years ago, when my children were young, my wife and I sent our son to a private school as soon as he was old enough. Naturally, we wanted the very best education for both of our children so Jessica was tutored at home by a governess. When she reached her teens we employed a private tutor for her. His name was Robert Chamberlain and he came highly recommended. He was a very personable young man in his early twenties when I first employed him, and I was more than satisfied with my daughter's progress under his tuition. Robert was an orphan, but as time went on, he became almost like one of our family.'

Samuel paused to glance at his wife, and when she nodded he gulped deep in his throat and continued, 'He stayed in my employ for some years and Jessica grew to be extremely fond of him. Perhaps a little too fond, but my wife and I did not see what was staring us straight in the face; she was falling in love with him.'

He stopped again as the memories came flooding back, then pulling himself together with an effort he went on, 'One evening, Jessica came to me in my study. At that time she was nearly nineteen years old and had turned into a beautiful young woman, in looks as well as in nature. I confess she was the apple of my eye and I had high hopes of a good marriage for her. But that night she dashed all my hopes to the ground when she told me that she was in love with Robert and asked for my permission for them to be married.'

352

By now Josephine was sobbing softly and he turned to her and gently squeezed her arm. 'What I did next was unforgivable, for in my ignorance I told her that I would rather see her dead than married to a humble tutor. She pleaded with me to change my mind, but her request had come as such a shock that I refused to be moved. In my rage I told her that I intended to banish Robert from the house the very next day and I forbade her from ever seeing him again. I also told her that if she disobeyed me, then she must go too.' He visibly shuddered as pictures of that terrible long-ago night flashed in front of his eyes.

'By the next morning I had calmed down a little,' he admitted. 'And so I sent one of the maids to ask both Jessica and Robert to join me in my study. But when she checked their rooms she found them both empty. They had run away together during the night. I was frantic with worry and regret, for I knew by then that I had behaved very foolishly. I scoured the town and all the outlying villages all that day and the next, looking for them – but they were nowhere to be found. It was as if they had disappeared into thin air, and despite all my best efforts, I have never been able to trace them from that day to this.'

His eyes were so full of torment that Molly's heart went out to him.

'So, perhaps you will understand now, Mrs Ernshaw, why the sight of Amy wearing Jessica's locket affected us as it did, and perhaps you will be kind enough to explain to us how you came by it and put us out of our misery?'

Molly lowered her head. It was time to confess to

the lie she'd lived ever since that fateful Christmas Eve so many years ago. She'd no doubt whatsoever that once the truth was told, her relationship with Amy would never be the same again, but what other option was there? The thought of losing this girl, whom she had loved as her own, was more than she could bear, but now the truth could no longer be avoided and so she looked at Amy with all the love she felt for her shining in her eyes.

'I'm afraid yer won't like what I'm about to tell yer, my love,' she whispered brokenly. 'And I just pray that when I've finished, you'll forgive me for the lies I've told yer, for I *swear* that anything I have ever done was in what I thought was your best interest.'

Wrenching her eyes away from Amy's she now raised her chin and looked Mr Forrester directly in the eye as she told him, 'Twenty-two years ago to this very night I was makin' me way home from the ribbon factory in Abbey Street where I worked. It were a wicked night, much as it is now, wi' the snow fallin' thick an' fast. I was tired out an' longin' for me fireside, so I decided to take the short-cut through the parish churchyard. It was as I sheltered in the doorway that I heard a whimper, like someone in pain. I don't mind tellin' yer, me heart were in me throat, but after a time I plucked up me courage and ventured nearer – an' that was when I found this poor young woman who looked to be in a right bad way. She were burnin' up wi' fever an' I thought she must be delirious, 'cos she kept askin' me to take her baby, though there were no baby to be seen. Anyway, I decided that I would have to run an' fetch help for her. There were no

354

way I could have carried her, so I set off, after taking the bag at her side, as she insisted. I were hopin' that there would be somethin' inside it that would give me an inklin' as to who she was, so I could contact her kin for her.'

The room was so quiet now that you could have heard a pin drop, and after wetting her dry lips, Molly forced herself to go on. 'I got back here as quick as I could, an' then I ran to fetch Bessie, Toby's mam.' She cocked her thumb at him. 'Then, after I'd explained what had happened, Bessie ran all the way back to the church, bless her heart, to see how the poor girl was before she ran to get a doctor for her. But when she got back there the doorway was empty, though how the poor lamb ever managed to walk away, I shall never know, 'cos I would have swore she were knockin' at heaven's door.'

Molly paused to dab at her eyes with the hem of her pinnie. She could remember the poor young woman's face as clear as day.

'Anyway, when Bessie got back we opened the girl's bag ... an' that's when we found Amy. Cold an' as still as death she was, an' at first me an' Bessie thought she was dead, but Bessie worked on her, rubbin' her little body an' warmin' her, an' eventually she let out a little cry. Then we were up against the problem o' what we should do with her. There was nothin' in the bag to tell us who she was 'cept for that locket, a shawl an' a few clothes. It seemed the only place for her was the workhouse but I couldn't stand the thought o' that. After all, the way I saw it, the poor little mite hadn't asked to be born. So me an' Bessie got our heads together an' decided that I should keep her an' say that she was me daughter's child. Since afore she could walk she's allus called me Gran, an' we've been together ever since. As for the locket, I'd forgotten about it until Bessie reminded me. I was going to give it to Amy last year, for her twenty-first but then your late mother, sir, had left her that beautiful necklace.'

She stopped as Amy gawped at her in amazement, and the silence seemed to stretch on forever until Mr Forrester suddenly said, 'But that still doesn't explain who the girl in the doorway was, nor how she came to have Jessica's locket.'

'I know who she was,' Josephine whispered and all eyes turned to her. 'That girl in the doorway was our Jessica.'

'But why would she be there? And where was Robert?' Samuel snapped indignantly.

'I fear we may never know the answer to that question, Samuel,' his wife told him softly. 'Unless, God willing, she is still alive somewhere and decides to forgive us and come home one day. But looking beyond that ... don't you see what this means?'

Samuel stared back at her in bewilderment. 'No, I don't.'

'*Look* at Amy, Samuel! Who does she remind you of, in both looks and nature? Can't you see it? If that poor girl in the church doorway *was* Jessica, then Amy must be our granddaughter. Haven't we always said how much she reminds us of our daughter?'

Samuel blinked as he stared at Amy's astounded face and the tears began to roll unashamedly down his cheeks. Of course, Josephine must be right. Amy had the same auburn hair, the same dark eyes, even the same nature as his beloved daughter, which would probably account for why he and his wife had always felt so drawn to her.

Samuel then addressed Amy, saying 'If you are in fact our granddaughter, my dear, perhaps you would like to come home with us?'

Amy kept her arm wrapped about her gran's shoulders.

'*This* is my home,' she told him firmly and ever the peacemaker, Josephine caught his arm.

'She is quite right, Samuel. And now I think we should leave. We all have a lot to think about, and we also have a houseful of guests back at The Folly.'

'Of course.' Instantly repentant, Samuel looked at Amy. 'Perhaps you could call at The Folly tomorrow and we can discuss this further? Mrs Ernshaw, I know it will be Christmas Day, but could you spare her for a couple of hours tomorrow? I can send the carriage at three o'clock. Amy, will you come?'

'Yes, sir.'

'Oh, I think we could dispense with the "sir" now, don't you? In future you can call me–'

'*Samuel!*'

'Yes, my dear.' Samuel meekly followed his wife to the door and after flashing one last smile towards his newfound granddaughter, the couple were about to go on their way when Molly spoke up feebly.

'The bag,' she said, almost at the end of her strength. 'Amy, love – your poor mother's bag –

357

the one we found yer in. It's still up in the attic where it's been these many years, with the clothes yer were wrapped in still inside it. Them clothes rightly belong to yer new grandparents, pet, an' so does the bag. Happen they'll like to have it – so run up an' fetch it, eh, like the good girl you are.' She wiped her eyes again on her pinnie, before going on, 'It's a tapestry bag, love – you'll see it in the corner.'

Without another word, Amy ran lightly up the stairs and the four people waiting below heard her move around above as she climbed into the attic; there was a silence, and then, more slowly this time, her footsteps came back down the stairs.

Reappearing in the doorway, Amy had a smudge of dust on her pale cheeks, and she had caught a corner of her evening dress on something in her haste, and ripped it. Advancing towards Josephine Forrester, she held out the bag, her heart too full for speech.

For a second, the woman hid her face in her husband's jacket, before taking a shuddering breath and opening the tapestry bag. One by one, she produced the items within – the pretty blouse and well-worn black skirt, the blue silk shawl ... and her sobs were heart-rending as she choked out, 'These are hers – these are Jessica's! Dear God, I want my daughter back! Samuel, where is she, *where is she?*'

Taking hold of his wife's shoulders, Samuel held her while she cried, then led her gently out of the cottage and into the swirling snow. The sound of her grief could still be heard as the carriage rolled away into the night.

As soon as they had gone, Toby also sidled towards the door. 'I reckon you two could do wi' some time on yer own,' he said, thoughtful as ever, and Amy nodded at him gratefully as he slipped away, closing the cottage door softly behind him.

'Whyever didn't you tell me all this before, Gran?' she whispered.

''Cos I wanted you to feel that you belonged,' Molly answered weakly. The evening's events had taken their toll on her. 'But just think who you really are. The Forresters will want you to move in wi' them now.'

'The Forresters have been very good to me and I am very fond of them,' Amy told her truthfully. 'But *you* are still my gran in my eyes, and you always will be. Things will go on as before.'

Molly nodded, but deep inside she wondered, would they?

The Forresters arrived home to find the party in full swing. The musicians were playing a romantic waltz and the noise of talk and laughter was loud. The guests were still having a wonderful time. By contrast, the atmosphere in the hall was extremely unpleasant.

Seeing his son there, Samuel burst out with: 'Adam, you will never believe what has happened! Amy was wearing your sister's locket this evening, and when we went to question Molly Ernshaw as to where she had got it, she told us the most extraordinary tale. I will explain it all in detail later, but the outcome of it is that young Amy is actually your niece – can you believe that?

She is your sister's child. Which means that Jessica might still be alive somewhere, so–'

He fell silent as he saw the plump figure of his daughter-in-law Eugenie standing on the staircase wrapped in a warm cloak with a suitcase at her feet. She had heard every word he had said.

'So, the brown-eyed girl will remain,' she snarled, her lips curled back from her teeth. 'Well, I hope she rots in *hell*. But then I should have expected no more of this family. You *all* came from the gutter and you shall return to it, if I have my way. My father always told me that I could do better for myself than marry into the Forresters and their vulgar life in trade, and now I wish that I had listened to him.'

'What's going–'

Adam held up his hand to stay his father's words. 'Eugenie is leaving, now that the coach is back,' he said, and Samuel saw that his face was drawn and anxious.

'He's turning me out – like a common parlour-maid,' Eugenie spat to her astounded in-laws.

'And not a second before time,' her husband told her coldly. 'Now kindly leave, and may I never have to look on your face again.'

'You are going to regret this night for as long as you live.' She gathered her cloak about her and sailed out into the night as Adam sagged against the wall. This was certainly turning out to be a Christmas Eve that they would all remember for the rest of time.

Over the next weeks, as 1852 was left behind, the scandalous news of Amy's true identity swept through the town like wildfire, and sometimes she wondered if life would ever be the same again. She was now acknowledged as Amy Elizabeth Hannah Forrester. Her newfound grandparents had already seen their lawyer and included her in their Will, and she was suddenly related to one of the wealthiest men in the country.

Her mother's old room at The Folly had been prepared for her and was kept ready for her at all times, but up until now Amy had not used it once. Molly's hacking cough had returned with a vengeance and, true to her word, Amy had remained at the cottage with her.

In many ways it had been a bittersweet time for all of them, each and every one had all had a lot to come to terms with, not least of all Adam, whose disastrous marriage was now well and truly over, all but for the marriage certificate that stated otherwise. Eugenie had returned to her father's stately home on the borders of Leicestershire, and rumour had it that she was turning into a hopeless drunk. Adam himself was not surprised, he had seen it coming for a long, long time, but even so his parents were concerned about him because he seemed to have slipped into a deep depression. He had said little about the connection with Amy, and still treated her respectfully when they met, but Samuel and Josephine had noticed that he seemed to be taking to his room more and more, as if he was avoiding her. They briefly wondered if he was concerned at having to share his inheritance with her, but quickly dismissed the idea. It was not in Adam's nature to be avaricious. They eventually decided that it could only be the break-up of his marriage that was affecting him. After all, they still remembered only too well how obsessed he had once been with Eugenie, and so they left him to his own devices.

Samuel was pleased to see that Josephine loved having a granddaughter, and there seemed to be a spring in her step once more, once she had recovered from the revelations of Christmas Eve. But he knew it wasn't just due to the girl. Josephine was now firmly convinced that Jessica was still alive somewhere, and had once again begun to hope that one day, they would all be reunited. She had contacted Mr Burrows, the private detective they had employed many years ago when Jessica first went missing, and informed him about Amy, urging him to resume his search for Jessica and assuring him that money was no object.

Because of the circumstances which had brought Amy into her life, neither Samuel nor Josephine had ever once blamed Molly for keeping the secret of Amy's birth, not for a single second. They accepted that she had only acted in what she had thought were the best interests of the child and had a huge admiration for her. They had offered her, as well as Amy, a home within Forrester's Folly, and when she refused that, they again offered her a cottage in the grounds. But Molly refused to leave her home and they bowed to her wishes with good grace.

Of them all it was Amy's life that had changed the most, and sometimes she found herself in a total state of confusion. The Forresters had begged her to refer to them as Grandmama and Grandfather, and this she tried to do whenever she could remember to. But mostly out of habit she would find herself addressing them as sir and ma'am, at which they would smile and gently correct her. From choice, she still accompanied her grandfather on his business trips to London, but he would no longer allow her to work as many hours as before. It never ceased to amuse her when the seamstresses and the staff in the townhouse in Sloane Street addressed her as Miss Amy, respectful of her newfound status. All that is except Nancy, who would never be able to think of her as anyone but the girl she had befriended. This more than suited Amy, who was finding it all rather overwhelming.

Her grandfather had written to Monsieur Laroque, who was delighted to hear of Amy's true heritage. François's letters had slowed somewhat lately, but now they began to come again with regularity, and his father had high hopes of the two families becoming united through the two young people. After all, Amy was now an heiress in her own right and a supremely suitable bride for his son.

Chapter Twenty-Five

One sunny afternoon, Molly, Josephine and Amy were taking a gentle stroll up the lane leading from their cottage when a spasm of coughing wracked Molly's body. Instantly concerned, Amy stopped and placed her arm about her shoulders.

'Come on, Gran,' she urged. 'Let's get you home, eh? It might be springtime but there's still a nip in the air and you ought to be indoors. Coming for a walk was a silly idea. I thought the fresh air would do you good.'

Molly nodded, her eyes streaming from the coughing bout as she banged at her bony old chest until her breath returned.

Josephine was also concerned and taking Molly's elbow she turned her about. 'Why don't you come and stay at The Folly for a few days, Mrs Ernshaw, just until you are recovered?' she pleaded. 'I could get our doctor in to take a look at you.'

Molly stubbornly shook her head. 'There ain't no place like yer own four walls when you ain't feelin' up to scratch, though I thank yer kindly fer the offer. An' will yer *please* stop callin' me Mrs Ernshaw? Me name is Molly.'

Amy and Josephine exchanged an amused smile as they helped the old woman towards the cottage and at the door, Josephine told them, 'Right well, I must be off now. Are you quite sure that there is nothing you need?'

'Nothing at all, thank you,' Amy assured her. 'I'll be up to The Folly this afternoon, so long as Gran is all right.'

'Then I shall get Cook to make you one of your favourite Victoria sponge cakes for tea, and another for you to bring home for Molly,' Josephine told her as she turned towards the carriage. 'Goodbye for now.'

'Bye,' Molly answered. She was getting to quite like the woman and found herself looking

364

forward to her popping in, which she seemed to be doing more and more of late.

Amy helped Molly hobble into the kitchen just as Bessie bustled towards them, wildly flapping an envelope.

'It's for you, Amy,' she told her breathlessly. 'Another letter from Paris, by the looks of it. I bet it's from that François. It came just after you'd set off fer yer stroll.'

Amy's heart missed a beat just as it always did when she heard from him. She slipped the letter into her coat pocket as Bessie looked at Molly leaning heavily on Amy's arm.

Noting her pale face, she asked, 'Has she been coughin' again?'

Before Amy could answer, Molly snapped, 'I ain't invisible, yer know, Bessie Bradley, an' I am capable of answerin' fer meself. I ain't quite in me dotage just yet. I can't understand why you pair keep fussin'. It's only a bloody cough when all's said an' done.'

Bessie nodded as Amy pursed her lips to stop herself from grinning.

'Aye, well, that's as maybe, yer stubborn old sod, but let's get yer sat down, eh?' With that, Bessie grabbed Molly's other elbow and she and Amy propelled her towards her rocking chair. Bessie went to fill the kettle at the sink as Amy sank down at the table to read her letter. As her eyes scanned the page her face lit up, and Bessie asked curiously. 'Had some good news, have yer?'

'I can hardly believe it,' Amy gasped. 'François is coming to England this summer to visit.' She read the letter again to convince herself that it was true as Bessie looked on with mixed feelings. She loved Amy almost as much as Molly did and wanted nothing more than to see her happy. But oh, what a shame that she couldn't have found happiness with her Toby!

'Gran, you'll be able to meet François at last,' Amy bubbled as she waggled the letter in the air. It was full of love and endearments, and the young woman's heart was singing as she launched into yet another description of his many virtues.

Molly and Bessie exchanged a glance, and, could Bessie have known it, Molly was feeling much as she did. But then, if this Frenchman was the one that Amy wanted, she was glad he was coming at last. Hopefully, his visit would set a seal on Amy's future, and although he wasn't the one Molly would have chosen for her girl, still she might live long enough to see her settled. After how she had been feeling of late she had sometimes doubted it. But then, she had the consolation of knowing that Amy would always be well cared for, no matter what the outcome with the Frenchman. It was already more than obvious that her newfound grandparents doted on her, and the knowledge gave Molly comfort.

Amy's excitement was still as great when she reached The Folly that afternoon, and her grandparents looked on with amusement as she waved François' letter at them, although they did not seem to be as surprised at the news as she had expected them to be. The reason why became clear when Josephine patted the seat at the side of her and told Amy, 'Come and sit beside me, dear. We have another piece of news that you might like to hear.'

Immediately curious, Amy crossed the room to sit at her grandmother's side and Josephine squeezed her hand affectionately.

'It just so happens that your grandfather and I also received a letter from Monsieur Laroque this morning,' she explained. 'He informed us of his son's visit and I must admit it got us to thinking, so your grandfather has already replied, inviting the whole of the Laroque family to accompany him. We have all had a lot of adjusting to do over the last few months and we wanted to somehow officially welcome you into the family – and what better way to do it than to celebrate with a ball that could coincide with their visit?'

Momentarily speechless, Amy gaped at them, and then for the first time she tentatively put her arm around the woman who she had so recently discovered was her grandmother and hugged her, causing Josephine to flush with delight.

'Oh, that will be wonderful!' she cried, clapping her hands with delight.

Her grandfather winked at her mischievously. 'I have a strange feeling that once François arrives, this could well turn into a double celebration,' he told her and now it was Amy's turn to blush as the meaning of his words sank in.

Josephine was in her element and every bit as excited as Amy. 'I intend this ball to be the best the town has ever seen,' she declared. 'We shall skimp on nothing, and of course, my dear, you shall *have* to design us each a new gown and then we can go together to choose the materials and your grandfather can set the seamstresses to work to get them done in time for us.'

The two women spent the next hour chattering on about the forthcoming event as Samuel looked on indulgently, but then glancing at the clock, Amy reluctantly took her leave of them, kissing them both shyly on the cheek as she slipped from the room.

She lay in her bed that night trying to picture François' face in the darkness, but try as she might his features eluded her. Still, she thought, that will soon be put to rights now, for in just a few short weeks they would be back together again. And on that happy note she drifted off to sleep.

The next few weeks passed in a flurry of preparation and activity but at last the day came when Amy found herself standing on the railway platform, along with Mr and Mrs Forrester, staring down the line as her heart hammered in her chest. At last the train appeared, belching thick black smoke into the cloudless blue sky. When eventually it drew to a halt she scanned the carriage doors as the stationmaster threw them open, and then at last there he was, stepping down on to the platform, even taller and handsomer than she remembered him. Mr Forrester hurried to welcome Monsieur and Madame Laroque and Adeline, and Amy and François stood there, their hands clasped, staring deep into each other's eyes. François kissed her hand tenderly with the smile that never failed to charm her as he told her, 'Ma petite, you have grown even more beautiful, if that is possible.'

'I can hardly believe you are really here,' Amy

whispered. 'So very much has happened since we last met.'

'Ah yes, but they are good things, no? Monsieur Forrester, or should I say your grandpapa, has informed us that he has discovered you are actually a part of his family, and we have rejoiced for you all. Now I am very much looking forward to seeing your home, Forrester's Folly.'

'Oh no, François,' Amy quickly corrected him. 'I do have a room there should I ever wish to use it, but I still live with my gran. You know ... the one I told you all about? I am longing for you to meet her. I'm sure you will like her.'

Slightly confused, he frowned and said, 'But surely, *ma petite*, now that you know that the Forresters are your true family, should your loyalty not lie with them? You will after all be very rich one day, will you not?'

'Of course I am loyal to them.' Her chin jutted indignantly. 'But you must remember that my gran is the one who brought me up – and as I once told you, I could never leave her. Were I to discover that I was the Queen of England herself, *nothing* will ever change that.'

Seeing that he had annoyed her, François was instantly penitent. 'Do not become agitated,' he implored her. 'I had no wish to cast aspersions on your guardian. But as for never leaving her... Well, I can only hope that by the time I am due to return home I will have changed your mind. And now, *mademoiselle*, allow me to escort you to your carriage, for I fear I have vexed you, and that was not my intention.'

Slightly mollified, Amy took his arm and as the

369

carriage rattled towards The Folly she reverted to her normal cheery self, yet somehow some of the joy had gone out of Francois' arrival and it had not been as she had imagined.

Nevertheless, the atmosphere in the dining room during dinner was pleasant and relaxed. The cook had excelled herself and they were served with a home-made vegetable soup and melon boats, followed by a succulent goose stuffed with herbs picked fresh from the garden that Monsieur Laroque declared was *délicieux*. The dessert was a mouthwatering meringue topping fresh baked apples from the orchard, and at last Monsieur Laroque sat back in his chair, and daintily wiping his little waxed moustache, he sighed contentedly.

'Ah, I am how you say? Fitting to burst!' he exclaimed and everyone laughed.

Shortly afterwards the women retired to the drawing room where they were served with small glasses of sherry whilst the men enjoyed a glass or two of Mr Forrester's finest port from the cellar and huge aromatic cigars in his study.

As the twilight beyond the window gave way to night, the men joined them in the drawing room and Amy rose. 'I shall have to be going now,' she announced quietly.

François' shoulders sagged. 'But surely not so soon, Aimée? We have so much to talk of. Could you not spend the night here, just for once?' His voice was sharp with disappointment but Amy would not be swayed.

'I am afraid that is out of the question,' she told him firmly, although she could not resist a smile at the way he pronounced her name. It never failed to amuse her and she was sure that she would never tire of hearing it. 'I am sorry to leave you so soon, but my gran has been unwell and I don't like to leave her alone for too long. But never mind – we have all of the rest of your stay before us, and tomorrow I shall take you to meet her.'

'You will like her, François,' Mr Forrester interrupted. 'She really is quite an incredible old lady. She has many of the traits that my late mother possessed, one of them being stubbornness, so it's quite hard to determine where Amy inherited hers from.' His eyes were alight with mischief as Amy grinned back at him.

'Then at least let me escort you home in the carriage,' Francois pleaded and eventually Amy agreed.

'Very well then, but just this once. I do actually prefer to walk, but if I do that, you may never find your way back.'

Mr Forrester left the room to order the carriage to be brought to the front of the house and shortly afterwards Amy and François left. The two ladies retired to bed whilst Monsieur Laroque and Mr Forrester discussed business over yet another glass of port.

Eventually, the Monsieur remarked, 'Amy is indeed a most fortunate young woman, I am thinking.'

'Actually, my wife and I consider ourselves to be the fortunate ones.' Mr Forrester flicked his cigar ash into a cut-glass ashtray. 'Amy is an exceptional young woman. She is beautiful, intelligent, talented and warm, and she had brightened our lives already.'

'That I can well believe.' The Frenchman peered at his host from the corner of his eye before proceeding cautiously. 'You may have observed that my son is quite taken with your granddaughter, *monsieur*. My wife and I are very pleased about this, as François has been – how do you English say? – "a bit of a one for the ladies" up until now. My wife was beginning to despair of ever marrying him off, but now that we have discovered that Amy is your granddaughter, we consider she would be a very good match for François and we have high hopes that before our visit is over, he will approach you to ask for her hand in marriage. How would you feel about this, Monsieur Forrester?'

Mr Forrester swirled his port about in his glass and peered into its depth, considering. 'Well, from a purely selfish point of view I would be sad to lose her so soon,' he admitted. 'But if François was asking her for the right reasons and it was what Amy wanted, then I would not stand in their way.'

Monsieur Laroque stared into the fire with a wide smile on his face. 'Then that is good, *monsieur,* and it would certainly cement our partnership. Why, with our two businesses combined there would be no stopping us. Come, let us drink to young love.'

And their glasses clinked merrily together.

The next morning, Amy arrived back at The Folly bright and early. There were just two days to go to the ball and she was buzzing with happiness. Also, today she intended to take François to meet her gran. She found him just leaving the dining room when she slipped into the hallway, and he instantly hurried to meet her. He noticed that she was looking extremely pretty in an elegant sky-blue day suit, with a jaunty little plumed hat perched on her head, and he gazed at her sparkling eyes and rosy dimpled cheeks admiringly.

'Today we shall spend the whole day together, yes?' he asked beseechingly.

Without hesitation she nodded. 'Yes, we shall, François. I am going to show you our shop in town and then I shall take you to meet my gran.'

He clicked together his heels and bowed gallantly. 'I am yours to command, *mademoiselle*.' He laughed as, hand-in-hand, they made their way out into the summer sunshine.

The day turned out to be very enjoyable. Amy gave him a guided tour of her hometown and introduced him to the staff in the shop as well as in the factory. The women were enchanted with him and blushed as he kissed their hands. François obviously found it all very interesting, if tiny compared to Paris.

Amy eventually led him back to the carriage, telling him, 'I shall take you to meet my gran now.'

'Lead the way, *ma petite*,' he agreed, and soon the coach was swinging through Attleborough on its way to the cottage.

When it drew up outside, François jumped out and stared at the humble dwelling. 'This is your home?' he asked.

Amy nodded as he helped her step down from the coach. 'Yes, it is. But do excuse my gran if she is a little quiet, won't you? She hasn't been at all well.'

When they first entered the cluttered little

kitchen, François had to screw his eyes up so that they could adjust to the gloom after the bright sunshine outside. And then he slowly looked around in amazement. The cottage was tiny. He noted the crude dresser and the flagstone floors with gaily-coloured peg rugs scattered here and there, and wondered how two people could manage to live in such a confined space. However, he also noticed that everywhere was sparkling clean and extremely comfortable. As he stood there with his hat held respectfully in his hands, Amy hurried over to an old rocking chair that stood beside a highly polished brass fender that was placed around a low burning fire. Sitting in the chair was an old woman who was eyeing him suspiciously, and advancing on her he held out his hand.

'You must be Madame Ernshaw.' He bestowed his most charming smile on her and then, taking the wrinkled hand that Molly extended to him, he bowed respectfully and kissed it.

'I am that, lad. But yer can call me Molly; everybody else does an' we may as well start as we mean to go on. Now sit yerself down there an' let me have a look at yer.'

Moving his coat-tails to either side of him, François perched uncomfortably on the edge of the sofa.

He saw the pride shining in Amy's eyes as she looked down at the old woman, and as their eyes met he sensed the strong bond between them. It was hard to believe that a young woman as intelligent and beautiful as Amy had grown up in such surroundings and with such a wizened old guardian, but she obviously loved her.

374

Molly brought his thoughts back to her when she asked bluntly, 'So what do yer think o' Nuneaton then?'

Francois flashed her another dazzling smile. 'It is most interesting, *madame.*'

She nodded before turning her attention back to Amy and barking, 'Well, have yer forgot yer manners, gel? Get that kettle on. I'm sure as François could manage a brew an' I know I could. I'm as dry as a bone.'

Not understanding her use of the local slang, François was perplexed, and Amy smothered her laughter with her hand as she told him, 'You will have to excuse Gran. I'm afraid she's not one for putting on airs and graces, as I'm sure you will discover over time.' Then, leaving them to chat, she hurried away to do as Molly had told her.

When the lovers left, Molly sat staring broodily into the fire, and it was there that Bessie found her when she entered the cottage a short time later.

'Well, I saw Amy turn up wi' her handsome Frenchman. What's he like?' she demanded.

Molly dragged her eyes away from the fire and looked up at her, her eyes bleak.

'He don't seem a bad sort, Bessie,' she admitted grudgingly, 'but I'll tell yer now, he ain't the one fer my Amy. They're from two different worlds, as different as chalk from cheese.'

Bessie hitched up her ample bosom before asking cautiously, 'Are yer goin' to tell Amy that?'

'No, I ain't.' Molly shook her head slowly. 'It ain't my place to interfere. Amy's old enough to make her own mind up an' she'll have to learn

375

from her own mistakes, same as we all do. She's movin' in different circles now; hobnobbin' wi' the gentry. O' course, there's no reason why she shouldn't, seein' as it's turned out she's gentry herself. I always told yer I thought she were a cut above, didn't I? But I just worry about her, that's all. She were brought up here, a world away from the types o' places she's visitin' now, an' it's a big change fer her.'

'Yes, you did always say that Amy were somethin' special.' Bessie's head wagged in agreement. 'An' it turned out that you were right. But yer know, Molly, I think underneath all her fancy clothes, Amy is still the same lass that you brought up as yer own, an' it will take a lot more than a fancy-talkin' Frenchman to alter that. She may have the Forresters' blood flowin' through her veins, but it's your morals that she lives by an' it's you that's made her the person she is. Amy's got her head screwed on, so don't go worryin' about her unnecessarily, eh?'

Molly sighed as she pulled her shawl tighter about her scrawny shoulders. At the end of the day all she really wanted was for Amy to be happy.

Chapter Twenty-Six

The day of the ball dawned bright and clear, and Amy skipped about the cottage as she prepared breakfast for her gran and herself. Her own gown and Molly's were pressed and hanging on the back of the door, and every time she looked at them she smiled. She could hardly believe that Molly had agreed to attend the ball with her, and could scarcely wait to show her off, although she was a little apprehensive about how Molly would cope with such a formal occasion. Molly was a home bird through and through, never happier than when she was sitting at her own fireside, but Amy hoped that she would view the event as a treat and enjoy herself.

Once the tea was mashed, she took a cup up to Molly – but the second that she set foot in her room she knew that something was wrong. Her gran's face was as white as the linen pillowcases that she lay upon and her chest was rising and falling rapidly.

'Gran, what's the matter?' Amy cried as panic gripped her.

Molly looked at her wearily. 'Oh, it's just this damn cough again, lass,' she told her in a weak voice. 'It's had me up half the bloody night, so it has, an' I don't feel as if I've been to bed.'

'Right, that's it then. Enough is enough. I'm going to fetch the doctor!' Amy declared, and when Molly began to protest she slammed the cup of tea down on the small chest-of-drawers at the side of the bed and glared at her. 'You can moan as much as you like, Gran, but this has gone on for *quite* long enough. I don't usually go against your wishes, as you well know, but this time I am going to fetch the doctor whether you like it or not.' And so saying, she swung about in a swish of skirts and hurried away.

Amy went through the back door intending to

take the short-cut across the fields and as she banged it to behind her, Bessie, who was in the process of putting a dripping sheet through the mangle in her back yard, called over to her, 'Where are you off to in such a tearin' rush, pet?'

Amy sped past her, shouting across her shoulder, 'I'm going for the doctor. Gran isn't well again so I've put my foot down. She should have let me fetch him weeks ago.'

Bessie nodded at her retreating back as she dried her hands on her coarse calico apron. 'Well, I'm with yer there, gel. You're right, but take yer time an' I'll go an' stay with her till yer get back.' And true to her word Bessie pottered away, leaving the sheet to steam in the warm sunshine.

The doctor arrived almost two hours later. By then, Molly was feeling slightly better. Bessie had helped her to wash and dress, and she was sitting in her chair by the fire.

Even so, the big man tutted when he had finished examining her. 'That's a rare bad chest you have on you there, Mrs Ernshaw,' he scolded. 'You should have seen me sooner and then I could have given you something to stop it from getting to this stage.'

'Pah! You know I ain't never been one fer runnin' to the quack wi' the least little ailment,' she grumbled.

The doctor winked at Amy. 'Happen this time you should have. Now I'm going to give you some linctus and I want you to take it three times a day. And just mind you *do* take it, otherwise Amy will tell me. Besides that, I want you to rest. You're not as young as you used to be, Molly, and

I'm sure that Amy is quite capable of seeing to anything that needs doing, so just do as you're told for a change, eh?'

Molly muttered something under her breath and when he had snapped his bag shut Amy saw him to the door.

'Does this mean that Gran shouldn't go to the ball tonight?' she asked.

The doctor looked at her regretfully. 'I'm afraid it does, Amy. It wouldn't do her any good at all in her present condition. If we are to clear that chest of hers she should stay in the same temperature.'

Amy was unable to hide her disappointment as Bessie squeezed her arm sympathetically. 'Never mind, love, there's absolutely no reason why *you* shouldn't still go. Me an' Toby will see as she's all right, I promise. Those grandparents of yours have gone to a lot o' trouble to organise this affair, so you just get ready an' leave the rest to us. Yer gran will be as right as ninepence, you'll see. An' she'd hate for yer to miss it.'

Amy looked at her kindly neighbour, feeling as if she was being torn in two. One half of her wanted to stay with her gran. The other half of her recognised the truth of Bessie's words, for the Forresters had pulled out all the stops to arrange this ball in her honour. It looked set to be an occasion that would be remembered for a long, long time to come, so how could she let them down?

Seeing the dilemma she was in, Molly, who had been listening intently, added her comments to Bessie's. 'Don't even *think* o' not goin', my gel,' she told her sternly. 'I shall be perfectly all right here wi' Bessie an' Toby. To tell yer the truth, I'm relieved. Yer know I ain't never been one fer fancy dos. But I ain't half lookin' forward to seein' you all dolled up in yer glad rags.'

Knowing when she was beaten, Amy sighed heavily then set about cleaning the cottage. She was no match for her gran and Bessie when they stood together, and well she knew it.

Amy was still getting ready in her bedroom that evening when Toby arrived at the cottage and she heard her gran chatting away to him. Molly loved nothing better than for Toby to sit and read to her, and it was a comfort to know that she would be leaving her in safe hands.

Turning her attention back to the reflection in the mirror, Amy eyed herself critically. Deciding that her gown was too sophisticated for her hair to hang loose, she began to pile it on to the top of her head. Once it was clipped into place she began to tease it into long fat ringlets that framed her heart-shaped face. The springing curls seemed to have developed a life of their own and she struggled with the style for some time, wishing that Nancy were there to help her. Nancy could do in minutes what it always took Amy ages to achieve. But at last it was done and rising from her dressing-table stool she shook out her stiff taffeta skirts and headed downstairs to the kitchen.

Molly and Toby were deep in conversation but they stopped speaking when she entered and gazed towards her in awe. Her gown was in a shade of palest gold, which complemented her thick auburn hair, and it was richly embroidered with silk burgundy thread all around its low-cut

380

neckline. Apart from the embroidery the dress was perfectly plain and she wore no jewellery whatsoever, which only seemed to add to the stunning effect.

Deeply embarrassed at the way they were staring at her, Amy flushed. 'It's very good of you to come round and stay with Gran, Toby,' she told him sincerely. 'I hope that Annie didn't mind.'

It was Toby's turn to flush now as he dragged his eyes away from her to stare at the copper pans that were gleaming in the firelight. 'I weren't seein' her tonight anyway as it happens,' he mumbled.

Now that Amy came to think of it she realised that she hadn't seen Annie around for some time. She was just about to comment on the fact when they all heard the sound of the carriage approaching and she dashed away to get her cloak and her evening bag from her room.

Toby was waiting by the door when she came back downstairs and he held her cloak for her while she ran to plant a gentle kiss on Molly's thinning hair.

'Goodnight, Gran. Don't get waiting up for me, I shall likely be late in.'

'Well, just be sure an' have a good time,' Molly said, flapping her hand at her. 'Now get yourself away, gel, an' leave an old woman in peace, eh?'

Amy stood as Toby draped her cloak about her shoulders and just for an instant their eyes met and she found herself thinking how incredibly blue his were... But then the moment was lost as the coachman rapped sharply on the door, and flustered, Amy turned away from him, her heart racing. With a final wave she was gone and Toby felt as if his heart was breaking.

All was in readiness for the ball and Mr Forrester, who was in his study with François, grinned at the poor young man's discomfort as he shuffled from foot to foot. After pouring them both a generous measure of whisky from a sparkling crystal decanter, he pressed a glass into François' hand and smiled.

'Come along then,' he teased. 'Spit it out, man. Whatever it is you wish to ask me must be important, but our guests will be arriving shortly so I suggest you begin.'

François took a great gulp of his whisky, then, raising his eyes to his host's he smiled nervously. 'The thing is, *monsieur*, as I am sure you will have guessed... I have grown extremely fond of your granddaughter. I am, I assure you, in the fortunate position to be able to offer her the best of everything, and as you are her nearest male relative I wondered...' He gulped again as he tugged at his stiff white collar. 'I er ... I have come to ask if you would give me permission to ask for her hand in marriage.'

Staring at Mr Forrester he held his breath as he waited for his reaction, and when the man smiled he visibly relaxed.

'I cannot pretend that this has come as a surprise,' his host stated kindly, hoping to put the young man out of his misery. 'And I thank you for the respect you have shown in coming to me first. I have no objections at all to you proposing to Amy, and I suspect that your proposal will be accepted as I happen to know that she is very fond of you too.'

François beamed before shaking Mr Forrester's hand until the man feared it would drop off. 'Thank you, *monsieur*. I shall ask her this very night and should she accept, you could perhaps make an official announcement at the ball?'

'It would be my pleasure,' Mr Forrester assured him. 'And a most fitting conclusion to your visit. To be honest, your father had already hinted to me of your intentions and I think, like myself, he would be delighted to see the two families united.'

François clicked his heels together and bowed respectfully. 'Thank you again, *monsieur*. And now with your permission I shall go and await Amy's arrival.' And under Mr Forrester's watchful eye he dashed from the room.

Soon after, the Forresters took up their positions at the front door with their guests of honour at their sides, and as the guests began to arrive they formally introduced them. The young women who arrived with their parents flushed and giggled as they were introduced to the handsome young Frenchman, but he simply smiled at them politely, oblivious to their charms as he waited impatiently for Amy to arrive. Samuel and Josephine had hoped that she would prepare for the ball at The Folly so that she could greet their guests with them, but as she had sent word that her gran was ill, and knowing how much she loved the old woman they were just grateful that she had still agreed to come.

At last she swept through the door like a breath of fresh air and hugged her grandparents fondly before taking her place at Francois' side. He guarded her jealously, determined that she should not spend a second with anyone but himself, and when the orchestra finally started with a graceful waltz he took her into his arms and swept her around the dance floor.

The two families looked proudly on as Monsieur Laroque murmured to Samuel, 'I am having the feeling that tonight shall be one to remember,' and he had no way of knowing just how true his words would prove to be.

Josephine positively glowed with pride as she introduced their granddaughter to their guests, while Samuel looked on with a broad smile on his face. The house and gardens were teeming with people and everyone was in fine high spirits. Champagne flowed like water and maids especially hired for the grand occasion flitted here and there replenishing the tables with mouth-watering treats and making sure that everyone's glasses were full.

Even Adam seemed to be making an effort tonight and was mingling with the guests instead of locking himself away in his room as he had tended to do since Eugenie had left. The moon winked as if in approval to hear laughter in the house that had seen so much sadness.

Amy had danced so much that she was breathless, so when the grandfather clock struck ten and François took her by the hand and led her out on to the terrace, she went willingly, glad of a chance of a little fresh air. It was a perfect night. The moon was sailing high in an inky black sky surrounded by millions of stars and Amy sighed happily as Francois' warm arm rested about her slim shoulders. Leaning on the ornate stone balustrade that skirted the terrace she smiled dreamily as she watched two snow-white swans swimming by in perfect harmony on the River Anker that snaked through the grounds. A sly old fox, his bushy tail flying out behind him, suddenly broke from the woods and after doing a quick tour of the lawns for any unsuspecting rabbit that might be loitering there, he disappeared back the way he had come, intent on finding his supper.

Amy smiled as she glanced up at François, but then noting his serious expression she asked, 'Is something wrong? Are you not enjoying yourself?'

'How could anything be wrong when I am with you, *ma petite*? If I appeared grave it was only because I was thinking how very lucky I am to be here with you.'

'Oh, François...'

He raised a finger to her lips and stopped her from going any further. 'No, do not say anything, Aimée, for I have something that I wish very much to ask you... But first I must show you this.'

Delving into his waistcoat pocket he withdrew a small box, and when he opened the lid she found herself staring down at a sparkling diamond ring. She gasped as the moonlight caught its many facets and reflected them a thousandfold, and François smiled at her reaction.

'This, *ma petite*, is for you,' he murmured. 'I had it especially made in Paris. Do you like it?'

'Like it? Why, François, who could *not* like it? It's beautiful,' she stuttered.

He lifted her chin until she was staring into his eyes.

'Aimée, you must know how much I love you by now.' To her consternation he then dropped to one knee. 'Aimée Elizabeth Hannah Forrester, will you please do me the very great honour of becoming my wife?'

Amy's mouth fell into a gape. It was strange. She had dreamed of this moment and yet now that it was actually happening, she felt only numbness. He stood back up and took her into his arms, his eyes gentle as she stared up into his face, perplexed. It was almost as if she was seeing him for the very first time. She was sure that she should be feeling something, anything, and yet all she could feel was this strange numbness, and for now words failed her.

'Come, Aimée,' he prompted urgently when the silence stretched on. 'Do not keep me in suspense. Let me put the ring upon your finger and then we shall go back inside and tell our families the joyous news. I have already spoken to your grandfather and he, like my father, is happy at the thought of our two families merging. Why, think of it – we could spend our lives living between Paris and England, and you need never want for anything again for as long as you live.'

Amy bristled. 'But I never *have* wanted for anything, François – my gran always saw to that,' she told him with a touch of ice in her voice. 'We may have been poor by your standards but what we lacked in material things she more than made up for with love.'

'Of *course* she did, *ma petite*,' he soothed. 'But come ... just think of it. My father is one of the wealthiest men in Paris. You could have everything that your heart has ever desired. Your gran is an old woman – she cannot live forever and I would employ a nurse to see to her every need for the rest of her days.'

'You obviously don't know my gran very well, François,' Amy said stoutly. 'She is a very proud woman. She would never agree to that.'

Seeing his stricken expression, her face softened as her eyes settled on the ring again. Surely there was no problem that was insurmountable? And he *was* very handsome and charming.

And then the words were out before she could stop them. 'Very well, François, I would love to be your wife.'

He gasped with joy and before she knew it he had slipped the ring on to her finger and kissed her soundly on the mouth, and then he was dragging her back into the house. He then left her side for a moment to rush over to Mr Forrester and whisper something into his ear.

Her grandfather looked towards her and smiled as she twisted the ring on her finger. It felt strange, but then Amy supposed that was to be expected. She had never been one for wearing a lot of jewellery.

The next minute, François was at her side again and marching her into the room where people were dancing. Mr Forrester went over to the orchestra and muttered something in the violinist's ear and then the music suddenly stopped while he clambered on to the platform.

'Ladies and gentlemen,' he boomed. 'Do excuse me for interrupting the dancing, but I have something to share with you all. I am delighted to announce that Monsieur François Laroque has just proposed to my beautiful granddaughter and she has agreed to become his wife, so could I ask you all to raise your glasses and drink a toast to the newly engaged couple, please!'

Before Amy knew it she was surrounded by people all kissing and congratulating her, and she suddenly had the urge to escape. Everything was happening so quickly and she felt that she could hardly breathe, but then a hush fell on the room and all the guests turned, their eyes fixed on the doorway. Amy, too, slowly turned – to find Eugenie, who was obviously very drunk, glaring at her.

'*So* ... you managed it then,' she sneered. 'Not only did you wheedle your way into this family but you pretended to be their flesh and blood too. And *now* you have landed yourself a wealthy husband-to-be into the bargain.' She began to advance menacingly on Amy, who could hardly believe what she was hearing. 'Well, let me tell you *this,* you common little trollop: enjoy your happiness while you may, because as God is my witness I can promise you it won't last for long. You just mark my words!'

She raised her hand but at that moment, Adam lunged forward and caught her around the waist, demanding, 'What are you doing here, Eugenie? Why don't you just go home and leave us in peace?'

'But I *am* home, *husband* dear,' she slurred as she trailed her finger down his pale cheek. 'Surely you prefer my company to that of this little guttersnipe?'

Adam began to forcibly drag her from the room as everyone looked on in horror. The wonderful evening had been ruined and besmirched, and they all felt sorry for Adam. Eugenie began to kick and spit as he heaved her considerable bulk out into the hallway and towards the front door.

'You'll be sorry for this,' she screamed as people began to whisper in little groups.

Josephine hurried over to Amy's side and asked anxiously, 'Are you all right, my dear?'

Amy nodded numbly, desperately wanting to run as far away as she could. François had come to stand protectively at her side, a look of complete and utter shock on his face.

'What a dreadful woman!' he shuddered. 'And for this to happen at such a time.'

Amy could feel everyone's eyes boring into her as she stood there, her cheeks aflame.

'I ... I think I should like to go now.' Lifting her skirts she fled into the hallway, completely forgetting her manners as she shouldered her way through the guests assembled there. She did not even stop to get her cloak, and once outside she saw Adam trying to manhandle Eugenie, who was fighting like a wild cat, into her father's carriage. She sped past them so quickly that Eugenie was not even aware that she was there, and then she ran across the lawns as if Old Nick himself was snapping at her heels. By the time she reached the shelter of the woods her chest was heaving and she stopped to lean against a tree as sobs wracked her body. The night had gone disastrously wrong and as the ring on her finger winked in the light from the moon that was filtering through the trees, she wondered if this was a bad omen for the life she was about to embark upon with François.

Inside The Folly, François was distraught and his hosts were trying to calm him as guests drifted silently away, aware that the party was over.

'I must go after her,' he told them as he paced to and fro.

'No, leave her,' Josephine urged. 'She must be feeling humiliated and she needs some time alone to recover. Eugenie has always been jealous of Amy, but what she did tonight of all nights is totally unforgivable. You may rest assured that my husband and I will be contacting her father at the earliest opportunity about her appalling behaviour.'

The young Frenchman moved to the front door and looked across the grounds. Perhaps Mrs Forrester was right. But at least Amy had agreed to become his wife before that dreadful woman had put in an appearance. That was something at least.

Chapter Twenty-Seven

Thankfully, Molly was fast asleep in bed when Amy finally stumbled through the cottage door. Her gown hung in tatters where the fallen branches and the bushes in the woods had torn at it. She pulled it over her head and flung it on to the floor as fresh tears started to her eyes. She supposed that she should not have run off as she had, but she had been so humiliated that she could not bear to stay at The Folly for a second longer. Surely François would understand? She shrugged. There was nothing she could do about it now; the deed was done.

Dropping heavily on to the settle she stared down at the ring on her finger. What was her gran going to say in the morning when she showed it to her and told her that she was now engaged to be married? And what would Toby say...

She shook her head to clear the vision of his face. She was François' fiancée now.

As her thoughts moved back to Eugenie she had to suppress a shudder. The woman was quite mad, but what had she meant when she said, *Enjoy your happiness while you may, because as God is my witness I can promise you it won't last long.*

It was probably just the drink talking, she decided, and snatching up the ruined gown, she wearily headed towards the stairs. She would hide it in the bottom of her wardrobe until she could sneak it out of the house. Better that, than risk her gran finding it. Molly must never know what had happened tonight, it might impede her recovery. Tomorrow morning Amy would tell her what a wonderful evening it had been – and with luck, Molly would never know any differently.

When she came down to breakfast the next morning, Molly was waiting for her, eager to hear how the evening had gone.

'Come an' sit down an' get some o' this porridge inside yer, lass,' she encouraged as she ladled a large helping into a dish. 'An' then I want to hear everythin'.' She noticed that Amy was looking a little pale but put it down to the fact that she had had a late night.

Amy meekly did as she was told; putting off the moment when she would have to tell Molly that she was now engaged to be married. But the opportunity never arose, for as she lifted her spoon, Molly, who was never one to miss much, spotted the glittering ring on her finger.

'Got something to tell me, have yer?' she asked caustically as her heart began to pound. Deep down she had half-expected something like this, but now that the evidence was staring her straight in the eye she was having problems coming to terms with it.

'I ... um ... that is... Well, François proposed to me last night, Gran.' Amy kept her eyes downcast. 'And the fact is, I accepted his proposal. We're engaged to be married.'

Molly tried to push away the memory of the young man's face when he had first entered the cottage. He had looked shocked, as if the place was far below him, but then in all fairness, compared to where he was used to living, it probably was. And Amy obviously loved him, so who was she to stand in their way?

'Let's have a proper look at this ring then,' Molly said, trying to sound cheerful. She lifted Amy's hand and sighed. 'By 'eck, that's a right old bobby dazzler an' no mistake,' she commented. 'An' when is the weddin' to be?'

'Oh, we haven't got that far yet,' Amy told her hastily, and then on a softer note, 'You *are* happy about this, aren't you, Gran?'

'O' course I am,' Molly retorted a little too

quickly. 'All I've ever wanted was to see you happy, an' if this here Frenchman is the one to do that, then that's good enough fer me.'

She sat down opposite Amy and they finished their breakfast in silence. Amy's feelings were in turmoil. She knew she should be feeling over the moon today, but instead she still felt that strange numbness. But then, she consoled herself, after Eugenie's disgusting display the night before, she could hardly expect to feel on top of the world. Eugenie had ruined what should have been one of the happiest nights of her life. No doubt the happy feelings would come in time, when she had had time to apologise to everyone at The Folly for running off as she had. And that would have to be sooner rather than later. It was no good putting it off, she would have to face them at some point and time was precious as François would be returning to Paris in less than two weeks' time now.

In less than an hour she was on her way back to The Folly again, slightly subdued and not feeling like a newly engaged woman at all.

As she approached Mary's cottage, she saw her old friend in the garden, pegging out a great basketful of washing to the line.

'Amy.' She spat a wooden peg out of her mouth and beamed from ear to ear. 'Congratulations. Joe told me about your engagement this morning. You must be floating on air, although I dare say that minx, Eugenie, took the shine off the night fer yer, turnin' up as she did out o' the blue like that.'

Amy suppressed a grin. News spread like wildfire in this neck of the woods and she had no doubt that everyone'd be talking about it today.

'It did rather,' she admitted.

Mary had already hurried over to the fence to join her, and grabbing her hand she admired the beautiful ring. 'Eeh, whoever would 'ave thought it, eh?' She sighed. 'Our little Amy related to the Forresters an' about to marry a rich Frenchman into the bargain!' She would have gone on but at that moment the sound of crockery smashing carried to them from within the cottage and she hastily turned about. 'Sorry, I shall have to go an' see what them pair o' little buggers is up to,' she gasped as she lifted her skirts and flew back the way she had come. 'I'll speak to yer later, Amy, eh?'

Amy watched her go with a sense of relief and hurried on before Mary put in another appearance.

Once inside The Folly she slowly made her way to the drawing room where she found the two families enjoying their morning coffee.

'Ah, Amy.' Josephine instantly rose to meet her and François also stood up. 'How are you this morning, my dear? We've been so worried about you and will never be able to apologise enough for what Eugenie did last night. It was absolutely unforgivable of her. I sometimes wish she lived a million miles away instead of a mere five miles as the crow flies.'

'It's all right,' Amy answered. 'And I'm sorry too, for running out the way I did.'

François had crossed to stand at her side now and she smiled tentatively up at him, feeling embarrassed.

394

'We quite understood,' Josephine assured her. 'You needed a little time on your own, which is why we didn't follow you. But come, we mustn't let what happened spoil the wonderful news. François has been beaming from ear to ear all morning and now we must speak about wedding preparations.'

'So soon?' Amy muttered as François possessively took her arm.

'Why not, *ma petite?*' He smiled persuasively. 'There is no point in delaying. Your grandmother and I thought the autumn might be a good time for a wedding. What do you think?'

Deeply conscious of the many eyes trained upon her, Amy flushed. 'I er ... it doesn't give us much time. It's only a matter of months away.'

As if she had not spoken, François went on, 'The next thing we have to decide is where the wedding shall be. Should we have the ceremony in Paris or in London?'

'I wouldn't want to get married in either of those places,' Amy spouted, before she had time to stop herself. 'The wedding should be here in Nuneaton. It's where I live and we have to think of my gran getting to it.' A pang of guilt, sharp as a knife, stabbed through her. And then what was going to happen to her gran when they *were* married? Amy had always vowed that she would never leave her, and Molly was getting too old to be living alone now. Everything was happening so fast and she was beginning to panic.

Thankfully, Samuel Forrester stepped in just then. 'For what my opinion is worth, I think you both ought to just enjoy being engaged for now,' he commented diplomatically, noting Amy's distress. 'There is plenty of time to think about the wedding.'

Amy flashed him a grateful smile but François looked less than pleased. 'Well, we shall see,' he said peevishly. 'Now come, Aimée. Let us go for a walk in your grandfather's beautiful grounds, *non*? I should like to have you to myself for a while.' He now turned to his mother and Mrs Forrester and after giving them a polite little bow, he asked, 'Would you be excusing us, please?'

'Of course,' the women answered in unison, and François took Amy's elbow and led her through the hallway to the front of the house. Once outside he tucked her arm into his and they began to stroll along the grounds

'You have made me the happiest man on earth,' he told her tenderly. 'Although I could have wished for a more pleasant end to the ball. *Quelle femme abominable!* How on earth did Adam put up with that Eugenie for so long? And why does she dislike you so?'

'I have no idea,' Amy said. 'Apparently she was exactly the same with Jessica, Adam's sister.'

'Well, we shall pay the incident no more heed. You have agreed to become my wife and that is all that matters for now. But tell me, *ma belle*, why do you drag your heels about setting a date for the wedding?'

'It's my gran,' Amy told him truthfully. 'I am very concerned about what will happen to her once we are married.'

'Could she not come to live with us?' François asked as he turned his head to look at her.

'She would never agree to that,' Amy said at once. 'She wouldn't even consider moving into a cottage on this estate when Mr Forre – when my grandfather suggested it.' She was still having difficulty in addressing the Forresters by their proper titles.

'Then what are we to do?'

'I don't know yet.' Amy stared off across the top of the trees. 'Could we not just enjoy being as we are for now, as Grandfather suggested, and talk about setting a date for the wedding sometime in the future?'

They were now walking beneath the canopy of trees and François was looking none too happy. Even so, he sensed that Amy was not going to be pushed for now, so he sighed heavily. 'If that is your decision, then for now I must accept it.'

They walked on for some time until they came to the edge of a deep ravine. There was nothing to be heard but the sounds of the birds and it was very peaceful.

'This is a beautiful place,' François remarked as he gazed down the steep incline, which was covered in bushes and wildflowers.

Amy nodded in agreement. 'Yes, it is. This place used to be a quarry but now it's a haven for wildlife. I often come here on a nice day when I have free time to sketch. I find it very peaceful.'

As he turned her to face him she looked up into his handsome face and her worries began to melt away. And then he tilted her chin and his lips came down on hers, and as she gave herself up to the pleasure of the moment she knew that somehow they would find a way around their problems.

Back at Forrester's Folly, Samuel was helping the Laroque family into his carriage to begin an inspection of his local businesses. Josephine meantime had made her way to the study where she found Adam sitting in a deep wing chair, staring out of the window.

'Oh, I'm sorry, darling. I didn't mean to disturb you,' she said. 'I have an appointment in ten minutes but I can always use another room if you'd like me to.'

'No, Mother, it's quite all right. I was just going out for a ride on Pepperpot anyway. Seth is saddling him for me now.'

'Oh, I see.' Her face creased with concern as she studied her son and realised for the first time that he had lost weight. He seemed to be living on his nerves just lately, and started at the least little thing. But then, she supposed the incident last night had affected him deeply. The end of a marriage, albeit a bad one, could not be an easy thing to accept.

He rose from his seat and as he passed her she patted his arm, saying softly, 'Try not to worry too much. Things have a habit of coming right in the end.'

'Yes, Mother,' he said dutifully, while knowing that nothing would ever be right for him again, but he refrained from saying so.

'Who do you have an appointment with?' he asked curiously, as he paused to place his arm affectionately about her waist. It was unusual for his mother to have callers, but then she had been so much happier lately, as if she was coming back from the dark place she had hidden in for too many years.

Instantly she became animated. 'It's with the private detective that your father and I hired to try and find your sister,' she said excitedly. 'I received a letter from him today saying that he had some news for me and that he would be calling to see me.' She clapped her hands together, her face a picture of sheer anticipation. 'Oh, just think of it, darling. Won't it be wonderful if he has found her? She can come back where she belongs, and her husband for that matter. I'm sure they would have married by now and if we can only find them and tell them that we are sorry for what happened, we can all be a real family again. It will be so wonderful for Amy to meet her mother at last.'

She watched a mixture of emotions play across her son's face, and then to her bewilderment he suddenly released her and strode abruptly from the room without so much as another word.

She wrung her hands together but then as she thought of how close Adam and his sister had been she slowly relaxed again. Her disappearance had affected him as badly as it had affected his parents, and he was probably just afraid that the detective's findings would lead to nothing but disappointment again.

Mr Burrows's attempts to find Jessica had come to nothing when they had first hired him shortly after Jessica had left home, but Josephine prayed that this time he would be coming with some good news – otherwise why would he be calling to see her? She hung on to the thought as she hurried to the window to look for a sign of his arrival.

By the time Mr Burrows finally did arrive, almost half an hour later, Josephine was beside herself with impatience. The maid showed him to the study as the mistress had instructed, and the instant he set foot through the door, Josephine demanded, 'Well, Mr Burrows? I believe you have some news for me.'

'Yes, ma'am, I do,' he told her solemnly as he removed his hat. 'But I'm not too sure that you will be happy with it.'

Remembering her manners, Josephine ushered him to a chair. Settling into the one directly opposite to him, she straightened her skirts and after folding her hands sedately in her lap, she raised an inquisitive eyebrow.

'I have had a measure of success,' he began tentatively, and when he saw her start he quickly held up his hand. 'Please, ma'am. Don't get too excited until I've told you the whole story.'

She gulped deep in her throat, silently willing him to go on as sweat broke out on her forehead.

'The thing is, I did discover where your daughter and Mr Chamberlain went when they first left Forrester's Folly. I initially made a number of enquiries that led me nowhere, and then I decided that if they had become man and wife there had to be a record of their marriage somewhere. I began to systematically work my way through church records, beginning in Nuneaton and slowly moving out further afield. It began to seem that I was on a fruitless mission but then after visiting a church in Coventry I was fortunate enough to meet an elderly gentleman who had played the organ at that particular church for many years. When I mentioned the names of the two young people that I was searching for he told me that he recalled them. They had attended the church for some time and he said that they appeared to be very much in love. He had assumed that they were married as the young woman was pregnant and wore a wedding ring. They were living in a rented room in a house in the back streets of Coventry and for a while he recalled that Mr Chamberlain had taken any job he could to support them, but then he got a job down the mines and they moved into a little tied cottage.'

'Oh!' Josephine's hand flew to her mouth and she had to blink to hold back tears as she imagined her beloved girl being forced to live in such a way, and with a baby coming too.

Mr Burrows, who was a great bear of a man with sparse grey hair and soft grey eyes, gave the woman a moment to compose herself before going on, 'The old gentleman could remember quite clearly how happy the couple were at the prospect of becoming parents. But then sadly, there was a pit cave-in and Mr Chamberlain was killed, along with four other men, all of whom had families. It must have been heartbreaking for the widows, your daughter included. Anyway, the old gentleman informed me that sadly, all five families were turned out of their homes as they were tied to the pit, and it seems that your daughter then rented a room somewhere in the town and for a time managed to earn a living sewing. If what the man told me is true, her landlord was a deplorable man and when your daughter was heavily pregnant she suddenly just stopped coming to the church. The old gentleman was concerned; he had become fond of her, you see? So he went to the room she had been renting, only to be told that she had been evicted on to the streets. And that, I'm afraid, is as far as I have been able to get. What became of her after that, I have no idea whatsoever, ma'am, and I regret that all my further enquiries have hit a brick wall.'

Josephine was sobbing by now as her heart broke afresh. After the story that Molly had told her of the night that she had found Amy, she could only piece together what must have happened. Perhaps Jessica had been on her way home, and had sheltered in the church doorway because she was too ill to go any further? And what had become of her when Molly left her to go and fetch help? Had she somehow managed to struggle away somewhere? If this was so, it could well be that Jessica was still alive. But in that case, why had she not tried to find her baby? Josephine's head was buzzing as she told Mr Burrows Molly's tale.

When she was done he too scratched his head in bewilderment. 'It's certainly a strange story, ma'am,' he told her respectfully. 'And going by what the old organist told me, your daughter was really looking forward to the birth of this child, as was her husband before his untimely death. She doesn't sound as if she would have just abandoned the child without very good cause.'

Josephine sniffed loudly. Her poor girl. She could only imagine what she must have suffered following Robert's death. But why had she not come home to them then? Surely she had known

402

that her father would never have turned his back on her under any circumstances, despite what he had said on the night he had forbidden her to continue seeing Robert?

Sighing, Mr Burrows rose from his chair and extended his hand. 'I am sorry I could not have brought you better news, Mrs Forrester,' he told her sincerely. 'And thank you for sharing the information you have with me. The jigsaw is slowly coming together and never fear – I will not stop searching until the last piece has fallen into place. Good day to you, ma'am.'

'Good day, Mr Burrows ... and thank you.' She placed an envelope containing a sizable amount of money, including a large bonus, into his hand and then the man quietly left the room leaving her to ponder on what he had told her.

Adam joined her over an hour later, following a ride on Pepperpot, his horse, and she immediately began to tell him of the detective's findings. He had intended to be gone for much longer but found that he could not wait to hear the news Mr Burrows had to impart to his mother. However, she was only halfway through her story when he suddenly rose from his seat and stormed towards the door.

'Oh, *Mother*,' he ground out over his shoulder. '*When* are you going to stop putting us through all this time after time, and accept that Jessica is gone from us forever? Is finding Amy not enough for you?' Without waiting for an answer he slammed out of the room, leaving her to stare after him in open-mouthed amazement.

Chapter Twenty-Eight

It was the last day of François' visit before he and his family returned to Paris, and he was not in a good humour, for despite all his attempts to get Amy to set a date for their wedding, she had refused. Oh, she was as loving and as affectionate as ever, but on this point she would not be swayed, insisting that for now she was happy as things were. François, who was used to getting his own way, was determined that he would change her mind before he boarded the train the next day.

They were sitting in the grounds of Forrester's Folly beneath a cloudless blue sky, and Amy looked enchanting in a soft cream linen dress that was adorned with little pink rosebuds, which only made him more determined to make her name the day.

The last two weeks had been fraught in some respects. Since Mr Burrows's visit, which Josephine had immediately told them all about, the poor woman had become obsessed with finding her daughter again, and that and the forthcoming wedding were all she seemed able to talk about. Almost daily, to Mr Forrester's deep concern, she would insist on visiting Mr Burrows's office in the town to see if he had managed to get any further along with his enquiries, and this left the entertaining of their Parisian visitors sitting very squarely on her husband's shoulders.

Adam was also giving him cause for concern, for since the night of the ball and Eugenie's untimely visit he had closeted himself in his room, often not even venturing out to eat or oversee his businesses.

When Mr Forrester visited the stables one day, Seth had commented on the fact. 'Is Master Adam all right, sir?' His face had shown his deep concern. 'Only it ain't like him to leave Pepperpot in his stall for such lengths o' time without taking him out to exercise him.'

Mr Forrester sighed. Old Seth had been his faithful servant since the day he had moved into The Folly and had worshipped Master Adam when he was a child. It was he who had taught Adam to ride his first pony after many patient hours on a leading rope in the small paddock at the back of the stables.

'I have to confess, I am concerned about him, Seth,' the man admitted sadly. 'He doesn't seem to be himself at all, but then no doubt the end of his marriage is taking its toll on him. But I have no doubt he'll come round when he's good and ready.'

'Let's hope as yer right, sir.' Seth had mumbled, but as his master walked away he was deeply troubled.

Now, François picked a buttercup and held it beneath Amy's chin, making her giggle. 'What would you like to do today, *chérie?*' he asked. 'We must make the most of every second, for this time tomorrow I shall be on my way home to Paris.'

'I know,' she answered, solemn again. It was

hard to believe that his stay was almost over. It seemed to have passed in the blink of an eye.

'Why don't you come with me to see Gran again before you leave?' she suggested. 'You have only visited her twice in the whole of the time you've been here and she has not had time to get to know you.'

François could have thought of many things he would much rather have done, but not wishing to upset her, he nodded. 'Very well then; it shall be as you wish.'

They pulled themselves up from the soft green grass and as François turned towards the house, Amy caught his hand and swung him about. 'Let's not take the carriage. It's such a lovely day. We could walk it.'

'But is it not some long distance away?' he objected.

Amy laughed. 'It's no more than a few miles, so come along. I walk it all the time. You'll turn to fat if you don't get your exercise and I don't want to be married to a fat husband.'

'Ah,' he said, seizing his chance, 'does this mean that you are having second thoughts and you will agree to setting the date for the wedding after all?'

'No, it does *not.*' Grabbing his hand she started to haul him in the direction of the woods. 'Now come along with you.'

It was some time before they turned into the lane that led to the cottages and by then François was complaining bitterly. Amy simply ignored him. It was Sunday and many of the cottagers were outside their homes. Some were just sitting on chairs that they had carried from the kitchen, enjoying the feel of the sun on their face, whilst others were tending the small vegetable plots that were allocated to each cottage.

It was as they approached Bessie's cottage that Amy saw Toby digging away in his garden. He had his shirt off and his muscled arms were gleaming with sweat as he upturned fresh vegetables for their dinner. He had heard all about François from Molly, but up until now he had not met him, nor if truth be known did he have any wish to. However, Amy had other ideas and she drew François to a halt merely feet away from him.

Toby stopped digging and looked towards her.

'François, I would like you to meet Toby Bradley. He and I have been brought up together and he is my best friend. It was Toby who taught me to read and write. Toby, this is my fiancé, François Laroque.'

The two men eyed each other warily, but then Toby wiped his hand down the side of his trousers and extended it. François eyed it reluctantly before shaking it and inclined his head.

'François is going home tomorrow,' Amy told Toby. 'So I thought it would be nice if he came to say goodbye to Gran.'

As François saw the different emotions flit across Toby's face, his arm settled possessively around Amy's waist. This young man was just a little too good-looking and familiar with Amy for his liking.

'Then I hope yer have a good visit,' Toby now said, and without another word he turned about and began furiously digging again.

Amy moved François along and seconds later

she was pushing him into the cottage, which once again appeared very dark and dismal to the young man.

'François has come to say goodbye to you, Gran.'

At the sound of Amy's voice, Molly, who was seated at the side of the fire busily knitting yet more socks for the twins, looked up and smiled. 'I didn't hear the carriage,' she commented, as she nodded pleasantly towards François.

Amy settled him at the table before hurrying to fetch the lemonade from the thrall in the pantry. 'We walked,' she told Molly as she poured some into three glasses. 'Though I don't think François was too keen on it.' Her smile was teasing and he smiled back at her before addressing Molly.

'I have been trying to persuade Aimée to set the date for the wedding before I return home, but as yet she will not be pinned down.'

If he had expected to find an ally in the old woman he was sadly disappointed when she answered, 'Well, happen she'll tell yer when she's good an' ready. There ain't no rush at the end o' the day from where I'm sittin'. Yer both young wi' yer whole lives stretchin' ahead o' yer.'

François' lips set in a straight line as he lifted his drink. If he were to be honest, he did not particularly like Molly. She was a little too outspoken for his taste and had no finesse whatsoever. In fact, he found it incredible that Amy, who was so beautiful and intelligent, could have been brought up by such a person, and in what amounted to little more than a hovel too. He also felt that Amy was being allowed to have too much say in the wedding plans. To his mind, her grandfather should have set the date by now and Amy should have obeyed his wishes, but it was more than obvious that Mr Forrester had no intention of forcing her into anything, so there was no help to be found there, nor here with Molly it seemed.

'Look at that lot Toby's brought fer us,' Molly said now, gesturing at the wooden draining-board, which was loaded with a selection of freshly dug vegetables. 'He's as good as the day is long, so he is,' she said, as she sipped at her drink.

Amy looked slightly embarrassed. Knowing her gran as she did, she had the feeling that Molly had not taken to François, whereas Toby could do no wrong in her eyes. But then, Amy was sure things would change once Molly got to know François a little better. He was so charming that it would have been hard for anyone not to like him. The rest of the visit proved to be hard work for Amy. Both François and Molly were both very quiet and she struggled to keep a conversation going, so much so that she was relieved when it was time for them to leave.

'Goodbye, Gran,' she whispered as she bent to kiss her cheek. 'Don't get waiting up for me tonight. I'm having dinner up at The Folly and I'll no doubt be late back.'

'Late back? But surely you will be staying? It is my last night here,' François objected.

'Oh, don't worry. I shan't come home until late and I shall be back first thing in the morning to see you off,' Amy assured him.

He shrugged as he crossed to Molly and kissed

her hand. '*Au revoir, madame*, until we meet again,' he said politely.

Molly nodded and once they were gone she wiped the back of her hand across her pinnie. Smarmy devil, she thought to herself, and then went back to her knitting and put him from her mind.

Later that evening, after dining with the two families, François and Amy slipped out on to the terrace. François was in a melancholy mood and Amy was doing her best to try to cheer him up.

'Don't be sad,' she whispered. 'We shall be together again before you know it.'

He stared off across the grounds. 'Who knows,' he muttered, and suddenly a wave of compassion swept through Amy. Perhaps she had been a little hard on him?

'Look,' she said hesitantly, 'I still feel that the autumn is a little soon for the wedding ... but what if I agreed to a spring one next year? Would that make you any happier?'

Suddenly his face was wreathed in smiles. 'That would make me the happiest man on earth,' he said. 'And now I shall be able to make proper plans.'

'Very well, but I still insist on getting married here,' she warned him.

He nodded eagerly. 'It shall be as you wish, and I have no doubt you will make a beautiful bride.' And then she was in his arms and everything else was forgotten.

'Goodbye, *ma petite*. Take care of yourself until

we meet again.'

Amy clung to François with tears in her eyes as the porter loaded the Laroque luggage on to the train. She could hardly believe that he was really going. The time had passed all too quickly.

'Just remember the sixteenth of May next year,' he whispered as he kissed her fingers. 'On that day we shall become man and wife, and with your talent and our two families united, our business will become world-known.'

Amy thought this was quite a strange thing to say but had no time to comment, for at that moment the stationmaster blew his whistle and François sprinted towards the door of the first-class carriage that contained the rest of his family.

'Goodbye, *mon ange,*' he called as he hung out of the window and Amy waved until she felt her arm would drop off.

'Ah, that's that then,' Samuel Forrester said, and Amy thought she detected a note of relief in his voice. But then in fairness, Josephine had been somewhat preoccupied in her quest to find her daughter and he had been rushed off his feet trying to keep his guests entertained.

Linking his arm through Amy's, he led her along the platform, and when they came to the entrance he suddenly drew her to a halt and asked, quite unexpectedly, 'Are you quite happy about this wedding, my dear? What I mean is, I would hate you to feel that because of my business association with Monsieur Laroque, you were obliged in any way.'

'Of course I don't feel obliged to marry François. I love him,' Amy assured him, but she was touched that he had cared enough to ask.

'Good, then in that case, your grandmother and I will make sure that you have a wedding to remember – and also, never forget that even after you are married, you will always have a home to come back to, should you wish.'

Amy said nothing now and allowed him to lead her to the carriage.

'Do you know,' he suddenly chuckled as they rattled through the town centre, 'it will be nice to be able to get back to work now. Not that the Laroques were anything but the perfect guests, of course. But my dear old mother had a saying: "I like the comers, and I like the goers, but I don't like the stayers".' And then he and Amy simultaneously erupted into laughter.

Chapter Twenty-Nine

It was now mid-July and already it felt to Amy as if François had been gone for years; although it was, in fact, only a matter of months. He wrote to her every week and his letters were full of endearments and excitement at the prospect of their forthcoming marriage. Amy had travelled to London three times since François had gone home and enjoyed each visit immensely. It was always a tonic for her, to see Nancy. The businesses were all thriving, and had it not been for Mr Forrester curtailing her working hours, she could quite easily have worked each day around the clock to meet the demand for her designs.

Now each week, her grandfather insisted that she should have at least two full days off, and while the weather was so nice she had taken to sitting at the edge of the ravine on the other side of the woods to do her sketching.

Today she aimed to do exactly that. It was a wonderful day with fluffy clouds riding in a soft blue sky. She had spent the morning with Mrs Forrester, who had now gone into town to see Mr Burrows yet again, so Amy collected her pad and pens and made for the front door. Lily was polishing the hall table and she smiled at her brightly as she passed.

'Off to do a bit o' sketchin', are yer, Miss Amy?' she chirped cheekily.

'Yes, I am, Lily. When the master and mistress come back, would you tell them that I shall see them tomorrow?'

'O' course I will,' Lily assured her obligingly and Amy smiled at her as she slipped out into the sunshine.

As she passed Mary's cottage, the children, who were playing with hoops in the garden, ran to the fence to greet her, and seconds later, Mary appeared in the doorway. She eyed the sketchpad in Amy's hand and smiled as she asked, 'Goin' to enjoy a bit o' sunshine, eh?'

'Yes, I am, Mary.' She ruffled the twins' hair. 'I can't see any point sitting inside working on a lovely day like this.'

'I couldn't agree more. Have yer started the design fer yer weddin' dress yet?'

Amy hastily shook her head. 'No, I haven't.

There's plenty of time for that.'

'Hm, that's what yer might think now but next year will be 'ere in the blink of an eye,' Mary retorted. 'Anyway, you get yerself off an' I'll see yer soon, eh?'

'You will that,' Amy agreed, and was just about to set off again when they looked towards the riverbank where a white horse was galloping along with a female rider on its back, riding side-saddle and with her habit flaring out behind her.

Mary squinted and shielded her eyes from the sun as she gazed towards the sight. 'Somebody's in a tearin' hurry,' she commented. 'Poor bloody horse, is all I can say.' And then she turned her attention to the little girls while Amy continued on her way.

Once she reached the other side of the woods, Amy sighed with contentment. It was so peaceful here and she loved to just sit and watch the wild-life and listen to the birds in the trees.

After dropping down on to the soft green grass at the side of the deep ravine she took the ribbon from her hair and shook it loose. For a while she sat letting the peace of the place wash over her and then she took up her sketchpad and in no time at all was lost in her ideas.

It was some time later when a commotion behind her made her turn startled eyes in that direction. It sounded as if a horse was being ridden through the trees, and she was proved right when a lovely white stallion appeared with a portly red-faced woman in an elegant green riding habit on its back. The poor horse was obviously distressed by the many bushes and branches that had clawed at him as he was forced through the trees, and she saw immediately that there were deep scratches leaking blood all along his flanks. The stallion was reined to an abrupt halt only yards away from her and Amy could see that the poor creature's eyes were wide and rolling with fright, and its nostrils flaring as it pawed at the ground in distress.

Dropping her sketchpad on to the ground she rose angrily, ready to give the uncaring rider a piece of her mind, but as her eyes settled on the woman the words died on her lips.

It was Eugenie and suddenly Amy felt very vulnerable. Even so she would have died rather than show it, and so she drew herself up to her full height and faced her defiantly.

'That poor animal is terrified,' she stated boldly, her angry eyes tight on Eugenie's.

Eugenie sneered. 'What if it is? It's no business of yours, guttersnip. And what would you know about horses anyway? Until you wormed your way into The Folly I dare say you had never even been near one.'

Amy bit back the hasty retort that sprang to her lips, not wishing to antagonise the woman further. The horse was still restless and she could see that it was taking Eugenie all her time to hold it steady. She suddenly shook the reins and slashed the whip across its flank; the terrified animal took another two steps towards Amy, forcing her to move closer to the edge of the deep ravine behind her.

Panic suddenly swelled in her chest and she

licked her dry lips before muttering, 'Look, Eugenie, I don't want any trouble. I came here to do some work, so why don't you just take that poor creature home and get his wounds attended to?'

'I shall go when I'm good and ready,' Eugenie ground out. 'Just who are *you* to tell me where to go? If truth be told, I have far more right to be here than *you*. And I probably still would be, if it hadn't been for *you*. Nothing was ever the same at The Folly since you came worming your way into everyone's affections.'

'That isn't true. I have never willingly done anything to upset or disrespect you, Eugenie,' Amy said – and now the woman's eyes flashed fire.

'How *dare* you address me by my Christian name?' she spat. 'Why, you should show some respect when you are talking to your betters. It's *Mrs Forrester* to you! I am *still* married to the master's son, though in name only now, thanks to *you!*'

At the sound of her raised voice the horse panicked and began to champ on its bit and rear on its hind legs as the woman fought to hold him.

Amy's heart was pounding with fear now as she inched yet closer to the gaping hole behind her, and then before she could do anything or have any chance of escape, the horse suddenly reared up again and as its front legs flailed wildly in the air, one of its hooves caught her cheek and she felt blood gush down her face.

She held out one hand beseechingly and the other rose to her cheek as pain swept through her. 'Please, there is no need for this...' Her words died away as she felt her feet slipping from beneath

416

her. She was on the very edge of the ravine now and Eugenie was forcing the terrified horse forward, her eyes shining with madness, whilst foam bubbled around the creature's mouth.

'I told you I would have my revenge.' She laughed maniacally as Amy plummeted over the edge of the drop. And then Amy's arms were flapping in thin air and she had the sensation of flying as she dropped like a stone into the deep gorge. She bounced sickeningly from the side of the ravine again and again as pain exploded behind her eyes like fireworks. And then after what seemed like a lifetime her body slammed on to the rocks below and a comforting darkness engulfed her.

It was now very dark as Molly once again hurried to the window to look for a sign of Amy. She should have been home hours ago. Her dinner was burned to a crisp in the oven and it wasn't like her to be late without warning Molly. Chewing on her lip, she stared out into the balmy night. Where could she be? Molly briefly wondered if she had decided to stay the night at Forrester's Folly, but then dismissed that idea almost instantly. Although the Forresters had a room that was kept ready for the girl at all times should she wish to use it, Amy had never taken them up on their offer, and usually she was as regular as clockwork at coming home. Had she decided to stay, Molly was sure that Amy would have informed her of her intentions.

Crossing back to the oven, she took Amy's meal from the range and scraped it into the pig bin as her concerns mounted. She stood chewing on her knuckle for some seconds then, snatching her shawl from the back of the chair, she slung it around her shoulders and painfully hobbled out into the lane. When she came to Bessie's door, she found it open and inside, Bessie, Jim and Toby were enjoying a last drink before retiring to their beds.

Bessie raised her eyebrow. It was unusual, to say the very least, to see Molly out and about so late at night. 'Somethin' wrong is there, Molly?' she asked.

'It's our Amy,' Molly told her without preamble. 'She ain't come home an' it ain't like her at all.'

'Happen she decided to stay at The Folly,' Bessie suggested, but like Molly, she knew that this was highly unlikely. Amy would have told Molly – and Bessie – had she intended to be away for the night.

'Ner.' Molly's head wagged from side to side. 'You know as well as I do that she would have told me if that were her intentions. Yer don't think she's been dragged off on her way home by one o' them there Mormons, do yer?'

Toby chuckled. 'They ain't monsters, Molly,' he told her. 'An' besides, there's only a handful of 'em left in the town now.'

'Then where is she?' Molly could not keep the concern from her voice as her eyes strayed to the open door.

Toby got up and lifted his boots from the side of the hearth. 'I'll go for a wander an' see if I can catch a sight of her,' he offered.

Molly smiled at him gratefully. 'Thanks, lad. I knew I could depend on you.' She then nodded towards Bessie and Jim and headed back to her own cottage to anxiously wait for his return.

It was well over an hour later when Toby walked into her kitchen.

'I went as far as the lawns of The Folly,' he told her. 'But there weren't no sign of Amy, though the lights were on in the downstairs windows.'

'Didn't yer knock an' ask if she were there?' Molly demanded.

Toby hastily shook his head. 'Did I hell as like. Why, they'd likely have called the peelers, had I knocked on their door in me work clothes, thinkin' I were a tramp. But I did see Seth and when I told him that I was looking for Amy he said that he hadn't seen her.'

Molly sighed and as she sank into her chair, Toby crossed to her and squeezed her arm reassuringly. 'Don't get worryin',' he urged. 'Happen it got late an' she decided to stay there after all. She'll be back in the mornin', bright as a button, you'll see. Now get yerself off to bed an' try an' get some sleep an' I'll see yer tomorrow, eh?'

'Aye, lad, I will, an' thanks,' Molly muttered but no matter how she tried she could not shift the terrible sense of foreboding that had settled over her, and all night long she tossed and turned.

By lunchtime the next day, Molly was almost beside herself with worry. Had she been younger she would have set off for The Folly herself, but she was only too aware that she would never make it. Her old legs were not as reliable as they had used to be.

'I'll get our Toby to go back there as soon as he gets in from work this evenin',' Bessie promised her and with that, for now, Molly had to be content.

However, she had no need to wait for Toby, for mid-afternoon, the Forresters' carriage rattled down the lane and Mr Forrester himself appeared at her door with a broad smile on his face.

'Good afternoon, Mrs Ernshaw, and what a wonderful afternoon it is, is it not?' He took off his hat respectfully and stepped into the kitchen, his eyes darting about the room. 'I was just going into the factory for an hour to see how they are getting on with Amy's latest designs and wondered if she would care to come with me?'

'What? Yer mean she ain't wi' you?' Molly's face was the colour of putty and now the smile slid from his face as he frowned in confusion.

'Why, no... My wife and I have not seen Amy since yesterday morning. She was up at the house but Josephine and I both had appointments, so we left her there, and Amy told the maid Lily when she went that she would see us today. Did she not come home?'

'No, she didn't.' Molly looked beside herself with fear. 'Where do yer think she could 'ave gone? It ain't like her to pull a trick like this.'

Hoping to allay the old woman's fears, Samuel forced a smile back to his face. 'I'm sure that there will be some rational explanation,' he assured her. 'I shall go back home immediately and try to find out what's gone on. Would you like to come with me, or would you rather stay here?'

'I'll wait here if it's all the same to you.'

'Of course. Rest assured I shall let you know

what's happening at the first opportunity,' he promised, then turning abruptly he strode back out to the carriage, leaving Molly to wring her hands and pray as she had not prayed for a very long time.

'What do yer mean, she *still* ain't home?' Toby asked when he arrived home from work that evening.

'Just what I said,' his mother informed him shortly. 'Old Molly is nearly beside herself wi' worry. Mr Forrester called in this afternoon an' told her that he thought Amy had come home last night. He then went straight back to The Folly just to make sure as she weren't still there. He sent word to Molly wi' the coachman that she hadn't been seen since yesterday mornin'. He's got his men out lookin' fer her now, by all accounts.'

Slinging his snap box on to the table, Toby swung about and told her. 'I'm goin' to go an' join in the search.'

'Ere, hold fire,' his mother objected. 'What about yer meal? Do yer really need to go harin' off like this?'

'Keep it warm fer me,' he told her, and without another word he stepped back out into the lane.

He arrived at The Folly to find the grounds teeming with people, Mr Forrester amongst them. Hurrying across to him, Toby held out his hand and introduced himself. 'I'm Toby Bradley, sir – a neighbour of Amy's. I just got home from work an' me mam told me that Amy is still missin', so I thought I'd come an' help yer search for her.'

'That's much appreciated, young man.' Mr Forrester shook his hand. 'I have every male member of staff out looking for her, but as yet there's not been a sign of her.'

They were standing at the bottom of the marble steps that led up to the door and Lily, who was just returning after her evening off, paused as she saw so many people about. She had been making her way round to the servants' entrance, but now she called Seth, who was searching amongst the topiary trees, and asked him, 'What's goin' on here then?'

'It's Miss Amy,' he informed her solemnly. 'She's gone missin'.'

'What do yer mean, gone missin'? Since when?'

'Since yesterday mornin', from what I can gather. She were here when the master an' mistress left the house, an' then when the master called to her cottage today, the old woman told him that Amy hadn't come home last night. We've been scourin' the grounds fer hours. Even Master Adam has left his room to help look fer her, but as yet we ain't had a sign o' the poor girl.'

Lily frowned. She could clearly remember Amy leaving the house yesterday morning and had passed on the message that Amy had asked her to give to the master and mistress about seeing them this morning. But where was it she had said she was going? Suddenly it came to her, and lifting her skirts she sped towards Mr Forrester.

'Sir,' she gulped, 'I just remembered. When Miss Amy left the house yesterday after you an' the mistress had gone out she said she were goin' to do some sketchin'. She had her pad an' pencils with her.'

'That is most helpful, Lily, but did she say

exactly where she was going?'

Lily sadly shook her head. 'Sorry, sir – no, she didn't. She just said as she were goin' to do some sketchin.'

'Thank you, all the same,' the man told her, and turning about she retraced her steps and went to join Cook in the kitchen.

'All we can do is continue to search,' Mr Forrester told Toby, and nodding, Toby set off across the lawns in the directions of the woods. As he approached Mary's cottage, he saw his sister with the girls one on each hip in the garden, staring at all the activity, and as he drew near she shouted, 'What you doin' here, Toby, an' what the hell is goin' on?'

He quickly told her and she frowned. 'Well, the last I saw of her yesterday, Amy were headin' towards the ravine, yon side o' the woods.' She placed the girls down and pointed in the general direction through the trees. 'She often used to go there to sketch on a nice day. Come to think of it, I didn't see her come by on her way back though.'

'Thanks, Mary.' Toby plunged into the woods. The light was beginning to fail now and he had to pause and blink as his eyes adjusted to the dimness. Eventually he moved on, his eyes searching this way and that through the undergrowth for a sign of her. It was some time later when he emerged on the other side of the woods and he stood there as his eyes played along the rim of the deep ravine. It was very quiet and peaceful here, but there was no evidence that he could see of Amy ever having been there. Slowly he began to tread the flattened grass that looped around the edge of the steep drop and he had gone some way when something on the grass up ahead caught his attention. Hurrying now he moved towards it and his heart plummeted as he saw what looked like Amy's sketchpad lying on the ground. When he drew close his heart dropped even further. Sketches that looked as if they had been trampled upon were lying here and there, softly blowing in the wind that was just starting to pick up. Her pencils were there too, scattered about as if she had dropped them.

Cupping his mouth with his hands he shouted, 'AAAAMY!' and the name echoed eerily back to him.

He stood perfectly still for a while listening, and then, dropping to his knees, he lifted first one sketch and then another. There was no doubt about it, they were definitely hers; he would have recognised her style amongst a million others. It was as he was kneeling there that he noticed a discoloration on a clump of grass and running his hand across it he then raised it nearer to his face and gasped. It was dried blood. But where was Amy? He began to shout her name again until he felt that his lungs would burst, but only silence answered him. Treading closer to the edge of the ravine now, he stared down into the deep gorge below but could see nothing but the wildflowers and the bushes that grew in profusion there. They looked as if they had been painted in black and white in the failing light and as he stood there, his eyes straining for a sight of her, the first drops of rain began to fall and everywhere grew ominously quiet. Next came the lightning, flashing in the sky overhead, followed a few seconds later by a clap of thunder as the downpour commenced. Blinking the lashing rain from his eyes, Toby began to inch away from the edge. Yet another crack of lightning flashed directly above him and it was then that he caught a glimpse of colour far, far below him in the bottom of the ravine. It was a deep sapphire blue – the colour of the gown that Amy had been wearing yesterday.

His first instinct was to try and scale the walls of the ravine to get down to her, but he quickly realised how foolish that would be. They were dangerously slippery now with the rain, and should he attempt it, he had no doubt that he too would end up laid out on the rocks far below. The only sensible thing he could do was to run and fetch help.

Toby plunged back into the woods, which were even darker now than when he had first entered them. The bushes and brambles snagged at his hands and face and his clothes as if they were trying to hinder his progress, but he raced on regardless. And all the time his heart was crying, *Oh, Dear God, please don't let me be too late!* For he knew that if Amy was dead, he would want to die too.

Chapter Thirty

As Toby burst from the shelter of the trees his heart was thumping painfully against his ribs. The men who were scouring the grounds held lamps aloft now as they poked at the bushes but

425

they all looked towards him when he shouted, *'Over here!'*

He saw Mr Forrester racing across the grass as he struggled to get his breath back and then the man was standing in front of him as Toby gasped, 'I ... I reckon I've found her, sir. In the old quarry. We're goin' to need a rope ... a long 'un.'

Mr Forrester swung about and said to Seth, who was standing close behind him, 'Get over to the stables, Seth, and bring me a rope. And be quick about it, man. We have not a moment to lose.'

By now the rest of the search-party was assembling behind him and he told Joe authoritatively, 'Wait here for your father, and then follow us through the woods as fast as you know how.'

'Yes, sir.' Joe tapped the tip of his peaked cap, which was dripping with water as the rest of the men set off back through the woods behind Toby.

At last they came through the other side of the trees and Toby strained his eyes into the darkness as he tried to remember where he had found Amy's sketches.

'It's this way,' he panted as he got his bearings, and as one they all set off again. Soon they came to the ruined sketches and Toby pointed over the edge of the ravine. 'I saw somethin' down there in the flash from the lightning. It looked like part of a woman's dress.'

Mr Forrester shuddered. If what Toby said was true and Amy had fallen over the edge, there was very little chance of finding her alive. How could anyone survive a fall such as this? Even so he now snapped, 'Where the hell is Seth with that damn rope? Someone is going to have to climb down there.'

'I'll do it,' Toby replied without hesitation and as the two men's eyes locked, the older one nodded.

Minutes later, Seth joined them carrying a long rope that the men started to fasten around Toby's waist.

'Are you quite sure that you want to do this, lad?' Mr Forrester asked.

Toby nodded, his face set in grim lines as he approached the edge of the drop. 'Yer goin' to have to take me weight in case I slip,' he told the men who were holding the rope, and they all nodded, bracing themselves as he lowered himself across the lip of the ravine.

Toby clumsily began his descent, gripping on to the slippery grass and finding footholds wherever he could. It was not easy with the rain blinding him but he never ceased in his efforts. Very, very slowly, the men lowered him down. More than once he lost his grip and swung out from the face, but they steadied him and held him fast until he was ready to be lowered again. The drop seemed endless and Toby began to worry that the rope was not going to be long enough to get to the bottom, but thankfully just then his feet hit solid ground and he sighed with relief.

'I'm there!' he shouted, for he knew that they could no longer see him so far below them. The night had come with a vengeance.

He unfastened the rope and dropping to his knees, began to feel around the ground, cursing the darkness.

'Amy, are yer here, lass?' he called but there was no reply. On and on he crawled until suddenly

427

his hand connected with something soft. It was the skirt of a dress. His hands moved upwards and as another flash of lightning lit the sky he saw Amy's beautiful face, although it wasn't so beautiful now for it was covered in blood and there was an ugly gash running from beneath her eye to her chin. One of her legs was sticking out at an unnatural angle and she was deathly cold and unmoving, and Toby feared that she was dead. He had come too late. Even so, he was determined not to leave her there, so climbing to his feet he shouted to the lights flickering above him, *'I've found her. I'm going to have to tie her to me and you'll have to hoist us up together. And we're gonna need a door or somethin' to carry her to the house on.'*

'Very well, Toby.' Mr Forrester's voice carried to him above the howling wind. *'Just tug on the rope when you are ready.'*

Toby caught at the rope and then after struggling to get Amy's inert figure into a sitting position he tied it about their waists so that her head was resting on his shoulder.

'All right!' he bellowed, then yanked at the rope and almost instantly felt the tension on it as the men above began to heave him and Amy upwards.

Keeping his arms tight about her, his feet braced against the cliff face as they were slowly inched up, Toby's face was grim; inside he was crying, for not once did she show the slightest glimmer of life.

The upward journey seemed to take forever, but at last the men's faces appeared above him and he and Amy were being heaved on to the sodden grass. He lay breathless as someone

428

undid the rope that tied them together and Amy dropped like a rag doll on to the ground.

He saw that Mr Forrester had a door all ready for her and it was on to this that the men now gently lifted her, although not one of them, if asked, felt that she stood a chance. That was if the poor lass was not dead already.

Mr Forrester clapped him on the back. 'Well done, lad.'

Toby was not sure if it was raindrops or tears streaming down the master's face. 'You did a good job. Are you all right?'

'Aye, I'm fine. You just see to her,' Toby flapped his hand weakly as the men lifted a corner of the door each and carried Amy towards the trees.

He felt emotionally and physically drained, but overriding everything was the fear that was coursing through him. What would he do if she were dead? It was more than he could bear to think about.

It was a solemn party which crossed the lawns that evening, with Amy lying still on the door that acted as a stretcher. In the time since she had been visiting The Folly she had touched the hearts of many, and they all thought it was a crying shame that the poor Miss should have had such a tragic accident.

When Mr Forrester had sent for the door, he had also sent word for his wife to call in the doctor, and now they saw that his pony and trap were already outside.

They were barely halfway across the grass when Josephine ran out to meet them, heedless of the atrocious weather. She began to sob when she saw Amy's ashen face. Her husband took her arm as they hurried along at the side of her, their hair plastered to their heads and their saturated clothes clinging to them.

'Take her straight up to the middle bedroom on the first landing,' Josephine ordered the men as they entered the hallway, and heedless of the mess they were making all over the highly polished parquet floors and fine carpets, they did as they were told.

Both Lily and Beatrice were waiting for her there, ready to remove her clothes, dry her and change her into a clean nightgown. The doctor was also present, and once Amy had been gently transferred to the bed he ushered the men and the maids away, keen to see if his patient would need a nightgown or a shroud. He did, however, allow Samuel and Josephine into the room as he felt for a pulse. For a while his face was grave but then suddenly he gave them a glimmer of a smile.

'She is alive,' he told them. 'But only just. Her heartbeat is weak and her pulse is thready. And now I will examine her properly.'

Josephine was crying softly as a vision of Amy's injuries flashed before her eyes. A bone had actually been protruding through the skin on her leg, and there did not seem to be an inch of her that was not bruised or cut. And then there was her face. *Her beautiful face.* Would it ever be beautiful again? Josephine doubted it after seeing the horrendous gash on her cheek. But then, she told herself, none of these things mattered, just so long as Amy lived. That was the best they could hope for now.

'Have you informed Mrs Ernshaw that Amy has been found?' Josephine's exhausted husband asked her.

She nodded, the overwhelming fear she was experiencing showing clearly in her eyes. 'Yes, I sent the carriage to fetch her. She should be here at any moment.'

Even as she uttered the words, they heard the front door open and Molly was helped inside by Lily. The first thing she saw was Toby sitting on a chair in the hallway, his hands dangling between his knees and his head bowed.

'Oh, Toby ... she ain't...'

He stared up at her from red-rimmed eyes. 'I don't know, Molly,' he told her truthfully. 'The doctor is upstairs with her now.'

Without waiting for an invitation, Molly hobbled along the hallway and wheezed up the stairs, ignoring her aching legs. She found the Forresters standing on the landing and as she approached them, Josephine took her hand.

'The doctor is in with her now, Molly,' she told her. 'She is alive but seriously injured. All we can do now is wait to see what he says.'

Molly's shoulders sagged and as Samuel pushed a chair towards her she sank on to it and screwed her eyes tight shut.

It was nearly half an hour later when the doctor strode from the room.

'I am afraid she is in a very bad way,' he told them solemnly. 'Her face I can stitch, although I have to be honest and tell you, with a gash so deep, she will be scarred for life. But that is the least of her problems. I found at least three breaks below her left knee, and I fear... Well, I fear that there is no way to save that leg. I shall have to amputate below the knee.'

'*Oh, no!*' Josephine burst into a fresh torrent of tears as Molly stared at the doctor from tortured eyes.

'But will she live?' This was from Samuel and now the doctor looked him full in the eye as he replied, 'That I cannot say. Who knows what internal injuries she may have sustained, as well as the ones that are visible? What I do know is I have to operate now whilst she is still unconscious. Do you wish me to proceed?'

Samuel and Josephine looked towards Molly and when she nodded numbly they then nodded their consent.

'Right then, I shall need a good solid flat-topped table to be carried into the room,' he told them brusquely. 'And also as much hot water and clean towels as you can supply me with.'

Josephine bustled away to see to his requests as Molly sat there feeling as if her whole life was falling apart around her.

Twenty minutes later, the doctor was ready to begin with his shirtsleeves rolled up to above his elbows. 'It is kinder this way,' he explained to them. 'Should she wake up, the pain of stitching her face would be excruciating and as for the amputation – well...'

They were standing in Amy's room. She had been transferred to a stout oak table that had been carried up from the kitchen. A smaller one was placed at the side of it and as Molly's eyes rested on the bottle of laudanum and the instruments lying there she shuddered, feeling as if she had been caught in the grip of a nightmare. Only the day before, her girl had been stunningly beautiful with a wonderful life stretching ahead of her. After today, if she survived, she would be maimed for life and a cripple. As Josephine led her from the room she began to sob.

The night hours ticked away on the grandfather clock in the drawing room as the Forresters, with Molly and Toby to keep them company, waited for news from the doctor. Both Beatrice and Lily had refused to go to bed and whilst Lily served the silent party at regular intervals with tea which was left to go cold, Beatrice volunteered to help the doctor. He would need someone to pass him his instruments, and being Amy's lifelong friend she wanted to be present.

At last, the doctor appeared in the doorway, his apron covered in blood, looking weary and sad.

'I have done all I can,' he said heavily. 'Now we can only wait to see if she wakes up.'

'How long is that likely to be?' Josephine asked fearfully.

The doctor shrugged. 'There is no way of knowing, I am afraid. She is in a deep coma and we have to remember that on top of all her injuries she had lain outside for a whole night. I would suggest that in the morning you employ two nurses. Should she survive, she will need constant care.'

Mr Forrester nodded. 'It shall be so,' he assured

the man huskily. 'And thank you for what you have done.' The words sounded ludicrous even to his own ears. Why was he thanking this man for cutting Amy's leg off and maiming her for life? But then had he not, the alternative was too terrible to even contemplate.

'Can I go in to her now?' Molly asked pitiably from the depths of the chair.

The doctor nodded. 'Of course you can, Mrs Ernshaw, but I should warn you that she will not be aware that you are there.'

Molly rose slowly as her back screamed in protest and Josephine accompanied her. Toby too now rose from his seat and addressing Mr Forrester he told him, 'I ought to be going now. There's nothin' more I can do here. Good night, sir.'

'Good night, Toby, and thank you. I don't know what we would have done without you tonight.'

Toby inclined his head and then strode past him with his mouth set in a grim line. This had been the worst night of his whole life.

Chapter Thirty-One

It had now been two days since Toby had rescued Amy from the bottom of the ravine but as yet she showed no signs of gaining consciousness. It had almost broken Molly's heart the first time she had stepped into the room and seen her. The gash on Amy's cheek had gone deep to the bone and the doctor had stitched it as best he could, but it still looked grotesque. If anything it looked even worse now than it had on the night the doctor had stitched it. Now the whole area around it was black and blue with bruises, and that side of her face was so swollen that the corner of her mouth and her eye were pulled down and she looked disfigured.

A cage had been placed beneath the sheets to hold them off her leg. The doctor explained that he had amputated halfway between the ankle and the knee, and assured them that once the stump was healed, Amy would be able to have a wooden leg made that would fit over it. But this was little consolation to Molly. She knew that Amy would never be the same girl again. Not that it made her love her any the less. If anything she loved her even more now and had not left her side once. She talked to her constantly and begged her to come back to her. If the girl died, Molly knew that she would have nothing left to live for.

Josephine had barely left the room either and she and Molly had taken it in turns napping in the chairs that'd been placed at either side of the bed. Two nurses were now in attendance and the only time the two women slipped away was when they needed to use the commode or when one of the nurses was changing the dressings on Amy's leg. Somehow, neither of them could face watching that. The doctor was still calling in three times a day but each time he would leave shaking his head. There was nothing more he could do now.

Samuel had written to François to tell him of the accident but knew that it would probably be at least another week before he could expect a reply, and with Amy as she was, anything could have happened by then.

Toby had called in to The Folly each evening on his way home after work to enquire after Amy, but had declined the offer to see her. For now, he preferred to remember her as she had been, not the broken girl he had lifted up the steep cliff face.

It was on this evening, as he was making his way home after calling in at The Folly, that he began to question for the first time how the accident might have come about. How could Amy, such a sensible soul, have fallen from the edge of the ravine if she was sitting sketching? And why had the sketches he had seen been trampled on and scattered about? But then, he asked himself, who would ever hurt Amy? She was loved by all. There was one thing for sure. Unless Amy woke up to tell them what had actually happened, they would never know.

By the fourth day, although no one admitted it out loud, everyone was beginning to lose hope of Amy ever awakening. Molly was so tired that she was sure she could have slept for a whole month straight through, but she was afraid of taking any more than a few moments' nap at a time in case Amy stirred.

Adam had been in to see her that morning, looking pale and pinched as they all did, but after hearing that there was still no change he retired back to his room.

At lunchtime, the doctor called in for his midday visit just as he always did, and for the first time after taking her pulse, he smiled tentatively. 'Her pulse is steadier,' he told them, not wishing to raise their hopes yet wanting to give them something to hold on to. 'And her heartbeat is more regular too.'

'Does that mean that she's goin' to be all right?' Molly asked hopefully.

'Well ... let us just say for now that it is a step in the right direction,' the doctor told her cautiously. 'I shall be back this evening. But if there is any change at all in the meantime, do not hesitate to send for me.'

The two women bade him goodbye, then sat back to continue their vigil. Molly's head was dropping by mid-afternoon, but she still clung firmly to Amy's limp hand. It was whilst she was doing so that she suddenly detected a slight twitch in the girl's fingers. Her head was up in an instant as she stared down at it, and sure enough a few seconds later it twitched again.

'Mrs Forrester ... I reckon she just moved her hand a little,' Molly muttered, praying with all her soul that she had been right. Josephine was up in an instant, and taking Amy's other hand, she gently shook it up and down.

'Amy, my dear ... can you hear me?' Her voice was little above a whisper. For long moments there was no sign that Amy had heard her but then she suddenly let out a low groan.

It was Molly's turn to try now. 'Amy, if yer can hear us, open yer eyes, pet.'

Again nothing for some long time, and then Amy blinked. It wasn't much but it told them that she had heard them.

'Blink again,' Molly urged, and this time Amy obeyed her almost instantly. Looking towards Josephine, Molly told her, 'Get someone to run fer the doctor. I reckon she's comin' round.'

With an excited smile on her face, Josephine lifted her skirts in a most unbecoming manner and ran to do as she was told.

Amy opened her eyes properly early the next morning, and groaned with pain. Molly was up and leaning over her in an instant as she soothed, 'It's all right, lass. Just relax an' take it easy.'

As Amy's eyes settled on the old woman's face her eyes fluttered shut again as she fell into a natural sleep. From time to time she would wake, flailing and crying as if she was caught in the grip of a nightmare, but then when she saw Molly she would settle again. This went on for two days, during which time her mouth would open and close as if she was trying to tell them something, but no words came out.

'She is probably just traumatised from the accident,' the doctor told Molly when she expressed her concerns. 'In actual fact she is doing very well, so try not to worry too much. Injuries such as Amy sustained are going to take a long time to heal, so please be patient.'

Molly nodded. She knew only too well that they had a long way to go. As yet, Amy had no idea that she had lost part of her leg; nor about the damage to her face, but Molly knew that soon they would have to tell her, and she dreaded it. Outwardly, her cuts and bruises were healing. Even the scar on her face was not quite so swollen now, but already

Molly could see that it would never disappear, and it ran in a jagged angry line from just beneath her eye to her chin. And the girl had been so beautiful; it almost broke her old heart to see her.

Josephine was just relieved that Amy had survived the accident, and chattered to her constantly about François and the forthcoming wedding. 'We shall have to get you well,' she would tell her as she spooned chicken broth into her mouth, 'so that you can get busy on the design for your wedding dress. I have no doubt that François will be coming to see you soon to make sure that you are recovering.'

But François did not come. The following week Amy received a letter from him, which Josephine read out to her. He expressed his regrets at her accident and assured her that he was looking forward to the wedding and counting off the days. Secretly, Josephine was a little peeved that he had not taken the trouble to come and see Amy personally. After all, he *was* her fiancé. But then as her husband pointed out, the Laroques were very busy people and could not just leave their businesses unattended without a great deal of preparation.

Now that Amy was showing signs of improvement, Molly finally accepted the Forresters' offer of a room next to Amy's where sometimes she went to rest but never for more than a few hours at a time. As yet, Amy had not spoken a word, and when she was awake she would just lie staring at the ceiling. Sometimes she would appear agitated and her hands would grasp the sheets, but when she was asked what was wrong she would simply purse her lips.

'Amy, lass,' Molly gently asked her one morning when the nurses had washed her and changed the dressings on her leg, 'can yer remember what happened? How did yer come to fall into the ravine?'

Amy merely looked towards the window without attempting to answer. Molly and Josephine exchanged a worried glance. All they could do was wait until the girl was ready to talk to them.

The doctor assured them that behaviour such as this was normal following a bad accident. He even suggested that Amy might not remember what had happened and so for now they had to be patient.

That evening, when Toby called in as was customary to see how Amy was, on his way home from the schoolroom where he had been working, Molly was waiting for him in the hallway.

'Come up an' see her, lad,' she implored him. 'Happen she'll speak to you.'

Toby hesitated but then after taking a deep breath he nodded and followed her up the stairs.

'She's in here,' Molly wheezed pausing at the bedroom door. 'Go on in, lad.'

Toby gulped before grasping the door handle and stepping into the room. A nurse was in the process of folding some linen but when he appeared she bobbed her knee and quickly left as Toby stood wringing his cap in his hands and staring towards the bed.

Amy's head turned ever so slightly, and when she saw him standing there, a tear squeezed out of the corner of her eye. He was at her side in a minute, grasping her hand as all the love he felt for her rose in him like a tide.

'Aw, lass.' His voice was strangled. 'Thank God you survived.' He did not see the ugly scar on her face or the cage above her legs, only the girl he had always adored from afar. 'You give us a rare gliff back there for a time, I don't mind tellin' yer. But it's over now an' all that matters is you gettin' well again.'

She returned the pressure on his fingers for the briefest of seconds but then her eyes fluttered shut and as she drifted off to sleep again, Toby hung his head and wept openly with relief.

Toby continued to call in at The Folly every evening on his way home from his shift down the mine or after his few precious hours per week spent in the schoolroom, and it was on one such evening when he was making his way home that he stopped by to see Mary. She had just put the twins to bed and she and Joe were enjoying a bit of peace and quiet.

'Come on in, love,' Mary welcomed him when she opened the door. 'Yer just in time fer a brew. Sit yerself down, there's plenty left in the pot.' She hurried to fetch another mug as Toby sank into the chair next to Joe and asked, 'So how was she today?'

Toby sighed. 'They reckon she's healin' as well as can be expected, but she still hasn't spoken yet.'

Mary glanced at him out of the corner of her eye as she spooned sugar into his drink. Knowing Toby as she did, she suspected that something was troubling him. After carrying it over to him she asked gently, 'What's troublin' yer, love?'

After chewing on his lip for a moment, her

brother confided, 'I've just got this feelin', an' I can't get it out o' me head – that what happened to Amy weren't an accident.'

Mary frowned. 'But what else could it have been? As far as I know, I was the last to see her afore the accident happened an' there weren't anyone else about...' Then an image suddenly flashed before her eyes and the colour drained from her face.

'There *was* someone else in the grounds, now I come to think of it,' she said. 'Me an' Amy were standin' at the gate, an' as we were talkin' we saw someone ridin' a white horse alongside the river. It was a woman dressed in green an' she were goin' hell fer leather. I remember commentin' on it to Amy just before she left me.'

As she and Toby stared at each other, a terrible thought occurred to them both simultaneously. 'Weren't Miss Eugenie's horse white?' Mary asked.

'Aye, it was.' It was Joe who answered with a deep frown on his forehead. 'Did she see you an' Miss Amy talkin'?'

'I ... I don't know,' Mary stuttered. 'There's every chance she did. Yer don't think she followed the lass, do yer?'

'It wouldn't surprise me,' Joe answered as he rose from his seat. 'It were common knowledge that she was jealous o' Miss Amy. I reckon we ought to go an' tell the master.'

'I'll come with yer,' Toby told him, and in seconds both men were out of the door and heading back to The Folly.

Once Lily had admitted them, Mr Forrester

took them straight into his study and listened solemn-faced to what they had to say.

'O' course, we could be quite wrong,' Joe admitted. 'But it's funny as it were a pure white horse, ain't it? What do yer think we should do about it?'

With his hands joined behind his back, the master strode up and down the room for a time as he thought about it. Then he told them. 'I think I need to ask Amy if Eugenie was involved in the accident and we'll take it from there. Please wait here and I'll be back shortly.' Without another word he left the room and once upstairs outside Amy's door he took a deep breath before entering.

Nodding at his wife and Molly who were sitting at either side of the bed he bent and lifted Amy's hand and smiled at her.

'How are you feeling, my dear?' he asked gently.

She smiled at him weakly in answer.

'Toby and Joe are downstairs,' he went on. 'And Mary remembered something quite interesting this evening. She remembered that on the day you had your accident, just before you left her, you both saw a woman on a white horse riding through the grounds. Is this right, Amy?'

He heard her sharp intake of breath and she pulled her hand from his.

'Please don't be afraid to tell me what happened, my dear,' he urged. 'Was that rider Eugenie?'

Mr Forrester's heart was thudding with rage. Could it be that Adam's wife had tried to kill Amy? He had known for many years that Eugenie was a jealous, possessive and self-centred woman, but surely she would not stoop to such levels?

When it became clear that Amy was not going to answer him, he quietly left the room, closely followed by his wife, who asked him in a horrified whisper, 'You surely don't suspect that Eugenie was involved in Amy's accident, do you, Samuel?'

'Well, it sounds very suspicious, don't you think? Eugenie made it more than clear that she hated Amy, and if it *was* her riding through the grounds that day, she could easily have spotted Amy talking to Mary and followed her. Also, how many pure white horses have you seen hereabouts? Eugenie sent one of her father's stable-hands for Snowflake within days of leaving here, much to Seth's dismay. He had raised that horse from the day that Adam bought it for her as a foal, and she liked the fact that no one else had a mount like hers. She and Seth had many a quarrel about the way Eugenie rode him, but at the end of the day he was her horse and there was little Seth could do about it.'

'So what are you going to do now?' his wife asked nervously.

'I am going to see Eugenie's father. If she did have anything to do with Amy's accident, the only way she could have got to the ravine was through the woods. You know as well as I do how dense the trees are in there, and if she forced the horse through them the poor creature would have been scratched to pieces. I shall demand to see Snowflake, and if her father refuses to allow me to, I shall involve the authorities. Although I doubt it will come to that. I always found Sir Edmund to be a reasonable man, and if she was not involved in any way he will be keen to clear her name.'

'And when will you be going?'

'As soon as Seth can have the carriage made ready for me,' he told her, and with that he strode off, leaving Josephine wringing her hands fearfully.

Mr Forrester, accompanied by both Toby and Joe, was on his way to Eugenie's father's home, Greyfriars Manor, within the hour. They each sat silent until the carriage drew to a halt at the steps of the magnificent residence just within the borders of Leicestershire.

Toby and Joe waited outside while Mr Forrester was admitted to the house, reappearing moments later with a manservant who led them to the stable-block at the rear of the Manor.

One of the grooms showed them to the stall where a pure white horse was tethered.

'Hello, Snowflake,' Mr Forrester cooed softly as the groom opened the stall for him, and the gentle creature nuzzled his hand as he stroked its silky mane. Snowflake had always been a great favourite of Samuel's, and he had been sad to see the stallion leave The Folly when Eugenie's belongings were removed.

'Fetch some lamps, please – I need more light,' Mr Forrester demanded, and the groom scurried away to do as he was told. Minutes later, as the lamps were held aloft, Mr Forrester ran his hands down the creature's flanks. There were cuts all along them that had obviously been inflicted recently.

'When did the horse get these injuries?' he asked.

The groom frowned as he tried to think back. 'Oh, it must have been about a week an' a half or so ago,' he mumbled. 'Yes, it was, I remember now – it were the night before we had that bad thunderstorm. The poor critter were in a right old lather when Miss Eugenie brought him back. Foamin' at the mouth he was, an' I had to bathe all the cuts meself. But thankfully she ain't been back out on him since.'

Grim-faced, Mr Forrester strode back towards the house, telling his companions, 'Wait outside for me, please. I shouldn't be too long.' He disappeared back into the Manor, where Sir Edmund Walton, Eugenie's father, was waiting for him.

Toby and Joe clambered back into the carriage to wait, and when Mr Forrester rejoined them some time later, he was in a towering rage.

'It was her all right,' he spat in disgust. 'Her father sent for her and she was so drunk she almost fell into the room. I actually felt sorry for the man. He obviously doesn't know how to cope with her. She's an only child and he's a widower, and he's out of his depth. Apparently she's drinking the second she sets foot out of bed in the morning now. She admitted that she had forced Amy over the edge of the ravine and actually laughed about it. Can you *believe* that? She showed no contrition – says she is only sorry that she isn't dead.' Samuel took a deep breath to get himself under control.

'So what do we do now?' Toby asked as his blood boiled.

'I'm not quite sure what to do yet,' Samuel admitted. 'I need to speak to Amy and Adam first. Her father has assured me that if we do not press charges against Eugenie, he will have her admitted to an asylum.'

'Best place fer her an' all!' Toby cried. 'Either that or she should feel a noose about her neck.'

The three men then lapsed into silence as the carriage bore them all back to The Folly, each locked in their own solemn thoughts. Their beloved Amy had been maimed and crippled for no good reason at all.

Chapter Thirty-Two

'Aw, lass, whyever didn't yer tell us that it was Eugenie who had done this terrible thing to yer?' Molly asked as she held fast to Amy's hand.

It was now three days since Samuel Forrester had visited Eugenie's family home and the whole of the town was alive with gossip about what had happened. News had a habit of travelling fast in this neck of the woods.

'I ... I didn't want to cause any trouble,' Amy said miserably. The nurses had just washed and changed her into a pretty lace-trimmed night gown and the process had exhausted her, although she was slowly grower stronger by the day.

'Well, all I can say is, it's a good job Mary remembered seein' her then,' Molly told her. 'An' at least she's had her comeuppance now, though I still don't understand why you didn't want the justices involved. Had you died, which you well could 'ave done, she'd have hung and that's a fact. As it is, it's doubtful she'll leave that asylum for some long time – so that's sommat to be thankful for, at least. They reckon they had to drag her out o' the house kickin' an' screamin' when they went fer her, an' serves her right, that's what I say. She don't deserve no better.'

As yet, Amy was still lying flat on her back and once Molly's chatter had died away, she suddenly asked the question that Molly had been dreading.

'Gran, why can't I feel my foot?'

Molly gulped deep in her throat. She had never willingly lied to Amy in her whole life and had no intentions of starting now.

'Well, the thing is, love ... yer leg were badly broken in the fall, an' in more than one place. It were a terrible mess an' so the doctor had no option but to...'

When her voice trailed away and her eyes filled with tears, Amy stared at her steadily. 'My leg is gone, isn't it?' she asked.

'Not all of it,' Molly told her hastily. 'He had to amputate halfway between the ankle an' the knee.'

'So ... I will never walk again?'

'Oh yes, you will, my dear.' Josephine took her hand now and her own eyes full, she told her, 'Your grandfather has already sent for a doctor from London to come and see you. He special-ises in people who have suffered accidents such as this, and he assured us that when you are strong again and the wound has properly healed, he will be able to make you a wooden leg. No one will ever know what has happened, once you get used to walking on it, and no one will ever see it.'

Both women had expected tears but Amy lay

448

unmoved before asking, 'And what about my face?' Her hand slowly rose to trace the jagged wound that she could feel running all down one side of her cheek.

The breath caught in Molly's throat but thankfully, Josephine answered the girl. 'The doctor assures us that the scar will heal in time. You must have done it during your fall.'

Amy carefully shook her head. 'No, I didn't. I remember how it happened quite clearly. Miss Eugenie was whipping her horse, and when it reared, its hoof caught me in the face.'

Molly visibly shuddered at the image Amy had conjured up, and not for the first time over these last long days she found herself thinking, Eeh, what I wouldn't do to have just half an hour alone locked in a room wi' that little minx an' a horse-whip. I'd let her know what it felt like to have it laid across her, an' that's fer sure.

'I would like a mirror.'

Amy's words startled them and the two women glanced at each other fearfully.

'I ... I shouldn't get lookin' at yer face just yet, pet.' There was a tremor in Molly's voice. 'It's still a bit swelled an' you'll be seein' it at its worst.'

'Gran, I *want* a mirror.' Amy's voice expressed that she was determined to have her way, so Josephine slowly crossed to the dressing-table and, lifting the silver-backed mirror that lay there, she carried it back to the bed.

'Just remember what your gran told you,' she said. 'There is still a lot of healing to come and in time it will get much better.' She handed the mirror to Amy and as the girl gazed into it, her

449

face was sad.

'I am so ugly now,' she stated flatly.

'*You ugly!* why, I never heard such a thing!' Molly snapped. 'It would take a sight more than that to spoil you, me lass. Yer still beautiful both inside and out.'

Even as the words were spoken she knew that they were exaggerated, but Amy shocked her now when she told her, 'It doesn't matter, Gran. At least I still have my hands and I will still be able to design. But what about François. Do you think he will still want to marry me?'

'Without a doubt, if his letters are owt to go by,' Molly assured her. 'Don't forget, by next spring when yer get wed, that scar will be hardly noticeable. All you have to do now is concentrate on gettin' well. The master has already had a crutch made for yer, fer when yer first feel able to get about, an' then the doctor will be here from London to measure you up fer yer new leg. Everythin' is going' to be just fine, I promise.'

Amy nodded and then further surprised them when she asked, 'Would you mind if I had a few moments on my own?'

Both Molly and Josephine moved towards the door, and as it closed behind them they heard Amy start to cry, and it almost broke both their hearts.

'Is Adam not coming down to breakfast again?' Samuel enquired as he looked across the table at his wife the next morning.

Helping herself to a kidney from a silver serving dish she sighed, 'It would appear not. I don't

450

mind telling you, Samuel, I am very concerned about him. He spends all his time either locked in his room, out riding Pepperpot, or talking to Seth in the stables. I don't think he's been into town to check on his business once this week. He just seems to have lost interest in everything.'

Samuel took a bite of hot buttered toast as he nodded in agreement. 'I have noticed,' he said. 'He seems to have gone steadily downhill since Eugenie's attack on Amy. He took it very badly when he went into her room to see her; no doubt he is blaming himself for what happened because Eugenie was his wife.'

'I have the feeling that there is even more to it than that,' Josephine replied with a worried frown on her face. 'There is something deeply troubling him, Samuel, and I don't know what it is.'

'No doubt he will tell us when he is good and ready to,' her husband replied, and the couple lapsed into silence as they finished their meal.

As autumn approached, and her wounds healed, Amy became adept at getting about on her crutch, and much to her grandparents' disappointment, she and Molly moved back into their cottage.

When they expressed their concerns, Amy had waved them aside. 'My leg is healing well,' she assured them, 'and I know that Gran is longing to get back to her own home. But I will still come and see you regularly, although you may have to send the coach for me if you have no objections to that. I don't think I could walk too far on my crutch just yet.'

'We shall miss you, my dear,' Josephine told

her, and she meant the words from the heart.

Amy was now busily sketching again and it had been a great comfort to her. So had Toby, who once again came to see her almost every evening. They seemed to have regained some of the closeness they had once shared, and it did Molly's heart good to see the two of them together. The girl had started to design her wedding dress, although it was not what Molly had been expecting. It was very plain – which she was quick to point out, but Amy just shrugged.

'You know I've never been one for anything too fussy, Gran,' she told her. 'And all the frills and furbelows in the world won't hide the scar on my face, will they?'

Molly's heart was sore for her. The cut was healing far better than any of them had dared to hope, but it was still very noticeable.

'Do you think I am ugly now, Toby?' Amy asked him one evening when her gran had retired to bed. His mouth gaped in amazement as he looked at the scar as if he was seeing it for the first time. 'You … *ugly?*' He laughed as his head wagged from side to side. 'You could *never* be ugly, not even if you were covered in boils,' he told her.

'But what do you think François' reaction will be when he first sees me like this?'

Toby considered his reply for some time before saying, 'I would hope he would see the same girl that he saw the last time he came here. 'Cos that's what I see. To be honest, I never even notice it.'

Amy had sighed, hoping he was right. But then, François was not Toby.

'The doctor that Mr Forrester contacted in

London is coming to see me in November,' she told him. 'He thinks that my leg should be healed enough to measure me for my wooden one by then, and he says that if I try very hard and persevere with it, I will be able to walk down the aisle without my crutch.'

Toby lowered his eyes. It was hard to think that Amy would be a married woman next year. His thoughts moved on to Annie. She had never made a secret of the fact that she was his for the taking, but lately he had got the feeling that she was growing impatient with him, so perhaps it was time that he did something about it. His life was going to be very empty once Amy was gone, and a lonely future stretched ahead of him.

Yes, he thought to himself. I'll call in an' see Annie on me way home from work tomorrow. He knew that he would be welcome, but he did not tell Amy of his intentions. She was too wrapped up in her own wedding plans to care.

Now that Amy was no longer staying at The Folly, time was weighing heavily on Josephine's hands and so she renewed her efforts at finding Jessica, badgering Mr Burrows almost daily.

Samuel was growing increasingly concerned about her. She seemed to be slipping back into the melancholy place that she had been in for years following Jessica's disappearance, and he had no idea at all what he could do to stop it. He was also worried about Adam. The young man seemed to have lost all interest in everything, even his businesses, which were being kept going now by temporary managers who Mr Forrester had employed both in London and Nuneaton to take Adam's place. There was no way that he could see to the running of them and his own as well. The only thing he could hope for was that it would be a temporary measure, but as time moved on he began to have his doubts.

It was on a bitterly cold Saturday afternoon in October, when the leaves were fluttering from the trees, turning the lawns of The Folly to russets and gold that Josephine returned from one of her frequent visits to Mr Burrows.

Samuel was sitting in the drawing room reading his newspaper and Adam was slumped in the bay window staring out across the grounds when she joined them and promptly burst into shuddering sobs.

'Why, my dear, whatever is the matter?' Samuel was out of his seat in a second and leading her to the settee.

'Despite all his best efforts Mr Burrows has still not been able to discover anything at all about Jessica's whereabouts since the night that Molly found her in the church doorway.' Josephine's sobs were echoing around the room and tears were spurting from her eyes. 'And today, he said he fears there is no more he can do. He said it might be as well if we settled up what we owe him and leave our daughter in the past. But how can I do that, Samuel? When our child might still be out there somewhere, in need of us. Oh, I just cannot bear it.' And she broke into a fresh torrent of sobs that were heartbreaking to hear.

Adam stood up from his seat and strode past

454

his parents without a word, his face set. Once in the shelter of the stable-block he dropped his head into his hands and began to weep.

It was there that Seth found him sometime later when he came to feed the horses. He had loved this young man almost like his own since the second he had drawn breath, and it hurt him to see him so upset.

'What's troubling you so, Master Adam?' He placed a gentle hand on his shoulder.

Adam turned tortured eyes to him. 'It's my mother, Seth. Searching for Jessica is destroying her. I ... I don't think I can keep up the pretence any more.'

Seth nodded understandingly. He had always dreaded this day but now that it was finally here, he felt strong enough to face it. 'Then let us go together an' put the poor woman out of her misery, eh? This has gone on fer long enough an' it's no good fer any of us. What do yer say?'

Adam looked at him long and hard before nodding tearfully. 'I think you are right, Seth,' he said. 'It is time.'

'Well, I can't say as I'm sorry,' Seth muttered. 'It's been hard to sleep of a night wi' such a heavy weight on me mind.'

Side by side, the two men walked from the stables and headed back to the house.

His parents were still in the drawing room when Adam entered with Seth and they both looked mildly surprised to see him enter with his groom in tow. Josephine had calmed down a little now, although her eyes were red-rimmed and swollen from crying.

Before either of them could comment, however, Adam told them, 'Mother, Father ... I have something I need to confess. Many years ago I committed a most heinous sin and I made Seth here a party to it. Before I go any further I should ask that there be no repercussions on him. Seth only acted on my orders like the loyal servant that he has always been.'

Adam's face was as pale as death and behind him, Seth shuffled from foot to foot uncomfortably as he wrung his cap in his work-worn hands.

'Perhaps you had better tell us what it is then, Adam,' his father told him, guessing that he was going to hear something of importance.

Drawing himself up to his full height and looking his father full in the face, Adam began his sorry tale. 'After Jessica and Robert ran away, they kept in touch with me,' he admitted, ignoring his mother, whose hand had flown to her mouth. 'Just as Mr Burrows informed you, they went to live in the back streets of Coventry and for a time, Robert earned them a living as best he could. They desperately wished to get married, but of course, that was out of the question because Jessica was not of age, so they were forced to live as man and wife without the blessing of the church. Things were not easy for them and then Jessica discovered that she was pregnant. She did not wish her child to be born out of wedlock, so she wrote to me begging me to speak to you and to ask you to forgive her so that they could marry.'

At this point Adam hung his head in shame before forcing himself to go on. 'As you know, at that time I had just become engaged to Eugenie and I was terrified of losing her. I was sure that if her father were to discover that I had an unmarried, pregnant sister, he would stop the wedding from going ahead. So I did the most deplorable thing. I sent Seth to Coventry with some money and a letter for Jessica, in which I told her that I had spoken to you on her behalf and that you had truly disowned her and never wished to set eyes on her again.'

'Oh, Adam, *no!*' His mother's voice held such pain that he wished he could die of shame there and then, but now that he had begun his terrible confession he knew that he must end it.

'Some months later, following my marriage, I received another letter from her telling me that Robert had been killed in an accident down the mine. She was totally distraught. She had used the last of their money to give him a decent burial and now the birth of her child was imminent and she did not know which way to turn. Again she pleaded with me to speak to you for the sake of her unborn child. She said she would throw herself on your mercy if only you would allow her to come home. So, once again I sent Seth off with some more money for her, but when he got to the address I had been given, the landlord informed him that he had thrown Jessica out on to the streets for falling behind with her rent.'

Adam's voice broke at this point and he was momentarily too distressed to go on, but then he calmed himself and continued, 'When Seth brought this news back to me I was beside myself and I ordered him to find her at any cost and stop her from returning home. On Christmas Eve he eventually found her wandering on the outskirts of the town and followed her, unsure of what he should do. After some time, he saw her seek refuge in the doorway of the church and from the sounds that were issuing from there he guessed that she was giving birth. Some time later, whilst Seth was still watching, Mrs Ernshaw came along and he saw her go to Jessica's assistance. All was quiet by then and when Mrs Ernshaw left a short time later, he crept into the doorway and saw that my poor sister's struggles were over. He presumed that the child must also have died inside her, for he had not heard an infant cry and there was no sign of a baby.' Adam's voice broke as he concluded the sorry tale. 'Jessica was dead, and so not knowing what else to do, Seth removed her body and shortly afterwards had her buried in an unmarked grave.' Adam faced his parents. 'And so now you know the terrible secret that I have been forced to live with, all of these years. You will probably disown me and I do not blame you. But I will tell you this: there is no punishment that you could inflict on me that could make me suffer a *fraction* of what I have suffered over the years. You could never loathe me or hate me half as much as I hate and loathe myself. What I did is unforgivable and I can truthfully say I will never forgive myself to my dying day. And all for a woman who turned out to be not good enough to lick my sister's boots.'

A terrible silence lay heavy on the room. The tale that Adam had just told them was so awful that no words for now could express his parents' feelings.

But then slowly his father's eyes found his. 'I can forgive you, Adam, because in my heart of hearts I know that I am just as responsible for this tragedy as you are. *I* was the one who ordered Jessica from the house in the first place, and like you I shall never be able to forgive myself for that. For me, there can be no excuse for my actions except for a father's foolish pride. But you were young and in love and could not foresee the terrible consequences of your actions. I have already lost one child through my pride and I do not intend to lose another.'

Adam now broke down and wept as his father looked beyond him to his wife, whose face was stricken.

'I am afraid that from this night on, we must accept that we will never see our beloved girl again,' he told her. 'We must also accept that she has long been dead and buried, but one thing we can do is rejoice in the fact that we still have our grand-daughter – and if Seth will only show us where Jessica is buried, we can visit her there and make our peace with her. Will you do that for us, Seth?'

'Aye, I will, master, an' be right glad to,' the man said humbly.

Throughout the confession, Josephine had not spoken one word, but now she surprised them all when she stood up and said quietly, 'If you did but know it, Adam, this confession is almost welcome. Now at last we can put the past behind us and look to the future. Deep inside, I have somehow known since the day we discovered that Amy was our granddaughter that Jessica was gone from us for good. She would never have abandoned her child and not gone in search of her, had she been alive. But still I clung to hope, not allowing myself to believe that she was dead. And now at last I can grieve properly and go on for Amy's sake.'

She seemed strangely calm, almost as if she had already done her grieving through the last long lonely years, as indeed she had.

Chapter Thirty-Three

On a bitterly cold November day in the corner of the churchyard in Caldecote, a magnificent tombstone was erected to mark Jessica's grave. It had been commissioned by Mr Forrester and carved in the shape of an angel from finest Italian marble, and was a fitting tribute to the young woman over whom she would now watch for all eternity. The sweet-faced angel appeared to hover, her marble arms held out protectively over the body of the soul that she guarded. Behind her, her wings stretched high towards the sun, making it seem as if she was about to take flight. At her feet was a plaque with an inscription carved into it, which read:

Jessica Amelia Forrester 1810–1830
Beloved daughter, sister and mother
Always remembered
Forever in our hearts

As the small group assembled there stared down at the snow-white lilies that had been heaped upon the grave, each of them was silent, locked in their own thoughts.

For Amy, who was leaning heavily on her crutch, there were deep regrets for the fact that she had never been privileged to know her mother. For Molly, sorrow that she had not been able to save the poor soul that she had found in the church doorway on that long-ago Christmas Eve. The master and mistress had their own feelings to deal with. But the one who was hurting most of all was Adam. He knew only too well that, had it not been for him, things might have turned out very differently. It was a truth that he would have to try and live with for the rest of his life.

Still, at least there was one feeling that they all had in common – and that was relief. Jessica could now rest in peace.

Behind them, the stonemasons who had erected the monument were busily loading their tools on to an open-backed cart, keeping the noise they made to a respectful minimum. Mr Forrester broke away from the little group to congratulate the men on their craftsmanship, giving them a hefty bonus. The men tipped their caps and mumbled their thanks as the gentleman turned and made his way back to the graveside.

It was then that a spasm of coughing wracked Molly's old frame and Amy placed an arm about her shoulders, waiting for the bout to pass.

'I think I ought to be getting Gran home now,' she said, unable to keep the worry from her voice. 'I did tell her not to come out today. The

461

cold air always sets her cough off.'

Molly's eyes were streaming from the violence of the attack she had just endured, and now Josephine stepped forward and asked her, 'Why don't you and Amy come and stay up at The Folly with us, Mrs Ernshaw, just until your cough has eased? I could get our doctor to take a look at you.'

'That's very good o' yer, ma'am,' Molly answered, thumping her chest, 'but I'll not take yer up on the offer, if yer don't mind. Soon as ever I get back to me own fireside I'll be fine.' Even so, she allowed Josephine to take her elbow and lead her back to the carriage. The two women were completely at ease in each other's company now and had been ever since Molly had stayed at The Folly following Amy's tragic fall.

Amy cast a last look at the grave before limping after them. The doctor that Mr Forrester had sent for from London had been to see her earlier in the month to measure her up for her new leg. He had returned two weeks later with the finished article, and ever since then Amy had practised on it every spare minute she had, determined that she would walk down the aisle on Mr Forrester's arm when she married François. Her leg had thankfully healed well, but since trying the wooden replacement she had been in extreme pain. The wood had rubbed against the tender skin to the point that Molly had begged her to leave it off, but Amy was determined to walk again without the use of her crutch.

The scar on her face had also healed well, but she would never again be the unblemished beauty she had once been, as she knew only too well each time she looked in the mirror. Still, she supposed that things could have been worse; at least she had survived. But how would François feel when he saw her? Her fiancé was so handsome and could have had any woman he chose. Would he still want her when he saw that her face was now permanently scarred? She could only wait and see. He had still not seen her since his last visit, and it looked suspiciously as if he would not do so now until he and the Laroque family arrived for the wedding in the spring.

She tried to turn her thoughts to happier things once they were all seated in the carriage, but still she worried about how François would react, the first time he saw her. She was no longer the girl he had fallen in love with, and there was nothing she could do about it.

She had been to London twice since the terrible day of her fall, accompanied everywhere she went by Mr Forrester, who watched over her like a hawk as she moved around on her crutch. On the first visit, Nancy had been heartbroken when she saw what Eugenie had done to her.

'Didn't I always tell yer she was a bloody little minx?' she raved indignantly. 'Why the hell didn't yer let the peelers deal wi' her? They'd've locked 'er up an' thrown away the key, or better still they'd've strung the cow up!'

Amy just shrugged. 'She *is* locked up,' she reminded Nancy gently.

Hands on hips, Nancy frowned. 'Yer too soft by 'alf, so you are,' she declared, but thankfully she then let the subject drop and loving Amy as she did, she was careful to never mention it again.

Now, as the carriage bowled away from the church, Amy thought of her friend as she peeped at her grandfather out of the corner of her eye. There was something she was longing to ask him, but how would he react to her request? Deciding that there was only one way to find out she began,

'Grandfather, I have something to ask you.'

'Then ask away, my dear.'

Amy glanced at Molly before going on, 'The thing is, during the time I have been staying at the house in Sloane Street, Nancy, your maid there, and I have become good friends.'

Samuel nodded, well aware of the fact.

'So I was wondering – and I know that this is very irregular – but I was wondering if you would object to her coming to the wedding to be a bridesmaid? Of course, I am having Beatrice as my matron of honour. We have grown up together, but–'

'Stop right there.' Samuel held his hand up and grinned. 'You really do not have to explain your relationship to Nancy with me. Be she a servant or a queen, if you want her at the wedding then it shall be as you wish.'

'Oh, thank you!' Amy sat back in the seat with a wide smile on her face as she thought of how thrilled Nancy would be when she asked her, and the rest of the journey was passed in silence, apart from Molly's occasional rattling cough.

The following week, Samuel and Amy set off for London. She had not expected to go so soon, but her grandfather had insisted that there was urgent business there that needed to be attended to and so she went without question, trusting him explicitly.

Amy wore her new leg for the journey and by the time they reached London she was in terrible pain, but even so she was determined to persevere with it. It was only six months to the wedding now and she so wanted to walk down the aisle without the aid of her crutch.

She was tired by the time they reached the house and finally removed the offending leg and resorted to her crutch as Nancy fussed over her. Her friend seemed unusually excited as she settled Amy into the chair in the drawing room and Amy noticed that she kept glancing towards the window.

'Are you expecting someone?' she asked.

Nancy flushed. 'Er ... no, I ain't, but I reckon the master's expectin' some visitors.'

'Oh, is he? He never mentioned it to me. Who is it? Do you know?'

Nancy breathed a sigh of relief when Mr Forrester suddenly entered the room and she was saved from having to answer. Flashing a nervous smile at Amy, she scuttled away as if she couldn't get out of the room quickly enough.

'Grandfather, Nancy just mentioned that you are expecting some visitors. Who...' Her voice trailed away as the doorbell suddenly clanged and she looked towards it.

She could hear Nancy admitting the mysterious visitors and wondered why her grandfather hadn't mentioned to her that he was expecting guests. And then the door opened and François stood there, looking devastatingly handsome.

Her grandfather smiled at her guiltily as he headed towards the door. 'I didn't tell you who our visitors were because I wanted to surprise you,' he told Amy. 'And now I will leave you two together whilst I go and welcome Monsieur Laroque. When he mentioned that he would be coming to London I could see no reason whatsoever why we should not all combine business with pleasure. But listen to me, you two have a lot of catching up to do, so I shall leave you alone now. Do excuse me.' With that he quickly stepped past François, closing the door behind him as Amy felt the colour drain from her face. She had only just arrived and had not even had time to tidy her hair.

But it was not her hair that François was staring at but the ugly scar on her face, and Amy lowered her eyes as she saw the look of horror that flashed across his handsome features. It was gone in an instant and then he was striding towards her, his hands held out to her.

'*Ma petite*, how are you now?' he asked solicitously. 'What a terrible time you have had, and what a dreadful woman she was, to do such a thing to you.'

'It's over now.' She was trying desperately hard to shut out the image of the look on his face when he had first seen her. Grasping her crutch, she tucked it under her arm and rose to face him as he planted a gentle kiss on her unmarred cheek.

'Yes, of course it is, and we should rejoice in the fact that you are still alive. And also, of course, the fact that you still have an outstanding talent.'

Amy found this quite a strange thing to say, but

did not comment on it. She should have realised that it would be a shock for François, the first time he saw her. Even so, she could not help but feel disappointed. She had hoped that François would react as Toby had and look beyond the scar. He now took a seat on the chair some distance away as he eyed her crutch.

'Did your grandfather not tell me in his letter that you would be able to walk without that?'

Amy nodded. 'Yes, he did, and I can. I have had a prosthesis made, but as yet it is too painful for me to wear all the time.'

'I see.' He eyed her full skirt as if he was trying to imagine what lay concealed beneath it, and Amy felt tears start to her eyes. This was not the way she had expected their first reunion to be at all. But then she supposed that she should give him a little time to get used to how she looked now.

'How long will you be staying?' Amy asked, hoping to fill the silence that had fallen between them.

The young man spread his hands vaguely. 'I am not sure. Papa will decide, I have no doubt. Oh, and Mama and Adeline send you their love.'

'That is very kind of them.' Amy felt as if she was talking to a stranger rather than the man she loved, and stifled a sigh of relief when Samuel and Monsieur Laroque suddenly joined them. Monsieur Laroque was his usual kind and urbane self, which made Amy feel a little better.

She rang for tea, and when a suitable time had elapsed she excused herself to go to her room to change for dinner, feeling strangely deflated.

Nancy was waiting for her and she pounced on

her immediately. 'So that's the 'andsome French-man, is it?' she giggled, helping her up the stairs, but then seeing Amy's solemn expression she settled her into her chair in her room and after taking her crutch off her, asked, 'You are pleased to see 'im, ain't yer? I mean, when Mr Forrester said how 'e was comin' an' that 'e wanted ter surprise yer, I thought yer'd be tickled pink.'

'Oh, I am pleased to see him,' Amy assured her, a little too quickly for Nancy's liking. 'But I think it was a bit of a shock for him ... seeing this for the first time, I mean.' Her hand rose self-consciously to her face and Nancy's tender heart went out to her.

'Well, all I can say is, if he loves yer that shouldn't matter. Just give 'im time to get used to it, eh?'

'Yes, I'm sure you're right.' Amy suddenly felt very tired. 'I think I might have a little rest before I come down to dinner,' she decided. 'And then I have something to ask you.'

'In that case I'm glad I agreed to work late.' Nancy's ready smile was firmly back in place, and after snatching a cover from the bed, she tucked it around Amy's lap and left the room with a cheeky wink.

Amy lay back in the chair, staring up at the ceiling. She knew she should be elated at seeing François again, but all she felt was embarrassment. There was no use trying to pretend that she was still the same girl that he had fallen in love with – at least, not to look at. Part of her leg was missing and her face was badly scarred. Perhaps when the right moment arose she should ask him straight out if he still wished to go ahead with their marriage? She certainly did not wish him to marry her out of pity. That'd be more than she could bear, and she would live the rest of her life as an old maid rather than that. Sighing, she closed her eyes.

Dinner that evening was a trial for Amy. Monsieur Laroque was his usual ebullient self and talked endlessly between courses about how well her designs were doing in Paris.

'Once our families are merged there will be no stopping us,' he told Mr Forrester, slapping him firmly on the back. 'Why, with Aimée's talents, our name will become known all over the world. There will be no other milliners to touch us.'

Amy let the chatter pass over her head. François was unusually quiet, and every once in a while she caught him looking at her from the corner of his eye, which caused colour to flood into her cheeks. He was still charming whenever he addressed her, but she began to get the distinct feeling that his father was far keener for their marriage to go ahead than he was.

The chance to speak to him alone finally came when Monsieur Laroque and Mr Forrester retired to the study after dinner.

'Would you care for a brandy?' François crossed to the cut-glass decanter on the small table in the drawing room.

'No, thank you.' Amy's hands were folded sedately in her lap as she watched him pour out one for himself. Once he was seated she swallowed nervously and began, 'François, there is something I must speak to you about.'

Raising an eyebrow he remained silent as she

went on, 'I realise that seeing me like this must have come as a shock to you.' She held up her hand to stop him when he opened his mouth to deny it. 'Of course it must have been a shock. I know I told you of my leg and the scar in my letters, but nothing could have prepared you for the reality. And the thing is ... well, you are a very attractive man and I would quite understand if you wished to end our engagement.'

'I would never do that,' he blustered. 'How heartless would I appear if I did such a thing? And you know we have fine surgeons in Paris, *ma petite*. People who may be able to improve the scar with surgery.'

'I do not wish to have further surgery.' Amy's chin lifted stubbornly. 'I have already spent many months being attended by doctors. I almost died, and am just grateful to be alive. I am assured that the scar will fade in time but I repeat, if you do not wish to go ahead with the marriage, I would quite understand. There would be no reason whatsoever why we could not still work together.'

'That is quite enough of this talk,' François told her sharply. 'Our wedding is set for the sixteenth of May and unless *you* wish to cancel it, it will go ahead as planned.'

'Very well.' Amy longed for him to come and take her in his arms and tell her that he still loved her, but François stayed sitting where he was and she felt the divide between them. They turned their conversation to other things and Amy was thankful of an excuse to escape to her room when the two gentlemen joined them a short while later.

'Good night, my dear.' Her grandfather kissed

her cheek as he saw her to the door and after in-
clining her head towards the other two men, Amy
slowly climbed the stairs to her room. She was
already in bed, exhausted, when Nancy joined
her after helping with the mountain of dirty pots
in the kitchen.

'Right.' She bustled cheerfully into the room
without knocking. 'I'm dead on me feet an' my
Billy'll think I've got lost if I don't get 'ome soon.
So what was it yer wanted to ask me?'

Amy grinned. At least Nancy never changed.
'Actually, I was going to ask you if you would be
my bridesmaid.'

Nancy was in the process of folding the clothes
Amy had laid across the back of the chair, but
now her mouth dropped open and she swung
around to stare at Amy incredulously. 'But I
thought yer were gettin' wed in the Midlands?
'Ow am I goin' to be a bridesmaid from 'ere?'

'You would come and stay with us until after
the wedding is over.' Amy chuckled. 'Billy would
come with you too, of course, if he can get the
time off work. I have already asked my grandfather about it and he is all in favour of the idea,
so what do you say?'

'Would it mean me 'aving to go on a train?'

'I'm afraid it would,' Amy admitted. 'But I'm
sure you'd enjoy it. They are not nearly so frightening as they look, I assure you. In fact, they're
very comfortable to travel in and I would pay all
of your travelling expenses. It would be like a
little holiday for you. You certainly deserve one.'

Nancy dropped on to the end of the bed as she
scratched her head. The Midlands sounded like

471

the other side of the world to her. 'Yer've taken the wind out of me sails good an' proper,' she said. 'It's just about the last thing I ever expected.'

'I dare say it is, but *please* say yes,' Amy implored. 'It would mean the world to me, to have you standing behind me at my wedding.'

'In that case, 'ow can I refuse?' Nancy was beaming from ear to ear. 'An' just wait till I tell my Billy. 'E'll be like a dog after a rabbit.' She threw her arms around Amy, but something didn't feel right. Amy didn't seem as excited about the wedding as she should have been. But then, Nancy told herself, the poor gel had gone through the mill over the last few months, so that was probably why.

'Wild 'orses wouldn't keep me away,' she promised Amy now, and after saying their good nights she floated home to tell Billy the good news.

The next few days passed in a blur of visiting Mr Forrester's shops and talking to the seamstresses for Amy. François accompanied her on many occasions and as always showed great interest.

Eventually it came to the eve of the Laroques' departure, and as they all sat at breakfast, Mr Forrester suggested, 'Why don't you and Amy go to the theatre this evening, François? You have both worked so hard this week and it is your last evening in London. I am sure I could get you a box if you tell me which play you would like to see.'

'That is most kind of you, *monsieur*,' François told him with his most charming smile, 'but forgive me for declining your most generous offer. I have actually arranged to visit some friends this evening.' He now turned to Amy and said

472

apologetically, 'I do hope you do not mind, *ma petite?* I have only just recalled that I had made these arrangements and meant to tell you before.'

Amy was actually feeling very peeved but she bestowed her warmest smile on him as she assured him, 'Of course I do not mind.' She'd had no idea that François had any friends in London. But then she decided that she was probably just being unreasonable. She could not expect him to spend every minute with her, after all.

Once the meal was over, Amy planned to ask Nancy to pop upstairs to fetch her coat and bonnet. She and her grandfather had yet another appointment with the seamstresses today, who were putting the finishing touches to a very elaborate wedding gown before the bride-to-be came in with her mama for her final fitting later that afternoon. It was easily the most expensive gown that they had ever made, and Amy wanted it to be absolutely perfect. The bride-to-be was the daughter of a lord, and her father had also commissioned Amy to design the bridesmaids' dresses, all eight of them. The bridesmaids would be each coming for their final fittings too, so it looked set to be a very busy day.

It was as they were all about to leave the table that Mr Forrester wiped his mouth on his napkin and told them, 'I have a little surprise for you both.'

Both Amy and François gazed at him curiously as he went on, 'The thing is, I know that Amy has expressed a wish to spend the majority of her time in England once you are married. And so this got Mrs Forrester and me to thinking. A newly-wed couple should have their own place in which to begin their married life. And so, even as we speak, the grounds of Forrester's Folly will be swarming with builders that I have appointed to build you your own home.'

'Why, *monsieur,* that is most generous of you,' François told his host.

'Your residence will be built some way away from The Folly,' Mr Forrester continued. 'And I assure you, it will be built with your privacy in mind. It will have its own drive, and internally there will be all the usual downstairs rooms as well as five good-sized bedrooms on the first floor. The second floor will be the servants' quarters, and, dare I say – the nursery, should you require one.'

'Oh!' Amy blushed and seemed momentarily lost for words. This latest kindness was just too much.

'And I thought perhaps, seeing as how you get on so well, you might wish to ask Nancy if she would like to live there as one of your maids,' he went on. 'Billy could choose to work either in the gardens or in the stables. There will be adequate servants' quarters for a married couple to live in, should they wish to, that is.'

Amy let out a deep breath as she tried to imagine what Nancy would say to this suggestion. She knew that Nancy was more than happy living with Billy's mother for now, but this would be a wonderful opportunity for both her and Billy should they choose to take it. A chance for her to get away from the smoggy streets of London to good clean air. But how would Nancy feel about becoming

474

her maid when they were friends? Amy herself would have no problem with the arrangement but she would have to ask Nancy what she thought of the idea. It was certainly worth considering.

'Th ... thank you, Grandfather,' she stuttered. 'I shall put your offer to her this evening.' Mr Forrester then went into a lengthy description of the house he had ordered to be built until it was time for them to leave for their first appointment and Amy said a hasty goodbye to François before limping out to the waiting carriage on her crutch.

For the rest of the day she was so busy that she barely had time to think of anything but what she was doing, and when she finally arrived back at the house that evening she was tired – then disappointed too, when Nancy informed her that François had already left for his evening out. But then, she consoled herself, she would see him the next morning before he and his father left to return to Paris, so it wasn't the end of the world.

When she put her grandfather's proposition to Nancy later that night just before she set off for home, the girl just gawped at her.

'*Stone the crows!*' she choked. 'Yer full o' surprises, ain't no doubt about it. But to *live* in the Midlands ... I'll 'ave to 'ave a serious talk to my Billy about that. I ain't never set foot out of London before so it'd be a big wrench. An' I don't know how Billy'd feel about leavin' his ma.'

'Of course you would need to talk about it. I understand that,' Amy said sympathetically. 'I can remember how nervous I was before my first visit to London. I felt as if I was going to the other side of the world. But I do hope you will both at least consider it, Nancy. The way of life is so much more peaceful where I come from. And I'm sure you and Billy would be happy there, if you would only give it a chance. Think how nice it would be for your children when they come along – to live in clean fresh air with fields about them rather than the murky streets of London.'

'Hm.' Nancy frowned. She would have a lot to think about in the days ahead. Hoisting herself off the bed she walked towards the door where she paused with her hand on the door handle to ask, 'It won't stop us bein' friends, will it? If me an' my Billy decide not to accept yer offer, I mean.'

'Of course it won't.' Amy shook her head. *'Nothing* would ever stop me thinking of you as my friend, *ever.'*

Nancy skipped back to give her young mistress a quick hug before leaving the room, her mind a whirl. She would certainly have somethin' to tell Billy tonight, that was for sure.

'So, this is it then. *Au revoir, ma chère fiancée.'* François took Amy's hands in his. 'The next time I see you will be when I return to England for our wedding in May.'

She nodded numbly. It still seemed unbeliev-able that in a few short months' time they would be married.

He had arrived back very late the evening before and when she had heard him on the landing out-side her room she had gone out to bid him good night. He had started guiltily when he saw her and, as she had leaned towards him to kiss him, she had thought for a moment that she had caught the scent of a woman's perfume on his coat. But then, tucked up in bed again, she had convinced herself that she must have been mistaken.

Now, he leaned to kiss her gently on her unmarked cheek and she realised then with a little shock that he had barely kissed her a handful of times during his entire stay. And then it had only been to peck her chastely on the cheek as he was doing now.

'Goodbye, have a safe journey,' she whispered, and then he was striding away to the carriage that was waiting outside and she waved until it was swallowed up by the smog.

Sighing, she hurried away to pack her own small valise. It would be time for her and her grandfather to leave in less than an hour if they were to catch their train home.

Chapter Thirty-Four

Seth snapped his braces into place and slapped his wife's bottom soundly as she stepped past him with a large pan of porridge in her hands.

'Do that again an' yer might find yerself wearin' this,' Winifred warned him as she plonked it on to the table, but for all her harsh words her voice was soft. Seth seemed to have been happier these last few months than she had known him to be for years. But then as she thought of the terrible secret that he had been forced to keep for Master

Adam she wasn't surprised. She just wished Master Adam would snap out of his melancholy now. The way she saw it, poor Miss Jessica was gone an' there could be no bringin' her back. The sooner Master Adam realised it and put the past behind him, the sooner he could get on with his life. After all, how could he have known, all those years ago, that refusing to speak to the master on his sister's behalf would have such tragic consequences? It was common knowledge that Adam had adored his sister and no one believed that he would willingly have done her any harm. He had just had his head turned by that minx, Eugenie – who, word had it, was now in the final stages of her illness in an asylum in Leicestershire.

'The master an' Miss Amy are due back from London today,' Seth informed her as she ladled some porridge into his bowl.

'Will you be takin' the carriage to pick 'em up from the station?' Winifred enquired, pulling her thoughts sharply back to the present.

He nodded as he looked across at her, considering himself to be a very fortunate man indeed. Winifred was a good woman and they had barely had a cross word in all their long married life. An' she were still a bit of a looker, an' all. A bit on the plump side now, admittedly, but he weren't complainin'.

When they had finished their breakfast, Seth stood up and yawned lazily as he stretched. 'I could just fall back into bed,' he told her meaningfully, but she wagged a finger at him.

'Yer wouldn't be able to, 'cos I'm just about to strip the sheets off it. So get yerself off an' get

478

some work done. I've got a pile o' dirty laundry to tackle an' I don't want to see yer ugly face again till dinnertime.'

'Yer a tartar, so you are, woman,' he teased, and snatching his coat from the hook on the back of the door he slid his arms into it and with a final wink at Winifred left the room.

At the top of the stairs he paused, enjoying the smell of the fresh hay in the stables below. Seth kept the horses' stalls as clean as a whistle and took a pride in his job, which he loved almost as much as the horses he tended to.

Halfway down the stairs, as he was buttoning his coat, he heard Pepperpot snorting softly. He frowned. The thoroughbred was usually a placid beast but this morning he sounded agitated. Hurrying now, Seth reached the bottom of the rickety staircase and moved in the direction of Pepperpot's stall.

'What's up then, eh, me old lad?' he asked, as he reached over to stroke the horse's mane.

The stallion pawed at the ground and tossed his enormous head as Seth tried to soothe him. 'Let's get yer some oats fer yer breakfast, eh? Happen that'll take yer mind off whatever it is that's botherin' yer.'

Seth lifted a large wooden pail and began to walk towards the other end of the stable-block where he kept the horses' food, and it was then that he saw them and his eyes started from his head as he dropped the pail. It rattled noisily across the floor as he stood there, rooted to the ground with shock. A pair of men's feet were dangling in midair. Forcing himself forward, he began to run – and as he drew closer, tears began to roll unchecked down his wrinkled face. It was Master Adam. He was hanging by a thick rope that was wrapped about one of the rafters. Seth could only suppose that he had climbed into the hayloft and crawled along the beam before securing the rope around his neck and jumping.

'Aw, no! Me poor lad.' Seth felt as if someone was ripping the very heart out of him as he stared at the young man who had meant so much to him. It was more than obvious that there was nothing to be done to help him. Adam's face was blue and his tongue was lolling out of his mouth as he stared ahead from sightless eyes.

Turning about, Seth ran up the stairs and bade his wife to remain within; he said he would explain as soon as he could. She knew that something was badly wrong, but wisely held her peace and carried on with her work. Seth then headed for the main house. He would have to break the news to the mistress, though God knew, he had no idea how he was going to do it.

It was Seth who inched himself along the broad oak beam and cut the poor chap down a short while later. The mistress was so distressed that Beatrice had been ordered to run into the village to fetch the doctor to her. And God only knew what the master would say when he got home. Some homecoming this was going to be.

When the doctor arrived and saw Adam's broken body lying there he looked at Seth gravely.

'A fall, was it?' he asked innocently, but with a strange emphasis.

Seth looked bemused for a moment but then latching on to what the doctor was thinking, he nodded quickly.

'Aye, it was that, sir. He must have fallen from the hayloft.'

And so word spread that Adam had died of a tragic accident, and the doctor, who had a high regard for the Forresters, was happy to go along with this, for he knew that if word got out that Adam had taken his own life, he would not be allowed to rest in consecrated ground. The way he saw it, these good people had already had their fair share of heartache.

Adam was laid to rest five days later beside his sister in the little churchyard in Caldecote and for a while, Samuel Forrester feared that his wife would shortly follow him. Her eyes were empty and she seemed to be locked away in a world of her own. The only time she spoke was when Amy was present. The girl had endless patience with her and gave of her time freely, encouraging the woman to eat tasty titbits and reading to her.

Sometimes she would lead her out into the gardens and walk her about, holding her by the hand as if she was an infant, insistent that her grandmother should get some fresh air. A dark shadow was hanging over The Folly once more, and every one of them, from the indoor staff to the gardeners, missed Master Adam daily. No one more so than Seth, who mourned the young master almost as much as his parents did.

There had been no note from Adam, so they could only assume that he had taken his own life because he could no longer live with the guilt of the way he had betrayed his sister. All they could do now was pray that he was reunited with her and that he and Jessica were both finally together again and at peace.

This sad state of affairs continued for some weeks until one afternoon when Amy was in the drawing room with her grandparents. Josephine was staring off into space as usual, and Amy and her grandfather were studying some designs that she had brought for him to look at.

'Grandfather, I've been thinking...' Amy was finding it hard to concentrate on what they were doing and began cautiously, 'I wonder if we should not postpone the wedding? What I mean is, none of us are really in the mood for a celebration and I'm sure François would understand. It doesn't seem right to have a happy occasion when we are all still in mourning and–'

'*What* was that you said?'

Amy and Samuel looked towards Josephine in surprise. They had not been aware that she was listening to them.

'I ... I was just saying that perhaps it would be wise to postpone the wedding for a time,' Amy faltered.

'You will do *no* such thing!' Josephine looked more her old self as she stared towards Amy indignantly. 'This house has seen enough sadness, and I know that if your mother and Adam could speak, they would both say they wished this wedding to go ahead. So let us hear no more talk of postponing it. In fact, I think it's high time we began to prepare for it. There is a lot to be done.'

'Very well, but only if you are quite sure.' Amy

wrung her hands as she glanced towards her grandfather for support but he merely shrugged, delighted that his wife was speaking to them again.

'I think your grandmother is right, Amy.' He winked at her with relief evident in his eyes. 'You are all we have left now, so let's work together towards making this a wedding that the town will never forget. Because you know, I have a strange feeling that there will be two guests that attend the church who we will not be able to see, and like your grandmother and me, I am sure that they will be very proud of you.'

Amy lowered her head as tears stung at the back of her eyes. She too missed Adam, although they had never become close. And now she finally understood why. Each time he looked at her he must have been reminded of her mother and the wrong he had once done her. She hoped it was not what Eugenie had done to her that had finally tipped him over the edge, and prayed that he would now find the peace in death that had so long been denied him in life.

Chapter Thirty-Five

Gazing from her late mother's bedroom window, Amy looked at an enormous tent that was in the process of being erected in the grounds of Forrester's Folly. It would house the deluge of guests that had been invited to the wedding in just two weeks' time. *Two weeks' time!* Amy could hardly believe it; the weeks had slipped by so quickly since the last time she had seen François in London – late last year. But soon she would see him every single day. Raising her eyes, she looked towards the woods and above the treetops spied the chimneypots of the beautiful new house her grandfather had had built for them.

It was small in comparison to Forrester's Folly, but elegant, and Amy loved every room in it; she was still marvelling at how quickly the builders had managed to complete it. It had been finished less than two months ago and since then she had been busily furnishing it to her taste, which was simple by most standards.

After their two-week bridal tour of the Lake District following the wedding, she and François would reside there with Molly for the most part of each year. It had taken a great deal of persuasion to get Molly to agree to leave her beloved little cottage, and the fact that she had, only made Amy love her all the more, although she knew deep down that Molly was not happy about it. But her health was failing fast now and she had finally had to acknowledge the fact that she could not live alone without being a burden to Bessie, and Molly couldn't bear the thought of that. Whilst Amy and François were away following the wedding, Molly had reluctantly agreed to have her few meagre possessions transported to her new home and she'd be waiting for them when they arrived home. Nancy and Billy were due to arrive in a few days' time, and they too would be taking up residence in the new house as Nancy had managed to persuade Billy that it would be a brand new start for them.

Stepping away from the window, Amy stood with her hands on her hips critically inspecting the wedding gown that was hanging on the wardrobe door. It was very plain and simple, but she loved it. The heavy satin was so fine that it seemed to shimmer with a life of its own. The top had a low sweetheart neckline and was slightly off the shoulder, with tiny sleeves and a tight-fitting waist, and then the skirt was full with a long train at the back. The only adornment was a row of sequins that were stitched around the neckline, and Amy reminded herself to thank the seamstresses yet again for the wonderful job they had made of it, the very next time she saw them.

Her grandparents had been insistent that this should be a wedding the like of which had not been seen in the town for many a long day, and not wishing to offend them, Amy had been happy to leave most of the preparations to them.

Her biggest regret was that Toby had declined her wedding invitation. He had made the excuse that he would feel like a fish out of water at such a grand affair, but Amy had her own thoughts on the matter. She was aware that he and Annie had been seeing a lot more of each other again over the last few months, and thought that was perhaps the reason he did not wish to attend. His mind was obviously channelled elsewhere nowadays, and the fact irked her more than she cared to admit. Every night for the last month when she had returned home to Molly she had expected to hear that Toby and Annie were going to be wed. The way she saw it, Toby was ready to settle down now, but as yet Molly had said nothing on the subject.

The room she was standing in now had been made ready for her to get changed in on her wedding day, and as she slowly looked around it, she tried to picture her mother Jessica there. After all, it had been her room many years ago. The fact that she had never known her mother still cut deep, although she knew that she could have had no better substitute than Molly. She often visited her mother's grave and told her of all her worries and concerns and her hopes and dreams, and when she came away she always felt better for the visit.

Now, she glanced for one last time through the window at the men who were scurrying about the enormous tent like industrious little ants before making her way downstairs to the kitchen to see how the cook was getting on with the unenviable task of icing the wedding cake. There were four layers in all, each one slightly smaller than the last, and the cook looked flustered as she refilled the icing bag.

'It'll take me a month o' Sundays to do this,' she complained, wiping the sweat from her brow with the back of her hand. 'Why the mistress wanted one this size I shall never know. There's enough to feed the whole bloody town here.'

Amy smiled as she passed her and stepped out into the sunshine. Her grandfather had forbidden her from visiting any of the *Forrester's Fashions* shops until the wedding was over, and Amy was feeling at a loss. She was so used to being busy that she was slightly concerned about how she would take to being a lady of leisure. François had already informed her that he did not think it was appropriate for her to be visiting any of the

486

businesses after they were married, although he was still keen for her to continue with her designing, which she supposed she should be grateful for.

She was now walking everywhere on her new leg and sometimes even forgot that it was there, until later in the day that was, when it would start to pain her. She still fretted about what François would think when she removed it for the first time on their bridal tour. The stump, although well healed, was not a pretty sight, and that, added to the ugly scar on her face, had taken away all of her newfound confidence. Still, she would think whenever she began to feel sorry for herself, at least I am still here. I could have been lying in the churchyard with my mother and Adam. And this thought always put things into perspective.

Now it seemed there was nothing more to do but wait for the big day to arrive. Josephine had all the arrangements in hand and was flying around like someone demented. Whenever Amy asked if there was anything she could help her with, her grandmother would flap her hand and wave her away, insisting, 'All I want you to do is rest so that you look beautiful on your wedding day.'

And so Amy drifted about like a lost soul counting the days and the hours until Nancy and Billy were due to arrive.

Nancy was awestruck by her first train journey, and even more so when Amy took her and Billy for a walk around the grounds and she had her first glimpse of The Folly.

'Why it's near as big as Buckingham Palace,' she

gasped as she clung on to Billy's arm. Amy laughed at the exaggeration as she led them round to the stables where Billy was to work as a groom.

Seth welcomed him with a firm handshake and a smile, and Amy knew instantly that they were going to get on. Billy knew absolutely nothing about horses but he was eager to learn, and Amy knew that he had found a good teacher in Seth.

The couple were absolutely thrilled with their living quarters on the second floor of Amy's new house, and Nancy clapped her hands in delight when she saw all the trouble that Amy had gone to, to furnish the three rooms for them. There were also two further rooms for extra staff should Amy require them, although she very much doubted that would be the case. The further two rooms would serve as a nursery and a schoolroom.

Everything in their living quarters was brand new, and as Nancy had never owned a new stick of furniture in her whole life, it seemed like a palace to her.

Within two days of being there, she felt as if she had lived there forever, and never tired of looking out at the wide-open spaces. It was like living in another world after knowing nothing other than the busy streets of London and she was often heard to remark to anyone who would listen, 'I reckon I've died and gone to 'eaven. But we 'ave to come up wiv a good name fer the place, so what about The Woodlands or Treetops?'

And so she would prattle on as Amy looked on indulgently.

Now that Nancy and Billy were settled, Amy

began to look forward to the Laroques arriving. They would be staying at The Folly, and Josephine already had all their rooms ready and waiting for them.

They came on a blistering hot day at the beginning of May and it was instantly obvious that Edwige Laroque was almost as excited as Josephine. She swooned with delight when Josephine showed her the tent, which had now had a beautiful wooden floor laid down for the dancing that would take place after the wedding feast.

'*C'est magnifique!*' she declared, clasping her hands together, and Josephine smiled at the praise as she pointed out the table-plan.

'But now, am I allowed to have a peep at the bridal gown?' she asked.

'Of course,' Josephine told her. 'I'm sure Amy would have no objections to me showing it to you.'

The two women wandered back across the lawns and Josephine led her upstairs.

'Ah, simple yet elegant,' Madame Laroque said approvingly as she studied the dress. 'And will Amy be wearing *un voile* – you know, a veil?'

'Yes, it's over there.'

The woman looked towards it and she nodded again. 'Good, good. It will hide her scar, will it not?'

Josephine bristled as the smile slid from her face. 'I suppose it will,' she conceded. 'Although I think Amy is still beautiful even with the scar.'

'Oh, but of *course* she is,' Madame Laroque said hurriedly, seeing that she had offended her host. 'But it is such a shame that her face was marked. She was such a beauty before that terrible attack.

Still, we should be grateful for small mercies, should we not? At least her hands are undamaged. It would have been a sin, had she not been able to continue designing. My husband assures me that Mademoiselle Aimée is the most talented designer he has ever come across, and he has great plans for her future.'

Josephine smiled. 'I will agree that Amy is talented. But what will happen if children come along? She may wish to devote her time to them then.'

The woman waved her hand dismissively. *'Non, non*, if this should happen, François would employ a nurse to care for them. In Paris, women of standing do not take on the menial tasks of caring for their *enfants*.'

'I see.' Josephine was concerned. 'And what about whilst they are tiny and need their mother's milk?'

'We employ *une nourrice* ... how do you say? The wet-nurse, who will come in to feed the *enfant* whenever necessary.'

'Oh.' Josephine was horrified as she thought back to when her own two infants had been born. She had treasured every moment she spent with them, and although she had had a nanny for them to see to the more menial tasks like washing and ironing their clothes, she had fed them herself and spent as much time as she could with them. Still, she decided that Amy would decide what she wanted, if and when that day came, and could see no point in upsetting Madame Laroque by airing her own personal views on the subject.

Outside on the lawn, Amy and François were heading for the new house. She was excited at the prospect of showing him their home and could hardly wait to see if he approved of her choice of furnishings.

They skirted the woods, and there it was before them. Amy held her breath as she waited for his first reaction. When it finally came it was not quite what she had hoped for.

'It is somewhat small, is it not?' he commented musingly.

Seeing as it was much larger than the whole row of cottages that she had been brought up in, Amy could not agree with him. 'It's very spacious inside,' she assured him. 'There are five bedrooms as well as the servants' quarters upstairs, and the kitchen is huge. There is also a study where we can both work and a drawing room and a dining room. I'm sure you will be surprised when we get inside. Nancy and I thought we might christen it Treetops – what do you think?'

François shrugged indifferently and once in the hallway, stood with his hands folded behind his back as he looked around critically. 'It is, as I thought on first glance, quite small compared to the residences I am used to living in,' he said. 'But then we shall be spending the majority of our time living in Paris, so I am sure we will manage very well for the time we are here.'

'But... I thought we had agreed to spend the majority of the time *here*.' Colour had flamed into Amy's cheeks and he saw that she was not pleased. Not wishing to cause a row before their wedding, he smiled at her charmingly.

491

'Let us not quarrel, *ma petite*. First we shall be married and then we shall worry about trivialities.'

'But where I live *isn't* a triviality, François.' There was a determined glint in her eye that he had never seen before, and he realised that she had more spirit than he had given her credit for. He had assumed that Amy would be easy to manipulate but now he wasn't so sure.

'I have to think of my gran,' she went on. 'She is an old lady now, and once she is living here the only person she will have for company when I am absent is Nancy.'

François kept his smile fixed firmly in place although he was beginning to get annoyed. It was bad enough that he had been forced to agree to Molly living with them. Now it seemed she would dictate their comings and goings. Still, he consoled himself. There was an easy way around that problem. Once they were married, Amy could stay here with her gran if she so wished and he would come and go to Paris as he pleased.

Taking her into his arms he slowly kissed her lips for the first time in months and suddenly all her misgivings melted away. No problem was insurmountable and she was sure that they were going to be happy. Relaxed again now, she gave him a guided tour of the rest of the house and now he was nothing but complimentary about it.

It was now less than three days to the wedding and Amy was beginning to feel very nervous.

'Stop pacin' up an' down, will yer,' Molly told her. 'My God, at this rate yer'll be a nervous wreck before the weddin' day dawns. What's up wi' yer anyway?'

'I don't know,' Amy admitted. 'It's just nerves, I suppose.'

Molly suddenly stood in front of her and peering closely at her asked, 'Are yer *quite* sure as yer want to go through wi' this, lass? It ain't too late to change yer mind, yer know.'

Amy snorted. 'Can you imagine what a scandal it would cause? And what would the Forresters say, after all the money and effort they've put into it?'

'The way I see it, it'd be a nine-day wonder,' Molly said stoically. 'While folks are talkin' about you they'd be leavin' some other poor bugger alone... An' as for the Forresters – well, if they loved yer, which I believe they do, they'd want what's best for yer.'

Amy laughed nervously. 'Oh, just ignore me, Gran. Every bride has doubts before her wedding, so I believe.' She began to limp towards the stairs and as Molly watched her go she frowned. Amy was doing really well on her new leg but she could not walk as far now as she had used to, and by the end of each day her limp was visible.

Even now, so close to the big day, Molly could not rid herself of the feeling that François was not the right one for her girl. But then as Molly's mother had been fond of saying, *We all have to learn by us own mistakes.* Amy was a grown woman now and old enough to make her own choices, be they right or wrong.

Chapter Thirty-Six

It was the night before the wedding and Amy was waiting for the carriage that her grandfather was sending to take her back to Forrester's Folly.

It was hard to believe that she had slept in the cottage for the very last time as she looked around her. Tonight she would sleep in her late mother's room and tomorrow morning the carriage would return to pick Molly up, so that she could help Amy to get dressed for her wedding.

She was lost in thought when a shadow suddenly fell across the open doorway and Toby appeared. His hair was still wet from his wash following a long day down the mine and when Amy saw him her face lit up. He had been avoiding her, these last few weeks, but she had been hoping that he would come to say goodbye. It didn't feel right to go off and start her new life without his blessing.

'Hello, Toby. Or should I say goodbye? I'm glad you came to see me off.' She held her hand out to him and he took it as he smiled at her.

'I just wanted to wish yer well, Amy.' She clung to his hand as she looked back at him and Molly discreetly slipped away to give them some privacy.

'So, tomorrow is the big day then, eh?'

Gulping deep in her throat, she said, 'Yes, it is. I can hardly believe it's come around so fast. I dare say it will be your turn next. Have you popped the question to Annie yet?'

His face flushed. 'Actually, me an' Annie... Well, the thing is – we decided to call it a day. Or what I should say is, *she* did.'

Amy blinked in surprise. 'But I thought you were getting on so well! I thought ... oh, I don't know. I thought you loved her.'

'Well, we all know what thought did, don't we? Truth o' the matter is she got fed up o' me keepin' her danglin', an' I can't say as I blame her. But Amy...' his grip on her hand tightened now... 'I want you to be happy above all things. You are *sure* you're doin' the right thing, ain't yer?'

She was saved from having to answer when they heard the sound of the carriage in the lane outside.

'I shall have to go,' she told him softly, and now there was a lump in her throat as she stared into his eyes. Molly came bustling back into the kitchen just in time to see Amy stand on tiptoe and kiss Toby on the lips, saying, 'Just remember, you have been my dearest friend, and my door will always be open to you.'

He blinked, and then before she could say any more he was gone and she felt strangely bereft. She'd miss their chats and the laughter they had shared. But more than that, she suddenly realised just how very much she would simply miss *him*.

'Come on then, let's be havin' yer.' Molly was ushering her towards the door. All of Amy's possessions had already been moved to her new home and all that remained to do now was deliver Amy to her grandparents' home.

Just before Amy climbed into the carriage,

Molly hugged her fiercely. 'Just be sure to get an early night,' she cautioned her. 'I want yer bright-eyed an' bushy-tailed when I arrive in the mornin'. Do yer hear me?'

Forcing a grin, Amy told her, '*Yes*, Gran, I hear you. Now you just be careful, and if you need anything, give Bessie or Toby a shout.' Her eyes suddenly filled with tears again and her voice dropped as she mumbled, 'I wish you were coming with me tonight.'

Molly shook her head. 'Don't let's start that again. I'll be in the new place soon enough. Let's go an' get tomorrow over with, an' get you away on yer bridal tour an' then I'll be there waitin' for yer when yer get back.'

Amy sighed. She knew of old that Molly would not change her mind, so there was no point in arguing. Heaving herself up the steps of the carriage she settled herself into the seat as she smiled at Molly from the window.

'I'll see you in the morning then. Good night, Gran.'

'Good night, lass.'

Amy waved as the carriage drew away, knowing that from this moment on, the humble cottage she was leaving would no longer be her home. It was a sobering thought.

As the carriage rattled down the long driveway leading to Forrester's Folly, Amy saw that the grounds were bustling with activity. Maids with their arms full of flower arrangements were hurrying towards the enormous tent. Lanterns were being strung all along the front of it and men were

496

also busily stringing them into the surrounding trees.

Yet more maids were inside setting the tables with crystal goblets and silver cutlery. And now she saw the cook bossily shouting her orders as flummoxed maids tried to set up the wedding cake to her satisfaction, on a table set to one side of where she and François would sit tomorrow. She shuddered involuntarily as the carriage drew to a halt. It would not be long now.

Her thoughts were interrupted when Nancy came haring towards her, her eyes bright with excitement as she helped Amy down from her seat.

'Cor, I think this is gonna be a weddin' to remember,' she chirped as she linked her arm through Amy's. 'It's like summink yer read about in fairy tales, ain't it?' she went on dreamily with a faraway look in her eyes. 'Not so long ago when I first met yer, yer were workin' fer the master, an' then it turns out yer his own flesh an' blood, an now 'ere you are, about to marry a dashin' Frenchman. Yer can't get much better than that, I don't reckon.'

'I don't suppose you can,' Amy said absently, her eyes still flitting about at all the bustle.

'The mistress 'as been runnin' around like a mad thing all day,' Nancy tittered. 'I think she'll drop in 'er tracks if she don't slow down soon.'

'Mm... Do you happen to know where François is?'

'What?' Nancy was surprised at how subdued Amy seemed, but put it down to pre-wedding nerves. 'Last I saw of 'im he was in the drawing room wiv his pa.'

'Right, well, don't get working too hard. I'll see you later.'

Nancy nodded as Amy lifted her skirts and headed for the back of the house where the French doors in the drawing room opened on to the lush lawns. Many of the maids that were rushing in and out of the front door had been hired for the occasion, and she decided to take this route to avoid bumping into one of them. Once she had turned the corner she sighed with relief and paused to compose herself before slowly moving past the flowerbeds. She had almost reached the open French doors when the sound of raised voices wafted out to her and she stopped abruptly. It sounded like François and his father.

'Mais Aimée sera une femme assez bonne. Elle n'est plus parfaite, mais son talent va vous rendre riche de toute façon.'

Her French wasn't good but she could understand some of his words. A good enough wife? No longer perfect? Make him rich anyway? Why was he saying such things? Was François having second thoughts? She blinked back her tears and then, drawing herself up to her full height, she hurried on as fast as her wooden leg would allow her. When she appeared in the doorway, Monsieur Laroque looked momentarily startled, but then coming towards her he held both his hands out and said, 'Ah, here you are, my dear. Our little bride-to-be. How are your nerves? My son seems a little tense.'

Amy looked towards her fiancé and he told her, 'Do not listen to Papa. Come and have a drink with us. Mama and Adeline have gone to lie

498

down for a rest before dinner, but they will no doubt be joining us soon.'

Amy sat down and sedately smoothed her skirts as François poured her out a small glass of sherry. If truth be told she had never acquired a taste for it, much preferring Molly's home-made wine, but she graciously took it from him and sipped at it all the same. The atmosphere seemed somewhat strained and Amy was relieved when Madame Laroque and Adeline appeared some minutes later.

Thankfully, dinner was a more relaxed affair, as Josephine was full of the arrangements and almost beside herself with excitement.

'I just hope that the weather will hold out,' she murmured fretfully as she looked towards the windows.

Samuel threw back his head and laughed aloud. 'That is something that even *you* cannot control, my dear.'

She nodded regretfully in agreement before grinning at Amy. 'But I *have* made sure that everything else is under control,' she assured her.

Amy smiled politely, suddenly wishing that everyone wasn't making quite so much fuss and then instantly felt guilty. Her grandparents had gone to so much trouble and expense, that she should at least try to feel excited.

After the meal the men retired to the study for a glass of port and a cigar whilst the ladies retired to the drawing room, leaving François and Amy to do as they pleased.

'Shall we walk for a while?' she suggested.

He nodded and fell into step with her as she

headed towards the copse. He walked with his hands joined behind his back and his chin down, and they had gone some way when Amy said uncertainly, 'There is something wrong, isn't there, Francois?'

'Of course not, *ma petite*,' he denied instantly. 'What could be wrong?'

She stopped walking and he stopped too to stare at her enquiringly.

'I don't think that you really wish to go through with this marriage,' Amy said with a forthrightness that astounded him.

'B ... but of *course* I do. How could you think such a thing?'

'Quite easily.' Amy supposed that she should be in tears, but instead she felt strangely calm. 'I am not a fool, François, and I have felt you cooling towards me for some time.' She recalled his visit to see 'friends' on his last night in London the year before, and realised with a flash of clarity that those 'friends' would have been a woman even though she had tried to deny it to herself. When she unconsciously raised her hand to touch the ugly scar on her cheek he shook his head in denial.

'If you are thinking it is because you are scarred now, then don't. You are still the same person I fell in love with in Paris.'

'Truthfully, I think your feelings towards me began to cool even before this happened,' she told him. 'Your letters began to come less frequently, and then I had my accident... I am a cripple now and no longer the girl you first met.'

His head was moving from side to side in denial but she smiled at him sadly. 'I think we both know deep down that it would be wrong of us to go ahead with this marriage, François. What we once had in Paris was wonderful, but I see now that it was merely an infatuation. I think we started to grow apart when I returned home. I just wish I had realised it before.'

She could hardly believe what she was saying and yet suddenly she felt as if a great weight had been lifted from her shoulders, and knew that she was doing the right thing.

Slowly withdrawing the glittering diamond ring from her finger she handed it back to him, saying, 'Forgive me, but I cannot go through with this wedding. It would be a mistake for both of us.'

The look on his face was incredulous and yet she thought she also detected a measure of relief in his eyes. 'You ... you are ending our engagement?'

'Yes, François. That is exactly what I am doing. But I hope that we will still be able to remain friends and that we will continue to work together. However, our engagement is at an end.'

'B ... but what will our families say?'

She noticed that he had not tried to persuade her to go ahead with their wedding – and that, more than any words, told her that she was doing the right thing.

'Please don't concern yourself with that. I shall do the explaining. And François ... be happy.' She reached up and brushed his cheek with her finger-tips before slowly turning and walking away.

Once back in the house, she beckoned to Beatrice and told her, 'Could you tell the master and the mistress that I need to speak to them on a matter of some urgency, please? Tell them I shall be waiting for them in the dining room.'

'Course I will,' Beatrice told her with a curious frown as she noticed Amy's flushed cheeks. And then she turned and hurried away to do as she was asked, wondering what could have happened, to make Amy look so solemn. She certainly didn't look like a woman who was about to marry the man of her dreams and that was a fact.

When Samuel and Josephine joined her only a matter of minutes later, Amy was staring from the dining-room window. She could see François talking to his father out in the garden and sighed as she saw Monsieur Laroque gesticulating agitatedly. She hoped François would not be in too much trouble.

'What is it, my dear? Is there something wrong?' Josephine asked as Amy turned to face her.

Suddenly she felt ashamed. These dear people had gone to so much trouble and expense, and now she was about to let them down, just as her mother had before her.

'I ... yes ... I'm afraid there is.' Lowering her gaze she then forced herself to go on as she whispered, 'Forgive me, but I have just told François that I cannot go ahead with the wedding.'

Josephine's hand flew to her throat as she sank heavily on to the nearest chair and it was Samuel who asked her, 'But why, my dear? I thought you and he were besotted with each other.' And then his colour rose as he asked her angrily, 'Is it because of what happened to you? Your leg...'

'No, no, it wasn't François that ended it, it was me,' Amy told him hastily. 'I take full responsibility for ending the engagement. François is a gentleman and he would have honoured the agreement. But it wouldn't have been right. You see ... I think we've both realised that we don't love each other. I see now that what we had was an infatuation, and a marriage without love would be doomed to failure. I know this must come as a huge disappointment to you both, and I also know how much work and money you have both put into all the preparations. But I will pay you back *every* penny, I promise. And if you wish to disown me, I shall quite understand.'

'*Disown* you?' Samuel was red-faced with indignation. 'We would *never* disown you no matter what you did. I once disowned my daughter and have been made to pay for such foolishness every day of my life ever since. I do not intend to make the same mistake twice, Amy. So if you are saying that you do not wish to marry François then I shall honour your decision. But tell me ... does he have someone else?'

'I don't know,' Amy answered truthfully. 'But *I* do!'

'*You* do?' It was Josephine speaking now and Amy looked towards her regretfully.

'Yes, I do – although I have no idea if the person I love feels the same way about me. I did not even realise that I loved *him* until this evening. And I must warn you, this person is not gentry. He is just a hardworking, kind, wonderful man.'

Samuel and Josephine exchanged a glance then rising, Josephine crossed to Amy and kissed her gently on the cheek. 'Then go to him, my love. And tell him how you feel and we shall pray that your feelings are returned. I will order the carriage to be brought round to the front for you immediately.'

Amy sighed. At one time she would have run all the way home without losing breath. But those days were gone. She was a cripple now and her face was horribly scarred. Who would want her now?

In no time at all she was rattling through Weddington in the carriage and suddenly she felt exhausted. So much had happened in such a short time that she realised now that she had been swept along with the romance of it all. It seemed only yesterday that she had been a cleaner in the factory and then she had worked her way up to becoming a designer before discovering that she was in fact the granddaughter of the factory owner. There had been the trips to London, the voyage to Paris and then the terrible day when Eugenie had tried to kill her.

Even that until now had not been enough to make her see what was staring her right in the face. She loved Toby with all her heart – had *always* loved him – which was why, she now understood, she had been so hurt when he began to avoid her.

Well, now it was time to try and make amends, and if she had missed her chance she would only have herself to blame.

Molly was just going to bed when the carriage drew up outside and she hobbled to the door in her nightgown holding a candle aloft.

'Why, whatever has happened?' she asked as Amy climbed wearily down and nodded her thanks at Seth.

Amy waited until the carriage drew away before telling her, 'I'm not going to marry François, Gran. I realised that I would be making a mistake, so I ended our engagement.'

'Well, I'll be damned.' Molly was deeply shocked, although also more than a little relieved. 'Yer'd better get yerself inside then, an' tell me all about it, lass.' As she held the door wide and stood aside, Amy stepped past her. But instead of sitting down as Molly had expected her to, Amy lifted her skirts and, removing the wooden leg, she threw it across the floor and snatched up her crutch.

She then limped towards the door as Molly shouted after her, 'What the 'ell are yer doin' now? Where are yer goin'?'

'I'm going to do something that I should have done a long time ago,' Amy flung across her shoulder and then she was gone, leaving Molly to scratch her head in bewilderment.

When Amy hammered on Bessie's door she heard movement from within the cottage and seconds later, Bessie appeared.

'Why, love, whatever are *you* doin' here?' she gasped. 'I thought yer'd gone to The Folly fer the night.'

Completely forgetting her manners, Amy pushed past her and once inside, her eyes came to rest on Toby, who was sitting at the side of the fireplace smoking his pipe. He looked as shocked as Bessie did to see her but remained silent as he eyed her warily.

'Toby, I need to speak to you urgently.'

Sensing that she wasn't wanted, Bessie bustled towards the staircase. 'I'll leave yer both to it then. Good night, loves.'

Neither of them answered her, so mumbling to herself she climbed the stairs to her room, where her husband was already fast asleep, judging from the snores, and the younger children were all abed, too.

Toby tapped the contents of his pipe into the fire and then laying his pipe aside he turned his attention back to Amy and said, 'I didn't reckon on seein' you here tonight. I thought yer were gettin' ready fer yer weddin'. What brought yer back?'

'You did, Toby.' There. It was said and she was glad.

'*I* did?' Toby frowned in confusion.

'The thing is...' Now that they were face-to-face, Amy's courage suddenly deserted her and she ran her tongue across her dry lips. 'The thing is ... I realised this evening that I don't love François. I never have. He was the first man to woo me and I suppose what with being in Paris and everything, I got swept along with the romance of it all.'

Toby's eyes had narrowed to slits as he leaned towards her and asked ominously, 'Has he left yer?'

Amy giggled at the outraged look on his face. 'No. Actually it was *me* that left him.'

'*You did what!*'

Amy flushed. 'I ended it,' she said tremulously.

'But why?'

'B ... because I suddenly realised that I loved someone else.'

'Oh, I see.' His face darkened as he straightened to his full height. 'So what'll happen now then?'

'Well, I'm rather hoping that the man I *really* love feels the same about me. Although I would quite understand if he didn't. I mean, I'm not the girl I was any more, am I? I'll never walk on my own two feet again, and as for my face...' Her hand reached up to cover her damaged cheek.

'Don't talk so daft, woman.' Toby looked enraged. 'You could still have your pick of any man yer wanted. Yer still the bonniest lass I ever clapped eyes on, an' you're an heiress now into the bargain.'

'I may well be, but what I've realised is that my roots are still here where I was brought up.' Her voice was loaded with sadness now. 'I am very fond of my grandparents,' she added quickly, 'and I would never willingly do anything to hurt them, but I think I lost track of where I belong somewhere along the way. All the trips to London, the fancy clothes...' She looked down at the beautiful gown she was wearing, which just happened to be one of her own designs.

'The money and all the riches in the world don't mean anything if you can't share them with the person you love, Toby. I'm just glad I realised it before it was too late.'

'So, what will you do now?'

'That rather depends on you,' she said softly, and now his head snapped up and he stared at her curiously.

'On *me?*'

'Of course, seeing as it's you I love. Didn't you

understand what I was trying to tell you? I love *you*, Toby. I think we were written in the stars but I was so caught up in making something of myself that I lost sight of what's important.'

For a moment he stood as if he had been rooted to the spot and in the glow from the lamp on the table she saw tears glistening in his eyes.

'Have I left it too late?' she asked fearfully. 'Could you ever consider marrying me?' And now he sprang forward and wrapped her in his arms, crutch and all.

'Aw, *lass*. I never dreamed I'd hear yer say that to me.' His voice was choked with emotion. 'Yer must have known that I've loved yer since yer were knee high to a grasshopper. Why, I'd go to the ends o' the earth fer you if yer asked me to.'

'Can you forgive me for being so blind?' she whispered, and suddenly they were both laughing, which caused Bessie to creep to the top of the stairs and peep down at them.

'An' was that a proposal, young lady?' His eyes were shining brighter than the full moon in the sky outside and Amy felt as if she might drown in them.

'I rather think it was, sir, so what's your answer to be?'

'Hm, well, I'll have to give it due consideration, of course,' he said with an exaggerated sigh, and then his lips came down on hers and a thousand fireworks exploded behind her eyes.

At the top of the stairs, Bessie grinned from ear to ear, *'An' about bloody time an' all,'* she whispered and turning about, she crept back to her room to wake her Jim and tell him the wonderful news.

Chapter Thirty-Seven

'Hello, Gran. Why, you look absolutely lovely!'

Molly tugged self-consciously at the jacket of the smart green costume Amy had designed and had made for her. She had just arrived at Forrester's Folly to help Amy prepare for her wedding, although she doubted that Amy would need much help. At Amy and Toby's request, it was to be a very quiet affair.

Samuel and Josephine had insisted that Amy should go to the church from their home and Amy had been only too happy to oblige. Her grandparents had been wonderful following the Laroques' departure, and after properly meeting Toby they were happy to welcome him into the family. He seemed like a sensible and kind person, and if he made their granddaughter happy then they were happy too. Better still, as part of their wedding gift to the couple, the workmen were now busily constructing yet another building next to Treetops which would become the new local school where Toby would be the full-time teacher. As Mr Forrester had pointed out, 'It's about time the local children had the chance of a decent education.' Toby was thrilled with the idea and could hardly wait to take up his new post. Josephine had promised to work alongside him – she could hardly wait for the school to open. She and Toby were going to make a grand team.

The Laroques had returned to Paris three days after the cancelled wedding, but thankfully the two families were still on good terms and continued doing business with each other.

Now as Nancy fiddled with Amy's hair, Molly felt a huge lump welling in her throat. She had always known deep down that Amy and Toby were perfect for each other, and was relieved that Amy had realised it too, before it was too late.

'Did you see Toby this morning before the coach came to pick you up?' Amy asked, as she peeped at Molly through the mirror.

'I did that, an' I have to say he looked right dapper,' Molly grinned broadly. 'I don't mind tellin' yer, if I were a few years younger I'd 'ave run off wi' him meself.'

Nancy giggled before asking excitedly, 'Now, 'ave you got yer somefink old, somefink new, somefink borrowed an' somefink blue? It's bad luck fer a bride if she ain't.'

'I rather think I can help with the something new,' Josephine piped up as she swept into the room. 'I'd like you to have this, my dear; it's a wedding present from your grandfather and me.'

She placed a long velvet box into Amy's hands and when Amy opened it, Nancy whistled though her teeth. It was a glittering diamond necklace.

'Oh...' Amy was lost for words at her generosity. As Josephine lifted the necklace from the box and fastened it about her throat they all stared at it admiringly.

'It's lovely, but you shouldn't have,' Amy objected. 'You have already had the house built for us, and now the schoolroom. But thank you. I shall treasure it.'

'An' now I reckon I can 'elp out wiv the somefink blue.' Digging into her pocket, Nancy withdrew a blue lace garter and dangled it in front of Amy's face. 'This is the one I wore on mine an' Billy's weddin' day, an' I only 'ope it 'as the same effect on Toby as it 'ad on my Billy.' Amy giggled as Nancy slid the garter up her leg, blushing furiously.

Now it was Molly's turn, and bending to Amy she kissed her on the cheek before slipping her thin gold wedding band off her finger. 'This don't look much, I know,' she whispered in her ear. 'But it ain't never been off me finger since the day me an' my Wilf were wed. Now I'd like you to have it, lass.' So saying, she put it on to Amy's finger as the girl's eyes welled with tears. The ring was Molly's most treasured possession and she almost hated to take it from her.

'Are you quite sure?' she gulped.

Molly nodded emphatically. 'Just as sure as eggs is eggs. While yer wear that, you'll always have a part o' me close by.'

'Thanks, Gran.' Their eyes locked for a moment but then Nancy broke the silence when she declared, 'But we still ain't got nuffink borrowed!'

'Oh yes, we have,' Josephine assured her. 'And I shall be giving it to Amy when she has finished getting ready.'

Nancy renewed her efforts with Amy's hair and some minutes later she stood back to eye it critically. She had gathered it on to the top of Amy's head and then let it fall in curls down her back.

'What do yer reckon?' she asked Molly.

'I reckon she looks bloody beautiful.'

'Then that's good enough fer me,' Nancy replied. 'Now come on, let's be gettin' yer into yer dress.'

Amy obediently stood up as Nancy lifted the dress over her head. This one, if anything, was even plainer than the one she had had made to marry François in, but Amy loved it all the same. It was of a very similar style but without the long train, and this one had no adornments of any kind. Not that it mattered now that she was wearing the lovely necklace that Josephine had given to her.

Finally, Nancy lifted a fine veil and clipped it into place on Amy's head.

'Wonderful. Now I think we're ready for the something borrowed.' All eyes turned to Josephine as she produced yet another box from a drawer at the far side of the room. When she opened the lid and lifted out a glittering tiara, everyone was speechless. It was fit for a queen.

'My grandmother and my mother wore this on their wedding day,' she told them. 'I also wore it on my wedding day. It is a heirloom and has been in my family for many generations, so now I am entrusting it to you, to pass on to your own daughter one day.' Sadly, Jessica had not taken her turn, but at least her daughter could do so.

'Oh!' Amy could think of nothing to say as her grandmother secured it in front of her veil.

'There.' Josephine's smile was haunted as she thought of the other two people who should have been here to share this special day with them.

512

But it was no use wishing; she simply prayed that her children were in a better place now.

Amy felt like a princess as she stared at her reflection in the mirror, but if truth be known she would gladly have married Toby in rags, if need be.

As she looked at the three women surrounding her, she felt truly blessed. There would be no matron of honour or bridesmaids at this wedding, but Nancy looked charming in a blue linen gown dotted with tiny white flowers, and Josephine was striking in a lilac suit that showed off her petite figure to perfection.

Amy felt tears start to her eyes as Josephine grasped Nancy's elbow and told her, 'Come along now, we should be getting off to the church otherwise everyone will think we've got lost. Molly, we'll be waiting for you downstairs when you're ready to join us.'

Molly smiled at her gratefully and as the door closed behind them she turned to Amy and took her hands. 'This is it then, lass. An' I couldn't be happier for yer. I reckon you'll have a good life wi' young Toby. He's a good lad.'

'Oh, I'm sure I will,' Amy agreed. 'But I wish you'd come to the house tonight, Gran.' She and Toby were to go straight to Treetops following the small reception that Josephine was holding for them at The Folly, but Molly wouldn't hear of it.

'I reckon it will be bad enough havin' to start yer married life wi' me underneath yer feet, so the least I can do is let yer have yer weddin' night in privacy.' If she were to be honest, Molly was looking forward to spending one more night in her little cottage. She was dreading moving into Treetops, and somehow knew that it would never be home to her – not that she would ever dream of telling Amy that, of course. She crossed to a small table and lifting up a small bouquet of white roses, she placed it into Amy's hand.

'There yer go, yer all ready now.' Her eyes were moist. 'An' yer look absolutely beautiful. I'm so proud o' yer, lass. You've made me life worth livin'. Never forget that.'

'Oh, Gran...' Suddenly Amy was in her arms and they were hugging each other fiercely. 'Thank you for everything,' she whispered.

Molly sniffed loudly and held her at arm's length before turning for the door. 'I'd best be off,' she murmured, and before Amy could say another thing she had slipped out on to the landing where she paused to noisily blow her nose. It wouldn't do to be blartin' all the way to church.

Amy waited until she heard the carriage pull away and then with her head held high she walked along the galleried landing and down the sweeping staircase to her grandfather who was waiting for her in the hall. He was pacing nervously up and down with his hands behind his back, but when he saw her he stopped abruptly. She looked so like her mother that his heart ached, and when she finally stood before him pride shone from his eyes as he gently took her hand, too full to speak.

Smiling up at him through her filmy veil, Amy squeezed his hand. 'If you're quite ready, Grandfather, I believe we have a wedding to go to,' she said with a twinkle in her eye.

'I believe we do – but are you quite sure about this, Amy?'

'I've never been surer of anything in my life.'

'Then come along, my dear. We don't want to keep the groom waiting, do we?'

She tucked her arm into his as he proudly led her out on to the marble steps. The pony and trap that was waiting for them was bedecked with flowers, and the brass handles gleamed in the sunlight as Mr Forrester helped her into it.

All of the staff who were not attending the wedding had assembled outside on the lawn to wave her off and wish her well, and Amy waved back, feeling like a queen.

Every single one of Mr Forrester's employees from the hat shops and the factories thereabouts had been given a day off with full pay to mark the happy occasion, and they lined the route by the dozens as they drove through Caldecote. The men tossed their caps high into the air as they passed whilst the women's good wishes echoed around them.

Very few people attended this wedding, which was just as Amy and Toby had wanted it. There were the Forresters, Seth and his family, Bessie and Jim and their brood, and lastly Nancy and Billy – all the people in the world who the young couple truly cared about. There would be no bridal tour either, as both of them had insisted that they would rather spend a few days settling into their new home. Toby had been initially quite unhappy about living in a home that he had not provided for them, but now that the schoolroom was being built he felt as if he had a purpose. He would be a teacher and hoped he would be able to make a difference to the children hereabouts. And, as Amy had rightly pointed out, it would have been ungrateful, not to live in such a fine house after the Forresters had gone to all the trouble of having it built for her, as she was all they had left and so Toby had bowed to her wishes.

As Amy entered the church on the arm of her grandfather, everyone agreed that they had never seen a more radiant bride. Amy was glowing, and when she saw Toby turn to look towards her, her heart skipped a beat and the whole day began to take on a magical quality. Everywhere she looked were flowers, and the sun shining through the stained-glass window had turned Toby's hair to gold. When the sound of *The Wedding March* struck up on the organ, her grandfather squeezed her hand for one last time and they slowly made their way up the aisle as happy smiling faces turned towards them.

As silence descended, the vicar solemnly began the marriage service that would bind them to each other for all time. They repeated their vows one to the other as they gazed deeply into each other's eyes, and Molly began to cry softly. The day she had always dreamed of had finally come to pass, and now she knew that when her time came she could die at peace, content in the knowledge that Amy would be loved and cared for. And yet as she gazed at the bride her joy was tinged with sadness as her thoughts flew unbidden to the angel-faced girl who had lost her fight for life so long ago in the church doorway.

Dragging her eyes away from the happy couple at the altar, she at least had the consolation of knowing that she had fulfilled the dying girl's last wish. She had taken Amy and loved her as her own. But oh, how she wished that Jessica Forrester could have been here to see her daughter today. She would have been so proud.

Molly pulled herself back to the present with a start as the choirboys in their snow-white smocks lifted their voices until the church rafters rang with their sweet singing. And then when the hymn had finished, a silence descended on the church as the vicar solemnly announced that Amy and Toby were now man and wife. Hot tears began to course down Molly's cheeks as Toby tenderly kissed his bride, and it was then that Molly saw her. At first she thought she must be imagining things, and she screwed her eyes up tight. But when she opened them again the vision was still there. Molly's heart began to pound in her chest. Amy's mother was standing silently at her daughter's side and her face was a picture of incredible joy as a mother's love shone from her eyes.

Molly gulped as she quickly glanced at Josephine to gauge her reaction. But she seemed to be oblivious to the vision as she was still firmly focused on the young couple. Panicking slightly, Molly looked around at the rest of the small congregation but again she saw only smiling guests looking on. With a little shock she realised that she was the only one who could see her; even Amy seemed totally unaware of her presence.

Jessica suddenly turned to Molly and smiled, and Molly's fear died away as she smiled back.

And then the vision simply faded away as if she had never been there at all, and Molly bowed her head. A feeling of peace had settled around her and now she knew that everything was just as it should be.

The church bells pealed joyously as the blissful young couple emerged from the church amidst a shower of rice and rose petals. Josephine took Molly's hand and the two women embraced each other, their mutual love of the bride binding them closer together.

Amy then walked through the churchyard to her mother's resting-place, and as she placed her bouquet on the grave, she uttered a prayer. But then Toby took her hand and she was smiling again as he led her back towards the pony and trap.

They then began the journey back to Forrester's Folly with Samuel, Josephine and Molly following them in the carriage behind.

Josephine had noticed that Molly was unusually quiet and leaning towards her she stroked her hand as she asked, 'Are you feeling all right, dear?'

Summoning a smile, Molly assured her, 'I'm fine. Just a bit tired, that's all. I ain't as young as I used to be.'

'None of us are,' Josephine replied regretfully, and then becoming serious she said, 'You know, Molly, I'm so glad we've had this chance to talk. Samuel and I want you to know that we will never be able to thank you enough for all you have done for Amy. God only knows what might have happened to her if you had not come across Jessica all those years ago.' She shuddered as she thought of it.

'Aw, stuff an' nonsense!' Molly flapped her hand dismissively. 'Wi'out that lass to keep me on me toes I've no doubt I would 'ave been pushin' up daisies long ago, so happen it should be *me* thankin' *you*.'

Amy's grandparents shook their heads in unison.

'No, that isn't true and well you know it.' Samuel meant every word he uttered. 'As far as we are concerned, Molly, you are part of the family now and should you ever need anything – anything at all, mind – you only have to ask and it shall be yours.'

Molly was deeply touched and after a moment she answered. 'Thank yer kindly, sir. But yer know I already have everythin' I could ever wish for, an' today has just been the icin' on the cake.'

When they arrived back at The Folly, Amy and Toby were already there with smiles on their faces that lit up the whole room and with eyes only for each other.

The cook had produced a wonderful four-course meal, and once it was over everyone chatted and laughed as daylight slowly entered into twilight. Maids replenished their glasses with the very finest champagne and the sound of laughter floated on the air.

Eventually, Amy and Toby opened their wedding presents before cutting the cake, and then it was time for them to go. They began to kiss everyone goodbye before they left to spend their first night in their new home.

Outside on the soft green lawns, Amy hugged

her gran to her and whispered, 'Good night, Gran. Sleep tight and we'll see you tomorrow, eh?' Suddenly she started to cry as Molly stroked her hair, savouring the closeness of her.

'Now we'll have none o' that,' she scolded. 'You've got a fine lad there, so you be sure an' be good to him an' make the most o' yer life. Do yer hear me?'

Amy grinned through her tears. 'Of course I'll be good to him, Gran. I know how lucky I am. But not just because of Toby – it's because of you too. Without you I would have been nothing, and as for making the most of my life ... well, with you behind me I couldn't do any other. You have been my whole life. And just because I'm married now, don't think that anything is going to change. When you come to join us tomorrow, things will go on just as before.'

Molly nodded, but deep down she knew that things could never be the same again. Amy had a husband now and she couldn't have asked for better.

'Go on now, lass.' Molly gently pushed her away. 'Yer husband is waitin' for yer.'

Amy paused to stare into her eyes one last time. 'I love you, Gran,' she said from the heart, and then turning she made her way to where Toby was waiting for her, and hand-in-hand they set off in the direction of Treetops.

Molly watched until the soft sweet night swallowed them up, and then Josephine gently took her elbow. 'Tired, love?' she asked.

'Aye, I am a bit, pet,' Molly admitted.

'I shall have the carriage brought round for you

immediately,' Josephine said. 'But be sure to be up with the lark in the morning. Seth will be calling to transport you and your possessions to the new house bright and early.' And with that she lifted her skirts and left Molly with Samuel, while she hurried away to arrange the coach.

He stood with her right until it arrived and then helped her inside, saying, 'Good night, Molly. It's been a marvellous day, hasn't it?'

'It has that, lad. The best!' And then with a wave she was off back to where her heart belonged as pictures of Amy's happy face flashed before her eyes. Everything had turned out just as she had prayed it would, and she knew that she could not have wished for more.

Once back inside the kitchen of her little cottage, Molly sighed with relief as she kicked her shoes off and lit the oil lamp on the table. She stared about her. Everywhere she looked were boxes and trunks packed with all her belongings. She smiled wistfully as she looked towards her old oak dresser; stripped of its china plates it looked as she felt – empty. And in that moment she knew that she could never leave this place. It was her home. She would explain to Amy in the morning and pray that she would understand. Somehow she felt that she would.

Epilogue

'I now christen you Benjamin Tobias Bradley, in the name of the Son, the Father and the Holy Ghost.' As the vicar solemnly made the sign of the cross on the tiny infant's head with holy water, Molly felt as if she would burst with pride.

Amy and Toby were beaming as they stared at their baby in his fine robes cradled in his mother's arms. He was a beautiful child, in both looks and nature, as was their three-year-old daughter, Sophia, who was now tugging restlessly at her father's trousers. Toby grinned as he bent to sweep her into his arms, and she gave him a mischievous smile.

She was so like Amy had been at her age that sometimes when Molly looked at her she felt as if she had been transported back in time. Yes, they were a fine family all right, and there was not a happier one anywhere, from what Molly could see of it. Sophia had come along ten months after their marriage and Amy had positively sailed through the pregnancy and the birth, much to Molly's relief. And now here was little Benjamin, who looked exactly like a miniature version of his father. Amy absolutely doted on her children and Toby spoiled them both shamelessly, which to Molly's eyes was just as it should be.

Nancy was there with Billy and their two-year-old son, Simon, who was Sophia's constant companion and, as the two youngsters linked hands, Molly wondered if she was seeing the beginnings of yet another future romance?

Bessie and Jim were there too, along with Josephine and Samuel, who couldn't seem to be able to stop smiling.

The christening was such a joyous occasion that as they all left the small church in Caldecote the sound of laughter floated on the air. They would all now go on to a small reception at Treetops and then Molly would return to her cottage.

Amy had not been at all happy at first at Molly's decision to stay in her old home, following the wedding, but Nancy now went along daily to do Molly's chores for her and Samuel regularly sent the carriage to collect her so that she could go to Treetops and spend time with Amy and the children, so all in all, things had worked out well.

Amy still produced her designs, which continued to sell successfully, although she no longer travelled to London, choosing to leave that part of the business to her grandfather; her time was too taken up with her children, and the arrangement suited them both.

Toby was like a changed man and had thrived in his position at the newly erected village school. It had been hard work at first as the locals had been cautious about their children attending, but now, thanks to his efforts and Josephine's support, the room was full each day and Toby had a newfound confidence about him.

Josephine was cooing over her new great-grandson as Samuel helped Molly into the carriage and Molly looked on affectionately. As the afternoon had advanced into evening, she had begun to tire and Samuel thoughtfully sent for the carriage to take her home. She would leave the young ones to their merrymaking now. All she wanted now was her bed. It had been a long day.

Amy reached up to kiss her soundly, then settled a warm travel rug about her gran's scrawny legs.

'Now don't you get doing anything,' she warned. 'Nancy will be there first thing in the morning to help, and I shall be along in the afternoon to see you with the children, do you hear me?'

'I hear yer, lass,' Molly replied with a grin. 'But now you get back to the party an' that lovely family o' yours, eh?'

Amy lifted her skirts and turned to do just that, but then she paused and turned back to say, 'Do you know something, Gran? I never thought it was possible to be this happy.' And then as she tripped away, Molly's heart swelled as she settled back in her seat.

When the carriage arrived back in the lane, the coachman lifted Molly down and escorted her into the cottage, and she looked about her contentedly. Everything was spick and span, thanks to Nancy's hard work. She thought briefly about making herself a cup of tea, but then the pain that had been gripping her heart more and more of late had her bending over the back of the nearest chair. When it had finally passed she lifted the lamp from the table and slowly climbed the stairs. The tea could wait till morning.

Once on the tiny landing, she entered the room where her beloved husband had spent so many hours, and as she held the lamp aloft, its light spilled on to Wilf's old dusty loom. She paused to stroke it lovingly before moving on to her bedroom, then stepping out of the fine new outfit that Amy had insisted she should have for the occasion, she slipped a long cotton nightgown over her head. After then, taking the pins from her hair, she wove it into a long grey plait and painfully clambered on to her comfortable new mattress, the latest gift from Amy. Reaching over to the small table at the side of the bed she extinguished the lamp and lay there as the moonlight spilling through the small leaded window cast a cold glow about the room.

Molly was totally exhausted, but the pain in her chest had returned again now, and for some reason sleep would not come. It was as she was lying there that a strange feeling of waiting settled around her. She found herself thinking back over her life, right from the time when she was a very small child. In her mind she saw herself as she had been on her wedding day with Wilf standing beside her, handsome and dashing with their whole lives stretching away in front of them. Then she was holding the three tiny daughters whom she had only been allowed to keep for such a short time, then there was Amy on the night she had fetched her back, all unknowing, to what was to become her home. From that day on, the child had become the centre of her world and all the love that Molly had stored away inside her for her own children had been poured into the tiny orphan. But now at last she could rest easy, safe in the knowledge that Amy was truly loved and content.

She sighed happily as the memories rushed back, but then the pain returned a thousandfold and Molly was afraid, for she suddenly felt very old and alone.

Fearfully she pressed her hands into her chest and that was when she noticed a strange light seeming to glow at the end of the bed. She shuddered, wondering if she had perhaps forgotten to turn the oil lamp off. But no, a glance towards the small table assured her that the lamp was extinguished. As she stared back towards the foot of the bed the pain became unbearable and the light seemed to intensify. And suddenly she found herself staring into a gentle face that she could never forget. Jessica was standing there smiling at her.

Trembling in her fear and pain, Molly pulled the blankets up under her chin but as she gazed into the girl's kindly eyes, peace of a kind descended on her, as it had during Amy's wedding, when the young woman had appeared to her before, and Jessica's eyes seemed to have the power to soothe the pain that was tearing through her.

'Don't be afraid, Molly.' The girl's voice was as sweet as a choirboy's as she held her hand out towards her, and now in the light behind her, she could vaguely see her Wilf waiting patiently. His eyes were full of love, and without fear now and with joy in her heart, she stretched out her hand to Jessica's and the pain was gone.

Hand-in-hand with her fallen angel she walked into the light, leaving her little cottage behind for the very last time without so much as a backwards glance, as she went to join her husband.

The publishers hope that this book has given you enjoyable reading. Large Print Books are especially designed to be as easy to see and hold as possible. If you wish a complete list of our books please ask at your local library or write directly to:

Magna Large Print Books
Magna House, Long Preston,
Skipton, North Yorkshire.
BD23 4ND

This Large Print Book for the partially sighted, who cannot read normal print, is published under the auspices of

THE ULVERSCROFT FOUNDATION